The Professor's Bet

K.M. Ringer

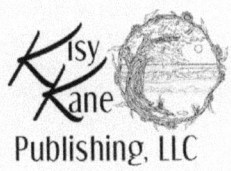

Kisy Kane
Publishing, LLC

DEDICATION

FOR ALL THE GOOD LITTLE SLUTS

YOUR MENTAL HEALTH MATTERS

If you or someone you know may be struggling with suicidal thoughts, you can call the U.S. National Suicide Prevention Lifeline by simply dialing 988 or the full phone number: 800-273-TALK (8255) any time, day or night, or chat

Crisis Text Line also provides free, 24/7, confidential support via text message to people in crisis when they dial 741741.

Content Considerations

Parental Death
Gambling
BDSM Aspects
Consensual Degradation
Pegging
Murder
Profanity
Sexually Explicit Scenes
Cheating (not main characters)
Violence
PTSD Flashbacks

Mass Shooting
Stalking
Mention of Drug Use
Torture
Kidnapping
Anal
Workplace Masturbation
Attempted bombing
Impact Play
Addiction

This book also containes
neurodivergent and plus size representation

NOTE FROM AUTHOR

This book is a story of dedication, forgiveness, and the willingness to try again and follow your heart. Don't forget to set boundaries, though, and stick to them. Remember that no matter what the past has given you, you are worthy of love.

This contains poker games randomly throughout the book. If you haven't played before, here is a quick list of the tiered winning system.

Poker Cheat Sheet for the your game!

combinations are listed in order from highest to lowest

10 J Q K A	**Royal Flush**	10 to Ace, same suit
3 4 5 6 7	**Straight Flush**	Any sequence of five in the same suit.
10 10 10 10 4	**4 of a Kind**	Four cards of one rank, and one unmatched card of another rank
J J 7 7 7	**Full House**	Three matching card of one rank, and two matching cards of another rank
2 6 9 Q K	**Flush**	All five cards are of the same suit
3 4 5 6 7	**Straight**	Five cards of sequential rank, not the same suit
9 9 9 6 2	**3 of a Kind**	Three cards of one rank, and two unmatched cards of another rank
4 4 J J 8	**2 Pairs**	2 cards of one rank, plus 2 cards of another rank, and one unmatched card of another rank
6 6 3 Q 10	**1 Pair**	Contains two cards of the same rank, plus three other unmatched cards
A K 4 10 8	**High Card**	No two cards have the same rank, the five cards are not in sequence, and the five suits are not all the same suit

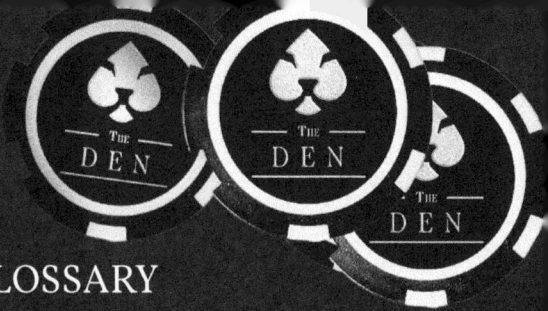

GLOSSARY

ante: A forced bet required, in some types of poker, of all players before the hand begins.

bet: Any money wagered during the play of a hand.

blind: A type of forced bet.

bluff: A bet made with a hand that is mathematically unlikely to be the best hand, either to make money or to disguise play patterns.

board: The set of .

call: To match a bet or raise.

check: To bet nothing.

chip: A small disk or tablet used in place of money.

deal: To distribute cards to players in accordance with the rules of the game being played.

dealer / croupier: The person dealing the cards.

felt: The cloth covering of a poker table, whatever the actual material.

flop: The dealing of the first three face-up cards to the board, refers also to those three cards themselves. This is very specific to Texas Hold 'em and Omaha.

fold: To discard one's hand and forfeit interest in the current pot.

jackpot: A game of jackpot poker or jackpots, which is a variant of with an from each player, no , and an requirement of a pair of jacks or better.

olalliberry: A berry that has the physical characteristics of the classic blackberry, but it is genetically about two-thirds blackberry and one-third red raspberry.

overbet: To make a bet that is more than the size of the pot in a no limit game.

river: The river or river card is the final card dealt in a poker hand, to be followed by a final round of betting. This is very specific to Texas Hold 'em and Omaha.

royal flush: A of the top five cards of any suit. This is generally the highest possible hand.

tell: A tell in poker is a detectable change in a player's behavior or demeanor that gives clues to that player's assessment of their hand.

The
Professor's
Bet

K.M. Ringer

Kisy Kane
Publishing, LLC

THE

DEN

DON'T LET THEM EAT YOU ALIVE

Chapter One

Jason

Running my hands through my hair, I gripped it tight. "Fuck!" I kicked the tire on my black Civic, barely registering the pain in my foot, then slammed my hand down on the roof. Getting into the driver's seat, I stared back at the district office building. My stomach had completely hollowed out as fear and anger went through my body.

What am I going to do?

Lanie. I need to talk to Lanie.

Starting the car and all but peeling out of the parking lot, I raced to her apartment. Buildings were a blur, and I wasn't so sure I paid attention to the lights as I pressed the gas harder, eager to get to her.

What right do they have?

Who gives a fuck who I—

I made the turn onto her street and parked in one of the guest parking spaces on the ground floor of the parking garage. Getting out, I slammed my car door way harder than I should have and hit the button to lock it as I went inside, and when I saw that the elevator was near the top floor, I turned and went to the stairs.

Taking them two at a time, I raced through my options. None of them were the best of scenarios. Flinging the large metal door open, it banged against the concrete wall as I broke through into the hall, striding quickly to her door. Knocking so I didn't scare the shit out of Kevin, I paced as I waited.

When she didn't answer, I knocked again, yelling, "Lanie. Open up. Please."

3

The door swung open, and Lanie was standing there with her eyes wide. "Jason, what is wrong?"

I rushed into the room, wrapping her up in my arms and holding her for a moment.

"Ahh. Okay. Hi." She stumbled over her words, obviously confused by what was happening. I set her down and gripped her head in my hands, kissing her hard. Letting the feel of her lips calm me down. Her fingers gripped into my shirt as she kissed me back. I pulled away, staring into her dark brown eyes. "Hello, and do you mind telling me what is going on?"

"Is Kevin home?"

She shook her head, and her eyebrows scrunched together in confusion. "No, he's with the tudor at the library. Now, again, what is going on?"

I took a deep breath and led her to the couch, sitting down next to her. I took a few more deep breaths before I told her about the meeting at the superintendent's office. She waited, trying to give me time to gather my words, so I looked her in the eye. "I received a call at two that I needed to go and meet with the superintendent as soon as he was out."

"Which is why you had to cancel our coffee date."

Nodding, I continued, "Well, remember how we took Kevin to the museum on Sunday and I noted that the superintendent's wife was there with some of the other PTO moms?"

Her gaze became weary as she dragged out the word, "Yes."

I clenched my jaw and took a breath. "Well, apparently one of those self-entitled, prudish, PTO moms had too much time on her hands. She called and complained to the school principal that I was fraternizing with one of the students after hours."

Rage went through her as she growled, "They tried to say that you were being inappropriate with *Kevin?*"

"No! Thank gods. However, they did say that they were greatly offended by the fact that we were engaging in public displays of affection and thought that it was highly unprofessional and inappropriate for a school teacher to be behaving as such with a student's family."

"Well, first, they can shove it. Second, if it's really a problem, we will be more careful about PDA then, as fucking stupid as that is."

Swallowing, I felt my skin go cold again, just as it had while staring down the superintendent. "They told me I have to end our relationship."

"Oh, how I would have liked to be a fly on the wall when you told them that wasn't going to happen." She laughed, but when I continued to stare at her, fear went through her face. "You did tell them to fly a kite, right?"

"I did, but then they told me that if we didn't, the parents who complained were going to bring it to the school board and get the media involved."

She stood up quickly. "Then fucking let them. We're grown, consenting adults. They can't tell you who to be with."

"Lanie . . . I'm still a new teacher. If I have anything on my record, I'll never work with kids again, baby girl."

My whole body started to tingle in fear, but I had to give him a chance to explain this to me. "Talk to me. Tell me what's going through that head of yours."

Standing, I paced in front of her. "I don't know. All I've ever wanted to do was to teach kids so they can learn from the past, so that they might be able to keep from repeating it."

I saw the hurt on her face. "Then you've made your decision. You aren't choosing me."

My gaze met hers as every ounce of me roared with the thought of not having her in my life, by my side. I strode up to her, and she backed up. Reaching out, I grabbed her by the throat, just under the jaw, and pinned her against the wall. Heat flashed in her eyes, but there was also hurt and anger.

"I didn't say that, baby girl. You are mine." I slammed my lips onto hers, but she bit my bottom lip, and the tang of iron hit my tongue. She pushed against my chest, but I only pressed mine against her body. Against her lips, I muttered, "I don't think I could ever give you up."

"You can't have it both ways."

Kissing down her neck, I pulled at her clothes and removed them as quickly as possible.

"We will figure it out, baby girl. Now, that anger in your eyes is sexy as hell." I hummed as she licked her lips and sucked in her bottom lip. "I'm going to fuck the ire out of you."

5

"You can try." She was still be pissed at me for even considering what they were demanding. "But the fact is, you didn't tell them to take a long walk off a short pier."

It wasn't like my baby girl to fight me, especially when it came to sex, but that was exactly what my Lanie was doing. When I went to pin her arms over her head, she ripped them from my grasp and tried to push me away again. My eyes darkened as I leaned in and rested my forehead against hers, forcing her to look into my eyes.

"Why is my little slut denying Sir access to her body to use for his pleasure?" I slid my hands down her chest, pinching her nipples hard. She cried out, and there was a battle of emotions in her eyes. Part of her was fighting to stay angry, but the other part wanted to melt into what I wanted to give her. What I needed to give her. "You know what to say if you want me to stop."

Lanie moaned and rocked her hips against me. "Yes, Sir."

"What's your safeword?"

She growled in frustration, but I didn't move anymore, waiting to make sure she knew she could stop this, no matter how bad I wanted to remind her that she was my everything. "Strawberry. It's fucking strawberry, you asshole. Now, are you going to try to fuck the ire out of me or what?"

I chuckled. "That's my baby girl." Lanie glared at me as I maintained the tense pressure on one nipple, slid the other hand down, and cupped her pussy. "Now tell me, who does this belong to?"

Her rage flared up as she fought her lust and bucked against me, trying to push me off her. "I'm not entirely sure since you don't know if you want to keep me or it in your life."

My lust burned brighter as I removed my hand from her pussy and undid my belt and jeans. "How can you possibly believe that your beautiful, delicious cunt would be anyone else's but mine."

"So it's just my pussy you want? Fine, I'll have it molded and made into a masturbator for you. Since you can't even stand up to a prudish bitch who probably couldn't ride a dick enough to get her man off."

I blinked at her and pulled my head back to look at her. Really look at her. There was no doubt she was pissed, but shit, she was vibrantly explosive even. I knew my eyes were wider than normal, but when I met her gaze, the sass, determination, and heat there were only barely covering the fear in her.

She really thinks I can walk away from her that easy?

"While it is entertaining to hear you say that shit about the superintendent's wife, you are not going to derail this discussion. You are *mine.*"

I pulled my cock out and then bent down, lifting her thighs then carrying her to the couch. Tossing her onto it, I took hold of her wrists and pinned them on the back cushion. Using my knees, I forced her legs open, and she instinctively wrapped them around my waist as I kicked my clothes off and onto the floor.

"You can't fuck the mad out of me, Jason."

Smirking at her, I rolled my hips and took pleasure in the fact that her eyes rolled back into her head and her hips rocked to meet me. With a hard thrust, I seated myself within her. "What was that, baby girl?"

"Prove to me right now that you will find a way out of this."

Pulling back and thrusting hard into her over and over again, I said, "I will find a way out of this. Your ire will be for fucking nothing. Now lie there and take this dick like you're supposed to, slut."

Lanie tried to get me to release her hands, and when she met my gaze again, there was a flash of anger, but her eyes were glassy and her hips rolled into every hard stroke I gave her. "I may be a slut, but I'll be a slut who fights for her man and will gladly walk into the district office and tell them where to fucking shove it."

"You will do no such thing. I'm the only one shoving anything into this pussy and ass. You are mine to use. Mine to worship. Mine to fuck. You are *my* cocksleeve." I felt my release building with each stroke, and there was something about the wrath and fight in her eyes that pushed me further and further. "Now, cum for me and tell me that you're mine to use. That you're my fucktoy."

Releasing one of her hands, she reached for my shoulder and dug her nails in hard as I slipped my hand between us and pinched and rolled her clit. Her moan filled the air, combining with the sound of our skin slapping together quickly. I could feel her pussy tightening. "That's it. Fucking . . ." I pounded into her with everything I had.

7

"You'll never forget who you belong too." She was mewling beneath me. "What are you?"

Her orgasm ripped through her as her pussy clenched my cock, spurring my own release as she screamed, "Your fucktoy! Your fucking slut to use."

Emphasizing each word with a hard stroke, I said, "Yes. You. Are."

Twisting, we lay onto the couch, with her over top of me. I idly ran my fingers up and down her back, trying to catch my breath.

I meant everything I'd said. My whole world was in my arms right now, and I wanted to spend the rest of my days with her. But that stupid woman and her friends had gotten their panties in a bunch, and now I was being threatened with my livelihood.

Fuck, what am I going to do? I have to keep this woman, but if I can't teach, how can I provide for my baby girl?

THE
DEN
Don't Let Them Eat You Alive

Chapter Two

Lanie

Jason and I had been arguing all week. The best solution was to hide our relationship for the next year and a half while Kevin finished up high school. Neither of us liked the thought of having to hide anything, but the only other option was to break up until then.

Kevin was working on his homework when the door knocked. Kami was supposed to be here pretty soon so we could hang out and watch movies, but it was still a little early.

Opening the door, I smiled as I saw Jason standing there. Only he had his hands in his pockets, and when his gaze lifted to mine, my entire body went numb.

"No."

He just stood there, staring at me.

"No, Jason."

"Lanie, we have to. They gave me an ultimatum. They threatened to not renew my position next year."

I took a step back and had to catch myself on the door. "So you're choosing your job over your heart. Over our love. Our dedication to each other . . . Over me."

His throat bobbed, and I saw the pain in his eyes, but he nodded once. "I love you and always will, but it is the logical choice. Because I love you, I can't ask you to wait. I can't ask you to hide. So, this is it. Please take care of yourself." Jason's throat bobbed as he held my gaze. Then he took a step forward and pressed his lips to my forehead and muttered against the skin, "Goodbye."

I stared at the stained tan carpet, my mind completely blank other than the thought of, *Jason gave up on us. He didn't choose me.*

Sure, we hadn't liked the options we'd come up with, but to go with a full break up? That wasn't a *we have to keep it hidden* or a *let's wait until Kevin is done with school and if we still feel this way, then we will try again.*

Goodbye.

Jason had said goodbye and then given me a final kiss before walking away.

A kiss goodbye.

I had no idea how long I stood there like that, but Kami's face materialized in front of me, and I looked up at her as a single tear fell onto my cheek. Someone guided me further inside, and Kami was in front of me again.

"What happened?"

I blinked, and another tear fell. "He said goodbye."

"What?"

I looked at her again, and then Kevin was in the living room asking if he had heard Jason. I barely registered Kami turning toward him and seeing her lips move. She must have said something because he disappeared down the hall. When my focus went back to her, I tried to take a deep breath, but nothing was there.

Goodbye.

I couldn't focus on anything anymore. Everything was blurred out. It was hard to breathe.

My parents were gone.

My job barely paid the bills.

For almost a decade, even before Mom and Dad had died, I'd been on my own. Was it so wrong to want someone to take care of me?

I'd taken on raising my little brother because there'd been no one else, and he deserved to know unconditional love.

Unconditional love.

I thought that was what Jason and I had. Instead, it was only conditional upon him being able to teach. It was a lot to ask, but again, we had options around that. I wasn't asking him to choose between us. I was asking him to allow us to have both.

But I wasn't enough.

I was, once again, disposable.

A black hole opened up under me and I crumpled to the floor. In the distance, there was someone screaming in outrage and sorrow. Slowly, that darkness crept up my body, turning it cold along the way. As despair rose, it tried to repel it, tried to keep it from taking over, but my heart crumbled to ash under its weight.

Once the ash was flying away in the wind, all I knew was darkness. It swallowed me whole, and then I was out.

San Diego: 1 Year Later

As I unlocked the door to the apartment, I groaned at the sore muscles that racked my body. I couldn't wait to take a hot bath. I'd been putting in applications for an office job that would give me something more consistent for Kevin, but for now the coffee shop marginally paid the bills. We got by, but it was tight.

Once inside, I kicked my shoes off and put my keys in the bowl and called out for Kevin.

"In my room, Sissy!" I took a deep breath and let out the stress of the day, reminding myself of just how far we'd come in the last few years. Kevin was doing well in school, there was food on the table for both of us, consistently now, and I didn't have to wonder how I was going to pay the electric bill anymore, as long as we didn't go crazy. Life was finally getting back to normal, and I was so relieved that for the last few months, when Kami came over, it was just to hang out again.

I didn't know where I would be without her. In the last year, Kami has proven her loyalty and devotion to our family in abundance. After Jason had walked away from me, I'd been in shambles. There were no memories from that first week. All I remembered was the darkness and the feeling of being empty inside. Kami had completely taken over my life. She'd made sure Kevin was okay, got him to school, made food, and helped him with his homework. She'd helped him through his emotions of losing Jason, all because there was no bandwidth from me to be able to do it. It had taken another week after that before Kevin had started to settle down and focused on me. Kami had told me later that Kevin had said that part of the problem was that he didn't know how to help me, so she started giving him things to do. Kami had called and told the café I was working at that there had been a family emergency and that I, unfortunately, had to take some time off. They'd understood and had even sent a bouquet of flowers in sympathy, without even knowing what had happened. Even after I'd gone back to work, Kami had stuck around for another month to help out. Getting through the day had been exhausting for me.

As I got to Kevin's door, I leaned on the doorframe. "Whatcha working on?"

"Calculus." He turned to smile at me, and I knew he saw the grimace on my face. "Don't worry, I'm not going to ask you to help. It will be done by the time I go to bed."

I nodded. "Did you eat something for dinner?"

"Yes, Sissy. It's pasta night, so I made some macaroni and cheese in the microwave."

"Okay. Kami is coming over to hang out. Do you want to join us or draw in your room?"

His smile was bright. "I want to draw. I'm feeling . . ." He hesitated for a moment. Kevin had a hard time expressing his emotions sometimes, so I gave him the space to be able to do it on his schedule. He was also seeing a therapist every week to help give him the tools to work through his grief of losing Mom, Dad, and Jason. They had been very close, and it had hurt him a lot when he'd decided to walk away from us. "Anxious. Drawing may help me work through it."

"You got it. Boop snoot."

His smile was electric as he turned back to his homework. I had no idea where the phrase had come from, but it was our special way of saying I love you. Heading back to the kitchen, I pulled my apron off and tossed it onto the arm of the threadbare, blue couch.

Once I was standing in the kitchen, I looked around, trying to decide what I wanted to eat. The mac and cheese didn't sound horrible, and it would be easy. So I pulled one from the cupboard, ripped the top off, and grabbed the powdered cheese packet out before adding some water to it and setting it for three minutes in the microwave. I leaned on the counter for a minute with my hands flat, stretched my back, and rolled my head, cherishing how my neck popped a few times with the movement. I reached for one of the stemless plastic wine glasses and opened the fridge, filling it about halfway with the cheap box wine I'd been able to get on sale. Lifting the glass to my lips, I took a small sip, letting the smokey, fruity flavor sit on my tongue before the microwave beeped.

Quickly, I finished making up my dinner, took it into the living room, and collapsed into the couch, being careful not to spill the wine. I just stared off into space, relishing the relative quiet while I ate. My phone lit up with an email notification, and I stared at it for a moment, not sure whether to open it or not. It was from Jade Forest, one of the places I had interviewed for, and I expected to hear back from them this week. I really wanted the position, but what if it was a form letter telling me that they had gone with someone with more experienced. Holding my phone in my shaking hands, I was about to open it when it rang with a 619 area code. My thumb swiped across the screen without conscious thought, and I lifted it to my ear.

"Hello?"

"May I speak to Melanie Carley please? This is Dezmond from Jade Forest Adult Care."

My heart raced. "This is she. How can I help you?"

"Well, we were very impressed with you at the interview. We would like to offer you the Assistant Program Director position."

"Oh– Umm– Yes. That would be amazing!" I stumbled.

"We are very happy to hear that," Dezmond said then continued to give me some of the details, including the full employment package. "You should be receiving a formal offer letter via email soon. If you could review it and please sign it, we can then start working on getting you into the system. I'm assuming you would like to give your two weeks?"

"Yes, sir. They've been really understanding about my schedule with my brother, so I feel it would only be right to make sure they have time to get someone lined up."

I could hear the smile on his face. "Very considerate. Great, we will see you in two weeks. If there are any questions about the offer letter, or anything else between now and the 26th, please don't hesitate to contact me."

"Thank you, sir."

"Please, call me Dezmond. We're pretty informal here."

"Thank you, Dezmond."

I squealed so loud when I hung up the phone, Kevin rushed in with me dancing around the living room.

"Sissy?"

"I got a new job! At Jade Forest."

He smiled big and bright at that one. "It's the one you really wanted, isn't it?" I nodded and he came over, giving me a quick hug before stepping back.

I blinked at him. He hadn't given me a hug since Jason had left. It'd been . . . tough on both of us, but we were healing, and life was getting better.

"Yes, it's the one I wanted. I'm going to call Kami and tell her to get over here with something good to drink." He nodded and headed back to his room. Just as I was about to hit the call button, there was a knock on the door. Opening it, I saw Kami standing there with a giant bottle of vodka and a bottle of watermelon juice.

"How did you know I needed this?" I was all smiles.

Kami looked legit confused. "How did you find out?"

"I just got a call. They're starting me out at $5 more an hour than I'm getting now, medical insurance, 401K, and it's a Monday through Friday day job, which will be more consistent for Kevin." Then I noticed that her confusion wasn't going away. "I got the Assistant Program Director position at Jade Forest Adult Care."

There were so many emotions on her face, I was having a hard time latching onto one of them. "Why aren't you happier?"

"I— I mean, I am." Her entire demeanor changed as she then jumped up and down, excited. "This is amazing for you, Lanie. I'm so happy for you."

She strode over to the kitchen and pulled out two shot glasses, filled them with a shot of vodka a piece, and then we slammed them back.

We were laughing and giggling as she made up two full drinks, and then we sat down on the couch.

"So, how are you doing? I know I haven't been able to talk much this week."

I smiled down at my drink as I lifted it and took a sip. The sweetness hid the burn of the vodka as it slid down my throat. "Okay. I even saw Jason at the home improvement store and didn't cry. So, there's progress!"

"I'm so proud of you." Her voice was hesitant, though, and I scrunched my eyebrows together.

"What's wrong, Kami? Wait, why did you think I would need to drink tonight?"

She stared at me a long time before she sat her cup down on the little cheap coffee table and then let out a long breath. "Jason's gone."

It felt as if my heart stopped in my chest. "What do you mean gone?"

Kami shook her head. "I don't know the details, only that he got a job in the valley and moved. Like, up and moved. Isn't even finishing the school year."

My brain was blank as I just stared at her and blinked. I was trying to process what she'd said, but he wouldn't leave without telling me, right?

"He moved?"

"Yes."

"But I just saw him at Home Depot the other day. Our eyes met and he nodded at me before he headed down an aisle." Standing and going to the kitchen, I was trying to reconcile the Jason I'd known with who he could be now.

Kami just nodded and took my hand, squeezing it.

My voice was barely above a whisper. "He didn't even say goodbye?"

Kami didn't say anything but shook her head no.

Leaning against the counter in the kitchen, I slid down the cabinets onto the floor, some of that old darkness and feeling of abandonment washing over me. Kami's hands were on my cheeks as she said, "Lanie . . . it's going to be okay."

I shook my head back and forth and hiccupped as I attempted, and failed, to keep the tears at bay. There were flickers of me lying in bed while Kami had taken care of Kevin. Flickers of just how hollow I'd felt. Picturing myself hiding behind a door, trying to shut it all back in.

No. No. No. I can't go back.

But he left without saying goodbye. That means he really is gone from my life.

I hadn't realized just how much I was holding onto that hope that once Kevin graduated in five months, we might be able to return to what we'd had. I looked at that space in my core that still had an ember of hope, and it was all I could do to not howl in agony as I watched it fizzle out.

Instead, I concentrated on the cool floor under me, the feel of Kami's hands, and the fact that Kevin was in his room.

You can't check out again.

You can't do that to Kevin.

You can't do that to Kami.

"Lanie?"

I looked up at her, up to where the bottle of vodka was sitting, and then back to her. "Start pouring."

She studied me for a moment, and I saw the fear and desperation in her eyes. "Okay, but I'm staying here."

"Whatever, just start fucking pouring."

CHAPTER THREE

LANIE

TRENTON: FOUR YEARS LATER

It had been eight months since I'd felt the warmth of Kami's hugs. Sure, as best friends, we video chatted constantly, but her hugs had the power to calm me in a way no one else had been able to do. She'd decided after a year of interning at a few museums, she wanted to go back for her master's degree in history and had transferred to California State University of Trenton from the University of Redlands.

Kami was planning on picking me up at the airport tonight, but since I was able to get the day off work, I decided to get a cab and catch an earlier flight. Once I landed, I double-checked her location, and I saw she was still at school. After I ordered a rideshare driver, I headed out to the curb. Moments later, I was settled into the back seat and heading toward CSU Trenton.

I stared out the window, watching the city go by, when the driver pulled around the entrance and down a few streets before making a left and parking in front of a large, off-white, stucco building. "Here you go. Have a great time."

"Thanks." I pulled my rolling dark red carry-on off the seat next to me and headed inside. Just beyond the main entrance was a long brick hallway with wood doors scattered along the length. A bulletin board held a map of the building, and I smiled when I found Kami's classroom on the second floor. She was going to either kick my ass for surprising her or be excited. Either was reason enough for getting up earlier this morning to be on the flight. The first door beyond the map was propped open, as well as one on the opposite side of the hall, near the end by the stairs. Just as I went to turn in that direction, a voice carried out of it that had me pausing in my steps.

Swallowing, I listened to the professor answer the student's question about the royal family of Bohemia in 1330. It instantly brought back all the hurt, anger, and abandonment of him leaving. My heart skipped a beat as it, too, recognized the voice, before I took a deep, ragged breath. I tried to make myself keep walking, but then I was peeking through the door. There he was. The man who'd made me feel like I was someone before he'd shattered my very existence. He was animated in his relay of information, his brown hair still cut short on the sides and longer on top, his bright eyes shining in excitement, and his fit, six-foot-three frame hadn't changed one bit in five years. Jason Rathborn, the man who'd held my heart for so long, was standing not fifty feet from me.

What the actual fuck is going on right now?

When we'd first met, he had been Kevin's junior year history teacher in high school. I had fallen for him hard, and I'd thought he felt the same. But that was five years ago, and it could have been yesterday for how my body was reacting.

A heat only he had been able to conjure spread through me, and I felt my pussy clench in anticipation. My gaze slid over his body, and I noted each of the muscles that bunched with his movement.

My hormones were overriding every rational thought I had. It pissed me off.

Jason continued on with his lecture, answering more questions from his students and going into more depth about Bohemia and their relationship with the Roman Empire. He'd always been so passionate when it came to teaching. It was one of the things I loved about him. Leaning on the wall watching him, I had to swallow hard against all the memories that flowed through my mind. The nights sitting on the couch, watching a movie, throwing popcorn at each other. The times we would go to exhibits with Kevin and I would see Jason's pride in him as he recited facts about either a painting or artist. All the nights of us watching the stars, listening to the waves crash against the beach. All the soft touches we would give each other that had me horny in seconds. All the memories of the best sex I'd had in my life. Five years hadn't been enough time to erase him from my mind or heart. I had tried multiple times to find pleasure like that again, but everyone had fallen flat. I'd still used a vibrator to get myself off after more than half of those encounters. Nothing and no one came close to Jason. There had always been an abundance of love in his eyes when he would look at me, but then I remembered the determination I'd seen when he'd told me we were done.

I took a step back as the anguish hit me in the chest, and my vision became blurry with the tears filling my eyes. I didn't remember much from the two weeks after we'd broken up except for the emptiness. Days and nights had bled together during that time, but Kami had always been a constant. I had just started to feel what would pass for normal again when I'd heard the news that he had been offered an amazing opportunity at a university in the valley. I'd never dared to ask which school wanted him, and I hadn't wanted to know. Knew if I did, it would be too hard not to drive out and confront him about leaving without saying goodbye.

My throat tightened as I swallowed back the tears. He wasn't obligated to tell me shit about his life. I shouldn't be feeling like this; we weren't together anymore, but hearing his voice brought all of it back. Swallowing hard, I checked my watch. I still had a few minutes until Kami was out of class and was debating how to kill the time. With one last look at the man who had been my everything, I grabbed the handle of my carry-on. Only, when I moved to turn in the opposite direction, his attention snapped over to where I stood. As his gaze met mine, I held my breath to see what he would do. His mouth dropped open, just the smallest bit, before my name was on his lips. His arm dropped from midair where he was pointing something out on the board, and I might have imagined it, but I thought I saw him pinch his leg and swallow hard. His attention never left mine before he announced, "Class dismissed. See you next week."

My heart jumped, and an explosion of nerves burst through my veins. There were looks and murmurs of confusion while they packed up their things, but Jason's attention was solely on me as the room emptied out. As the students walked by me at the doorway, there were a few polite nods and more than a few confused looks, but when the last of them left, I forced myself to step into the classroom. I couldn't help but let my gaze travel up and down his body again. His chest was just as broad, but his hair was a little lighter than it had been a few years ago. My heart was pounding, and my throat dried out as he continued to stare at me in disbelief.

Should I leave?

I shouldn't be here. I interrupted his class. I really should go.

Only, I couldn't get my feet to move. I could almost feel imaginary hands pressing on my shoulders to hold me in place.

"Hi." My voice was a little squeaky with nerves, but I got the greeting out.

He let out a hard breath, his shoulders sagging just the littlest bit. He took a tentative step toward me. "It's you. It's really you."

"It's me." I smiled at him, silently hoping he wouldn't turn me away. I hadn't come to see him, but now that he was standing before me, I couldn't walk away.

I needed to talk to him. We had to clear the air, get closure. Sure, it might have been a huge mistake to stand there and watch him, but . . . it was Jason. *My* Jason.

He moved quickly toward the door, shut it, and closed the blinds on the small window before turning to me. "Lanie . . . what are—"

I cut him off. "I'm here to see Kami. I took an earlier flight to surprise her at the end of her class upstairs. I was walking by and heard your voice."

"So you aren't going to be attending school here as a student?"

I shook my head as he took a step toward me, slowly and tentatively. When I simply let my suitcase go, he took another one, obviously testing the waters. It didn't matter that it had been five years. I felt my nipples tingle with each of his steps. Just being in his presence was enough. I pressed my legs together to relieve some of the throbbing as I was flooded with memories of his tongue there, his hands on my hips, around my throat . . . not to mention how he was the only man to make me orgasm repeatedly, just by calling me his dirty little slut.

He closed the distance between us as my back found the wall. My breaths were ragged at the sight of the heat in his gaze. Jason caged me in, forearms on the wall behind me, and leaned his forehead against mine as he stared at my lips.

The man who had walked away from me, without a word, was looking at me like he could devour me here and now.

What am I doing? I can't let him in again. He broke me.
Steeling my nerves and pressing my palms into the wall behind me,
I met his gaze. Instead of telling him to step back, I asked the question
that had been plaguing me for years. "Why didn't you say goodbye?"
Pain filled his eyes as he swallowed hard, and his breath hitched.
"I thought about it. Gods, I did nothing else but think about it, Lanie.
I was a chicken. A coward. I knew saying goodbye would have killed
me. I've thought about calling, but I guess I thought it would be easier
for you to move on with life without my interference. Easier to find
someone who made you feel alive."

"*You* made me feel alive, Jason. Only you have ever done that." My
voice cracked at the end of the statement, but I hardened my gaze and
took a long breath through my nose. It was already too hard for me
not to wrap my arms around him and have him call me his dirty little
slut again. No. I was going to get through this without crying, without
falling apart.

He twisted his head to the side as he gritted his teeth. "We talked
about it. You understood why we had to separate. Besides, you were
taking care of Kevin. He needed to be your focus."

I shook my head again, feeling all that hurt flash into simmering
anger. "It didn't mean you had to walk away from me. It also didn't
mean you needed to make decisions *for* me. We could still have talked
while I took care of him and helped him finish high school while you
continued to teach. We could have been friends until he graduated.
You didn't have to cut me out completely."

Jason pulled back and lowered one of his hands from the wall down
my sides, until it rested on my hip. "How is he doing?"

"Really well. He graduated high school with a 3.8." Smiling at the
thought, I lowered my head. "He's in a day program he really loves. I
couldn't be prouder of the man he's becoming."

"He's a smart kid."

"He is."

Jason's thumb and finger gripped my chin as he studied my face.
"Lanie, time and space away from you hasn't changed anything. Not
for me. I think about you all the time. I know you're here to see Kami,
but please, let me take you to dinner tomorrow night."

I studied his as his grip tightened. I could see the hope in his eyes, but could I trust him again?

"I . . . Jason, I really want to. Gods, I've missed you so fucking much in the last few years, but you abandoned me. You leaving without a trace broke something inside of me. You have no idea how many times I've sat on my bed, looking at my phone, wondering if you would even answer if I called. How many nights I would lie in bed, staring at where you used to sleep, and cry. Every time I walk downtown in San Diego, I would see us sitting at the restaurants, walking along the street hand in hand, going to the theater together . . . . Your memory is everywhere. I loved you, Jason. I thought I'd found my person with you."

"Lanie—"

Putting my hands on his chest, I pushed him back a few inches. "Listen, I didn't expect to see you again, and I'm floundering right now. So don't ask or tell me how I feel. I—"

The next thing I knew, Jason's lips crashed onto mine as he pulled me close. Once the shock melted to belonging and comfort, my body relaxed, and I kissed him back with vigor. His tongue danced with mine as I pressed myself against him, my arms wrapping around his neck. Electricity trailed in the wake of his fingers sliding up my back. His warm scent surrounded me, making my heart clench then relax at the realization that this was Jason Rathborn. My Jase.

He pulled back just enough to whisper against my lips, "Dinner. Please?"

Taking a couple shuddering breaths, I could feel his muscles tense as he waited for my answer. My attention bounced between his eyes as I thought about it. He had rarely said please in our relationship before. He would ask me questions and push for answers, but please . . . It hadn't been something in his vernacular very often.

I opened my mouth and then closed it, unable to get words out. Could I give him another chance? Would one dinner hurt?

"Lanie. I fucked up. Royally. I knew what I had, but I wasn't strong enough to fight for it. I never thought I would see you again, never thought I'd hear your voice again. I chose my job over you, and it was without a doubt the worst decision I've ever made in my life. Please, as much as I would love to have you be mine again, right now, I'm only asking for dinner. Please, Lanie."

Flashes of desperation shone in his eyes, and I swallowed. My heart and mind were at war with each other. One was screaming that my Jason was here, begging me to just go to dinner with him. Then there was my mind, reminding of all the hurt that he'd put me through. How it had taken a long time to just function again. In the end, despite all of that, I whispered, "Okay."

His lips slammed onto mine again as he pulled me closer against him. "Thank the gods." Giving me another quick kiss again, he asked, "Same phone number, or did you change it?"

"It never changed, you?"

Jason shook his head as he leaned his forehead on mine. I closed my eyes, trying to center myself.

"I'll send you the time and place."

I swallowed and slowly opened my eyes to see his burning into mine. With my heart racing, I stepped away from him and grabbed hold of my suitcase next to us. "Just dinner, Jase."

"For now," he teased, and I shook my head at his smirk. "Seriously, let's have dinner. Then I can work on fixing what I broke and prove to you I'm worth the risk. How long are you here?"

My fingers tightened on the handle of my suitcase, and I reached out to take his hand in mine. "I'll be here for a week. Then I have to get back home."

"I'll see you tonight."

I shook my head. "Tomorrow. I'm spending time with Kami tonight." *And I need to sort out what I'm feeling right now.*

His fingers squeezed tight around mine as he pulled me in for a quick kiss. "Okay. I'll let you know when and where."

As I turned to leave, I could have sworn I heard him mumble that he was not going to waste this chance. My heart leapt for joy, but I had to remind myself it had been years, and while I still loved Jason Rathborn, he had also shattered my very core when he'd left. He was going to have to fix what he'd broken and earn my trust again . . . and that wasn't going to be easy to do.

Only, as I walked out of that classroom, the emotions I had secured deep inside of me reawakened, and that scared the ever-living fucking hell out of me. I didn't know if I could let him back in, but first things first. Time to surprise Kami.

CHAPTER FOUR

LANIE

TRENTON

I walked in a daze to where Kami's classroom was, wondering why the universe was flinging Jason back into my life. I waited in the hall and leaned against the wall, my lips still tingling from his kisses, my clit still pounding in anticipation for what only Jason could ever give me, and heat still bloomed in my cheeks as I tried to get myself back under control. I took long, deep breaths for what seemed like only a moment before the door to her class opened. Grad students flowed through the threshold, and when she walked out, she was talking with a guy who had his arm protectively around her. Her eyes were bright with happiness I hadn't seen in her for a long time as they walked down the hall.

That bitch has a boyfriend and didn't tell me?

"Kamille Jane Robins!"

Both of them halted in the hall, and I crossed my arms over my chest and pasted an annoyed look on my face.

"Lanie!" She ran for me and jumped into my arms. I held her, and we swayed back and forth with her held tight against me.

Gods, it feels good to have her in my arms. This is what I needed. My best friend, my soul sister.

I could already feel myself becoming more balanced from the craziness downstairs. I opened my arms, and the man who had his arm around her was smiling brightly at us as people filtered down the hall. I couldn't let go of her yet though.

"Don't you *Lanie* me. You knew I was coming today."

She squeezed me tighter. "Yeah, later. I was supposed to pick you up tonight! Why did you come early?"

I chuckled as I held her. "To surprise you, obviously." Eventually, she released me, and I looked between the face of my best friend and the assumed man in her life. "Who is this guy that obviously makes you incredibly happy?"

Both of them blushed, and she smiled at him, saying, "Well, I guess we tell her now. Lanie, this is Eric. We've been together for a bit."

"What's a bit?"

She looked appropriately sheepish and muttered, "Little over a month."

My eyebrows went up and I smacked her arm. "A MONTH! Robins, what the hell! We're supposed to be best friends. You better start talking if you want to keep it that way." She winced at my use of her last name. "Seriously. Start talking! Why the hell didn't you tell me?"

"Well, Eric and I were talking and then hanging out more, and I guess we got a little distracted."

Raising my eyebrows at her again, I shook my head. "He must be pretty talented to distract you to the point of forgetting to tell your best friend."

Kami's cheeks went a deep red, telling me everything I needed to know. I looked up at Eric. "I suppose I can't be mad about you taking care of my best friend."

"Well, she's pretty freaking amazing. I might be biased though."

Kami huffed, but I nodded. "She is. Just don't let her cook for you."

"Hey! I've gotten much better. Not as good as you or Kevin, but I at least don't burn the bread anymore or overcook the pasta."

"Yeah, okay. Sure," I teased.

"Nice to meet you." I leaned in and whispered, "I'm not really mad. She knows that, but she can kiss my ass for keeping you a secret from me."

He ran his hand through his hair nervously. "I'm sorry about that. If it helps, she talks about you all the time . . . to the point I think my best friend, Chip, has a crush on you already."

I took a deep breath as I looked at Kami and thought about the conversation I'd had with Jason downstairs. I had to tell her and Eric so I wasn't a hypocrite. "Give Chip my regards. I already have a date tomorrow night."

Kami jumped up and down in excitement, but then froze and tipped her head to the side. "What? With who? You've been here for all of five minutes and have a date? Who's keeping secrets now?"

"Who do you think?" I watched her run through anyone I might know up here. When several seconds passed, I shook my head. "Kami, why didn't you tell me Jason was teaching here?"

She went ghost white. "How did you find out?"

My eyes went wide. "You knew?"

Kami nodded slowly and then responded, "Chip is a history major as well and is in his ancient civilizations class."

"What?"

Eric looked between the two of us before asking, "You know Professor Rathborn?"

It was my turn to nod. "I do. What do you know of him?"

This was a chance to find out what the rumors were about him. Was he a playboy? A monk?

I let out a little snort at the thought of him as a celibate man.

"Chip loves his ancient civ class. Says the girls are always hitting on the professor. Apparently, someone was trying to set him up, but he said he was still hung up on someone from home."

Eric studied me a bit, confusion written all over his face as he tried to put the pieces together, and I sighed. I really didn't know what to do with that information. *Am I the one he's hung up on?* From the way he was downstairs, maybe I was the reason, but maybe he had been with someone else between the time we'd been a thing and now. I took a deep breath when my attention went back to Eric. "Let's just say, we were both surprised when we saw each other downstairs."

Kami's eyes were lined with worry as she asked, "You okay?"

My chest felt tight again as I looked at Kami. Balling my hands into fists to keep them from obviously shaking, I swallowed. "Not in the least. Fuck, I'm a swirling mess right now." I looked over to Eric. "I'm sorry, but do you mind if I steal her?"

"I have practice so it's fine, not that she needs my permission to hang out with her best friend or anybody else." He turned to her and gave her a soft, sweet kiss. "I'll text you later."

As he walked off, she stared after him like a smitten, little schoolgirl. "That is adorable. I'm happy for you, Kami."

A half smile crossed her lips. "He's pretty amazing." She turned and faced me, though, and sighed. "Now, let's start over. You said you have a date with Jason?"

"Yeah . . . tomorrow."

"We need drinks." Then, she took my hand and we headed out.

THE
D E N

Don't Let Them Eat You Alive

CHAPTER FIVE

JASON

TRENTON

Lanie Carley was in Trenton. The stunning woman who had haunted my dreams since I'd left San Diego, by pure circumstance, had stood in my classroom doorway. Gods, she was more beautiful than I'd remembered. Her long black hair and deep chocolate-brown eyes with flecks of honey in them were still the picture of perfection. Those full lips were still just as alluring, and I couldn't keep myself from kissing her. I could still taste and smell the sweet strawberries that had filled my scenes. For years, I'd been trying to move past her, but in that moment, every ounce of my essence belonged to Lanie Carley. Having her soft, round hips in my hands and against me was like being home.

She's here.

She agreed to dinner tomorrow.

She didn't slap me when I kissed her either. She'd wanted to fight it, but when her body had finally relaxed against me, I wasn't going to let her go again. It had been instinct to pull her to me, but it had taken restraint not to rip her clothing off right there and show her just how much I'd missed her.

I need her.

I'm going to fight for her.

It's her or no one.

I stared at her as she'd picked up her carry-on, walked out of the lecture hall, and headed up the stairs. I knew her best friend was a student here, and I'd done everything I could to stay away from her. Once, we had locked eyes, and I'd felt the daggers in her gaze pierce through my heart. It wasn't that I hadn't wanted Lanie to find me. Gods, my heart hurt after endless nights lying in bed, waking up, and reaching for her, only to find it cold and empty.

 The school district I had been teaching at had given me an ultimatum: stay with Lanie or lose my job and be reported to the state for inappropriate interactions, which would likely mean losing my license to teach. I loved her too much to have her sit back and wait. When I'd told her, the devastation in her eyes had almost made me crumble, but without my job, how could I have provided for her? Helped her provide for Kevin?

 I'd known almost right away that Lanie was the one I wanted to spend my life with. It almost killed me to walk away. When I'd gotten the offer to teach here, closer to my parents, where I could help Mom with Dad before he died, I instantly agreed. It would give Lanie time, distance, and ability to move on with her life. If we didn't share longing looks with each other when she picked up Kevin, then she would be able to, even if it hurt like hell. She could be the amazing sister she was. When I'd gotten settled here in Trenton, though, Mom and Dad noticed how I'd turned into an empty shell, and truth be told, helping them was the only thing getting me out of bed every day.

 Only, Lanie was here in Trenton. She had stopped at my door, watched me teach, and then . . .

 I took a deep breath, running my hands through my hair. Grabbing the door and shutting it behind me, I made a sign that classes for the day were canceled and set up the online classroom with assignments for them to complete. After sending an email to administration to let them know I'd be out for the rest of the day, I grabbed my things and headed to my car. I was almost there when I saw Kami and Lanie heading toward the student lot.

 Fucking hell. Adjusting my raging hard-on in my pants, I had to take a deep breath. Her kiss had lit up a dark part of my heart that I'd killed in cold blood when I told her I didn't want her to wait for me. My chest tightened as I watched her laughing and smiling.

 I wonder how long it took her to laugh like that again.

 First things first, I'd set something up for tomorrow night, and we would talk. As I opened the door and slid into the driver's seat, my phone pinged. Looking down at it, I sighed.

Kai: Game tonight. Some big rollers. Want in?

I lifted my eyes to look back at Lanie as she disappeared behind a row of cars. Hope started to bloom in my chest as I watched her, but the way my body was feeling alive again was something that was going to take getting used to.

My phone pinged once more, and I wondered what she would think of my time at The Den? I didn't need the money anymore. Mom and Dad's bills, my house, and my car were all paid off. My kids, if I ever had them, were set for retirement, maybe even their kids, if they were smart. With what I made at The Den, I didn't need to teach, but I needed to be in a classroom for my soul. Passing on the history of the world to eager minds was its own kind of bone-deep satisfaction.

Sure, teaching could be a pain in the ass at times, and a whole lot of unnecessary drama and politics, but when I had a history major sitting in one of my lectures and their eyes lit up as I told them about ancient Babylon, Thailand, or the royal families of Russia, it had my blood pumping. While playing poker had its own brand of satisfaction, it was also currently giving me a way to distract myself until tomorrow. Starting the car, I decided that I'd go. If I won anything, I knew just what I wanted to do with it.

Jason: Deal me in.

When I walked downstairs into The Den, one of the city's most profound and worst-kept secret cardroom, Kai met my gaze and smiled. Anyone who didn't want to drive up the mountain to Tahoe or Reno, and was any good at poker, came here. It was owned by a local businessman, who thought he was pretty hot shit, Cyress Dazar. I'd won and lost against him many times, but in the end, I'd taken him for millions. He didn't like me much, but he seemed to respect the table.

Most did, especially if they wanted the ability to continue being allowed to come play. If a fight broke out, the bouncers at the door quickly threw all parties out and their cash went into The Den's coffers.

Most of us wanted to keep our winnings, so we restrained ourselves, no matter how pissed we would get at losing a game.

My eyes met with none other than Cyress Dazar's as he weaved his way through the large room with multiple black-and-grey tables, each with their own glass chandelier hanging over them, and his lip twitched up slightly before he nodded in recognition.

I was led to a table already populated by a few other players who I'd beaten easily over the last couple years. One of them even groaned. "Fuck, Jason. Why do you have to be at my table? My kid needs a new car."

Shrugging, I looked at the croupier, whose eyes tightened just slightly before he said, "Good luck, gentlemen," and walked away.

That was strange. I can't help but wonder if he isn't going to deal the table tonight.

Looking over at Sam, I leaned forward on the card table and folded my hands together. "A new car?"

"Yeah, damn thing went out this weekend while she was heading back to school. Car just stopped dead in the middle of the highway. She'd barely gotten on the 5 before it stopped. Damn lucky she didn't get run over pushing the thing to the side of the road."

When the final person arrived at our table, I suppressed a smile. I knew all their tells. While I liked Sam, his eye would twitch slightly when he was bluffing, Mike would tap his middle finger, Kirk would play with his beard, and Chantel, the lone woman, would swallow hard just before making her bet.

"I'm sure you'll get it figured out, Sam." I sat back in my chair and waited for my cards.

A few moments later, Becca, one of the croupiers who'd been here for a couple of years, walked up to the table, saying, "Good afternoon, gentlemen, ma'am. I trust you all will abide by the rules of The Den." She made eye contact with each of us and waited for us to nod in agreement. "Okay, then. Let's get started."

Quickly, she dealt two cards each and waited. Lifting the corners of my cards, I schooled my features as I saw the ace of diamonds and king of clubs. The blinds and opening bets were made, and then she laid down a jack of hearts, six of spades, and king of spades.

Bets were once again made, but Kirk folded. Grabbing the required chips, I called and looked to Becca. Sam studied at the pile and then his cards again. Folding his hands in front of him, he sighed and sized-up Chantel. His eye twitched, and then I focused on Chantel as well. He went ahead and called the bet, and we all waited for the turn.

When a king of diamonds was laid down, I waited for Chantel, who had a small smirk on her bright red lips. Looking around the table, she swallowed hard, made her bet, and looked at me. Sam and I called it, but Mike folded.

When a two of diamonds was placed down on the felt, I stared at it for a long moment. Three kings. Grabbing the chips, I tossed them into the pot and looked to Sam. "Eighteen hundred."

His focus went to my eyes, where I held his stare. "No way. Fold."

I looked down at my hole cards again before looking up at Chantel. Her throat bobbed as she glanced over the community cards and then at hers. Long fingers, with blunt red nails at the tips, reached for the chips as she called.

"Three kings." I flipped the cards.

She simply nodded, her long blond ponytail bobbing with the motion. "Pair of kings on the table, five high."

The pile was sent to me, and I stacked the chips. Round after round was played, and soon there was a crowd. We were evenly matched against each other. Mike, the only one who had fallen out after almost two hours, stood behind his chair to watch. I folded this hand and then watched Kirk push Sam out of the game.

His face fell, but as was the rules, he got up and stood behind his chair to watch the rest of the game. Kirk and Chantel continued to give me a run for my money. With a hand that even had me worried I'd lose with Chantel going all in, I somehow missed her tell. When I called with a full house, she grumbled, having nothing but a pair of fours in her hand.

Finally, it was just Kirk and me staring down a two of diamonds, four of clubs, eight of hearts, five of hearts, and a king of spades.

I studied Kirk and while he scratched at his beard, he was steady. He went all in.

Well then.

The room went still. There was a low straight probability lying there if he had the three and six. Would he still be in the game, though, with a three and six in his hand? Sure, I had a three of a kind, but was it enough to beat what else he could have in there? My eyes met his, and I decided to roll with it. "Call."

He blinked and threw his cards down. Pair of fives, king high. I looked at the table again, trying to see if that was right.

All in on a pair of fives? Was he really just trying to bluff me out?

"Three eights." I flipped my cards over, and through the gasps of surprise, I asked, "Why?"

He shrugged. "Why not? It was something. You were twitching your fingers. Thought you might be bluffing. Figured if I beat you, I'd have some bragging rights playing one of the best. No hard feelings." Kirk reached out his hand, chuckling, and I took it. "Well played."

Standing, I went to the counter and cashed out. Once I was done, I headed to Sam and gave him some cash for his daughter's car. His eyes went wide, and he tried to fight me about it, but eventually he just thanked me and gave me a huge hug.

"You play a good game. Besides, Andi is a sweet kid." Then I turned and walked out the door. Smiling, I knew exactly what I was going to do with the money from tonight's winnings, and any other winnings I would get from private play—set up a bank account for Lanie's little brother, Kevin, should he ever need it.

THE

DEN

Don't Let Them Eat You Alive

Chapter Six

Lanie

Trenton

"Okay. I've been more than patient," my best friend said as she stuffed half a slice of pizza in her mouth. I took a bite myself and stared at her, trying to figure out how I felt about everything that had happened today. "You just stared out the window the entire way back to the apartment. I've watched that mind spin all afternoon. Not to mention that you have avoided the Jason conversation and I've let you. Now that we are eating dinner, tell me, Lanie. What's going through that head?"

"I'm happy to see you." I smiled at her, and she rolled her eyes.

"Of course you are. I'm the best thing in your life," she teased but also raised her eyebrow at me, waiting for my answer.

Slowly, I picked at a piece of pepperoni on the slice of pizza on my plate and ate the bits as I thought about it. "I don't know. I saw him today by chance. I had no idea he was teaching here. It isn't like you told me he was. How could you not tell me, Kami?"

She shifted herself on the couch and tucked her feet up under her tighter. "You had moved on. I didn't want to bring it back full force again. I didn't think that even with you coming up here, we would ever cross paths. I saw him once. Our eyes met *once*. He looked devastated when he saw me, and before I could confront him about it, he was gone. So after that, I ignored him. I'm sorry."

Kami fidgeted with the edge of her plate and had a hard time meeting my gaze, keeping her head down the entire time. I could see

43

how torn she was about it. I understood it to a point, but she knew everything. "You knew how much I loved him."

"You mean *still* love him? I don't know if you will ever be over Jason. You can try to move past him if you want, but that man . . ." She let out a sigh and shook her head. "I've never seen you so happy as when you two were together."

"I *tried* to move past him. More than once. It never worked. No one ever came close to making me feel as alive as Jason did." My chest expanded with the ragged breath I took, and I nodded at her. "I didn't know what to think when I saw him there. He was completely in his element, so happy. Then he saw me and the world tilted again. When he kissed me—"

"I'm sorry, what? You kissed him?" She sputtered out some of her pizza and caught it in her hand as she covered her mouth.

Stealing myself, I lifted my eyes and looked at her. "I did. Well, he kissed me and I leaned into it."

"And how did that make you feel?"

I chuckled. "You my therapist now?"

"Bitch, I'm your best friend, of course I am. Now, did you freak out after he kissed you or not?"

"No freaking out. I got horny as hell and melted in his arms. My body completely betrayed me. I still want to be mad at him, but from the moment I heard his voice, it might as well have been like we never broke up." I realized just how much I needed Jason back. How much I still loved him.

Kami just sat there, watching me process it. And boy did I need to process that. I truly thought I had moved on. Put Jason's abandonment and, yes, even all that love for him in a box and shoved into the furthest corner of a dark closet in the back of my mind. Here I was, though, right back where I'd been the day he'd said we had to break up.

"So, what happens now? Are you really going on a date with him tomorrow night?" I was still staring off into space but nodded. "Are you two getting back together?"

Taking in a large breath and letting it out slowly, I leaned my head back on the cushions of the oversized, grey couch. I looked around her apartment, and it felt warm, comfortable, and homey. Macramé hung on the walls, and accents of greenery in both big and little pots were all over the place, not to mention the little yellow resin ducks in little unassuming locations. It all helped brighten up the place subtly.

"He wants to pick up where we left off, but I told him that it was only going to be dinner. He, of course, said for now, but I don't know."

Her eyebrows pinched together as she looked at me like I was crazy but wanted to give me a chance to talk. "Umm . . . okay."

"But I don't know if I should still go. I'm messed up just from seeing him. Hell, I couldn't barely get through saying hi before I was kissing him."

My thoughts played back that moment and how he'd felt pressed against me. How his hands had seared my flesh through my clothes and sparked my insides alight. How the feel of his lips on mine had my head swimming and cleared out every thought. There was no denying I was still madly in love with the man.

"Do you want him back?"

"Yes." Then I paused, surprised at the immediate answer as I looked at her and let out a tense breath. "I don't know. You saw how I was when he left the first time. I don't know if I have it in me to go through that again."

Her head tilted to the side and her eyes narrowed, making her look like a puppy trying to figure out what you were trying to say. "Okay, let me ask you this. What are some of your concerns?"

"Other than him hurting me again?" She nodded, and I leaned back. "Kevin. If I bring anyone in and they leave again, that's going to set him back. He's just getting to be able to trust others again."

"That's fair. So, let's say you and Jason get back together, what about Kevin? He's doing really well down there. Are you going to move him? Tell Jason to move down there?"

"That's the crux, right? He is perfectly capable of living on his own but says he doesn't feel comfortable doing that. I'm all he has after Mom and Dad died. I can't leave him."

"And no luck on finding out who his biological father is?"

Shaking my head, I turned to face her. "No. The only thing I found was the diary entry that says that no matter how much she loved him, she wasn't going to tell him about the baby. Apparently, Uncle Thom knows. Walked in on her in the bathroom and saw her staring at the pregnancy tests she had on the counter."

"Why would she tell her brother, but not the father of the child?"

I lifted a shoulder. "Hell if I know. You remember what she said before she died. Mom wanted me to know that Kevin was my half-brother in case something happened. Otherwise, I would have never known."

Nodding, she took another slice of pizza from the box and took a bite. I could see the wheels turning in her head so asked, "Whatcha thinking? I can smell the turning of the gears inside that brain of yours."

Kami tossed her napkin in my face. "Why don't you find Uncle Thom or your cousin, Chase."

"I don't even know where to start."

"Still have Chase's number?"

I shook my head. "Mom deleted it from my contacts when she found out that we were still texting after the big fallout."

We sat both staring at the floor, eating our pizza, when a text message came in.

Jason: Mickie's Burgers, 15784 Northstone Blvd. Best burgers in town. 7 tomorrow night.

There was no way I was able to keep the smile off my face. He knew how much I loved just a basic cheeseburger. If there were french fried onions on it with barbeque sauce, even better.

"He remembered your obsession with burgers." She was reading over my shoulder. *Nosy bitch.*

Glaring at her and huffing, I groaned. "It's not an obsession."

"He still remembered, Lanie. Go. I'll go out with Eric or have him come over and keep me company."

"Alright." Stuffing another piece of pizza in my mouth, I texted him back.

Lanie: I'll be there.

Jason: I can't wait.

When I turned my attention back at her, I noticed how happy she looked. Happier than she had been in a long, long time. "Speaking of Eric, I need all the details. I can't believe you hid him from me for a month!"

Her head tipped back as she laughed. "Remember that frat party I went to about a month and a half ago?" I tipped my head to the side that I did. "Well, he was there. We were drunk. And I mean druuunnnkkk."

"And when you are that wasted, your clothes tend to fall off."

A large smile crossed her face. "Well, we fucked each other until we both sobered up. Then on the way out, we exchanged numbers."

"I take it he was a good ride?"

Her cheeks went bright red, but she smiled brightly. "That man can go for hours. I never leave the bed with less than four orgasms, and that's only if I *can* leave."

"Well, good to know my bestie is getting laid *and* satisfied."

Kami smirked and crossed her arms. "You are just jealous."

"Oh, absolutely! Not even going to deny it. There hasn't been anyone that has even come close to satisfying me like Jason could. That man ruined me for everyone else. Enough about him, though, tell me more about Eric."

"Twenty-seven, working on his second master's. His first was in anthropology, but those jobs are few and far between. He said it's really in who you know, along with what you know. So he's working on his master's in psychology now."

"That's a switch."

"Yeah, if he can't dig up the past, then he wants to help the future, or at least that's how he said it." She smiled, and I could see the happiness he gave her shining through. Pride even.

"I'm happy for you, Kami. I really am. I hope it lasts. If not, then my car has a really big trunk, and your family's farm isn't too far away. They still have the hogs, right?"

She chucked. "I love your ride-or-die attitude, bestie."

"Hey, you threatened to feed Jason to hogs after we broke up, and I had to lock you in a closet until you promised you wouldn't make him disappear." I pointed at her, and there was that mischievous glint in her eye again. "Kami . . ."

"I promised!"

After that, we discussed going to dinner and maybe out to a bar, but eventually, we decided that neither of us really wanted to go out tonight. Instead, we elected for a movie night. Jodi Foster had just said that if there weren't aliens out there, that it would be an awful waste of space, when my phone rang.

"Hello?"

"Hi, Ms. Carley, this is Mrs. Blackworth."

My heartrate picked up at the sound of Kevin's new caseworker at the center calling. "Hi, Mrs. Blackworth. What can I do for you? Is something wrong with Kevin?"

"No. No. No. Kevin is fine. Do you remember the painting of Yosemite Falls that Kevin painted?"

"Yeah?"

"It was selected to be in the Los Angeles Art and Sculpture Exhibit. We wanted to get your approval to allow it to be shown."

I blinked in confusion. "Why are you asking me?"

"Well, you are his legal guardian." I heard her going through papers. She was relatively new and didn't know the parameters. Sure, legally I was his guardian, but Kevin was highly functional. He just needed a little extra help here and there.

"Mrs. Blackworth, Kevin is capable of making decisions on what he wants to do with his art himself. He owns the rights to them, and I will let him do with it as he wishes. If there is something that I need to sign as a formality for it, then fine."

"Yes, please. I'm sorry to have bothered you. I'm still trying to get my bearings." A few more shuffles of paper and she hummed through something she must have been reading. "And I see here that he can make minor decisions regarding his health?"

"Yes. If he has a headache, he can take medication without me signing off. If Velas believes he needs to go to the hospital, I'm to be called. Otherwise, he's perfectly capable of making decisions on the day-to-day things. Same on his living arrangements. He chooses to live with me."

"Yes, ma'am. If you could sign the paperwork as a formality, I can add some language at the bottom regarding him having full control over his works, without notification or approval from his legal guardian."

"Thank you. Email it over to me, please, and I'll sign it tonight so you'll have it in the morning. I'll call Kevin and let him know we spoke. Have a good night, Mrs. Blackworth."

"Night."

I stared at the phone for a moment and realized just how much of my life was taking care of Kevin. I didn't mind it, but was there even room for a relationship if I decided to give Jason the chance?

My best friend was staring at me as I ended the call. "What was that about?"

"Yeah, so one of Kevin's paintings was selected for the LA Art and Sculpture Exhibit." I rolled my phone around in my hands. "I'm going to go call him and let him know. I'll be back in a bit."

"You going to tell him you have a date with Jason tomorrow?"

As I stood, I nibbled on my thumb. "No. I need more answers because you know Kevin is going to ask all the questions. So, I want to see if it goes anywhere before I involve him."

"He's not a child, Lanie."

I turned to face her. "I know that, but I still feel like I have to protect him. He was there with you in the aftermath, Kami. You saw how protective he was. You also told me how much he cried in his room and didn't understand how Jason could do this to our family. I have to protect him from that again."

"Fuck that. The man is an adult, who does very well for himself. You even defended that in the phone call. Now you have to protect him like a baby? Make up your mind, Lanie. You can't have it both ways."

My jaw worked back and forth for a moment before I agreed. "You are right, but I'm still not going to tell him about Jason yet. Besides, this is *just* a dinner, not a fucking proposal!"

"Is it though?"

A smile crept onto my face at the thought of being with Jason again . . . . A forever with Jason? I hadn't been lying when I'd told Kami he had ruined me for every other man.

My heart was screaming for him now that we had seen each other. My head, though, was remembering all that hurt, all that agonizing pain, and the chasm of emptiness he left behind when we'd broken up. How it had all surfaced tenfold when I'd found out that he had moved away without even a goodbye.

When I stepped out onto the balcony, I closed the slider shut and leaned on the railing. As I stared out over the city, it was like my heart had walked over and thrown a blanket over all of that hurt, soothing it away with the knowledge that he said that he still wanted me.

Taking a deep breath, I pushed Jason from my mind and quickly dialed Kevin's number.

"Hi, Sissy! Did you make it to Kami's house okay? How was the flight? I stuck crackers in the small pocket of your backpack in case you got airsick. Did you need them?"

"Hi, Kevin." I smiled brightly. Gods, I loved him. "I didn't need the crackers. Flight was very calm. Thank you for thinking of it."

CHAPTER SEVEN

LANIE

TRENTON

Waking up early the next morning, I rolled over to cuddle with my bestie, but I was greeted with nothing but sheets.

What the hell? We always cuddle in the morning.

Groaning, I threw the blankets over my head, and next thing I knew, Kami was pouncing on the bed. "Sorry, I had to pee. Snuggle time!"

We wrapped around each other and sighed.

"I love my bestie."

"Yeah, duh. I'm adorable. Of course you do."

I huffed out a laugh as I started playing with her hair and scratching her scalp. She hummed a satisfied sound, and after a few minutes, the tension in her shoulders released.

There we go, bestie.

An alarm went off on her phone, and she grumbled. Kicking her feet in a fit, she rolled over and turned it off. "I have a test today I can't miss. I'll only be gone for an hour and a half, tops. What do you want to do after that?"

I shrugged and sat up as she got out of bed and started getting dressed. "Maybe go for a walk somewhere?"

"Oh, I plan on taking you to Lake Jackson. It's beautiful up there. You have your date with Jason tonight, right?"

"Yeah. You were there when he texted me."

She pulled a clean tank top out of the dresser and switched out the one she was wearing before turning back toward me and leaning back on the edge of the dresser. "Now, hear me out."

"Oh, for fuck's sake. What is it?"

Kami left the room for a minute, and just as I thought to get up to go after her, she came back in and handed me two small, folded cards with the name Renreg and Sango Spa written in an elegant font.

"I bought them when you first told me you were coming. Wanted to make sure to have the money to go and be completely extra at the spa."

"Okay, so you wanna go after your test?"

She ran her fingers through her hair and smiled as she put it up in a messy bun. "I want you to go this morning. I'll call Maria and let her know that you will be in right when they open at nine. And wipe that sassy look off your face. She's a friend's auntie."

"I didn't even realize I was making a face. I just thought it would be fun to go together, that's all."

Chuckling, she came over and took my hands. "Honey, when was the last time anyone did your nails? When was the last time you had a facial? And I mean a cosmetologist facial, not one from some one-night stand."

I couldn't help but laugh with her. "Honestly? The last time you and I went. It's sort of our thing. Plus, I'm so busy between work and making sure that Kevin has everything he needs that I've barely made time to get a haircut."

"Exactly. So I want you to go. Get a facial, mani-pedi, a full body massage. The works."

"But—"

"Don't make me fight you on this."

I studied her for a long moment and realized in the determined set of her mouth that I wasn't going to win this one. "Only because you are so insistent."

"Perfect." Dropping my hands, she went to her phone, and with a few swipes and touches on the screen, she was lifting it to her ear. "Maria, it's Kami. I'm sending Lanie over alone. Give her the works. If there are any charges over the gift cards, just put it on my card on file." She was smiling at me and then said, *"Muchas gracias."*

"You are a pain in the ass, you know that?"

My best friend grinned. "Yeah. *Your* pain in the ass. Maria said to go ahead and come in at nine so she can get started. Now, go get in the shower. I'll have a cup of coffee and breakfast ready for you when you are out."

I tipped my head to the side, studying her. "Why are you spoiling me?"

"Because you are a badass who doesn't take a fucking moment for herself. So yes, I am going to spoil you. Now, shower!"

"Yes, Mom."

She threw her head back and laughed. "Someone has to do it."

Putting some jeans on, she winked as she headed down the hall.

Quickly, I grabbed my toiletries bag, headed into the bathroom, and jumped in the shower. I washed and shaved everything. If people were going to have their hands on me, the least I could do was shave my legs and not have a forest growing between my legs or from my underarms. That might work for some people, and no shame, but I just couldn't. The water was starting to get cold as I finished rinsing the conditioner from my hair, shut the shower off, and stepped out. Since I knew I would end up in a robe once I got to the spa, I slipped on a pair of leggings and an oversized sweatshirt. By the time I got into the main room of the apartment, the bestie was handing me a cup of coffee.

"Thank you."

She smiled. "You are welcome. You know I'm just trying to take care of you, right?"

I let out a sigh and nodded. "Yeah. Can I ask you something?"

Huffing, she rolled her eyes. "Will you stop asking silly questions? You and I made the rule long ago that we would be straight with each other."

"Do you want Jason and me to get back together? You are the only one who stood by me in the aftermath. You saw how I was. I was a worthless mess. Kevin and I wouldn't have made it without you. There were days I couldn't get out of bed or hardly function."

Kami looked down into the cup of coffee sitting on the counter before she softly said, "Lanie, I have wanted nothing else than for you and Kevin to be happy, safe, and healthy. I have never seen you as happy as you were with Jason. It really shook my world when you broke up. I really thought you two were made for each other. It was my hope to have a relationship as pure and real as the two of you. In the aftermath, I wondered if a happily ever after was even a real thing."

Slowly, she lifted her head and met my gaze. "And for as pissed as I still am at the man for everything he did to you and Kevin, there has to be a reason the universe threw you two back into each other's paths."

"You really think our story isn't over?" I asked.

"I'm not saying immediately dive headfirst back into a relationship with him. I'm saying give him a chance to show you he's not going to run off on you again. He hurt you, Lanie. He broke your heart into a million jagged pieces. Pieces I had to help put back together. Jason has a lot of shit to fix. He has a lot to prove, and not just to you. He has to prove to me that he's worth my best friend's time again. That man needs to beg and grovel on his hands and knees." Kami took a deep breath and let it out slowly. "As intrigued as I am to see how you two reconnect, I won't stop myself from throwing hands if he fucks you over and hurts you or Kevin again. I don't care how good he is in bed."

I stood there a moment, slightly taken aback by her rant. It shouldn't have surprised me, though. I had made her promise not to go after him all those years ago and ruin his life. Kami was my ride-or-die bestie. She really only had my best interests at heart.

My phone buzzed, temporarily pulling me from my thoughts, and I looked down at the screen to see Jason's name.

Jason: Good morning, beautiful. I can't wait to see you tonight.

I rolled my eyes. *What a kiss ass. Is this what Kami wants to see?* I turned my phone so she could see it, and she rolled her eyes, shaking her head.

"Let the groveling begin."

Lanie: Morning. I'm not sure beautiful is the right description.

Jason: You know I've always adored how you look when you first wake up. Send me a photo. Let me judge.

Lanie: Oh, hell no. You can wait until tonight, after I've put some effort into my appearance and, most of all, had this coffee Kami is using as a bribe to be vertical this morning.

Jason: Damn. Kami is resorting to bribing you out of bed? How much did you two have to drink last night that you don't want to get up?

Lanie: I'm on fucking vacation. Can't a girl just lie around? And no picture.

Jason: Baby girl, it doesn't matter to me how long you stay in bed. Just be there at Mickie's tonight.

Oh, hell no. Not yet, mister. There'd been a time where he was my Sir and I was his baby girl, but that honorific had been earned with time and trust. I was not handing that over just yet. Kami was right. He still had a lot to prove. But damn if my heart didn't race and my body heat with need at the use of the honorific. I immediately loved and hated how much he still affected me.

Lanie: You have not earned the right to call me that again. Dinner first. Then we can discuss if there will even be an us again.

Lanie: We can discuss dynamics again should things go well.

Jason: Loud and clear. However, my statements still stand. I'll see you tonight, Lanie.

Kami headed back toward the bedroom, and I sat there with my phone in my hand, not even remembering when I put the cup of coffee on the counter. I let out a long breath as emotions crashed into me. Excitement, fear, hesitation, sadness, all of it. I swallowed hard when I read through the text exchange again and froze where he'd called me baby girl. Yes, my initial reaction had been that he had no right to that moniker, but I couldn't lie and say that it didn't make my insides swim.

I couldn't deny anything. I still wanted him. Needed him. This was so much more than he was the best fuck I'd ever had. Of course my body would react to him calling me his baby girl. The chemistry was obviously still there, or at least the memory of it.

The question was, could I trust him with my heart again?

THE
D E N

Don't Let Them Eat You Alive

CHAPTER EIGHT

JASON

TRENTON

The day dragged on. It seemed like every class was running through a vat of peanut butter. I didn't even remember the drive home. My mind had been totally consumed by her since I saw her standing in the doorway of my classroom. I'd thought I had died or imagined it, but when I had cleared out the classroom, my heart being hard, I'd known I couldn't let her leave without talking to her. Once I'd been within arm's reach though, my whole body had come alive. Sure, I should have probably held off on kissing her, but . . . that kiss. The love and need had burst to the surface as soon as her delicious lips had touched mine. My cock had swelled with the need for her, and my body had tingled with excitement. There was never going to be another woman who filled my heart and soul like she did.

The entire way home today, my mind was swirling. I was going to have dinner with her tonight. I was going to have a chance at getting her back. When I walked into the condo and leaned on the closed door, I took a deep breath, willing myself to calm down. Distraction, I needed a distraction. Putting my bag down, I looked at the pile of papers I needed to grade and wrinkled my nose. Instead, I went over to the bookcase and grabbed the photo album that I had made after I moved to Trenton. It was a way to try working through my feelings and put her in the past. Only, when I'd been done with it, that hole in my heart had felt larger, like a black hole sucking any will to move past the woman who had totally consumed me.

Sitting on the couch, I flipped the cover open, and the pages fell to one of our trips to the beach. I smiled at a picture of her sitting on a towel in the sand, leaning back on her hands, head tipped back, eyes closed as the sun warmed her skin. My fingers traced the lines of her jaw and down her body. She'd once been my baby girl, but she was a bona fide queen—a goddess. *My* goddess.

I lost her when I'd walked away without a word, like a complete moron. I'd dove headfirst into taking care of my parents to avoid my broken heart and depression. It had worked for a while, but then I'd lost both of them in a one-two punch. Once they'd passed, I couldn't stay in my childhood home anymore. It had hurt too much. Everywhere I looked, there had just been memories of my parents, of the life that would never be again. When the lawyer came over to help arrange the estate sale, he'd asked if I wanted to keep it for my future family.

I had looked around the house and couldn't see Lanie in the kitchen, or even curled up on a couch in the living room. That hadn't been the house she would have wanted to live in. It had been a stab to the heart to instantly picture her as my life partner, my wife, and then remember that I was the one who had fucked it all up. So, I had instructed the lawyer to sell everything inside, after I had taken what I'd wanted and cleaned out all the trash.

Lanie was the only woman I could see my life being shared with. I wanted our home to reflect her joy, not be a constant reminder of what I'd lost. Then there was her brother, Kevin. I'd closed my eyes and known at that moment that it wouldn't just be Lanie and me.

I had looked around the place and felt nothing. Not a single emotion to tie to the future. Sure, there'd been memories of my mom and dad in there, but I didn't need the house to keep those. If I couldn't see Lanie in that house, then there was no way I would keep it.

My phone dinged, and I instantly tensed at the thought it might be Lanie canceling our date tonight. When I saw the message, I sagged in relief to see Kai's name on the preview screen. The man had become more than just someone who ran The Den—he had become a friend in the years since my parents' deaths, and with another long look at the photos of Lanie and me smiling at the camera, I opened my texts.

Kai: Lightweights tonight. You want an easy haul?

Jason: I'm good. Got plans.

Kai: You sure? You could walk out with six figures.

Jason: Gonna try to get my woman back. Keep that to yourself, though. I love you, man, but I don't want her in anyone's sights.

Kai: What? I'm sorry, you were breaking up.

Jason: Thanks, man.

Kai: I gotcha. Wait. The girl from San Diego is here?

Jason: She is, and I'm not going to pass up this chance. Just like you shouldn't with Amber. Stop pining over the bar manager and shoot your shot.

Kai: What? I can't hear you.

Jason:

Kai: Sorry, you were breaking up there for a moment.

Jason: Whatever, man. You keep living your delu-lu life.

Kai: See you soon and good luck.

I went back to looking through the photos and reliving all the good times Lanie and I had back in San Diego. The silly selfies at concerts, bars, dinners, walks downtown, at the beach, or even just hanging out at our apartments. My heart skipped a few beats as I landed on a page with her lying in my bed, her dark hair spread all over the pillow as if she were floating on clouds. The blankets were around her full waist, and the tank top she wore had a low-cut neckline, giving me an ample view of her chest. Her face, though, was serene and calm.

It had been the morning after her birthday, and Kevin had been asleep in my guest room. We had spent the evening before playing board games, eating pizza, and having drinks, and when Kevin had gotten tired, we had gone to bed and gone more than a few rounds. There were faint marks on her wrists from where the restraints had pulled tight, and memories of how there were matching ones on her thighs and ankles raced through my mind. She had looked sexy as hell bound like that while she'd looked up at me as I'd fucked her face. She'd been my everything. Would be again, if I had my way. My fingers traced the lines on her face as I let out a long, sad breath. It was a mere two months before I'd made the stupidest decision of my life.

Then, just a few months after walking away from her, the position at CSU Trenton had been offered. I knew why I'd made the decision to take it, even if it did take me from her. Mom had needed help paying for Dad's cancer treatments, and yes, I'd chosen my job over the woman who was going be my wife. Yes, I'd walked away when things unknowingly had gone downhill quickly with my dad. Yes, I'd been a total and complete dumbass. No, I wouldn't feel bad about helping my mom. But, I could have had both. I could have continued to see Lanie while helping my parents. It would have been difficult, but it could have been done. I was just too much of a chicken shit to do it.

Now out of the blue, she'd literally shown up at my door.

I rubbed my thumb over her hair in the picture. First things first, I needed to grovel and beg for her to take me back, to prove I was worth trusting again. I had to show I deserved to hold her heart again, that I could be the man she deserved. With the success I've had at the tables, she would want for nothing. If my queen asked for it, heaven and hell would be relocated by my hand to make it happen.

My eyes flicked up to the clock on the dark wooden mantel over the electric fireplace on the other side of the room. Where had the last two hours gone? Nerves started to tingle throughout my body. Taking a deep breath, I tried to remind myself it was going to be okay, no matter what happened. Only, my heart and brain fought me on it, saying that I had to make it up to her. I was determined to get her back.

In an hour, I would pick her up at Kami's apartment and start proving to her I was serious about making this right. I would never be worthy of her, but I could show her that it was her or nothing. Setting the photo album on the coffee table, I took one more calming breath before heading to the bathroom to shower.

THE
D E N
DON'T LET THEM EAT YOU ALIVE

THE

DEN

Don't Let Them Eat You Alive

CHAPTER NINE

JASON

TRENTON

When I pulled up in front of Kami's apartment building, I didn't expect to see Lanie waiting for me outside. To my delight, she was standing there in a dark blue dress that reminded me of something from the 30s or 40s. The belt sat in the perfect spot on her waist to accentuate her ample hips and draw your eye down to her fucking fantastic legs. I stopped for a moment, just to take her in, while she stood there talking to someone on the phone. My focus was glued to her legs as she walked back and forth, and my thoughts went to the last time they'd been wrapped around my waist. It also didn't help that her long, dark hair was half up, half down and in light waves that I desperately needed to thread my hands through. *Fuck, how did I walk away from this woman?* She was everything to me, and I didn't want to fuck up my second chance at this.

Memories of her coming undone for me all those nights had all the blood rushing to my crotch. After adjusting my cock so that it wasn't completely apparent to everyone within a country mile that I was hard as a rock for her, I took a step out from behind the cars and headed toward her. I made my way up onto the porch, keeping my position so her back was to me, stood behind her, and whispered in her ear, "You look absolutely drop-dead gorgeous tonight."

She jumped and turned around. When she saw who it was, she glared at me. "That's wonderful, Kevin. Hey, the car got here to take me to dinner .... Of course .... Love you, too."

Giving her a smile that looked like the cat got the cream, I said, "Good evening."

"I swear, you gave me a fucking heart attack. If I hadn't been on the phone with Kevin, I probably would have socked you in the face."

"So, Kevin saved me from having a bloody nose on your last first date?"

Her eyes narrowed at me in suspicion. "Mighty confident, aren't you?" I shrugged before she said, "Fine, I guess so."

I was mildly grateful for her not calling me a presumptuous asshole. I knew I had one chance, and if I had anything to say about it, I was the last man she would ever date for the rest of our lives. She was mine, and I wasn't going to be stupid enough to make the same mistake twice.

"Well, sweetheart, shall we?" I reached out and offered my hand to her.

Lanie looked at it and then put hers in mine, pulling me to her. Instantly, her lips were pressed to mine, and I froze in shock. *Lanie was kissing me.* But as quickly as it happened, she pulled away and started wiping away the lipstick that had transferred to my lips. "There. Now, we can go."

"As you wish." My heart was racing, and I tried to hide the deep breath I took to keep myself from pulling her back to me and kissing her like she deserved. Instead, I threaded my hand with hers and headed back to my car. I didn't miss the small bit of confusion in her eyes as she slid into the passenger seat. After she was in and secured, I walked around the back of the car, adjusting myself again, and then slid into the driver's seat. Turning the car on, I backed out and pulled onto the main road.

We were sitting at the first light when she finally broke the slightly uncomfortable silence. "Jase?"

"Yeah?"

"Why didn't you kiss me like you always did when you picked me up?"

I looked at her, smiled as I gripped her chin, and pulled her in for a soft, teasing kiss before pulling back just in time for the light to turn green. "Because I didn't know if you would have wanted me to. That was then. Before I did the one thing I have regretted most in my whole life. So, since you decided to give me a chance to go to dinner with you, I didn't want to mess it up. I pushed too far at the university. My conscious brain turned off, and the primal side of me came forward, demanding that I have you in my arms again."

Her words were breathy as she said, "Jase, I-I'm not mad at you for being you when we saw each other yesterday."

Without much conscious thought, I reached over and laid my hand on her thigh. "Why did you agree?"

She looked out the window, watching the buildings go by and the people walking along the street. After a long moment that had me on edge, she sighed in resignation. "Because our story isn't done."

I held my breath, trying to convince myself not to read into that too much, but she laid her hand on top of the one that was resting on her thigh, and I squeezed it softly. There was a small smile on her face as she watched the world go by, so I took it as a positive sign.

So far, so good.

I parked in the gravel parking lot next door to Mickie's Diner, and when I turned the car off, I let out a long, deep, settling breath. My chest was tight, and it felt like a swarm of bees had made my stomach their hive. Without focusing on that, I grabbed my leather jacket from the back seat and stepped out of the car. I was glad that winter was on the way, taking the hot, humid days away. I got out and walked around to let Lanie out, relieved that she'd waited for me to open the door for her.

"I know it doesn't look like much, but they have the best burgers in town." As she stood, I didn't move, and it brought her right up against me. Bending down, I brought my lips to her neck softly and whispered, "They even have the fried onion strings."

"Jason, are you teasing me?" She chuckled, and I stood up and just shrugged. I took her hand, and we headed for the door.

My favorite waitress opened it just as we stepped up the stairs. "Hey there, Jason. Go ahead and sit anywhere. I was just stepping out for a smoke."

"Thanks, Peggy. This is Lanie."

She stopped, a cigarette halfway out of the pack as she looked at me, slightly stunned. "A lady friend?"

I nodded and chuckled. Peggy had taken over the business from her father, Mickie Ramel, almost twenty years ago and knew everyone in town. "She's from San Diego. Don't go getting ideas." Turning to Lanie, I suggested that she sit anywhere she liked. I watched as she headed in before I turned back to Peggy.

After lighting her cigarette, she smirked and blew the smoke out the side of her mouth. "This the one you told your momma that you left behind and felt like it was a mistake?" I nodded, and a bright smile crossed her face. "Your momma and I were best friends for over thirty years. The fact you are finally trying to get back what is yours—admitting your mistakes and trying to correct them—she would be so proud of you."

"Thanks." I could feel the heat in my cheeks as I turned to head inside. I took in the familiar smells of the special blend of seasonings they used while grilling their locally sourced meat. It released some of the tension in my shoulders, especially when I saw Lanie sitting in the booth that had always been my favorite spot. Slightly hidden in the back corner, it was quieter and more private than the main room. Flashes of hanging out in this place with my friends as a teenager, and the number of times we had all almost gotten caught being wildly inappropriate in that booth, brought a smile to my face.

How many times did I come in here drunk and sit at this table, stuffing my face with a burger and fries, without a care in the world.

This place was filled with memories of my childhood, and I wanted to share them all with her. I wasn't sure if she would want to stay in San Diego or if she would even be open to moving here. I didn't care where I was, as long as she was there. That was going to be home. I knew there was also Kevin to consider. They were a package deal.

"Hi, my queen." Even I heard the heat in my voice as I ran my hand along the edge of the table before sliding into the booth next to her. My hand fell to her thigh and gripped the inside of it tightly, and I kissed her temple.

"Jason . . . ," she chastised.

I knew there was a sparkle of mischievousness in my eyes when I pulled back and met her gaze. "What? You said that I couldn't call you my baby girl anymore. I understand that because you aren't a baby girl. You are my queen."

"It sounds like a moniker in the same context, Jase. Please don't. Not yet. We have a lot of talking to do first."

I pinched her chin to lift it toward me and leaned forward to kiss her softly on the lips. "That's fair. Now, what do you want to drink?"

"Water is fine."

I rolled my eyes and gave her an even look when Peggy came up, took our drink orders, and left. I was going to ask Lanie how her day was, but before I could, she blurted, "What is your end goal, Jason?"

"What?"

Gesturing between us, she asked again, "What is your end goal? Is this just a friendly get-together? Are we reminiscing about the past? Or do you want to go back to belonging to each other?"

Oh, baby, you are mine. You just don't know how much I am already yours. If I were in charge of this, there would already be a ring on her finger and her name would be changed. There was no doubt, but I had to make sure it was all on the straight and narrow. "What do *you* want?"

"I can't take that kind of loss again, Jase. If this is just a fling to you, then—"

"Melanie Anne . . . you listen to me very carefully." I held her gaze for a long moment, making sure she was listening. "You are mine, and I have always been yours. You will be my wife, and we will have those kids you said you wanted. We will be sitting on a beach somewhere, old and grey, bickering about where we are going to go for the four o'clock senior special for dinner."

She studied me, and when her mouth opened slightly, I reached over and took her hands in mine. "Breathe." When she didn't look so panicked, I continued, "You asked what my end game was. So I'm telling you, in no uncertain terms, what my plan is."

"What about Kevin?"

"What about him? You mentioned yesterday he is doing really well in a new program. Do you want to keep him there? Stay close? Move him?"

She shook her head. "No, Jase. You know that I'm all he has. He could live on his own, but it would feel wrong to just abandon him."

A crease formed between my eyes. "I would never ask you to do that. You two are a package deal. You know how much I adore him. I'm just asking, after we marry, where do you want to be? Do you want to stay in San Diego? Move up here? Go somewhere else? Do you want to have Kevin stay with us? Live with us and our kids?"

"Jase . . ."

"Yeah?"

"What about your job?"

I smiled at her and reached over to wipe a tear from her cheek that had escaped. "It's just a job. I'll take pay cuts, never make tenure, anything it takes, just as long as I can have you and Kevin by my side."

"But you and I broke up before because your job said we couldn't be together. You pushed me aside before for *your job*. How can you guarantee it won't happen again?"

"And it was the stupidest, most ignorant thing I have ever done in my life. I took you for granted. You are more important than *any* job. I made that mistake once, and I will never repeat it. I will always choose you. I—"

Peggy walked up just then and handed Lanie her ice tea. "Did you decide on what burger you want, sweetheart?"

Lanie blinked and a couple more tears fell down her cheek. "I . . ."

Instantly, Peggy went on the defensive and smacked me in the back of my head with a menu. "You shithead! What did you do to make her cry? I know your momma and pa taught you better than that."

"Peg—"

Lanie started chuckling. "Ma'am, I appreciate the concern, but I'm crying because he's actually being sweet."

Peggy narrowed her eyes at Lanie. "You swear it? Don't think I won't take him out back and whoop his ass for hurting you. I'll make him find his own switch, too."

"You know him well, then?" She was smiling up at Peggy, and I sighed, knowing that woman had way too much on me to get out of this without some embarrassment.

A bright smile crossed Peggy's face. "His ma and I were best friends for over thirty years. I could tell you stories that would make you die from secondhand embarrassment."

I couldn't help the whine that came out of me. "Peggy, please don't."

"I won't because I know that I have plenty of time to tell her all about the night you came in here drunk off your ass and passed out in this corner. Had to call your pa to come and pick you up." Lanie started laughing, and I just sat back and rolled my eyes, gesturing to her to continue. There was no stopping this. She turned to Lanie and went on. "When George got here, he hauled him over his shoulder, and this guy here immediately threw up all down George's back and onto my floor."

"Dad made me come back here every week for a year to mop the dining room." I had a small smile on my face at the memory.

"He was seventeen at the time. Was lucky the sheriff looked the other way because George had helped his son out a time or two at the grocery store." I nodded, and then Peggy looked at me, smiling. "You were a kid figuring out his life. Moving on, you want your usual burger with no peppers?" When I nodded, she looked to Lanie. "And what would you like, sweetheart?"

"I haven't even had a chance to look at the menu yet."

I took her hand across the table and squeezed. "She'll have the buffalo barbeque burger. Fried onion strings."

With a quick nod, she turned and left us alone. When I looked back at Lanie, her eyebrow was cocked up in questions. "You just ordered for me. You know how much it annoys me."

"I know, but you're hungry, and I knew that's what you would choose."

With a sigh, she shook her head. "It does sound good."

"So, what have you been doing the last few years?"

She huffed slightly and played with her fingers. "Getting by. Working my ass off. Making sure Kev has everything I can provide him."

Lifting an eyebrow in confusion, "*You can provide him?*"

"Well, I can't provide him a male role model." Her voice was clipped, but she let out a harsh breath. "Sorry. That was a low blow."

I swallowed and kept my voice down. "But not untrue. I *am* truly sorry for all the hurt that I caused you and Kevin."

She squared her shoulders and looked me dead in the eye. "I hope so, because if we are trying our relationship again and I get hurt, then I get hurt, but we both have to protect Kevin."

My breathing hitched as I felt the sting and promise in her words. "Agreed, but let me make it clear. I have no intention of walking away again. Till death do us part is starting now."

She studied me for a long moment, and I saw the confusion and worry cross her face before she nodded. "Noted."

My breath loosened and my chest didn't feel as tight, so I took that moment just to watch her. The red booths with silver and laminate tables were the perfect background for Lanie tonight. Pendant, silver lights hung down over each of the booths, causing her eyes to sparkle. "Could it be possible you've gotten more beautiful in the past few years?"

"I could say the same about you, but I could just be hallucinating." She chuckled, and I let a small smile dress my lips.

"What else have you been doing, other than working and taking care of Kevin?"

"Seriously—" She took a long drink of her tea, sucking it in through the straw. It took a lot of focus not to think of what those beautiful red-painted lips would look like wrapped around something else much bigger. "Nothing."

"Nothing?" I narrowed my brows in confusion. "You seriously could not have spent the last five years only working, sleeping, and taking care of Kevin. You had to have gone to dinner with friends or at least spent time with Kami."

She moved her head back and forth as she bit the inside of her bottom lip and shifted in the booth. "After . . ." Lanie took a deep breath and let it out slowly, never taking her focus off the napkin she was currently shredding. "After you and I broke up and . . . then you disappeared, I didn't *want* to go out." Pain shot through my heart at what I had done to her. "It took a long while for me to want to get out of bed, and the only one who stood by me was Kami. So it's just

Kevin, Kami, and me." She took another drink of tea and then swirled the straw around in the glass, watching the liquid intently. "Like I said, I didn't expect to see you yesterday. But the universe puts us where we need to be. So, here we are."

Her eyes lifted to meet mine, and I had to hold back the tears at the pain I had caused her. I also had to hold back those three words that were too early to say again. I knew them to be true. They had never stopped being true, but I needed to prove myself.

"So, what about you? What have you been doing since you left San Diego?"

Besides regretting leaving your side every single day? I rolled my shoulders and steadied myself to tell her about my parents. "As you know, Dad had been fighting cancer for a while but was doing okay. Until he wasn't. Mom didn't let on how bad he was."

"You two video chatted every week, though."

I took her hand and squeezed it in recognition of her remembering that detail of their lives. She had always given me the space to talk to them if we were together for our regular video chat. "They covered it up. I noticed he looked more tired, but they just said one of the treatments was kicking his butt. It wasn't until after we separated that she told me that Dad's treatment wasn't working and there weren't any other options. He was terminal. That's when I applied for the position at CSU Trenton. They needed someone right away, so when they offered it to me, I packed up and came home to help Mom with taking care of Dad through treatment. I'd been home about six months when Dad called to say Mom hadn't picked him up from chemo.

"I had just gotten Dad settled on the couch when the sheriff pulled up in front of the house. I knew something bad had happened. I met the sheriff outside, not wanting to have him tell Dad. They told me how a drunk driver was speeding and hit Mom's car from behind so hard the car flipped end over end three times before it landed on the center concrete divider. The driver's side was the point of contact, and then Mom's car slid down another fifteen feet along the center divider before being stopped by the pole for the traffic control."

"Holy shit. How fast was he going?"

"Sheriff said they last clocked the drunk at a hundred thirty and he was pulling away from them. Had been chasing him since Stockton."

"Fucking hell. I'm so sorry."

I twisted and kissed her on the temple. "They told me the impact killed her instantly. So, small miracle in that, I guess."

We sat in silence for a moment as I gathered my thoughts. "When I told Dad, the sheriff was standing just behind me. Dad sobbed the rest of the night. I handled everything. I had to claim her body, or what was left of it, and organize the cremation and memorial service for her. For the next four months, my dad just stared at that damn urn as he shut down. He stopped eating and refused to continue to go to treatment. Said he didn't want to fight any more if Mom wasn't here."

I remembered thinking how I wanted to have a love like that again. Preferably with Lanie.

"What about you, though? Why wouldn't he fight for you?"

I rested my head on hers and tightened my hold it. "I understood it. He didn't want to live without her. Just as I had already realized I didn't want to live without you. Our lives were not complete without our people by our sides."

Lanie pulled her head back and twisted to face me. "So why didn't you ever call me?"

My throat was dry and it hurt to swallow. I had to take a calming breath not to have the walls close in around me and to keep the panic away. I had to admit this to her. "I was ashamed. I figured that this was my penance for hurting you. I deserved to lose it all. When I sold the house, I still had a shitload of my dad's medical bills to pay off. Not to mention dealing with the probate."

We sat in silence for a moment, giving me time to get my emotions under control. "The debt was astronomical, even after insurance, and so I did what I could to get them paid off as quickly as possible."

I took a deep breath and couldn't look her in the eye as I said that. I had no way of knowing how she would react if she knew *how* I had paid all that off. I would have to tell her one day, especially since I had more than enough to ensure she would never want for anything.

Her eyebrows scrunched together as sorrow filled her face. "I'm so sorry, Jase." I could tell she meant it and knew that she would have wanted to be there, if I hadn't been a stupid ass.

I just nodded in acknowledgement and squeezed her hands. "I'm okay now, though. I'm teaching and just trucking along, as they say."

Lanie threaded our fingers together. I cupped our joined hands with my other one and swallowed down the ball of emotion as I remembered that day.

"I'm sorry you had to deal with that all alone."

"It's okay, sweetheart." I kissed the top of her head again, then Peggy came out with dinner. Our conversation went on to more pleasant things, like Kevin's continued growth in art and how he recently got accepted to have a piece at the LA Art and Sculpture Exhibit. Seeing Lanie's excitement warmed my heart.

When we were done with dinner, I asked, "Feel like getting ice cream at Marianne's?"

She rolled her eyes. "I can't believe you'd ask such a stupid question. Let me use the restroom and I'll meet you out front."

"Alright, I'll pay Peggy and then we'll go and get it for you.

Chapter Ten

Lanie

Trenton

"Single scoop of strawberry sorbet, please," I told the kid behind the counter at Marianne's. The open-air shop was adorable, with its red and white striped facade. Jase had just taken a bite of his coconut ice cream when he looked at me confused. "What?"

"I thought for sure you would have gone with the root beer float. They use a local root beer so the sassparilla is rich."

"Next time." I smiled at him.

He stopped in his tracks, and when I turned to look at him, he was blinking at me with an odd expression on his face. "Next time?"

Slowly, I turned from the counter after Jason paid, and walked toward the street, taking a small spoonful of the sorbet, that was just enough flavor, rich, creamy, and just down right delicious, I took another bite and sucked on the spoon a moment. I took my time looking him up and down while making a show of contemplating it. I'd known before I'd started this date there would be many more *next times* if I had any say.

His eyes brightened as I slowly removed the spoon from my mouth. Before I knew it, he had me in his arms and was kissing me, hard. "Really? I promise you won't regret it."

I cupped his face in my hand. "Jason Rathborn, I never stopped loving you, even after you broke my heart. It took so long for me to even be able to think about you without crying. I'm giving us one more chance." I paused and made sure his eyes cleared of some of the euphoric glaze. "But, I need you to hear me when I say you won't get a third. You fuck this up and we are done. Forever. Clear?"

"Crystal clear." A bright smile crossed his face, and I felt my heart warm at the expression. He pulled me close, as I rested my head on his chest. "Thank you."

Jason kissed the top of my head and then pulled back, but he kept his arm around my waist. We crossed the street to a small park with a grove of trees, a walking path winding through them. It was well-lit, and I loved the clean air and smell of the earth here. When Kami had told me she was going to Trenton for her master's, I'd wondered why she hadn't picked one of the other schools with a more prestigious program, but she'd said it wasn't just about that. She loved the area and could see herself having her home base here, regardless of where her career took her. When I'd first visited her at the beginning of the summer for a long weekend, I'd seen what she did. Beautiful trees, atmosphere, and a mountain vibe, with all the amenities of the city. An hour northwest to Sacramento, yet you were still able to get to one of the lakes in less than an hour.

We ate our treats in silence as we made our way through the park, and when I was finished, I dropped the trash into one of the bins along the path. Jason tossed his in right behind me and instantly took my hand in his. The feel of it sent butterflies alight in my core.

"Lanie . . . ?"

"Hmm?"

"I wasn't just spewing bullshit at you at dinner."

"Which part are you referring to specifically?"

He took hold of my arm, made me stop and face him, and pulled me close. "I fully intend on legally making you my wife. I'm willing to wait until you are ready, but I'm not letting you go again."

My heart was racing. "Wife?" I didn't know what to say to that. Sure, I loved him with every fiber of my being, but that was a step I wasn't sure I could take yet.

"I know I have to prove to you that I'm not going anywhere. I'm not asking you now. I just need you to know where I'm at. As far as I'm concerned, you are my wife."

"Is that so?" I slid my hands down to his waist, wrapped a couple of fingers around his belt, and pulled him close to me as I rested my forehead on his chest. He rested his chin on my head, his arms sliding around me, and we stood there like that for a long minute. Occasionally, I could feel my hair move with his breath, and soon, I used his breathing to calm my heart that had started racing at his declaration.

Wife? He thought of me as his wife? Already?

Inhaling his scent, I let it wrap around me. It reminded me of walking into an old library with a fresh cup of coffee. Of study sessions that went late into the night. I took a deep breath again, letting it calm my ragged nerves and the tightness in my chest. He was so ready to go all in, and here I was absolutely terrified to take that step.

"What are you thinking about?" he murmured against the top of my head before placing a gentle kiss on my hair.

"I'm scared. I don't want to get hurt again. It almost killed me the first time. I know we are living the high of seeing each other again, but let's just take it day by day for now. See if the feelings last and if we still need each other as much as we thought we did back in San Diego."

Jason tightened his grip around my waist and let out a long breath. "Alright, but I know I want that family with you. I want us to have the kids, the dog, the house, all of it."

"I know." Pulling back, I looked up at him. His eyes were warm as they took in my face. "But I need time, Jason. You keep telling me that you want this forever for us, but I need to see that your words are more than just talk."

He gave a sharp nod, then we turned to keep walking through the grove. His arm was tight around my waist, like he was afraid I was going to disappear into the night. The silence through the trees was calming as we made our way down the path. We were circling back around toward the entrance when his arm tensed up around me.

"What's wrong?"

He shook his head.

Oh bullshit, mister.

I leaned into him but tried to make it look like it was a loving moment before I called him out on it. "It may have been five years, but don't forget just how well I know you. Don't lie to me. What is it?"

He kissed the top of my head again and whispered, "There is someone following us."

"Well, it is a trail through a park. I would make the assumption that there would be other people out here."

"You're right. Of course." He paused and looked over his shoulder again, and I saw him narrow his eyes before he turned forward. "Sorry, I'm just being silly."

I didn't like his body language one bit. What I didn't know was whether it was because he was hiding something from me or if he just didn't want to scare me.

Oh, hell no. No more trying to play it off. I stopped in the middle of the path, crossed my arms, and stared him down. "Jase, don't hide shit from me. Whether you feel like it's the right call or not. You have to trust me."

He stared at me, and I could see him warring with himself over how much to disclose. I knew things had changed over the years, but this was part of trying again. Learning to trust each other. With the way he was hesitating, I wondered what kind of shit he might have gotten into since his parents had died. I was just about to ask him about it when he let out a heavy breath.

"They look familiar, but I could just be imagining it." He put his hands on my biceps and squeezed, trying to be comforting. "Like you said, it's a public path. I'm sorry."

I nodded and took his hand as we headed back toward the diner. I would let him have this for now. "So, tell me about teaching at Trenton. Is it different than down south?"

"In some ways. Even though there are schedules, everyone here runs on mountain time."

"Mountain time?"

He chuckled, and the sound had me smiling. I had missed this. Hearing him laugh did things to me. There was something about it that was like a warm hug on a cold winter's day.

"You've heard of island time, where things will happen, when they happen?" I nodded. "Mountain time isn't as bad, but it's not uncommon for someone to be late, and no one thinks twice about it up here. If someone says they will be over today for something, it's likely they could be tomorrow."

"Okay, so what does that have to do with class?"

He squeezed me. "It means that by the time I am ten to fifteen minutes into a lecture, that is when half the class comes in. It's a bit annoying, but I don't dare wait 'cause then they will be in thirty minutes late."

"Alright."

"I like it up here though. Because things run at a little slower pace, I don't feel like I have to rush to get everything done. Yes, there are still deadlines, and those will never go away, but the day-to-day things just happen when they happen." I nodded, and we walked for a couple minutes in a weird kind of silence before he asked, "Can I ask you something? I know it might be weird, considering . . . "

"Go ahead. If I'm going to demand no lies from you, I will give you the same."

He sucked in his bottom lip, and his hand slid up and tightened on my shoulder before he continued. "How . . . Was there anyone after me?"

I stopped, and he let his arm drop as he turned to face me. I didn't meet his gaze, but I took his hand, lacing our fingers together. "No one significant. There were guys who tried to satisfy, both emotionally and sexually, but . . . no one could come close to what you gave me."

He chuckled and got sassy, saying, "Oh, so I'm the best you've had, huh?"

"Oh, don't make me pop that head of yours."

"Oh, sweetheart. You know exactly how to pop my head."

"Jason!" I lightly smacked his stomach and tried to hide the humor in my voice. "That isn't what I meant and you damn well know it."

"I know, but it was worth it to see the look on your face." He pulled me close and kissed me. His tongue danced with mine, and I felt lightheaded by the time he pulled back. "For the record, no one has come close to you either. Now, there were only a couple, but they couldn't even scratch the itch."

Heat burst across my cheeks, and I couldn't help but smile. "Only I can be the perfect little slut?"

When he tugged me closer against him, I felt exactly how my words had affected him. His hard, long length pressed against my stomach, and I couldn't help but lick my lips. I wanted to pull him into the trees and swallow him whole, but instead, I balled my hands up in his shirt to ground myself. Not yet. I couldn't give in yet. Not that I knew when yet was.

This is basically day one all over again.
I will not sleep with him on the first date.
I will not sleep with him on the first date.

Pulling back, I bit the inside of my lip and continued down the path. "I'm sorry. I shouldn't have said that."

"You aren't wrong, though, Lanie. You are the only one who can be in that role." He kissed my temple again. He was being so affectionate, and I wasn't sure how to take it. Was he just happy to have me back in his arms, or was this something he had developed over the years? He'd been affectionate and attentive before, but it was different. He had never been one for much in the way of PDA, unless it was sex.

Ultimately, it didn't matter. It was still just so easy with him. We sat on one of the wood benches cut from a fallen tree, and talked about Kevin some more, but we both realized pretty quickly that we had just settled into the monotony of the day to day. There wasn't anything really special about anything on any given day.

We were almost back to the car when he said, "So outside of work, everything is about Kevin?"

"Yeah. Kevin is worth it though. I really have enjoyed watching him thrive and grow into the man he is. I try to encourage and support his art as much as I possibly can. I'm also lucky that my boss is willing to allow me to work from home at times when I want to go to something they are doing at the center. I know that's a privilege."

When he opened the door to his car, he pinched my chin between his fingers, lifting my chin toward him as he bent down, his lips ghosting over mine before he kissed me softly. As he pulled away, my breath hitched at the same time my nipples hardened and my clit pulsed. "Fucking hell, Jase."

We drove in comfortable silence, his hand on my thigh, but I noticed how his attention kept bouncing to the rearview mirror. I tried to convince myself he was just being cautious and hypervigilant, but even though his shoulders weren't at his ears, they were still stiff, not to mention I could feel the tension in his hand on my thigh. The problem was that I saw a large white truck that had stayed a couple of cars back since we'd pulled out of the diner parking lot.

Once we drove up to Kami's apartment building, I narrowed my eyes at him. "What in the hell is going on, Jase?"

"I don't know, but I need to hear your voice once you are safely back inside her apartment, okay?"

I nodded but asked, "Is this just a protective boyfriend thing, or do you think there is something more here?"

He let out a long breath. "I don't know. I think we were being followed back at the park. I know I tried to brush it off earlier, and I would have continued to if not for the truck that followed us and parked at the other end of the parking lot."

I swallowed and tried to keep my breathing even. "The white truck?"

"You noticed it too?" I nodded. "Alright. Now, go inside and call me when you are upstairs."

He stopped right in front of the main door to the complex and got out of the car. I stayed where I was seated. Jason opened the door for me, and I gave him my hand to help me out, but he pulled me into his arms and pressed his lips to mine.

It started slow, but when I pulled him closer to me by his shirt, he deepened the kiss. His tongue pushed through my lips and tangled with mine. He pressed against me, wrapping an arm around my waist and pushing a hand through my hair. Jason swallowed the moan that escaped me, and I pressed my hips against him. Slowly, he pulled back, both of us breathing hard. "Lanie . . ."

"I'll call you when I get upstairs." I kissed him again quickly before he reached behind me and opened the door to Kami's apartment building.

While I knew he didn't mean to, what Jason had said put me on edge. I normally loved the dimmer hallways and decor of the building, but tonight, it gave me the creeps. I'd only been here a couple of times and was seeing things that weren't in the dark shadows of the stairwell and corners. My feet moved faster as I rushed upstairs to Kami's apartment. By the time I got inside, I leaned against the closed door and locked it, breathing heavily. A chill went up my spine, but the only thing that had happened was the possibility that we had been followed through the park.

Then a white truck followed us back to my best friend's house.

No. That's nothing to worry about at all.

"Lanie?"

My attention snapped to Kami and Eric sitting on the couch, one of the *Family Vacation* movies playing on the TV. She sat up straight, and Eric had his arm resting on the couch, a bottle of beer in his other hand.

"Sorry. I'm going to bed. I'll talk to you tomorrow." I pushed off the door and muttered, "Have a great evening."

I stripped when I got to the only bedroom in the apartment and changed into my PJ's. Before jumping into bed, I looked out Kami's window that overlooked the parking lot. The white truck that had followed us from the diner was still sitting there. Moving back so I could lie down, I pulled my phone out and called Jason.

"Sweetheart, you make it up okay?"

"Yeah, but the truck from the diner is still parked at the other end of the parking lot. Driver is on his phone in the cab. Jason, I'm not one to easily get rattled, but this does." I could hear the shakiness in my voice and forced myself to take a deep breath as Jason turned around to face where the truck was. When he did, the driver put the phone down and tore out of the parking lot and down the street without even looking for oncoming traffic.

"Okay. I'll reach out to some friends of mine and see what the deal is. I'm sure it was nothing. Just a coincidence."

"So you are just going to brush all this off? You were tense the whole way back, and I get it, Jase, but you are talking out both sides of your mouth right now."

"You're right. I'm sorry. I'm just trying not to worry you over something that might not even be a thing. Now, get some sleep and we will talk tomorrow. Sweet dreams."

"You too. Night."

I had just plugged my phone in when Kami opened the door to the bedroom, Eric right behind her, but she dropped his hand and he didn't cross over the threshold.

"What happened? Did Jason hurt you?"

I couldn't help but laugh. "No. He was great, actually. It was like we just stepped back into where we had been. Everything was simple and easy, natural. I'm going to give our relationship another try." When I smiled at her, she raised an eyebrow, waiting. "Don't worry, I told him that this was his last chance. He doesn't get a third."

"Good. Good." She nodded but then looked over her shoulder at Eric before looking back at me. "So what is wrong?"

"After we ate, we got ice cream and then took a walk through a park. We had circled back around toward the cars, and Jason said he thought we were being followed. Then on the way back here, a truck followed us all the way. It could be a coincidence, but it parked at the other end of the parking lot. When I called Jase to let him know that I got upstairs okay, I told him that the driver was still in the cab, and he turned to look. When Jase saw him, he squealed out of the parking lot onto the street, so not likely to be a coincidence."

"Did you see the make and model of the truck?" Eric's voice was comforting but firm. When I gave him a questioning look, he gave me a lopsided smile, heading for the window. He pulled the curtain back and looked out. "My dad is Trenton PD. I can ask him to check into it for you."

"Just that it was a big white truck. Jase said he was going to check on it as well." I turned back to Kami. "Go finish your movie. I'm going to try to get to sleep."

Kami reached over and pulled me into a hug, just as Eric said, "I'll stay on the couch tonight, just in case. I'd feel better if you two weren't alone." He took his phone out and pushed some buttons on it before he lifted it to his ear. "Hey, Dad. Yeah, I'm gonna stay at Kam's. Her friend was followed home tonight, and I'd just feel better— Yeah. No, she couldn't tell . . . . Okay. Love you, too. Night."

"Your dad instantly jumped on board with trying to find things out?"

"Trenton has grown a lot in the last twenty years, but there are still some hometown ways of thinking. We help each other."

"Thanks. Now please, go finish your movie. I'm gonna crash."

Kami kissed the top of my head and headed back out. "Love ya, babes."

"Back 'atcha." She shut the door, and I took a deep breath.

Stop overreacting. This is silly. It was just a coincidence. Now lie down and get some fucking sleep, you dumbass.

For once, I listened to myself and lay down. I pulled a pillow close against me as my mind replayed how Jason could still turn me on like a light switch. I smiled and before long, I was drifting off to sleep.

THE

DEN

DON'T LET THEM EAT YOU ALIVE

CHAPTER ELEVEN

JASON

TRENTON

Jason: C there all night?

Kai: Left a couple hours ago.

Fuck! I ran my hand through my hair and paced the living room. The shadows had obscured him pretty well, but if he'd wanted to stay completely hidden, he would have. *What game is he playing at?*

My phone rang, and when I saw who it was, I let out a long breath. "Hey, Kai."

"What's going on, Jason?"

I rubbed the back of my neck with my free hand and shook my head. "Fuck if I know. I took my girl out tonight—"

"She agreeing to be with you again? What the fuck, dude? Why didn't you tell me?"

"Remember how I told you much I fucked up?" There was an affirmative hum on the other end of the line. "We talked, and she's giving me a chance. I'm bound and determined to have her be my wife. Well, once I prove myself to her. I'm not fucking this up, Kai. She's the one, has been, and . . ."

"I get it, man. But what happened tonight?"

"We were walking in the park, and I swear I saw Cyress following us. I know he hasn't been happy about all the times I've won against him."

There was a dark chuckle on the line, then he said, "That's the understatement of the night for sure. He's pissed. Been trying to catch you cheating for months."

"You and I both know I don't."

"Seriously though, if that was him tonight, then he's got something planned. You know how he operates."

"Down and dirty." I ran my hand through my hair. "He doesn't just get you back, he destroys you."

"I like you, Jason, and I don't want anything to happen to you."

A huff of a laugh came out. "You just like your cut of my winnings."

"Well, when you win, you win big." After a moment, he continued, "He's been on edge lately. I will say that. Also overheard something about collecting a debt, but there are a number of clients who owe The Den. You are not one of them."

"Alright. Thanks, Kai."

There was a light hum on the line before he hung up. I sat on my couch and flopped back, resting my head on the back cushions. I'd won every dime from him fair and square. There wasn't a single inch of The Den that didn't have at least two cameras on it. Not to mention the cameras on each table to ensure you didn't switch cards from your sleeve.

My head rolled to the side, and a pile of assignments stared me down. Letting out a large sigh, I realized I was too wound up to be able to go to sleep anytime soon, so I forced myself to get up and grade at least a few of them.

Chapter Twelve

Lanie

TRENTON

The next morning, I didn't wake up until almost nine and then lay in bed doom-scrolling on my phone before I got up, grabbed some breakfast, and went back to lying in bed. Scrolling through the books on my e-reader, I decided to read a cute story of a girl who met the cover model she had been drooling over for months. It was an adorable little novella, and I finished it in one go. It was early afternoon before I heard the key turn in the door, and Kami and Eric walked in.

"Lanie!"

"Still in bed." I shouted. A moment later, she and Eric were standing at the doorway. Kami shook her head at me with a smirk on her face.

"Don't look at me like that. I'm on vacation, and I can lie in bed all day if I want to."

"You can, but you are going to have to get cleaned up. We are going out tonight."

Raising my eyebrows, I looked between her and Eric.

Eric tried giving me an out. "It's only a suggestion, Kam. Chip will understand if you aren't there."

Kami winked at me and turned toward him, resting both her palms on his chest. "He's your best friend, though. The besties should meet."

"I'm not going to a frat party, Kami. Sorry, Eric, but that's where I draw the line."

"It's not a frat party. It's really just a bunch of our friends meeting up at a local bar. It's not just the boys, if that makes it an easier decision.

You can leave at any time." I smiled at him. Eric was being real sweet about it. "Really, no pressure at all."

I let out a sigh. *One night out won't kill me.* "Alright. What time do we need to be ready?"

Kami turned, and I could see the excitement written on her face. "Really? You'll go?"

"I'm here to spend time with you, goofball. If you want to go to this birthday party, then we will go."

"Thank you."

Eric smiled at me and nodded before turning toward Kami. The love and adoration in his eyes were all I had hoped for my best friend. She needed someone in her life who looked at her like she was the moon and stars.

She turned toward Eric, who kissed her slowly and softly. I smiled as he wrapped an arm around her waist when she fell into him. When he pulled back, they whispered something I couldn't hear, and he nodded to me, saying, "I'll see you tonight, Lanie," before heading out.

"See ya tonight."

Kami watched him as he walked away with the most smitten look on her face.

After I heard the door click shut, she came over and sat on the other side of the bed and studied me for a moment. "Are you sure about this? I wouldn't even suggest going if it wasn't Eric's best friend. I've told him I'm not here for the frat parties, so we usually stay away from them. The night I met him was the first and last one I've ever been to since coming to Trenton."

I waved her off. "No problem. This whole thing with Jason is making me realize just how much of my life is wrapped up in making sure Kevin has everything he needs." Readjusting how I was sitting, and tucking my feet up under my butt, I continued, "If it weren't for the sponsor, I don't know where he would be right now. Velas ain't cheap.'"

"Velas? How could you keep that Kevin was at *Velas* a secret? Velas is reserved for the richest of the rich who need to take care of their loved ones, but don't really want to do it themselves."

Wait, what?

"I'm aware of their status and I didn't intentionally keep it from you. How could I have? Maybe I just never used the name of the facility before?"

"Seriously, something that prestigious, how did you not tell me?"

I narrowed my eyes at her in complete confusion. "I don't . . . How . . . . No, I must have told you." There was no way. She was my best friend. Hadn't I called her when I'd found out to freak out? I had, hadn't I?

Her befuddled expression morphed into a sassy smirk before she started laughing. "Of course you told me. Gods, you *are* tired if it was that easy to make you lose your mind."

"You fucking bitch!" I smacked her arm. "You fucking gaslit me! I did think I was losing my mind. You are my best friend. There was no way I wouldn't have mentioned to you. Fucking hell, Kami."

"Come on, I need to get some dishes done." She pulled me out of bed and down the hall, chuckling the whole way to the kitchen before she started working on the dishes.

The main room was small enough that we didn't have to yell at each other while we were talking, but I did raise my voice just slightly so she could hear me over the rushing water. "I still can't believe it. I never filled out an application, only received a call that said he was accepted and that there was a benefactor for his charter. I am only responsible for a thousand bucks of it a month. Which is a hell of a lot cheaper than rent."

"And you still haven't found out who it was?"

Shaking my head, I rubbed my forehead, realizing I hadn't really eaten today. "Nope. When I tried to push and ask them to have someone else use the donation, they said it could only be applied to Kevin. No one else. Which I still don't get. I don't know anyone with that kind of cash."

I stood up and headed into the kitchen when my stomach growled. The bread was already on the counter, so I pulled some butter, cheese, lunch meat, and a pan out. I prepped the bread by spreading the butter out and went into her cabinet to get the parmesan, but it wasn't there. I double-checked the fridge, and when I still didn't see it, I asked, "Where is the parmesan?"

Looking over her shoulder, she winced. "I'm out. Fuck! Are you able to make a grilled cheese without it?"

"Guess you aren't getting the crunch like you want." I stuck my tongue out and made do with the imposter grilled turkey and cheese sandwich, as she liked to call it. Once hers was done, I cut it diagonally and then set it next to her as she finished up the last of the dishes.

"If you weren't making me food, I'd be pissed. I just finished the dishes and here you are, dirtying more."

I rolled my eyes, grabbing half of her sandwich and stuffing it into her mouth. "Oh, shut up and eat. If you plan on drinking tonight, then we are going to make sure you are well fed and hydrated beforehand."

She scrunched her nose and shook her head, chewing on the bite she took. "Nah. I won't. Maybe one, but since Eric and I got together, I don't really have the want to drink much anymore."

"Alright then. I didn't realize you had cut so far back."

She studied me as I flipped my sandwich over, and she took a bite of hers. "You aren't even going to grill me about it?"

"Why should I? We are in our late twenties. We are, for the most part, past our binging phase. College is where you get to live, binge drink, have fun, make stupid decisions, learn, grow, and let loose on occasion, but also try not to forget that your education is important."

"I know. Preaching to the choir, honey." Her phone chimed, and she picked it up, reading the message. I watched as her eyes went wide. "Holy shit!"

"What? Is everything okay?"

She sent a reply with shaking fingers and then took a deep breath as she set her phone down on the counter. "Yes. Remember me telling you about the history museum wanting a curatorial assistant?"

"Yeah. You were going to put in for it." I smiled in realization as I pulled my sandwich off the pan and put it onto the plate. Absently, I turned the stove off and set the pan to the back to cool down. "You get a callback?"

"Yeah. They want to do a video interview this afternoon." She looked down at her phone as it buzzed, and she opened the email app again. Her eyes went wide as she lifted her gaze to mine. "In an hour."

"Well, let's get you interview ready."

Chapter Thirteen

Lanie

Trenton

We had been dancing for over an hour out on the dance floor, and I was a sweaty mess in need of either water or another drink. I had a tight teal dress on that laced down the sides, and with the way it was cut, it made my chest look spectacular. Now, I was a couple of drinks in and I was less self-conscious than I'd been when leaving the apartment in it at first.

I made my way back to the bar and was leaning on it when Chip came up next to me.

"Happy Birthday, Chip." I smiled at him, and he blushed, nodding in thanks. "Can I buy you a birthday drink?"

He waved me off. "Nah, better not. Since you are already taken, I don't want anyone to get the wrong idea and think that I have a crush on you or something."

"Eric may have mentioned that a crush may have been forming." I chuckled, trying to make light of it.

"Well, Kami talked nonstop about you, so can you blame a guy?"

"Of course not. Have you met me? I'm amazing and hot to boot!"

His eyes went up and down, and as he nodded his head, eyes going wide for a second in agreement, then chugged the last of his beer and slammed it on the counter. "You could say that. That boyfriend of yours is a lucky man."

Now it was my turn to blush. "Thank you."

"I'm going to see about that blonde over there who has been shooting daggers at you since we started talking."

99

I smiled at him and leaned against the bar again when one of the guys who had been eyeing me came over and ran his hand down my arm. I shook my head, and it took more concentration than I had to keep the sneer off my face. His hair was styled as to desperately trying to hide the hairline that was receding down the back of his head. Not to mention the shirt that was open almost to his belly button, showing off matted, oily, and who knew what else was in it chest hair. I did my best to ignore him. In a stroke of luck, the bartender walked up.

"What can I get you?"

Before I could say anything, the ass next to me answered, "Get her a cosmo."

"Ewww. No." I grimaced but didn't miss the chuckle the bartender gave. "First, I can buy my own drinks, and second, I'm very much taken. I won't be taking any drinks from strangers."

"You're taken with me?"

I rolled my eyes. "You wish. I am spoken for."

"Yet, he isn't willing to be seen with you at a bar?"

"My relationship is none of your concern."

He reached down and played with the strings at the side of my skirt. "I could slide my fingers right in here and make you cum in front of everyone. You would like that, wouldn't you?"

"Yeah, no." I lifted my hand in a stop signal. "I'm not interested in whatever don't know what a clit is, limp-dicked, two-pump, *wild time* you think you are going to get with me tonight." Then I looked back to the bartender and asked for a bottle of water. With a nod, he turned and handed it to me but stayed within a few barstools distance.

"Oh, I would be more than a two-pump chump, baby."

I started to laugh and saw Eric and Kami dancing behind him, laughing and very much into each other. "So you admit you don't know what a clit is and that you have a limp dick. Perfect. Thank you for that."

"Whatever, bitch. You're fat and ugly, anyway." He took another drink of his beer, that spilled down his chin and dripped into that matted chest hair. When he finally walked off, I met the bartender's eye, and when he lifted an eyebrow, I gave a quick nod of my head, letting him know I was fine as I opened the bottle of water and chugged half. Seriously, if the worst insult he could give me was about my weight and that he thought I was ugly, it was no skin off my back. The man needed to work on his vocabulary.

A chuckle met my ears as the man next to me said, "I think you were being generous with the two pumps."

"Guys like him are all the same."

He tipped his head in agreement. He had dark hair, a short goatee, and light-colored eyes. He had just enough of a sleaze factor going for him that could almost be tempting for someone. Just not me. Hell, I couldn't breathe too deeply from the overwhelming smell of the cologne coming off him. That poor leather jacket was probably saturated with the stuff.

"Rathborn, too?"

I froze, the bottle of water halfway to my lips. In slow motion, I turned to face the man sitting on the barstool next to me. "What?"

"Is Jason Rathborn just like him? Is he a two-pump chump? Does he treat you like that? Or do you shield your eyes from his wrongdoings?" He smirked as he took another drink from his tumbler.

"What do you know of him?" My heart was racing, and I slowly screwed the cap back on the lid of my water, placing it on the bar as I leaned against the polished wood edge, trying to hide just how much this was freaking me out. How did this guy know that I was with Jason? I looked past the guy and looked for Kami, who was dancing with Eric, Chip, and that blonde that had been sending daggers my way earlier. Swallowing, I forced myself to look at the man next to me.

"More than you, doll. The mess his life has been since he stepped foot in Trenton, the debt he owes . . ." His eyes looked me up and down as he licked his lips, all of which sent a chill down my spine, before continuing. ". . . to some very powerful people. You shouldn't trust him, and be very careful with who you think are friends."

"I'm very careful with whom I associate with. You're not going to be one of them."

His menacing chuckle accompanied the darkening of his eyes as he leaned forward and whispered into my ear, "Think about how well you really know that man you are inviting into your bed. Into your brother's life. Is he really who you think he is? Should probably make sure he's not into anything nefarious before pushing into that relationship. A lot can change in a few years, doll." He backed away slightly so he could meet my gaze under dark eyebrows. "You'd be better off with someone like me. I'd protect you. Make sure no one hurts a hair on your pretty little head . . . or Kevin's."

Forcing myself to stand up straight and set my shoulders back, trying to hide the fear that was quickly rising inside of me, I glared at him and said, "I'll take my chances."

"Not a smart move, doll. Heads are going to roll in this town. If you don't rethink your actions, yours just might be one of them." Then he stood and looked me over one last time before shaking his head. "Really is a shame. I don't care what that other idiot said, you are one helluva sexy woman."

As he walked away, I scooted up against the wall and sat on the stool next to it, leaning my back against the cool concrete. Closing my eyes, I let the chill seep into my back and calm my racing heart. I pulled my phone out without thinking, and my fingers flew across the screen.

Lanie: I need you to pick me up.

The response was immediate.

Jason: Where?

Lanie: Revolution. I'll be right outside the door.

Jason: You hurt?

Lanie: No.

Not physically anyway. My breathing had picked up as I remembered the guy threatening Kevin.

Kevin.

How did this random guy even know Jason, let alone Kevin.

Three bubbles went across the screen and then stopped before starting up again.

Jason: I'm on my way. Where are Kami and her boyfriend?

Lanie: On the dance floor. I'll explain when you get here. Please hurry.

My focus went to where my best friend was on the floor, and just beyond her was the man who'd made the threats. There was a sly smile on his lips as he lifted a glass in my direction as he continued talking with someone. I closed my eyes as my breathing hitched and concentrated on the cold concrete at my back.

In and out.

I'm not injured. I'm okay.

In and out.

I'm okay. Jason is on the way. He will make sure I am safe.

In and out.

Jason is coming.

In and out.

My breathing still hitched as my chest tightened and my head swam. *How does he know that I'm with Jason already? We've been together for all of twenty-four hours.*

Twenty-four hours. How were we publicly linked already?

"Lanie?" I jerked, and Kami was standing next to me. "You okay?"

I shook my head and met her gaze. "Jase is picking me up."

Her whole body went on the defensive. "Why? What happened?"

I discretely took her hand and squeezed, telling her what happened with the creep. A moment later, Eric was there, stumbling a step and tipping back the last of his beer before leaning down to kiss Kami on the top of the head. When he looked at me, his face was flushed and his eyes were completely glazed over. The corner of her lip lifted at the affection, but the worry etched in her eyes didn't leave.

"I need to talk to Jason. He's picking me up. I–I need to be just outside the main door for him when he gets here."

"Eric, sober up a minute and walk us outside."

He blinked and stood up straighter. "Wait. What's going on?"

Kami turned to him and gave him the abbreviated version. His eyebrows rose, and the man was noticeably sober in about ten seconds. Reaching into the pocket of my dress, hidden near the lacing, I grabbed two twenties and handed to the bartender, who nodded and wished me a good night. After telling him to keep the change, I turned to face my best friend again.

"I don't want to ruin your night. I'll stay with Jase. You guys stay and have fun. I'll be fine. I promise."

"Alright."

Flanking me on both sides, they walked with me outside, and once we were at the door, Eric turned me to face him. He lifted his hands to rest on each of my shoulders. "Did one of my guys say or do something? If so, I will beat their ass."

"I–I don't think it was one of your friends. He was probably in his fifties. He was hitting on me, and then he mentioned Jason, said something . . ."

"What, Lanie? Tell me."

I shook my head back and forth. Fight or flight had set in and I was determined to run. My muscles were twitching, and I could feel the sweat roll down my back. While he had walked away, I just needed to get away from the man who was threatening my brother. I looked up and saw Jason getting out of his car and jogging up the walkway.

The bouncer stopped him, and when he tried to explain why he was here, the guard shook his head. I reached over to get the door, and just as it cracked open, I heard the bouncer say, "Sorry, man. If she's not out here, she doesn't want you. Sorry to be the dick to tell you that."

"Jase . . ." I swung the door open wide, and he rushed toward me, the bouncer turning, which gave Jason just enough room to allow him through.

"Lanie." His arms enveloped me as I buried my head in his chest and leaned into the safety of his arms. Some random, greasy guy had threatened Kevin. It didn't bother me to have him threaten my head, but Kevin? How did he even know him? Jase was here. I vaguely heard Eric tell the bouncer that we were okay and with him.

Jason was holding me tight, his heart racing. "Kami, why the need for the pickup? What happened?" I could hear the worry and fear in his voice.

"I'm sorry, Jase. I don't know exactly. She went to the bar to get another drink, and the next thing I know, I saw her leaning against the wall, eyes closed, looking like she's about ready to lose her shit. There was something about someone flirting with her." His arms tightened around me as Kami continued, "Then she mentioned you and Kevin, but I don't know what is going on beyond that. She said no one messed with her, but my bestie isn't the type to suddenly want to run away. Maybe you can get something out of her?"

His head moved up and down against mine before he kissed the crown of my head and whispered how everything was going to be okay. His thumbs moved along my back in soothing movements, and I vaguely heard them talking, but all I could see was the dark viciousness in the man's eyes who'd told me heads were going to roll in this town.

And what did he mean about having Jason near Kevin? They loved each other, and Jason had always doted on him.

Was this real or just some sick joke a random guy was playing on me? But how would he know I was involved at all with Jason? How would he know about Kevin?

We were moving, and Jason carefully got me into the front seat of his car. He reached over, took my hand, and held it as lights flew by.

I just kept hearing that man's voice in my head.

How well do you really know that man you are inviting into your bed? Into your brother's life? Is he really who you think he is? Should probably make sure he's not into anything nefarious before pushing on that relationship. A lot can change in a few years, doll.

When the car stopped in his condo building's parking garage, I looked over at Jason and tilted my head to the side to study him as he took a deep breath, running a hand through his hair before squeezing my hand tighter.

Jason seemed like the same loving and caring person he'd been all those years ago, but what could the guy have meant?

He brought my hand up to his lips, and they moved against the skin as he closed his eyes and took a deep breath. A moment later, he kissed my knuckles and got out of the car.

Jason led me from his spot in the parking garage to a bank of three elevators, holding my hand tightly the entire time. I was too in my thoughts to register where we were, so I just trusted Jason was taking me to safety. Probably to his place.

It wasn't until we were in the elevator and he'd pressed the 18 button that some of the mental fog cleared.

"Holy shit. I didn't even ask if you were busy. I just asked if you could come get me without—"

Jason's lips slammed to mine, cutting off my rambling sentence. "I will never be too busy for you. I know I still have a lot to prove, and the fact that Kami let me take you home without a fight is a huge step, but I know I'm still proving I'm a man of my words."

I nodded and took a shaky breath as I rested my head on his shoulder and stared at the wall. Jason had come to my rescue, no questions asked.

Has he really changed? Am I really the priority?

Jason held me close, rubbing his hands up and down my back until the elevator dinged, indicating that we had reached the 18th floor, and the doors opened. After kissing the top of my head again, he shifted me so I was tucked under his arm and led me down the hall, stopping in front of one of only two black doors, with a simple silver number identifier, "18B," on it.

Jason took a deep breath and let it out slowly before unlocking it and pushing it open. "Welcome home."

I walked in and looked everywhere at once. My heart wanted to soak in every detail of my Jase, but my brain was screaming for me to proceed with caution. I vaguely heard the door close behind me and felt Jason's hands slide down my arms and over to my hips. "What do you need, Lanie?"

"I'm sweaty and feel icky from being in that club. Would it be horrible if I wanted to shower?"

He kissed the side of my head and then just below my ear, sending goose bumps racing down my back. "My shower is your shower, my queen."

My breath hitched at the nickname. I both loved and hated how it made my body heat and pulse in all the right places "Jase."

He let out a tense breath and rested his head on my shoulder. "I'm trying to not freak out here, Lanie, but it's hard when you put out the SOS pick up request. You are mine to take care of, and I'm trying to prove I'm still worthy of the task." After another moment, he laced his fingers in between mine. "The bathroom is this way."

He led me down a wide hall where there were multiple photos of us in San Diego hanging. I swallowed and squeezed his hand in mine as he led me into and through a large, spacious bedroom, bringing me into the en suite bathroom. My mouth dropped open at the size of the massive walk-in shower. Letting go of my hand, he walked over to a small closet and pulled out two fluffy towels, hanging them on a small hook next to the shower door. "You can use anything in here. I . . . I'll be in the bedroom."

He jammed his hands in his pockets, turned, and walked out of the bathroom, closing the door behind him.

I wanted to ask him to stay but stopped myself. My heart was both saddened and relieved he hadn't even asked if I wanted him to join me. With a sigh, I kicked off my heels. *Finally.* I hated wearing those stupid things, but Kami had insisted. Pulling the strings to the side of my dress, I released it and was able to peel it off, roughly folding it onto the counter. I took a deep breath and started ripping the tape off my boobs. Wincing and groaning, I finally got the last piece off after about five minutes. I turned on the water and, once it wasn't freezing, stepped into the shower.

The hot water beat against my shoulders and I lost time to the feeling of it. Way too soon, the water started to cool, so I washed up quickly, stepped out, and wrapped myself in one of the towels, immediately falling in love with how soft it was. It was a far cry from the decade-old towels I had at home.

I felt so much better after washing the smell and stickiness of the bar off my skin. The woodsy scent of Jason's soap helped a bit, as I thought through everything that had happened tonight. Without thinking, I reached out to grab some clothes from the counter but realized I didn't have any. I stared at the counter that only had the dress on it, wondering what I was going to do.

"Jase!"

Almost instantly, the door opened, and I wondered if he had been standing just behind it. "What do you need, my queen?" His eyes were pleading and filled with worry.

"Some clean clothes? I don't suppose you have anything that would fit, do you? I can go ahead and wear my underwear, but I was taped in for a bra."

He smiled sheepishly and turned into the bedroom's walk-in closet. A moment later, he came out with one of my old sweatshirts and a pair of basketball shorts.

"How . . ." I ran my hand over the old stitching. "Why would you keep this?"

There was a slight reddening of his cheeks as he fiddled with the fabric. "It was one of the things I kept of yours." He smiled but shifted on his feet, like he was a little embarrassed. "On really hard days, where I was missing you terribly, I would put it on to just feel closer to you."

My vision started to blur as tears filled my eyes. It was a little overwhelming but heartwarming as well. "Jase."

He pressed his lips to my forehead and brushed some of my wet hair back behind my ear. "I'm going to give you a minute." Then he took a deep breath and ran his hand through his hair before walking out of the bedroom into the living area.

I dressed quickly, and after combing through my hair, I looked for anything I could use to keep it up. Of course, this was his bathroom, and there wasn't a single hair clip or tie to be found. I felt a little silly for assuming there would be one, but I tied my hair in a knot and went out to the living room.

I lay down on the couch next to him and used his thigh as a pillow. He instantly undid the knot in my hair and started running his fingers through my hair as he looked down at me, meeting my gaze.

"I'm better, Jase. Thank you for coming to pick me up."

His fingers tightened in my hair, and as he scrubbed my scalp, a wave of tension released from my body and a soft moan slipped out.

His thigh muscle went taut under my cheek, and he narrowed his gaze.

"Sorry. What you're doing feels good."

There was a quick nod before he asked, "What happened, Lanie? You scared me."

Looking straight ahead at his hip, I let out a long breath. "There was this guy at the bar who, after I had pushed off a drunk saying he was a two-pump chump, asked if that meant you, too."

Jase froze. "What?"

Slowly, I looked up at him. "He asked if you were also a two-pump chump or if I looked the other way when it came to your wrongdoings. It was strange because I don't know who he was, but he seemed to know you. Told me to think about how well I really knew that man I was inviting into my bed and my brother's life. Said something about how I should make sure you aren't into anything nefarious before moving forward with you and that people can change over a few years."

"He knew about Kevin?" His gaze back at me was one of distress. I nodded.

"How could anyone know I'm connected to you? We've been on exactly *one* date since we met back up. How do they know about Kevin? Jase, who or what have you gotten involved with out here?"

"I've been here for four and a half years, so I've met a lot of new people. I've taken some side jobs to help pay the bills, but nothing has ever ended up at my door." Jason took a deep breath and let it out slowly, resuming running his fingers through my hair. "I don't know who that was. As for how they know how you are connected to me and about Kevin at all? I have no idea. Someone is moving fast."

Who would care this much about a college professor?

I narrowed my gaze at him and shifted some as his fingers stopped moving in my hair again. "Do you have an idea of who it could be that threatened me tonight?"

He nodded and slowly looked down at me as his hand slid down the back of my head and gripped my neck firmly. "Not everyone loves me, my queen."

Oh, fuck. That voice. Whether he'd meant to or not, he had slipped into dom mode, and my entire body heated. I could almost feel my pupils blow out in lust, and when I shifted on the couch, the thigh under me twitched. My breath hitched, and I looked up at him through my lashes.

"Fuck, Lanie. I'm sorry. I didn't mean . . ." Then he stopped and studied me. The anxiety of the night slipped away and was replaced with the internal battle of whether or not I should let my guard down again and ride Jason like the slut I was for him. The man could make me feel so much better so quickly. He was my grounding rod, and the electricity he fed me went straight to my clit. I hadn't forgotten that I had nothing on under the sweatshirt. Lying down like this, it barely covered my butt. I hadn't bothered with the shorts he'd brought out.

"Jase."

He pulled his hands out of my hair and lifted them in surrender. "Seriously, I didn't mean to go there."

"You did, though." I moved and lifted to my elbows, purposefully letting my hand run along the length of his cock, which was hard under my fingers.

"Fuck, Lanie. I'm trying to be good and respectful, and you are sending a million mixed messages."

I dropped my focus down to where my fingers were and slowly moved them up and down along the zipper before meeting his gaze. I was a goner. This man had me wrapped around his finger, and the wall I had put up to slow myself down crumbled to ash.

"What if I don't want you to be good and respectful? What if I want you to fuck my throat right now?"

He completely froze except for the twitch of his cock.

"Lanie, once we start, we are both cumming multiple times if I have any say, and you will be mine again forever. I can't . . ." A groan slipped through his lips as he tipped his head back as I leaned forward and wrapped my lips over the bulge in his jeans. I knew that would be answer enough for him.

In one swift movement, he was up and leaning over the arm of the couch, his lips a whisper from mine. "Same rules as before? Same limits?"

"Yes."

"What's your safeword, my queen?"

The word came out as a whisper, "Strawberry."

"Louder."

I grinned and sat up on my knees as my heart cheered in triumph. "Strawberry."

He removed my sweatshirt, reached back, pulled his T-shirt off, and then tossed them both toward the glass slider that led to the balcony. I reached to help him with his belt, but he took my hands in his and stopped my progression. Leaning forward, he licked down my throat, kissed my collarbone, and licked and kissed his way back up to my lips. "And when your mouth is full of my cock?" His lips slammed onto mine, and I tapped him on the shoulder three times.

"That's my dirty girl."

The

DEN

Don't Let Them Eat You Alive

CHAPTER FOURTEEN

JASON

TRENTON

As she rolled over onto her back, I released her hands and watched as they made their way to my belt, releasing it, and undid my pants. Her pupils were black in need, and as I stared into her eyes, I couldn't believe I had her again. My queen. The only woman who could satisfy me. Sure, I'd slept with other woman, and while I'd had release, it hadn't given me the satisfaction that Lanie provided me. Taking my hand and running a finger up and down her elongated body, slowly going lower and lower, I watched as the soft curves of her moved under the pressure. Her skin pebbled in the wake of my touch.

Just when her hand wrapped around my cock and squeezed through my boxers, I let my middle finger swipe down the seam of her pussy. Her hips lifted as she begged for more of my touch, and I chuckled low in my chest. "Oh, you haven't changed at all, have you?"

"No, Sir."

"You still my little slut?" I let my finger run across the seam again as she wiggled, chasing the point of contact.

"Only yours." She panted.

I let my finger dip just between the lips and graze across her clit. The gasp from her was glorious. "Horny, horny, horny girl. You said you wanted me to fuck your throat?"

Circling and pressing quickly on her clit again, I ran my finger up across her stomach, between her breasts, and held her gaze as I ran it along the artery of her neck. I couldn't wait to see her neck bulging with my cock. Slowly, I traced her full lips with the tip of my finger and waited for her to answer me. Her chest was moving in quick, short breaths as I smirked. "Answer me."

"Yes. Use me for your pleasure, Sir."

"Fuck." I groaned and stood straight, stripping my boxers off as quickly as I could before bending over and taking her mouth in a hard kiss, running my tongue along her bottom lip. She opened for me and our tongues danced across each other. Holding her chin with my finger and thumb, she moaned into the kiss.

I cherished her taste and nipped her lip as I pulled back. "Scoot down."

She slid down the couch as I positioned my knees on either side of her head. Taking my cock, I studied her, her attention fully on my hand moving in slow, deliberate strokes. When she sucked her bottom lip and looked up at me, I smirked.

"Tell me. When was the last time you had a cock down this pretty little throat?" Her eyebrows pinched together quickly, and I explained, "If it's been a while, then I need to let you get used to it again."

Her cheeks flushed as I stroked myself slowly and squeezed back toward the tip. "A year, but he wasn't as long." She swallowed, and there was almost shame on her face.

"I don't care that there were others after me." I gripped the side of her face and rubbed her cheek until she nodded in understanding. "You are mine now, and I won't let you go. I will fight for you, for us, every step of the way."

"Yes, Sir."

Leaning forward, she tilted her head back and stretched out her tongue. "Nuh-uh. My little slut needs to beg for it."

I ran the bulbous head of me along the seam of her lips, and she pouted. "Please, Sir."

"Words. Use all your words." My voice was needy, even to my own ears. I wasn't sure who wanted this more, me or her. The last girl who'd tried couldn't take me all the way down, and they didn't hold a candle to my Lanie. That was the bottom line. No one could suck my cock like my queen. No one was going to let me fuck their throat like my little sex toy laid out in front of me.

"Please fuck my face."

I lifted an eyebrow and ran my cock along her lips again. "Just your face? I thought you said you wanted me down your throat. To use you for *my* pleasure."

Her lips pursed together and sucked in the head of my cock, and it took all I had in me not to let her take me in. To sink myself into her warm mouth. She whimpered when I pulled away again.

"Beg me to fuck your throat, slut. Beg me to spill my cum down your throat. Beg me to use you." Lanie's hips rolled as she pressed her legs together, trying to get some relief, but I smacked the outside of her thigh and she stopped. "No relief until you beg."

Her tongue snaked out and wet her lips as she looked up at me and did just that. "Please fuck my throat and make me swallow every drop. Use me as your personal sex toy. Please, Sir. Please use me. I'm your whore to fuck and play with."

"There it is." I let her suck me in and then slowly moved in and out of her warm mouth. Pleasure I hadn't had in over five years washed over me as I groaned. "Fuck."

Her tongue rolled around me as I moved slowly, until I hit the back of her throat. When I pulled back, she moaned and the vibration settled in my balls. "That's my girl."

I thrust into her mouth a few times before I held myself at the back of her throat a moment, and when she nodded her head, I had to remind myself not to thrust hard. If she hadn't had anyone like me for a while, she needed to get used to it again.

Reaching down, I held her along the back of her neck as she waited. Slowly, I buried myself balls deep into her, without so much as hesitation, a gag, or anything from her. Lanie's tongue snaked out and licked the base of my cock, and I shuddered as my arm tried to keep me up. The satisfaction that went through me hadn't been felt in years.

I withdrew and pressed back in, watching her throat expand as I slid back down. I went slow, but my barely restrained control was slipping. With a pop, I pulled from her and leaned forward to slide my tongue through her pussy. Her lips wrapped around my balls and sucked at the same time I sucked her clit in, causing a moan to slip from her and straight into me. Flicking her a few more times, I pulled back.

"Naughty, greedy, little slut. Sir was giving you something to enjoy and you couldn't just take it. You had to go for more."

She smiled brightly at me as she said, "I love how you force me to swallow you, though. Why do you think I'm so wet for you, Sir?"

Oh, this woman is going to be the death of me. "You want my cock so bad, then open your mouth and fucking take it."

Shifting back so that the head of my cock slipped between her lips, she sucked it teasingly. Lanie was a fucking goddess at this. The moment she tipped her head back, I thrust hard and fast into her throat. Stroke after stroke, I cherished the feel of her around my cock. The way her throat contracted against me, the silkiness of her . . .

Thrusting and holding myself in her wet warmth, I opened her pussy up with my fingers and rolled my tongue around her clit. She moaned, and my hips moved involuntarily.

"My little slut is begging for my cum down her throat, isn't she?" My cock popped out, and she took a gulp of air.

"Yes, Sir." Her hands reached around to my shoulders, and she dug her nails in. "Please. Your slut needs to know she can please you even after all these years."

"Fucking hell, Lanie. There is no doubt you can," I muttered against the tender skin of her pussy. I was hanging on by a thread.

"Cum for me, Sir. Please."

With another quick swipe of my tongue through her, I leaned back far enough so that I could see her face glistening with pre-cum and spit. My cock jumped at the sight of it, and the head of me was turning purple with the amount of blood pooling there. Gripping her chin, I met her gaze. "I'm not going to last much longer. It's going to be hard and fast, and my little cumslut is going to swallow it all, isn't she?"

"Yes."

I stroked myself as I guided my cock back to her lips, and she sucked me softly and rolled the head of me around on her tongue. She gave me a nod, and it was like the cable holding me back sprang loose.

I thrust hard and fast into her, loving the way her throat bulged with my cock on each stroke. My hips moved with purpose as I chased my pleasure. I pulled out once for her to breathe. "Fucking come for me, Sir."

She wanted it, and I would give her anything. Every stroke now was bringing me to that brink. When she reached down and fingered her clit, I couldn't hold it back. I buried myself into her throat and spilled every drop. She worked quickly to swallow it, but the force of my orgasm was so strong, some of it blew back against my balls, coating both of us in my cum.

Sliding out of her, I bent down to kiss her. "Fucking hell."

She was licking her lips and breathing in slow, efficient breaths. "Was your sex toy still good enough for you, Sir?"

"My queen will never be replaced. She has and will always be utter perfection." I kissed her again and smiled at the taste of my release on her lips. "I think she needs a reward. What does my queen think?"

CHAPTER FIFTEEN

LANIE

TRENTON

I was still reeling with heat and pleasure at being able to let him use my throat like that. Fuck, I'd forgotten how much I loved him using me. He would manhandle me, fuck me hard, fast, rough, but it never left me scared or made me feel I was in any danger.

Jase was still catching his breath over me, and when he climbed off the couch, he disappeared from view. I knew from our previous relationship not to move, so I waited. Water ran in the bathroom, and then Jason reappeared, wiping my face up and pulling me to a seated position. Meticulously, he cleaned me up and ran his hands through my hair. "So fucking beautiful."

He pulled me onto his lap and held me, kissing my temple and running his hand up and down my side. Every movement kept my body alive, and I was sure he knew exactly what he was doing. This man had always known how to get me going within moments. That being said, if we just curled up and went to bed right now, I would be fine with that, too. I had wanted to please him. Give him something to show that I was really willing to give *us* a go again. I wasn't going to let some asshat who happened to know about us get in the way.

When his lips nibbled on my ear, I moaned and squirmed in his lap.

"I meant it when I said that you deserve a reward."

"I don't need it, Sir. I wanted to please you."

"Lanie, you please me and make me happy just by being here." He kissed my cheek and then cradled my head against his shoulder. "I had a taste of you, and I hate to admit that I had forgotten how delicious you are."

I huffed a laugh and let myself settle into his hold. He didn't stop moving his fingers across my skin, his touch setting a fire in its wake. He was recovering quickly. His cock was already hard against my thigh. When his fingers traced intricate designs down my side, along my outside hip, and onto the top of my thigh, I pulled away from him and straddled his lap.

His head nestled into my neck, licking and sucking. I tipped my head to the side and let his hands and tongue wander while I gripped his shoulders tight. I took in the feel of him igniting pleasure throughout my body.

"My good girl. My good little slut loves when Sir takes his time, doesn't she?"

"I do, but I'm not going to lie. I really want you to fuck me."

He chuckled along my neck and muttered against the skin, "Beg for it."

"Sir, please. Please fuck me with your cock."

"Since you asked so nicely." In a simple rock of my hips, he thrust up into me, and my head fell back as burning pleasure filled me. A moan slipped from me as my nails dug into his neck and shoulders as his lips wrapped around one of my nipples, and he sucked and licked.

"Fuck." Rolling my hips, I moaned as he moved with me. As his hands moved from my side and splayed across my back, pulling me closer, he hit every spot and brought me closer and closer to my peak.

Euphoria rolled through me as his hand slid farther up and threaded into my hair. Gripping near the scalp, he pulled, lighting my nerves on fire, and I let out a sigh of pleasure as my pussy squeezed his cock.

"That's it, my dirty little whore. Take what you need from me."

"Fuck me, Sir. Fuck me hard."

His free hand gripped my thigh as he lifted his hips and jackhammered into my pussy. The sound of our skin hitting each other filled the room, and the edge was in sight. When his hand lifted from to cradle my boob, I groaned in pleasure.

He twisted my nipple in his hand and ground out, "Fucking cum for me, whore. Drench my cock." He pinched harder, and I threw my head back as my vision narrowed and I saw lights dance before my eyes.

"Fuck yes. Your pussy is so tight around my cock." Then he was grunting and spilling his release deep within me.

When we both came down, my chest heaved as I collapsed against him, and his arms were tight around my waist. This. This was where I wanted to spend the rest of my life.

Chapter Sixteen

Lanie

Trenton

Jason brought me home a few hours later after Kami had called, worried about me, then he kissed me good night and told me he would talk to me in the morning. I didn't want to leave him, but Kami had sounded pretty freaked out. I was dreaming of our time together when the blankets flew off me and I groaned.

"Look, just because you had a spectacular night reconnecting with Jason, doesn't give you the right to sleep in all day."

Grabbing my pillow from under my head, I pressed it against my face and whimpered. I was pleasantly sore, but I had at least been smart enough to drink some throat coat tea last night when I got back to Kami's and then took a couple spoonfuls of honey to coat my throat, so it wasn't too sore in the morning. There was still some scratchiness, and it was a little achy when I swallowed, but totally manageable.

Kami pulled the pillow off my face, looking down at me. "Oh, stop being a baby. Get up. We are going to stretch those sore muscles out. Wear your comfy shoes. We are going on a hike."

Forcing myself to sit up, I stared down at my feet. "Just what exactly do you have planned? Not complaining because, yes, I'm all about bestie time. I'm just wondering what I'm in for."

"Hiking and swimming at Lake Jackson." Her smile was bright as she slipped a tank top on and turned to look at me. "The movement will be good for you. I know how out of practice you are with Jason, so I figured it would help you out some."

"Fuck you. It's not like I haven't had sex in the last five years."

She threw her head back and laughed. "Yeah, but we all know that none of those guys compared to him."

"I still had sex."

"But not good sex. Now get up."

I glared at her, and she stuck her tongue out. "Get me coffee and we can discuss it."

A few minutes later, she came in with a cup, and with the first sip, I felt my shoulders drop in comfort. "Now that's what I'm talking about."

"Addict."

"I am and not even ashamed." It didn't matter if she was talking about the coffee or Jason. Both were equally true.

We finished getting dressed and packed up our backpacks for the trip. An hour and a half later, we were pulling into the parking lot. "Hike or swim first?"

Tipping my head back and letting the sun warm my face, I breathed in the smell of pine and earth. I let it spread through my body before I answered her. When I opened my eyes and met her gaze, she was smiling at me.

"Let's do the hike first. The water will feel even more amazing after we're all hot and sweaty. Besides, once we swim, we only have to go from the lake up the path to the parking lot."

"Long or short?" She was smiling mischievously, and I knew it was a trick question.

I took a drink of water from my pack and narrowed my eyes. "So, are you asking if I want the hard ass shorter hike with spectacular views of the valley or Sierras or the longer, easier hike with lots of trees, rivers, and cliffs?"

"You know me so well."

"While I would love to see the panoramic views, I'd like to stay in the trees a bit. I've been to Hauser Canyon the last few times and have gotten plenty of the expansive mountain views lately."

She let out a sigh as we headed down the path. "I miss Hauser's trails. Great to go to when it's fogged in at the coast. Next time I'm down there, let's go. I love being able to look over the fog from the hilltop."

"Well, let's see what this trail has in store."

Smirking, she headed to the left and into the trees. Three river crossings, a waterfall that we stood under to cool down, and three more miles of gentle ascents and descents later, we were at the top of a small hill looking down over Lake Jackson.

"You greatly downplayed this trail. It has been absolutely beautiful, and then to crest that climb to this? A+, bestie."

She smiled. "It's one of my favorites, for sure."

The sparkling lake was surrounded with tall pine trees, and I knew that it was full of wildlife. Hell, the signs all up and down the trail warning about mountain lions and bears were a testimony to that. Movement along the tree line by the lake caught my eye, and I watched as a hawk swooped down into the water and pulled a fish out with its talons.

While there were occasionally the sounds of kids playing down on the lake, it was mostly quiet, and I took a deep breath, appreciating in the clean, clear air. "This was exactly what I needed. Thank you, Kami."

She poked me with her elbow and tipped her head down the trail. "Come on. I'm hot, and you know that water is going to be ice-cold."

Following after her, I laughed. "Maybe because it is literally melted ice!"

"Race ya!" She shouted over her shoulder as she booked it down the path. When we got closer to the shore, she tossed her backpack on the ground and stripped in record time. I wasn't far behind her as we rushed toward the waterline. Unlike me, she had kicked off her shoes and was now running on the rocky shore. The hesitancy in her steps to protect her bare feet slowed her down.

I bolted past her, into the water as it splashed around my ankles and around my calves before I dove deeper. The surface was cool the first few inches, but by the time I broke through into the deeper water, it was like a polar plunge. My lungs constricted almost instantly, but I forced myself to stay under, pulling myself along the bottom a little farther, cherishing the cold skimming across my skin, soaking into my muscles.

Finally, I pulled myself across a log and into the deeper, murky water. Kicking, I pushed myself down toward a row of rocks. Holding onto one of the larger ones, I pulled myself into a sitting position. Head tipping back and looking toward the surface, I saw Kami a few feet to my right, swimming down toward me. When she reached me, she shook her head and smiled.

My lungs were screaming at me, but I held tight a little longer as she surfaced. My eyes closed, and I rolled my neck but finally pushed from the ground, bursting to the surface. Tipping my head back as I broke through the water, I took a large breath of air.

"I always forget how long you can hold your breath. No wonder Jason loves your blowjobs," she teased and then immediately splashed me. If my best friend thought that would go unanswered, she was grossly mistaken.

After a thorough water fight, we swam back to the beach, laid out towels from our backpacks, lying out in our underwear, and made ourselves comfortable.

"Thank you for this, Kami."

She rolled her head toward me and smiled. "Anytime, bestie. You were looking a bit stressed. While I know that you enjoyed your time with Jason, I could also tell that you have been running the whole situation through your head a million different ways."

I let out a sigh as I rolled onto my side. "Am I doing the right thing by giving him a chance?"

She let out a large breath of her own and shrugged. "Time will tell. I know I haven't seen you as happy as you were when you came home last night in a very, very long time."

"But it's not just about me. I have Kevin to think about."

"And you are. I know you are thinking of the potential fallout of a second breakup with Jason. For you *and* Kevin."

I rolled over onto my stomach and rested my head on my hands, facing Kami. "He is my responsibility. Whoever I bring into our lives has to realize that he will be my priority. He's—"

"Stop right there. You need to take a moment and not be Kevin's caretaker or Jason's girl. You need to just be you today, okay? You can't take care of everyone at the loss of who you are, bestie."

"But—"

She sat up and glared at me. "No buts. Just lie there, soak in the sun, and chill out. On the way home, we will stop by and get dinner and drinks. There is a great dive bar with the best burgers in all of Placer

County." I opened my mouth to complain, and she lifted a finger and glared at me again. "You are on vacation. Please take at least today to chill the fuck out."

"Yes, ma'am."

Stumbling into Kami's apartment, we wrapped our arms around each other to keep upright. Dinner had been amazing. The burgers had been to die for, and once we tasted the watermelon & vodkas, we knew we'd be drinking a lot of them. Two or three drinks in, Kami had realized there was no way we were going to be able to drive and had made a call. Another drink or two, or three, or six later, her boyfriend had strolled into the diner, shaking his head at us.

Once we collapsed on the couch, laughing our asses off, we looked up at Eric and smiled. "Thank you for picking us up, babe."

He shook his head. "No problem. Chip's downstairs to take me back." He took a few steps toward Kami, gripped her chin firmly, and kissed her, commanding, "Drink two glasses of water before bed. You have an early morning."

He kissed her again, and when he pulled back, her whimper was not hidden at all.

"Do I need to stay out here with my headphones while you two take over the bedroom?"

Eric's gaze slid to meet mine as he said, "I'm not fucking her when she's this drunk. I need her aware of everything I'm doing."

Even through the drunken haze of my mind, he earned a bit more respect from me. He had already had it based on what I'd seen this week, but that pretty much clinched that he was a good human.

My phone was ringing as he walked over to the kitchen and pulled out two glasses and turned toward the sink. I pulled it out and started giggling. Sliding my finger across the screen, I said, "Hey there, Sir."

"How was your day with Kami?" There was shuffling and what sounded like keys hitting the bowl next to the door.

"It was greaatt. We were up at Lake Jaacksonn. Hiked, swamm . . ."
He let out a hard sigh. "You're drunk."

I giggled like a little girl at the obviousness of it and leaned back on the couch, head against the back cushions. The room wobbled around me, but I continued, "It'sss been a long time, but yes, I am."

"Gods, woman." There was silence on the other end for a moment before he continued, "Who is there?"

"Kami. Eric picked us up"—the p popped at the end—"and brought us home."

Eric handed me one of the glasses of water and ordered, "Drink."

"So bossy."

"Lanie . . . ," Jason warned over the phone before he sighed. "Hand the phone to him."

"Fiiine."

Eric took the phone and walked into the other room. I heard them talking, but my head was a cloud right now so I couldn't make out a single word. I looked over at Kami, whose eyes were filled with lust as she looked at him.

"You really like this one, huh?"

She smiled, and even though her eyes were glossy drunk, they sparkled as she nodded and said, "Yeah. I think he's my version of your Jason."

I lifted my eyebrows. "And what does *that* mean?" There was no way I was going to analyze her love life that much while three sheets to the wind.

She gave me an even look and whispered, though I wasn't sure it was really a whisper considering how drunk we were and she could hardly stand on her own right now, "I think I love him. I think he's my person for life."

When I looked back at Eric, his back went straight as he turned, and I swore his cheeks were a bit redder than normal. I had no doubt he'd heard her. "No problem, Jason. I'll see you in the morning."

I narrowed my eyes in confusion, and he said, "I'm staying here tonight. I'll sleep on the couch so you two can have the bed. Jason will be here in the morning, Lanie."

I glared at him a bit and tried to put on a front that I wasn't a second from just sleeping on the floor, but it was hard when his face was blurring and my head was swimming. Finally, letting out a deep breath, I relented. "You go ahead and sleep next to her. I'll be fine on the couch."

It was his turn to stare at me a long moment, and I tipped my head toward her. It was a silent confirmation that I was giving him the chance to talk about what she had just said. He had absolutely heard that.

"You sure, Lanie?"

I smiled at my best friend. "Yes. Please sleep next to your man."

She blushed, but he turned her to face him, and it was like he was searching something in her face. "I love you, too. Now, will you please let me carry you to bed so you can sleep this off?"

She froze, her eyes going wide. I chuckled and got up to make my way to the closet for a pillow and blanket. I stumbled a step, and Eric caught me. "Jason would kill me if you hurt yourself. For fuck's sake, Lanie, please sit down."

"Just need to get a couple things from the closet."

He turned me back to the couch and sat me down before collecting what I needed. Then he lifted Kami from the couch and kissed her softly before carrying her off to bed.

As I watched them, I couldn't help but smile.

THE DEN

D E N

DON'T LET THEM EAT YOU ALIVE

Chapter Seventeen

Jason

Trenton

I'd been on edge for the last couple days, ever since my and Lanie's date. I kept looking over my shoulder at work and just couldn't bring myself to eat my lunch, I was so worried. On the way home, I texted Lanie:

Jason: How you doing?

Lanie: I'm okay. Just reading and waiting for Kami to get home.

Jason: Good.

Lanie: What's going on, Jase?

Jason: Nothing. Just wanted to check in with you.

Three bubbles went across the screen, stopped, moved again, and then she answered.

Lanie: Okay.

She didn't believe me, and I had to admit, I didn't either. Since I'd walked in the door, I'd been pacing my living room and trying to figure out what the hell was happening. Someone had known Lanie and I were back together before *we* had even really had the opportunity to absorb it. We had gone on one date and hadn't even made the decision to be in a relationship for more than a week before someone had come to threaten her.

But could it really be tied to Cyress? Would Cyress really resort to hurting Lanie, just because he'd lost a shitload of money at my hands?

I laughed. *Of course he would.* Who wouldn't be livid over losing a few million dollars to one person all because he could read you like a book? It wasn't my fault the others hadn't picked up on his tells and taken him to the cleaners.

I need to distract myself.

Flopping down on the couch, I pulled a bunch of papers out to grade. It was the last of them for the week, and once they were done, I could concentrate on sorting all of this out.

The first paper I pulled out was obviously a copy and paste from a paper writing website, and I put it aside to deal with later. That was a whole lot of plagiarism paperwork that I didn't want to get into at the moment. The next paper had things that I hadn't even discussed, and when there was clearly a statement in the middle of the paper that said, "written by webwriteai.com," it was a pretty clear indicator that the student gave less than two shits about the grade.

I got through three or four more before my phone went off, and I cringed when I saw Cyress's name pop up. After opening the text, I saw a picture of Lanie and me at Mickie's. She was smiling and laughing, and even I noticed how much more relaxed my shoulders were sitting there with her. All of that went away, though, in the millisecond that it took for me to remember who sent this picture and then read the text underneath.

Cyress: Piccolo. Thirty minutes at Piccolo Bistro.

Cyress: We need to talk. Wouldn't want this beautiful girl to pay for your disobedience.

Jason: She has nothing to do with us or The Den. Leave her out of this.

Cyress: Oh, she has everything to do with The Den. The person they are connected to has stolen so much.

I stared at my phone for a few minutes. Was he really going to take his anger out on Lanie? Sure, he blamed me for his financial issues, but Lanie didn't have anything to do with The Den. She didn't even know of its existence. I'd have to tell her how I'd paid everything off eventually, but she didn't know about it right now.

My phone went off again after a few minutes.

Cyress: 25 minutes

Then there was a picture of Lanie and Kami laughing at a park on a bench with coffees in their hands, the Piccolo Bistro just behind them.

Cyress: Tick tock

Jason: OTW

Twenty minutes later, I was striding in and sitting down across from Cyress at a table in the back. Regardless of how fast my heart was racing, I wasn't going to let him have the upper hand. Yes, he had threatened Lanie to get me here, but I was going to put a stop to that here and now. I was going to keep my cool, make my point, and then head home. Maybe a few rounds on a punching bag would help ease some of this energy.

"What do you want, Cyress?"

"You've taken me for a lot of money, Jason." He lifted his cup of coffee to his mouth and took a sip, his dark eyes not moving from mine. "I don't take kindly to those who cheat in my establishment."

"If you really thought I was cheating, then I would be dead by now. Since I'm not, I'm going to be bold and say you don't have shit. News flash. I'm. Not. Cheating. I can't help if you are just shit at cards."

His head tipped to the side as he studied me, completely ignoring what I'd said. "How did you do it? I've watched you. I can see that you aren't counting. At least, you lose too many hands for that to be a possibility. Though, I would expect you to throw a few hands to keep us off the trail, but . . . it still doesn't add up."

"I'm not counting cards, Cyress. I promise you that. If I was, I wouldn't have taken you for so much without being caught. Probably would have taken you for a lot more or I would be taking a permanent dirt nap. The fact is I'm just very good at reading people at the table. You watch enough games, you can figure out what people's tells are. Just like everyone knows, including Maureen, that if she twirls her hair more than twice, she's bluffing."

Cyress nodded and traced the top of his coffee cup with his finger. "So what's mine?"

I huffed a laugh and let the corner of my mouth lift. "I'm not giving that up to anyone. Many have asked, but I will take that secret to the grave."

His eyes narrowed as his voice dropped into a deep threat. "I can make that happen on a much earlier schedule than you were planning."

I shifted so that I was leaning on the table with my elbows and threaded my fingers together as I met his gaze once again. "I'm sure you could. I'm not concerned about my lifespan. What I want from you is to leave my girl out of this. Your beef is with me, not with her."

"Any plans on returning to The Den soon?"

My shoulder lifted as I ran my finger in a circle on the polished wood table. "I have no immediate plans, but who knows? I might just get bored."

"Where is the money you've won?"

"What is this, an inquisition? It's my money—"

His hand slammed down on the table, catching the attention of half the bistro. "It's *mine*."

I tsked at him as people in the line to order their food jumped and watched us carefully. "See, it's not. Even by the rules of your own club, I won it fair and square. You have all games recorded for proof and security. Everyone who plays, plays by the same rules. You've said so yourself. Just because you own the damn place, doesn't mean you get special treatment." Cocking my head to the side, I poked at the anger that was itching to burst out again. "Unless you are changing the rules to fit your narrative. I don't think that would go well for you, though, would it? People would stop coming if they knew the rules changed on a whim."

"It's the business. Everyone knows the house's odds are stacked." I lifted the corner of my lip and huffed a laugh.

A hum came out as I agreed. "We do, but we all sign the same contract when we sit at the tables, Cyress. You included. You have bound yourself to your own rules. It's one of the reasons The Den has been so successful. You even have Don Kingsley there frequently. And two others that stop by on occasion. I believe it's been designated as a neutral location, even though it's firmly within Kingsley territory."

He shifted in his seat. "How do you know that?"

I rolled my eyes. *Why wouldn't I know that?* "People talk. You don't think the Dons aren't going to use The Den as a way to work out negotiations, settle scores, and have a drink together?" He continued to stare at me like he didn't realize I had been that observant. "I've been at tables where two Dons settled business over the game. Seen deals be on the table, and they leave it to chance."

Red creeped up his neck in anger, and I had to stifle the satisfaction that rolled through me. I was playing a very dangerous game. I knew more because of my association with Don Kinglsey and continued to go because Kingsley needed information. Information being transmitted only over felt.

"Watch yourself, Rathborn."

I had pushed my luck about as far as I could but reiterated, "Leave Lanie out of it. This is between us."

His glare deepened, and I saw the rage and fury he tried to keep under control radiate through his body. Slowly, he stood from the table. "I *will* get my money back one way or another."

"If you can't afford to play . . ."

Cyress stood and his hands balled into fists. Just when I thought he was going to take the swing, his attention snapped to the window and he stormed off. As he left the bistro, he kicked the door open, almost hitting a man coming in. I hadn't recognized him at first, but then shook my head when I saw that it was Chase Kingsley, Don Kinglsey's son.

I was a little surprised that Chase hadn't put him in his place right there. I would have paid to see that, actually. When he came inside, he went to the counter and placed an order for a sandwich and grabbed a bottle of water. Turning, he saw me sitting there and shook his head and laughed before making his way over, sitting down in the chair that Cyress just vacated.

"Professor."

I shook my head. "Chase, I'm not your professor anymore. You can call me Jason, just like your father does."

He ran his hand through the hair at the top of his head and then said, "Eventually, but it's only been a year. Maybe after I graduate."

"You have, what, another two or three semesters?"

"Yeah. Added a history minor. So maybe more." He smiled brightly at me, and I couldn't help but smile back.

"History, huh?"

He twisted the lid off his water bottle and took a long drink before setting the bottle down with a sigh. "I blame you. Got me too interested in dead people."

"Well, it *is* one of your specialties."

With a shrug, he shifted topics. "Dad and I needed to talk to you, so I'm glad I ran into you here."

"Happy accident?"

A wily smile blessed his lips, and I could see how he could win over a lot of girls that way. "I have heard that Don Westwood is going to be at The Den in a couple days. We would like you to play him. We will finance it, of course. You keep the cash if you win the pot."

I nodded. "Anything you want me to keep an ear open for?"

"See what he's into these days . . . What he's moving."

"This sounds a bit like the conversation I just had with Cyress." I let out a long breath, and when I met Chase's gaze again, he lifted an eyebrow. "He's convinced I'm cheating and that I couldn't have won that much just from him. Thinks I'm counting cards."

Chase let out a chuckle. "No way you would have gotten away with that."

"Well, he refuses to accept that and is now threatening my girl."

He lifted his head and his eyebrows pinched together. "A girl? I didn't know you were involved."

I took a deep breath before letting it out slowly through my nose. "We were involved a number of years ago. I fucked up and left her. Ghosted her even. I knew then she was mine and that I wouldn't love anyone else, but I didn't stop myself from making the stupidest mistake ever."

"Want us to watch her?"

Yes. No. I paused a moment before answering. "I don't really wanna ask a Don for a favor. I know the strings that come with that kind of request. Besides, we only recently reconnected. Like this week. I don't want to scare her off. Plus, she's from San Diego, would be a bit difficult for you to keep an eye on her down there, ya know."

Only, the smirk on his face gave me the impression that it wouldn't be all that hard. One of the employees came and gave him his sandwich as he leaned back to look at me. After a moment, he sat up and unwrapped his lunch. "San Diego?"

"Yeah, that's where I'm from. Was teaching down there when I met her. She has a brother who needs a little extra assistance getting through life. I was actually his high school teacher when we met."

Chase pulled the onions out of the sandwich as he asked, "And I'm assuming the school wasn't too happy when they found out you were dating one of the kids' siblings?"

"Nope. That's where I fucked up. After we broke up, which I thought would be best for her, I left without a word. I came here, started teaching at Trenton, and did my best to restart my life. Fast forward a few years to her showing up at the school to see a friend who is working on her master's. She's only here for a couple more days. I can't fuck this up again"

"Noted." He picked up his sandwich and asked, "What's her name?"

"Lanie. Well, her legal name is Melanie Carley."

He froze, and veggies fell from his sandwich onto the paper wrapping on the table. His face was carefully blank. "Melanie Carley, and she's from San Diego?"

"Yes? Why?"

He set his sandwich down and swallowed. His eyes shifted across the table as he thought something through. "Consider it done. No strings. She's under our protection. We have some associates in San Diego who can help."

The slip of his cool, calm, and collected mask was unnerving. So was the free gift of her protection. "Chase, why? What is going on? Do you know her?"

"Glad we were able to catch up. Um, text me where she is staying so we can keep someone close. Don't worry. She won't know we are there . . . just to be sure. What's her birthday?"

"July 22nd." His face was completely unreadable except for the anxiousness in his eyes. "Chase, what's going on? Do you know her?"

He stood and wiped his hands. "I can't discuss it. I need to talk to Dad."

"This is my girl, Chase. Please. Is she in any trouble with you or your people?"

The man shook his head, and the determined look in his eyes confirmed the truth. "No. I can guarantee we will protect her. I swear it to you. Now, please be at The Den in three days at three. I'll wire the money to your account for the buy-in."

Thoroughly confused, I watched him hurry out the door, and his phone was to his ear before he made it to the end of the sidewalk and jogged across the street. I stared out the window after him, trying to make sense of what had just happened. There was nothing that I could think of that connected Chase and Lanie. What else was happening in the underground that her name had been brought up?

My phone buzzed and pulled me from my thoughts.

Lanie: Any chance I get to see you today?

Speak of the angel.

Jason: Well, I'm not sure about that. I am a busy man.

Lanie: Twerp.

Lanie: Do you want to go to dinner tonight?

I smiled at my phone. This was what I needed. Her in my arms. Her vanilla scent wrapping around me like a security blanket.

Jason: Asking me out on a date, my queen?

Lanie: Yes, Sir.

Jason: Come over. I'll make dinner. Be there in two hours.

Lanie: Bit early for dinner, don't you think?

Jason: I need to spend as much time as possible with you before you have to go home.

Lanie: Okay. For the record, Kami is being really understanding. Though, she wants Eric to come over tonight, and I'm thinking it might be better to be with you.

Jason: Tell her thank you for me, if I don't see her beforehand.

Jason: Wait, *might* be better? Does my little slut need a reminder of who she belongs to?

Lanie: No, Sir. Not going to complain if you want to demonstrate how well you can use me again tonight, though.

Fucking hell, this woman. I couldn't help the growl that came out of me just before her next text came in.

Lanie: See you soon.

Jason: Don't wear underwear and plan on spending the night.

Lanie: Yes, Sir.

Putting my phone in my pocket, I readjusted my cock before I headed to the grocery store to get what I needed to make dinner.

THE

DEN

DON'T LET THEM EAT YOU ALIVE

Chapter Eighteen

Lanie

Trenton

"Holy fuck!" Kami exclaimed. "You look hot as hell. Eric, honey, you have competition."

Eric came around the corner, wrapped an arm around her waist, kissed her on the top of her head, and looked at me. "I mean, I couldn't really be mad at her if she left me for you, especially in that. You look good, Lanie."

Kami elbowed him in the ribs but chuckled. I looked down at the emerald-green, empire-waist, knee-length dress and smiled, pressing it down in the front, trying to flatten out a wrinkle that didn't exist. "I don't know. You don't think it accents the rolls at my waist too much? Or shows too much of my thighs?"

"Ah, fuck no. Shit, the off-the-shoulder look is . . ." Kami whistled and bit her knuckle. "Not so sure that he's going to be able to keep his hands off you."

"I hope not." My voice was low, but Eric chuckled at it. "Anyway, I'm stealing your nude flats, Kami. If they don't make it back, I'll buy you new ones. What time should I wait to come home tomorrow?"

It was Eric who answered. "Unless you want to see her suspended from the ceiling as I fuck her, then you probably should just stay at Jason's until ten."

"Eric!" Kami was shocked and bright red at what he had just said.

"What, Kami? I know *exactly* how much you love suspension. If I remember right, I bought your first toy box for your birthday *and* your first one hundred feet of silk rope."

Her eyes were wide as she turned her attention back to me. "Lanie! Seriously?"

I smiled and nodded at her. "What? Did you think you could tell me about Eric and I *wouldn't* make the assumption that he was into the same things you are?"

She sputtered for a moment before burying her head in her hands. Eric pulled her close and smiled at me. "Have fun tonight."

As I grabbed my stuff and opened the door to leave, Kami said, "Don't forget to stretch and hydrate."

"You, too."

Memories of Jason thrusting his cock down my throat flashed through my mind, and I had to press my legs together. I had followed his instructions to leave the underwear at home, but the bra was a must. It was a strapless bandeau, though, so it gave the illusion I wasn't wearing one. There was no way the girls were not going to be contained in some way. My phone dinged when I got downstairs, alerting me that my rideshare vehicle was here. After verifying the ride, I slid in and leaned my head back on the tan leather seat.

Slowly, I opened my eyes and rolled my head to look out the window at the buildings flying by. Only Jase would be able to get away with calling me a filthy slut and using me the way he did. Anyone else, I would kick in the balls. They wouldn't get to talk to me past the initial degrading comment.

I'd never forget the time we'd been at the La Brea Tar Pits and he'd pulled me into one of the closets by catching it just before it had closed behind a janitor. All of those people on the other side of the door and he'd been on his knees, my foot on his shoulder and his tongue buried deep in my pussy.

I shifted again and pressed my thighs together, resisting the urge to put my hands between them. I let out a long breath, trying to calm myself down, but I could feel myself getting wetter.

I opened the window to get some fresh air, and the cool spring wind came in and my nipples tightened as if ice cubes had been rubbed on them. One deep breath after another, and the knowledge that I was just a couple minutes from seeing Jason kept me in check. The fact I was in a stranger's back seat? Nope. Not that at all. No one else had ever been allowed to see or hear me cry out in pleasure.

When we pulled up, I quickly thanked the gentleman for the ride and hurried inside. With each step, I felt my wetness seeping down my thighs. A couple held the door to the elevator for me, and I thanked them as I walked in and pushed the button to his floor. I tried not to move, but I couldn't stop my legs from rubbing together to alleviate the need there.

The elevator stopped, and they stepped off with a nod. When the doors shut, I sent a text to Jase.

Lanie: Your dirty little slut needs you on your knees when she walks in.

I watched the numbers above the door grow higher and higher. When it stopped at his floor, I rushed out of the doors and down the hall to his condo. I had barely knocked when there was a, "Come in, my queen," from the other side.

Opening the door, I found him not on his knees, but flat on his back on the living room floor with nothing on. His cock was hard and twitched as he glanced over my body appreciatively.

"Come here," he said in that voice that I couldn't ignore. I locked the door, dropped my things on the counter, kicked my shoes off, and stood over him, my feet on either side of his hips. "Damn. You look amazing." His hands wrapped around my ankles and slowly ran up my calves. He took me in slowly, but my clit was pounding and I needed release.

"Thank you, Sir."

"Free your tits for me."

Lifting my hands to the top of my dress, I was thankful that the chest area was stretchy enough. My fingers wrapped around the hemmed edge and bando, then I pulled them down so that my breasts popped out. The cool air of the room had my nipples pebbling instantly.

"That's my girl, now lift your skirt so I can see that you followed my directions." I did, and I didn't miss the way his cock jumped or the way he took his bottom lip between his teeth. "My little whore is already wet and swollen for Sir's cock, isn't she?"

I moaned at his words. "Yes."

"Well then, sit on my face. Let me make sure you whimper in pleasure like the cockwhore you are."

I didn't realize I was moving so quickly, but when I straddled his head, facing his cock because I really wanted to suck it, he wrapped his arms around my hips and growled. "I said to fucking sit, slut. Don't you tease me by fucking hovering."

"Yes, Sir." He pulled me down, and when his tongue ran from one end of me to the other, I almost lost it. My hips moved unconsciously, and he slapped my ass over and over again as I rode his face.

When he sucked in my clit, I couldn't help but gasp as his fingers dug into my ass and sent waves of pleasure through me. My entire body tensed as I saw stars. "Fuck." I groaned.

Jason didn't relent and just rolled and flicked it over and over again, never letting up on the pressure he was building inside of me. Just when I thought I was going to career off the cliff, he backed off and licked me from end to end again. His tongue teased the entrance of my pussy before he dove back in like a starving man.

When he made his way back up toward my clit, his right hand slipped between my legs. There was no warning as he thrust two fingers into me and found my G-spot, rubbing it. "Jason, I'm gonna cum!"

He froze, pulled back, and lifted me off him. "What was that?"

Groaning, I tried to lower myself back to his mouth, but he held me firmly in place. "Who do you think you are, chasing an orgasm and screaming that name as you cum?"

"Sir, please, let me cum all over your face." He wanted me to beg for it. I was begging, and he knew it. Knew I knew it.

"Ordering me to my knees before you came through that door, screaming your boyfriend's name. When my cock is in you or when my face is between your legs, you don't use that name. My slut will use the right moniker as I make her cream all over my face." There was a slap on my ass, just hard enough to cause me to bend over and shake with restraint. "Is that understood?"

"Yes, Sir."

"Now beg. Beg for me to eat your pussy until you cum."

My whole body was shaking with need. I was so close, so desperate for release. "Please, Sir. Please let me cum. Please eat my pussy until you are drowning in my cum."

"That's my whore." Then he pulled me down and gave me exactly what I wanted. Within moments, the world caved in, and my legs shook violently with the force of trying to stay upright.

He took my weight as my legs finally gave out, but he didn't stop. I didn't even have time to overthink how I was likely squishing him. He continued until I was on the edge again and held my hips as he sucked and licked me through another orgasm. "Sir!"

Blinking, I was lying down beside him, my head on his arm. "Hey there. Was starting to wonder how long you were going to be out."

My inner thighs were still twitching in the aftermath, and I took a deep breath and let it out slowly. "How long?"

"Maybe thirty seconds? Long enough for me to realize you went out and to get you settled next to me. Haven't even had the chance to clean up yet. Don't move, baby."

All I could muster was a nod. I watched as he got up, went into the kitchen, and cleaned up himself before coming over with a warm towel, rolling me over onto my back, and wiping my thighs and core.

"Thank you."

"You are welcome, my queen." He tossed the towel into the kitchen and curled back up next to me. "What brought that on? You've never demanded I be ready for you."

Heat filled my cheeks, and I looked down to his once hard cock to see it softer between us. His thumb and finger pinched my chin, and he lifted it up so I would look at him. "You coming in like that, demanding to take your pleasure but in the scope of our dynamic. That was sexy as fucking hell. When you came the first time on my face, I just about lost it. I had to keep tasting you. I was a starved man, needing you. I came when you had your second orgasm. After dinner, you can have my cock and I can have your pussy milking me dry, okay?"

I couldn't help but just nod.

He pulled me closer to him, and I rested my head on his chest. "We still have another thirty minutes until dinner is done cooking, so we don't have to rush. Besides, I think the dress needs to come off. What do you say? Clothes free date night?"

My clit pulsed again. "Anything you want. I am yours, Sir."

He chuckled. "I mean, generally speaking. While sex with you is amazing, we have normal time, too. I'm just suggesting we just do that, sans clothing."

I looked up at him, and he was smiling. "Normality? I like the sound of that."

He nodded. "As long as we are together."

My heart leapt. "Not just sex, then."

"Not just sex, Lanie. I want everything. The good, the bad, and the ugly."

"Speaking of the ugly, I leave the day after tomorrow." I was tracing the lines of his abs and chest. The lower I got, I couldn't help but smile at the way his stomach would clench and his cock would twitch as it lay between his legs.

His fingers were running through my hair again, and I let out a long breath. "We will make it work. Nightly calls or video chats. Both. Whatever it takes. We will work on getting you up here again or me down there. Breaks, long weekends. Hell, during the summer, I can go down there." His arms tightened around me, and I slipped my arm all the way around his waist. "Just give us a chance again."

"I think we agreed on that the other night, Jase." I looked up at him and smiled. "Unless you throat fucking me was just fun and games."

The growl he let out was primal, and I recognized that spark of lust in his eyes. "You are incredible, you know that?"

"I do. And you know that one of my favorite things is for you to throat fuck me like that."

He kissed my forehead. "I know, and I appreciate it because fuck, you are so good at it. It's a tie for me. Either being buried in your throat or deep in your pussy with you bound to the bed, unable to move away from me pleasing you."

I pressed my core against him at the visual it gave me, and then I thought of something. "I have a question." He lifted his eyebrow, waiting. "Would you be open to trying a couple new things?"

"I'm listening."

"I have a list of things that I want to try. *If* I like it and want to do again, I can guarantee it would only be with you." I sat up and stripped my dress the rest of the way off, rolled over onto my stomach, and propped myself up on my elbows.

"You have a list?" He rolled over to face me, propping himself up on his elbow and moving his fingers up and down my spine. "Please tell me. I'll give you just about anything you want in the bedroom."

Studying him for a moment, I saw he was completely at ease. There was no tightness in his shoulders, his face was soft, and his eyes were intrigued.

I'll take those all as good signs.

"I want to try shibari."

"The art of rope bondage."

"Yeah."

I could see the wheels turning, but he looked at me and asked, "Do you just want the bound part of it or full suspension?"

"I know it's super complicated, so start with the binding. It will take time for us to learn to do it right before we go for suspension. I kind of walked in on Kami a couple of years ago as she was being hoisted up and have been intrigued ever since."

"Done. I'll start researching. What else?"

I blinked in surprise at just how quickly he'd agreed to it. There had just been a few clarifying questions and then approval. He didn't show any hesitation. His eyes were attentive, his jaw relaxed. "Oh . . . okay. Let's go one for one. What's something on your list? You can't tell me you don't have a sex bucket list."

He studied me for a moment. It was almost like he was trying to gauge what my reaction would be as he reached a hand out and caressed my cheek. His thumb moved back and forth as his focus bounced between my two eyes. "You know, it's a bit stereotypical, but I'd kind of like to try a threesome. The difference with that stereotype is that I'm not concerned about whether it's with two girls or two guys."

"Interesting." I sucked on my bottom lip. I'd never thought he would consider being with a man before. *He's always been so territorial of me.* "Okay. I'm on board with that. Either way, as long as everyone plays with everyone. Are you okay with either giving or receiving anal on a guy?"

His head tipped to the side as he thought about that. "I mean, an ass is an ass. So no problem fucking a guy. During blowjobs, you know a finger is okay, but I just don't know about taking a dick."

I looked down at the floor for a moment, thinking it through. "Okay, so you up for trying pegging? It gives us both a safe space for you to explore that. It's just you and me, and—"

Jason leaned forward and kissed me hard and fast. "Perfect. What else you got?"

Holy shit! Jason just enthusiastically agreed to me pegging him.

Taking a breath, I continued not wanting to stop this open momentum. "Sensory deprivation. No sight or sound. Only your touch."

He huffed a laugh as he traced my arm with his finger. "Done deal. That's an easy one."

"You next."

He thought for a moment. "Well, I'm going to have to do a lot of research on it, but electrostatic play. "

"Explain please?"

"Playing with electricity. It's a type of stimulation play. They have special wands for it that give a type of electric shock, sort of like when you rub your socks on carpet and zap someone. After a while, it can be used with sensory deprivation."

I smiled. "I've never thought about it, but let's talk after we know more. I'm intrigued."

He kissed me again and murmured against my lips, "How did I get so damn lucky?" Jason tipped his head back. "Anything else, my queen?"

"I have a full list written out back home, but those are some of my top. Do *you* have anything else?" He completely sat up and crossed. There was a line of worry in his eyes, so I mirrored the position. "This is going to be pushing one of my hard lines, isn't it?"

He winced. "Yes, so I'd like you just to think about it for now, and we can talk some more later."

"I promise to keep an open mind." I folded my hands into my lap and waited.

Taking a deep breath, he continued, "One of your hard lines was exhibitionism. Don't want us to have sex in public where we can be seen."

"Where we can be seen, yes. I'll watch others, but I'm not comfortable enough with myself to let others look at me. Please continue, though."

He studied me carefully, but I was trying to keep an open mind. He had never once asked to push a line. *Where is he going with this?*

"I would like to go to a sex club, but only with you by my side. I have no wish to be there *without* you. I want to go and be at one where people just have sex anywhere. There are shows where people on stage have sex, and I'd like to be able to watch one and fuck you while we watch."

I studied him and took a slow inventory of my own feelings at the moment. It didn't immediately scare me off. My body was not instinctively calling a no go on this. I opened my mouth to tell him I would consider it, but he continued, "I wouldn't want anyone else touching you, though. The only one who would be able to touch you would be me. Any changes to that would have to be thoroughly discussed."

Again, nothing was screaming no. "Find a show. Bring me information, and I agree to keep an open mind."

His eyes were wide in shock. "Seriously?"

The childlike look on his face had me chuckling. "An open mind, Jase. Not saying yes, not saying no."

"I'll take it." He leaned in and kissed me softly, languidly, and somehow it was that much sexier. Just as Jason threaded his hand into my hair, the oven timer went off. He let out a groan and glanced at the kitchen, then turned his attention back to me. "That timer had horrible timing."

I chuckled as he stood and then helped me up. With a seductive flourish, he pulled me into his arms and kissed just below my ear. I momentarily looked at my dress, but he had said he wanted a sans clothes night, so I would give it to him. Backing away, he headed into the kitchen, that fine ass of his teasing me the whole time. A smile crossed my face at the thought of fucking it. It surprised me how much I loved the idea.

He bent down to pull dinner from the oven, and then there was a growl that filled the room. He stood up quickly, an odd look on his face as his hands were balled up and pressing against the sides of his thighs. The heat in his eyes seared me in place.

"Fuck, I need to feed you before you can be mine to play with. Food and water," he said more to himself than anyone. "Food and water, *then* sex."

"What?"

"Are you okay? How did you make that jump?"

I followed him into the kitchen as he very carefully pulled dinner out of the oven, this time with oven mitts, and when he put the pan down to cool, he hissed. "Fuck, fire play may have to be on the list. The heat on my dick . . ." He turned, and there was a long drip of cum sliding down the length of him.

Walking over to the sink, I got a paper towel and got it wet. When he pressed against my back, I turned and wrapped his cock in the cold paper towel.

He groaned and leaned his forehead on mine, and it looked like he was trying really hard to distract himself by asking me, "What is first on your list?"

I let my thumb rub along the head of his cock and said, "I'm not sure what is highest on the list, but if we want to entertain the idea of a threesome, then how about the next time we see each other . . ." I took my free hand and grabbed his ass. "I fuck you for a change?" His cock jumped at my words, and I smiled. "Something tells me you are going to like that."

"I think I just might." Then he kissed me hard.

THE

DEN

DON'T LET THEM EAT YOU ALIVE

CHAPTER NINETEEN

JASON

TRENTON

Waking up with Lanie in my arms was pure perfection. *How did I forget how heavenly it was?* She looked so peaceful with her dark hair spread out on the pillow behind her. A small bunch of strands fell across her face, and I gently reached over and moved it behind her ear.

"Jase." Her word was a soft whisper.

"I'm right here, my queen."

Then, there was a soft snore from her, and I couldn't help but smile at how completely relaxed and at peace she looked. *Utter perfection.* During dinner last night, we'd talked about Kevin and how well he was doing, her job, and her hope to be able to move a little more up the ladder, or at least be able to get a remote job so that she could work from home to be a little more available for him and any kids she might have. Then we'd curled up on the couch and watched a movie, where she'd fallen asleep on my shoulder. I had ended up carrying her to bed, but the second her ass had hit the mattress, she'd wrapped her legs around me and rolled so that she'd been straddling my hips. We'd proceeded to have sex for hours. If there was a position that could be done in this room, we'd done it.

The next twenty-four hours were going to kill me knowing that she was going to still be in town, but not with me. We had talked about that as well, and she'd told me she was going to be spending it with Kami. I understood. I just didn't like it much. I didn't want her to go back home at all. I wanted her to stay here. With me. Forever.

Yes, I was still wholly in love with this woman. Her chest expanded, and she opened her eyes. "Good morning, Sir."

A small smile sat on my lips as I leaned forward and kissed her forehead. "Good morning, my queen." She stretched, and I looked down at her delicious curves. "How do you feel?"

"A good kind of sore."

I crawled out of bed and grabbed clothes from her bag for her. When I handed them to her, she thanked me and crawled out herself.

After she slipped on the shorts and sweatshirt, Lanie headed into the kitchen. "Coffee. I need coffee."

I chuckled and followed her out after throwing on a pair of pajama pants myself. Stepping inside the kitchen, I walked up and wrapped my arms around her, kissing her neck. "I could get used to this sight."

She laughed. "In time, Jason. In time."

Pulling away, I watched as she pulled eggs, bacon, and the sourdough bread out and started making breakfast sandwiches. My heart swelled with the hope of a future with her. I didn't say a word as she cooked, just watched her glide around the space just like she owned it. She did in a way. She owned me. Lock, stock, and barrel.

My phone rang in the living room, and I turned to go grab it. I silently cussed as I saw the caller ID. "Hello?"

"It's Chase."

"What can I do for you?"

Don Kingsley's voice was in the background, but he finally grunted and then trailed off. "Is Lanie Carley with you right now?"

"Yes. Is that a problem?"

"Thank God, and no, it's not a problem. I'm glad to hear she is." Then he was yelling in the background to someone and came back to me. *What the hell is going on?* "She going back to her friend's house today?"

"Yes." I was trying to not sound cryptic, but I didn't want to alarm Lanie. "Did you find the connection?"

"I am not able to say yet." He let out a hard breath. "It's complicated, and Dad is keeping it real hush-hush. She's heading back to San Diego in the morning, right?"

I groaned in frustration. "Yes, sir."

"Make sure *you* are taking her to the airport. Our guys are going to follow you and then head on the same flight to San Diego to keep an eye on her and her brother."

"No problem. I'll make the arrangements." Lanie lifted a plate toward me and put it down on the bar. "Anything else? My girlfriend just finished making breakfast."

She smirked at me, and the red that colored her cheeks was stunning.

"Just tomorrow at three, and you will be at table three. Everything is set up."

"No problem. Talk to you tomorrow."

After hanging up the phone, I put it down on the coffee table before going back into the kitchen. Giving her a kiss on the cheek and then sitting down next to her, I started eating.

"Everything okay?"

I nodded. "Just some work things."

Her eyes narrowed just the slightest before she shook it off. "Jason?"

"Humm?"

"This week has been amazing, and fuck, the sex has been out of this world." Her voice dropped a moment as she muttered, "It always is with you."

My heart dropped, and I instantly lost my appetite. I sensed a "but" coming. She wasn't going to call this off, was she? After the conversation we'd had last night, was she having second thoughts? *I . . . I don't know what I would do if she walked away forever, not after we finally reconnected.* I turned toward her and swallowed. "Lanie, my queen. What are you saying?" As much as I tried, I couldn't keep the wobble out of my voice.

I reached out and pulled her chin so she was facing me. Her gaze met mine, and there was fear there. Real fear.

"Jason, are you truly willing to do the long-distance relationship thing this time?"

I pulled my eyebrows together. "What? Of course." I'd walked away once before, and I was not going to make that mistake again.

"Are you willing to involve Kevin at some point in our relationship?"

"Yes, of course. My queen, talk to me. What is going through this pretty little head of yours?"

She held my gaze and swallowed. It took a long moment before fortitude set into her eyes. "Are you serious about trying a relationship with me again? One that could end with us forever?"

I felt the smile on my face spread as I cupped her face in my hands and kissed her. Pulling back, I whispered against her lips, "Lanie Carley, will you do me the honor of being my girlfriend? I don't want anyone else but you for the rest of my life."

She started chuckling. "Yes, Jason. I'll be your girlfriend. I mean, you already called me your girlfriend on the phone. So, it's sort of a done deal."

I kissed her again and then rested my forehead against hers. "Wasn't a done deal until you agreed to it. We may claim that you are my little dirty slut, but I recognize that doesn't mean the same thing to everyone. You are mine in every way possible."

A bright smile crossed her face as her cheeks bloomed red. I reached out and cupped her cheek, running my thumb across her cheekbone. "Now that *that* is settled, I'm going to drop you off at Kami's so you have another day with her, and *I* will be the one taking you to the airport tomorrow. What time do you need to be there?"

"Jase, I can get a cab or something. Don't you have to work?"

"And miss taking my girlfriend to the airport? No way. Now finish up breakfast and drink your water. You are probably dehydrated from yesterday." Her cheeks flushed red, but she did what I said. "That's my girl."

THE

DEN

DON'T LET THEM EAT YOU ALIVE

CHAPTER TWENTY

LANIE

TRENTON

When I opened the door the next morning, Jason had his hands behind his back and he looked at me from my feet right on up my body. "Lanie, you . . . fuck. If we didn't have to leave for the airport in ten minutes, I'd show you just how much I appreciate that look."

"I'm in leggings and an oversized sweatshirt, Jase. It's not lingerie or a ballgown. Also, I didn't wash my hair last night, so it's just up in a messy bun. And yes, I do have to go home. I need to get back to Kevin." I stepped aside as he walked into the apartment.

"One, I will always think you are sexy. I love every ounce of your curves, my queen. Second, where is Kami?"

I have a hard time believing he loves my curves, even if he doesn't seem to mind them all that much. I've gained weight, though, and hate the way my stomach hangs out more. I headed to the couch and sat down, looking down at my hands. "Kami already left for school."

A moment later, he set something on the coffee table and knelt before me, lifting my chin so I was forced to look at him. "What's going through your head?"

Searching his gaze, I swallowed. We'd had this conversation years ago, but I still didn't get it. "You know how I feel about my body."

"Melanie Anne Carley." His voice was soft, and he let out a long breath. "I told you then, and I'll say it again now. I love your body. I love being able to hold onto your hips and pull you close. I don't feel like I'm going to break you when we have rough sex. I love the way your eyes shine when you are happy. The way your whole body comes

159

alive when you talk about Kevin. The way your thighs press against my head to keep my ears warm—"

I couldn't help but laugh at him. "Seriously, Jason?"

"Well, I figured if the other things I love about your body didn't change your mind, then maybe that visual would get you out of your own head space."

"But if I lost like fifty pounds—"

He shook his head. "No, Lanie. If you want to change your body, I respect that. It is your body. But don't you dare change it because you think that I am disappointed in your looks because I assure you, it is *quite* the opposite." His eyes dropped to my lips before the tip of his tongue peeked out and wet his bottom lip. "Each and every part of you is perfect."

I looked off to the side, his finger still on my chin. "I'm not a size eight."

"Let me ask you something. Do you want to be thinner because you think you would be healthier like that? Do you think you will feel better about yourself? Or do you think it will make me happier?"

My focus snapped back to him, and I tilted my head. A million things were flying through my brain, but when I went to lock onto one and give him an explanation, it disappeared and crumbled to dust. His smirk had me shaking my head and smiling. "Yeah, that's what I thought. You are my badass queen. Understood?"

"Yes, Sir."

"Now, would you like a present before we head out?"

Narrowing my eyes suspiciously, I stared at him. His face was filled with a confidence and dominance that no one else could assume with me as he slipped deep into that Sir role. Reaching back, he grabbed the bag on the coffee table and handed it to me.

I didn't take my eyes off him as I reached in and pulled out a hot-pink silicone egg with a three-inch tail and a small bulb on the end. "Press the bulb and hold it for a second."

When I did, the larger egg vibrated quickly. My focus snapped back to him, and my eyes went wide. "Sir."

"It's already programmed into my phone." My mouth dropped open in shock. "You'll follow my orders to wear that one day and keep it on. You will endure the punishment of your pleasure at my whim."

"When?"

He shook his head. "I will let you know because there will be a time, I'll have to remind you that you're my little slut."

"Sir?"

He leaned forward and kissed me softly on the lips. "Behave or I'll have to punish you, my queen."

Moving my head up and down, he smiled, just as my alarm went off, reminding me that we needed to leave for the airport. We both groaned at the sound, and when he pulled back, I pouted. "I don't wanna."

He took my present, placed it in the bag before getting up, and put it into my suitcase. When he zipped it up, I watched his shoulders drop with a heavy breath. Standing, I went behind him and wrapped my arms around his waist, laying my head on his shoulder. Jason's hand rested over mine and squeezed. I heard the ragged breath he took against my cheek. I squeezed him a little tighter and inhaled his tobacco and old-book scent.

His voice was low and full of emotion as he said, "I know that you need to go and that Kevin needs you, but I don't want you to."

I smiled against his back. "We'll have visits, remember?"

He nodded, took my hand, and grabbed my suitcase in the other. "Let's head out."

Jason didn't let go of me until I was firmly in the passenger seat of the car. His lips pressed to my cheek softly, igniting butterflies within me, before he moved back, shut the door, and walked around to the driver's side. *Gods, I'm going to miss him.* Once he was situated, he tangled our fingers together again and brought them up to his lips for a soft kiss before starting the car.

We were silent for the whole drive, but as it was with us, it wasn't uncomfortable. The silence wasn't the problem. It was how loud the sadness of my departure was. I had him again. He'd said he wanted to continue long distance. Find a way to make it work. The present in my suitcase was confirmation of that.

I twisted slightly in the seat, not taking my eyes off him the rest of the drive. Every line, hair, and movement, I committed to memory. By the time he pulled into the parking garage, grabbed the ticket from the machine, and glanced over at me, there was a dark lust in his eyes. I didn't know what I had done to start it, but there simply wasn't time for us to enjoy ourselves. My flight left in two hours, and who knew how long the security line was going to be. His thumb moved against my skin again, rubbing the thin silver band on my finger, and when he licked his lips, I asked, "Jase?"

His words were tight when he gritted out, "My little slut has been teasing me the entire way here."

I leaned back, completely confused. "What? I didn't say or do anything. I literally just sat here holding your hand. In silence even."

"My queen, you don't have to do anything. You just are. You are sexy, beautiful, brilliant, and I will never not want you. So yes, you *just sitting there* is still a huge tease. One I have to do something about."

He didn't stop driving through the garage, even though there were tons of places to park. "Jase, where are you going? Nothing you are saying makes any sense."

He pulled into the spot on the far end of the top level, where there was no one around.

"Back seat. Now." I blinked at him, and when he lifted an eyebrow, I got out of the car and climbed into the back seat. "Lie down."

I did as he got out and opened the back, driver's side door. Sitting up on my elbows, I looked at him, and he growled as he came forward, crawling over me. His head lowered as he kissed my stomach, his eyes looking up at me.

"I need one more taste of my play toy before she leaves."

Fuck.

Chapter Twenty-One

Lanie

San Diego

No thanks to Jason, I barely made my flight and was just grateful to have only a carry-on. If I had to have checked my luggage, there would have been no way it would have made it home otherwise. They shut the doors behind me, and as I settled into my seat, exhaustion took over. I didn't remember takeoff, nor most of the flight. Even the drive home was mostly on autopilot. Once I was inside the apartment, I was going to talk to Kevin and then crash out the second he went to bed.

I could hear Kevin playing video games on the TV as I stepped up to the door. Sliding the key into the lock, I turned it, but before I could get the door opened, I heard the game pause and Kevin's, "Ms. Jones! My sissy is home."

By the time I opened the door, he was standing there smiling from ear to ear. "Did you have fun with Kami?"

"I sure did. We hiked up at Lake Jackson and went swimming. It was fun to see her again."

"Can she come down here next time?"

"I'll ask her." I thought it was sweet that he cared for her so much. She'd been around most of the time I'd been his legal guardian, so it made sense. "Did you have fun with Ms. Jones?"

"We did a puzzle, and then she let me paint it." He pointed to the wall where a large circle picture now hung. I took a few steps toward it and heard Kevin pull my luggage into the apartment. I blinked and looked at Ms. Jones, who was smiling.

"Kevin finished it last night and insisted that we hang it up for you." A confused, questioning look came across her face, but I looked back at the almost perfect representation of the flower garden we'd had at the house we'd grown up in. The vines along the back wall, with the honeysuckle along the sides and the double begonias, chrysanthemums, honeysuckle, and violets all in bloom. "He said you would know what it is?"

Tears filled my eyes as I looked at my brother, who was shifting on his feet and looking off to the side. "Kev, it's beautiful."

He smiled. "After we finished the puzzle, I went and got my paints. I have been thinking of Mom and Dad a lot. Wanted something to remember our old home."

When I nodded, a tear slipped out, and I quickly wiped it away. "It's perfect. I love that you hung it up here so we can see it anywhere in the apartment."

Kevin had been mentioning our parents more and more lately. Despite everything that had happened, they had raised us. He had been just an infant when Mom and Uncle Thom had had their falling out. I'd thought about my cousin Chase on and off for years, and after talking to Kami about them, I couldn't shake the feeling that I needed to find them. I stared at the intricate lines of the petals of each flower that Kevin had painted, remembering all the times that Chase and I had run and played in the backyard.

"How long had he worked on this? "Kevin, did you go to Velas this week?"

"Yes, Sissy."

I looked at Ms. Jones and then back to the painting. "Did you sleep? This is amazing."

Ms. Jones put her arm around my shoulders and said softly, "He was adamant that I not say anything. He wanted it to be a surprise. Said he had good memories there."

Nodding, I let out a long breath, pulling back all the emotions threatening to take over. I missed my parents, and while Kevin was a lot sometimes, he was worth every moment. As my thoughts drifted to the other man in my life who was a lot, but also worth it, I sighed. So much time had passed and so much had changed since Jason had last seen my brother. If he was serious about us trying again, he had to understand that Kevin would always come first. Hopefully, if Jason and I progressed, he would understand that.

"Now that you're home safe and sound, I'm going to head out. Kevin was a charmer, as always. He even tried to get me to have coffee with Mr. Klein down the hall." She gave him a pointed look.

"He's nice. You're nice. You need family, Ms. Jones," Kevin said as he headed back to the couch to continue his video game.

I smiled at her. "He's not wrong. Also, I've seen the way Mr. Klein looks at you."

Her cheeks blushed as she turned and grabbed her purse from the counter. "Well then, it's a good thing that I set up a lunch date with him tomorrow, isn't it?"

I chuckled and walked her to the door. "It is. Thank you again for staying with him. He's usually fine for a night or two, but I know it makes him more comfortable when there is someone in the house with him."

"My pleasure. Did you have fun at least?"

"Yeah. It was good to see Kami." I looked back at Kevin, who was fully back into his game, and then returned my attention to Ms. Jones. "Can I ask you a personal question?"

"Of course."

"If someone hurt you, would you give them another chance?"

She studied me for a moment, tilting her head to the side. "Are we talking *found him in bed with someone else* kind of hurt you or *someone backstabbed you* kind of hurt?"

"The kind where he sort of disappeared off the face of the planet." I lifted an eyebrow. She'd helped Kami with the fallout of everything that was Jason, and I would forever be appreciative.

"Jason?" Her eyes were wide, but she managed to keep her voice down. I nodded and chewed on my bottom lip. "You ran into him?"

I took a deep breath and let it out slowly, nodding again. "I shouldn't have been surprised. I knew that his parents lived in Trenton . . . and yet I didn't think of all the places I could run into him, it would be while I was visiting Kami."

"You loved him so fiercely, Lanie. What does your heart say?"

"My heart was all in the second that I saw him standing in that classroom. It's my brain asking if it's worth risking it. Mostly because of Kevin."

She smiled at me. "Of course you are going to be concerned about him. He's your brother."

I turned to look over my shoulder at Kevin. Sadness filled me, and I swallowed hard around the ball of emotion in my throat. "I'm all he has left."

"Just make sure that Jason knows that Kevin is your priority and you two are a package deal. If he wants this with you, then he will happily accept that."

"Thanks." I reached out and gave her a hug. "For everything."

She pulled back, smiling, and then shouted, "Kevin, be good for your sister, okay?"

"Of course, Ms. Jones. Thank you for the company this week."

"You are welcome, young man."

I smiled at them both as my heart warmed. She headed out, and as she shut the door behind her, I leaned against the wall, taking a deep breath. I watched Kevin as he made his character move through the world, and I half-wondered how he didn't get motion sickness from it. Slowly, my attention slid back to the painting that Kevin had done of our parent's garden.

Memories of Chase and I laughing as we swung on the swing set that would be just out of view of the area Kevin painted flowed through my mind, and my heart hurt. We had been close enough to be siblings, until Uncle Thom had come by to pick him up one day when we'd been playing in the yard and they'd never come back. The look on Mom's face as she'd told me I couldn't talk to him anymore . . .

Would he even remember me? Now that we are adults, why hasn't he tried to find me? Would he and Uncle Thom even want anything to do with Kevin and me?

Grabbing my carry-on, I rolled it toward the bedroom and kissed Kevin on the top of the head as I went by. "I'm going to shower. It's pizza night. What do you want? Double pepperoni or barbeque pineapple chicken?"

His head tipped to the side as he laid waste to a mob of creatures and then turned to look at me. His brown eyes narrowed at me mischievously before he smiled. *Oh boy. I'm in for it.* "Barbeque pineapple chicken . . . with jalapeños."

I winced and he smiled big. "Whatever you want. I'll order it after I take a nap. First, I'm going to jump in the shower."

"Welcome home, Sissy."

His voice carried down the hall, and my chest relaxed at the sound.

THE

DEN

DON'T LET THEM EAT YOU ALIVE

CHAPTER TWENTY-TWO

JASON

TRENTON

"Table three, Jason. Sorry to tell you that you'll be playing with two Dons." Kai's voice was the same even, careful tone he always carried when he gave these instructions, but he gave me a careful look when he handed me my chips. "Ante will be double the usual amount."

"And why am I specifically at *this* table?" I knew exactly why. I was here on Don Kingsley's orders, but Kai had to say it, and I had to play the game, make it seem strange.

His gaze met mine for only a second before he explained that it had been a special request of the house. With a nod of acknowledgement, I headed toward the table. When I sat down, I made sure it was so that the Dons were on either side of me, with an empty seat in the middle. I needed to be able to watch them both. Don Morliano, a tall, slender woman with bright red hair slicked back in a tight ponytail, perfect makeup, and bloodred nails, was to my right. Her lip twitched up as she gave me a single nod before looking across the table to the large, plump man with a receding hairline that almost reached the crown of his head. Don Westwood was the classic image of a Don, right down to the ostentatious watch and the cigar he was puffing on. When the other two players sat down, I sat up straighter, agreed to the terms and conditions again, and placed my blind.

When the flop was dealt, a six of spades, ten of diamonds, and three of hearts were laid face up. Looking at my cards, a three of clubs and a jack of diamonds, I laid them back down and looked around the table. Jerry, a man I had played against many times, sat to my right. He itched his temple, likely trying to distract from the shift of his hip, telling me that he currently had nothing. Don Morliano's long red nail tapped on the felt as she made the opening bet. Don Westwood was harder to read. I couldn't get a feel for him, either. He called the bet and raised two grand. Danny, who was next to me, groaned and called, saying, "I should at least see what the turn says."

Jerry and I both called the bet without hesitation, and so did Don Morliano. The dealer laid down a queen of clubs and looked to Don Westbrook. The Don's gaze traveled around the table, then he nodded and threw a six thousand dollar bet down. Danny folded, and so did I. With only a pair of threes, there was no way I was spending that cash. Jerry, who apparently had decided to bluff, called and raised another two thousand.

"Ten thousand on what is lying on the table? You got balls, Danny." Don Morliano's chips landed in the center with a click.

The Dons were paying very close attention to each other and didn't notice the wince from Danny when the river card was dealt and a three of diamonds lay there. Three of a kind, had I stayed in. But after looking over at the Dons, the odds would not have been in my favor. Danny placed his bet, and the Dons called easily. When he was forced to lay down his cards, there was nothing there. Don Morliano had three queens, and Don Westwood a pair of tens.

Don Westwood chuckled. "That's one way to start a game."

For thirty minutes, we continued, with Danny quickly being eliminated. When I was the one to beat him out, he let out a long, ragged sigh. There was something going on that he needed the cash, but he hadn't played smart. Too desperate.

"Thanks for the game," he said as he stood, tipped his head to the table, and went to take his place behind his chair. Rules stated you couldn't fully leave the table until it was over. So each player was forced to stand and watch to see who won the game.

It took a few more hands for Jerry to be eliminated. That was a hard loss. Holding a straight, only to be beaten out with a flush, I could understand the frustration. After another hour, I was trying to determine what exactly Don Kingsley had wanted me to learn at this game. There was definitely some boasting, but nothing stood out to me. A few times, there were add-ons of ammo and other supplies, but considering their business, I didn't think too much of it. I think at this point, they had evened out the ammo, which I found ironic.

Then, when the bet became non-monetary, I paid a little more attention. I had folded with a pair of nines and waited for the two to be done. The Den had mostly cleared out at this point, those left waiting for us to finish before opening the tables back up. They were taking the security of the Dons very seriously, and even I was surprised when they excused Danny and Jerry, allowing them to leave. I surveyed the room, security at the door, Kai leaning on the counter, and the waitresses in their uniforms, standing against the walls.

My eye caught Westwood's foot moving under the table. It was a solid tell, but if you couldn't see his feet, you would never know. I had caught it a few hands ago, and using the information had greatly reduced his chip load. He puffed out the last of his second cigar of the game and then extinguished it in the tray between him and the dealer.

"All in, plus three cases of *nightwhispers.*"

The sleep aid being sold in the underground? I thought Vispania had mostly cleaned it off the streets. Shit.

"You sure you can cover that, Westwood?" Morliano was tapping her long finger on the table when he nodded once. Her head tipped to the side as she said, "Three cases comes out to a cost of about $350K, so I call the overage with two cases of the tech you requested. Win the hand and you don't have to pay for that shipment."

Westbrook smiled as he laid down his straight flush, nine high. Morliano shook her head with a smile. "That was a close one."

Lifting her gaze to meet his, she slowly laid each card down. Straight flush, jack high.

Westwood stood, red as an apple, fat lips pursed tightly. "We will be in contact regarding delivery."

"Thank you." Her gaze was stoney as he walked away, but then she turned to me, her eyes softening slightly. "One more hand. Winner takes the pot. No over bets."

I chuckled. "Like I have anything to over bet with. I'm just a teacher at Trenton."

"That you are, Mr. Rathborn, but I also know you are very good in The Den. Heard you've made a few enemies along the way."

I ran my fingers lightly over the felt and smiled at her. "Really only one, but that's because he's shit at cards."

It was just a tip of her head, but she acknowledged the comment. "If you need protection, I'm willing to help."

"At what cost?"

The dealer dealt the cards, and Don Morliano smiled. "You are smarter than he told me you would be."

My stomach turned. *Does she know that I'm here for Kingsley?*

Peeking at my cards, I saw a pair of jacks. Not the best, not the worst, but it was enough to hold onto. The flop gave me another jack of diamonds, a six of hearts, and two of hearts.

"I'm not sure whether to take that as a compliment or not." I threw my chips in. "Twenty thousand."

"That's a big bet. Maybe you aren't as smart as I thought." She smiled, but her long nail tapped against the edge of the table. She had something, but what? There was a chance at a straight, but the right cards would have to show. "Call."

The turn was an eight of spades, so if the straight was there, she would still need the perfect card. "Forty thousand."

I didn't hesitate and called it. Her eyebrow lifted as her finger continued to slowly tap on the table next to her chips. "It's the last hand. Either you get everything anyway or I get all yours. It's just down to one card now, ma'am."

She leaned forward and studied me. "You know who I am." I nodded once. "You know who the fat man was."

"Everyone in this room does. The Den released the other players and it stayed empty because two Dons of Trenton were playing."

She chuckled. "You're observant, too." Holding my gaze, she stated, "I assume you are not going to discuss our over bets?"

"Didn't seem out of line, considering your professions. Business is business."

"Indeed." She nodded to the croupier, who put the last card down. "Obviously, all in."

"Obviously." Our gazes flicked down to the table to see a ten for a high full house in my hand. Casually, I looked back up at her. She had stopped tapping the table, and I smiled at her.

"So, what does a teacher at CSU Trenton have in his hand? There are only a pair of tens for the community."

"There are, and I intend on having them contribute to my winning hand."

"You are very confident in yourself."

Smiling at her, I laid my jacks down. "Full house. My pot because you didn't get what you needed for your straight."

Flipping her cards, she confirmed she didn't have the nine for an eight–queen run. "How did you know that?"

I looked around The Den and smiled at her when my eyes met hers. "Now, if I told everyone what their tell was, that wouldn't make me a very good poker player, would it?"

Her whole face lit up when she tipped her head back and laughed. "Oh, I like you, Rathborn." With the grace only a female Don could portray, she slid from her chair and walked around the table so that she was standing before me. I stood as she held her hand out and continued, "It was very nice to meet you. Though, I hope I don't sit at your table again anytime soon."

"Oh, I will gladly take your hard-earned cash from you." She smirked. "Fair and square of course."

She leaned forward to kiss my cheek but whispered, "Tell Kingsley about the nightwhispers. Westwood was dumb for letting that information out so publicly. Have Kinglsey destroy him."

She pulled back as a kind smile spread across her face. With a wink, she turned and headed out the door. It wasn't until she was out and probably halfway down the block that I collapsed onto the chair I had been sitting in for the last six hours.

Fucking hell. She knew why I was here.

THE

DEN

DON'T LET THEM EAT YOU ALIVE

CHAPTER TWENTY-THREE

JASON

TRENTON

It had been almost two weeks since Lanie had left, and even though we'd video chatted every day, I missed her terribly. She'd been a little more stressed out and jumpy lately, but she wouldn't give me the full story. Just said it was stress from work.

I was trying to hold out just another three weeks until the break, so I could drive down to see her. Just a few more papers to grade and I could stop for the night. Thank goodness the trimester ended just before break. It had taken some getting used to a trimester versus a semester, but it was actually easier for me to prepare lesson plans. The downside was the pile of term papers that were now stacked in front of me, waiting to be graded and entered into the system.

Reading through one of the papers, I groaned at how wrong the student had gotten Elizabeth of Bohemia's death and line of succession.

She wasn't stabbed. She died of tuberculosis. Did you even pay attention in class? Fuck!

Leaning my head back on the couch cushions, I ran my hand through my hair in mild frustration. My phone rang with a video call, and when I answered it, I almost dropped the phone at the sight before me.

"Lanie . . ."

Her voice was soft as she spread her legs farther. "Yes?"

"Fucking hell. My slut is asking for it, ain't she?" I shifted in my seat.

"She is. She's begging for you to make her cum. Your dirty slut needs you to make her cum so freaking bad." She groaned the words as she tipped her back and one of her hands trailed up her body and gripped one of her tits, her fingers pinching her nipple. A delicious moan from her lips had blood rushing to my cock. "Jase . . ."

"Sweetheart, you are killing me here." The look she gave me was all I needed to throw the papers on the coffee table and quickly undo my pants. *She wants this, so she's going to get it.* "Are you wet for me?"

She hummed that she was as her fingers slipped under the fabric. "Eyes on me." When she complied, I continued, "Now show me how wet that pussy is."

Lanie's cheeks turned red as she slipped her fingers from under her panties, lifted her hips, and slid the garment down her legs before tossing it to the side. Pinching her bottom lip between her teeth, she slowly widened her legs again and gave me one of the most spectacular views. The seven wonders of the world held nothing compared to what I was looking at right now. The only thing that could have made this better would have been me actually being there to dive in and lick her from ass to clit.

"That's my girl."

I saw her breathing hitch, and then she froze. She seemed to watch over the phone for a moment, as if she were listening for someone about to come in, before then looking back down at her phone. "Wish you were here."

"Soon, sweetheart. Everything okay?" My queen nodded. "Alright then, now play with your clit." She did, and I grabbed the base of my cock, moving the phone so she could watch me as well.

"Yes, Sir. Do you know how hot it is to watch you stroke yourself?"

"I have an idea." My gaze trailed down her body and homed in on where she was now sliding two fingers in and out of her, the sounds of her wetness coming through the call. "That's it, fuck your fingers, you horny, dirty whore."

I stroked harder, and a bead of pre-cum gathered at the head and slid down my shaft. Her wetness dripped down, pooling and soaking the sheets under her. I grunted as I jacked off to her before me. I could see her on the edge of losing it, and I stroked the head of my cock harder and faster, feeling my balls draw up tight. "That's it. Who does that pussy belong to?"

"You." She was panting and struggling to keep her eyes on me.

"Say my name, slut. Who does that pussy belong to?"

Her eyes flashed as her legs started to twitch at the edges of the screen.

"Sir. My pussy belongs to my Sir. Only him."

A smile crossed my face, and pride burst through me. She was the only woman for me. I wouldn't have anyone else but her. She was mine.

"That's a girl. Now cum for me."

She tensed, her feet pressing into the mattress, lifting her off the bed. Her release flowed down her plump ass to the sheets, and her moan filled the room. Beating my cock harder, I watched as she slowly came down. When her heated gaze met mine again, I couldn't hold back anymore.

"Fuck, Lanie." I growled as thick ropes of my release coated my hand.

We both lay there for a moment before she held up a finger and crawled off the bed. I took that time to go clean up myself before tucking my cock back into my pants and sitting back down on the couch.

When she sat back down on the bed, I smiled at her. "Good evening to you, too."

Her checks were still glassy from her euphoria, but they darkened slightly and she smiled. "Hi. I probably should have given you warning."

I shook my head. "Well, now I know not to open a video chat around others when it's you on the phone."

She giggled. "Thank you."

"Now, how was your day?"

CHAPTER TWENTY-FOUR

LANIE

SAN DIEGO

I took a slow, deep breath and tried to keep my heart rate down as I looked in the rearview mirror. I swore the white sedan a few cars back was following me. My attention went back to the street and down the road to where Velas was. It was a beautiful building with its tall white columns, elaborate plasterwork, and glass windows. If nothing else, I was lucky to have Kevin enrolled there. My gut was screaming in panic that the car behind me was staying with me, and I didn't want Kevin wrapped up in that mess. Not that I knew what mess I could be in, but when I took a right at the next light, the sedan followed.

Coincidence, right?

A few blocks down, I turned left and headed toward the grocery store parking lot. After parking, I watched the sedan drive in behind me and park near the cart stalls. I sat in that spot for a moment, contemplating my options.

One: Go into the store, but then I could be trapped in there, but I would also have people who might help.

Two: I could get out and go confront him, but then what if he was just some poor guy who needed tampons for his girlfriend?

Or he could be trying to kidnap you.

I tried to shake off that dramatic thought.

You have no reason to think anyone is after you! What is with the dramatics?

Carefully, I looked in that direction to see if he was out of the car yet, but instead, he was staring right at me. My heart was beating hard enough that I was surprised I couldn't see my shirt moving at my chest. Before I had a chance to overthink anything, I peeled out through the parking stall and down the row.

I didn't even pause at the stop sign, causing a large black truck to have to slam on his brakes to keep from clipping me. I blew through the back streets, barely paying any attention to anything or anyone. Before I knew it, I was behind the locked gate and near the keyed entry of the center. Taking deep breaths after I sandwiched my car between two lifted pickups, I leaned my head on the steering wheel. My phone was going off, but I ignored it for the moment, figuring it was probably Kevin wondering where I was. I needed to get myself under control before I went inside for him. He would pick up on my uneasiness immediately. He noticed everything.

After a few more minutes, I stepped out of the car, and after I didn't see anyone else around, I headed for the entrance. The glass doors shut behind me, and I rushed down the hall to the office Kevin was working in. Before I stepped inside, I took a moment to take another breath to calm myself down.

Come on, Lanie. This is ridiculous. Pull it together!

Quickly, I knocked on the doorframe before walking in, where I was instantly accosted by Kevin, arms crossed and glaring eyes. "Where were you? You are seven minutes late, Sissy."

I looked at the woman who was standing next to him, eyes wide. I didn't recognize the brunette and looked back at Kevin. "Got caught in traffic. You ready to head home?"

He nodded and grabbed his backpack from beside him. "Ms. Akin said that she wants to talk to you about moving me up to a teacher's assistant in one of the advanced art and math programs."

"Of course she does. You are brilliant and talented." I couldn't be more proud of him. He was a freaking art and math wiz. "I'll call her tomorrow."

"No need," said a sweet Southern voice behind me.

Kevin was studying the ground again, and I couldn't help but smile. There was still pride in his face, and while I was working on eye contact with him, when he was high in his feels, he forgot.

"Kevin, why do you call Lanie Sissy, and not her real name?"

His head popped up, and his eyebrows scrunched together. "Because she *is* Sissy. I've always called her that."

"But doesn't it sound a little childish?"

Excuse me? Who does she think she is telling him what he can call me. If he wants to call me Strawberry Shortcake, he fucking can.

"She is Sissy. I don't care how it sounds to other people. I'm an adult who can make my own decisions on what to call people, as long as it is okay with them. She told me a long time ago it was fine." *Damn right you can!*

I smiled at my brother. It really didn't matter what he called me. I was so damn proud of him. He was standing up for himself and drawing a line. Turning back to the woman, I tried not to sound smug. "Ms. Akin, Kevin mentioned an advanced art and math program you wanted him to be an assistant for?"

She nodded and, immediately, her face softened as she looked at Kevin. "Yes, ma'am. I'm sure you realize just how talented your brother is. Velas wants to move him into a TA position if that is okay with you."

"Of course it is, but it isn't my decision. It's Kevin's." I turned to him. "It would be more work."

"Would you let me?"

"Kevin, this is one of those things that is up to you. Do you want to be a teacher's assistant? If not, it's okay, but if you do, then I don't care. This is your decision."

He smiled and met my gaze, nodding, then looked away quickly. He didn't look at Ms. Akin but said, "I would like to help."

"Okay then, since that is set, I just got back from a scholarship meeting. We recently received a grant specifically for Kevin to attend an advanced art program, where he could earn his bachelor's in fine arts. He would also have the opportunity to get his master's in art if he wishes through the University of California, Los Angeles. The math program would have the same degree options but is through Stanford."

My mouth dropped open. I'd never thought about my brother pursuing a college degree. He'd never mentioned wanting one, and I'd never thought to bring it up. "I know you said it's a grant, but it can't possibly cover everything. I don't have—"

Ms. Akin lifted a hand and continued, "It's for Kevin only. He was specifically selected."

Looking at her in confusion, I asked, "How? We didn't apply for anything like this."

She nodded. "Remember the painting that was placed at a charity event a few months back?" I nodded, remembering how proud Kevin had been that someone had bought it for almost ten thousand dollars. He'd been so happy because the funds were going to help kids like him get services they needed. "The gentleman who purchased Kevin's painting has received so many compliments on it, that he wants to help him be able to get an education."

I looked at Kevin, whose cheeks were red. "Do you want to get a college degree in art and math?" He shrugged slightly, so I turned back to Ms. Akin. "Can Kevin and I talk about it and get back to you? I think there is a lot to take into consideration with that offer."

"Absolutely, Ms. Carley."

"Thank you." I turned back to face Kevin. "Ready to head home?" He nodded, and I took a deep breath as we walked down the hall. That was a lot to process. First, someone had sponsored him so he'd even be able to come here during the day, then he'd moved up to teaching art to some of the more challenged kids, and now someone was providing the chance for him to pursue a college education for free?

What is going on?

The entire way, I couldn't keep from thinking that we had a fairy godmother or father, and I wasn't sure how to feel about it. There was a part of me that felt like there were going to be strings attached or that I was taking advantage of someone else's hard-earned cash. There was also a part of me, a large one, that was thankful, and I just wanted to give them a hug to show my appreciation. I would never be able to repay the tuition and fees that would be due. Just the center alone cost more than my lifetime of saving, but to add in a potential double bachelor's and then double master's degree for him? I would never be able to finance that kind of loan.

It's for Kevin. Just be thankful someone is willing to give him the life he deserves.

Days passed, and I still had this itch on my shoulder that I couldn't get rid of, metaphorically speaking. I kept seeing people watching me at the grocery store, at the department store, and even at the big box warehouse store when I'd gone to stock up on necessities. I had pulled a bag of Kevin's favorite orange chicken from the freezer when I'd seen a man in a blue jacket who'd looked like he was on his phone about twenty feet away. I'd tried to brush it off, telling myself it was just another shopper, but when I'd looked again, his eyes had been fixed right on Kevin and me. As we'd made our way through the different aisles, I'd seen him in every one, and when we'd checked out, he'd been a lane over, with next to nothing in the bag he'd carried out.

It's fine. People don't always have to buy a lot when they come here.

I had almost convinced myself it was a coincidence, until I'd seen the same guy at the pharmacy down the street, and the next day when we were taking a walk in the park.

While I hadn't seen the white sedan since Friday, today there'd been a smaller grey SUV that followed me all the way to work, sat in the parking lot all day, and followed me back to the apartment. And no matter how I'd tried to lose him, he'd still found my bumper.

My phone buzzed, and I sighed as I looked down where I was rolling it between my hands.

Jason: How did it go?

Lanie: Haven't talked to him yet.

Three dots rolled across the screen, and I knew he was trying to find a nice way of telling me to get on with it.

Jason: We have talked about this, Lanie. If you need to wait, that's fine, but he needs to know that we are dating again before he finds out when I walk in for my visit.

Lanie: And when will that be exactly?

Jason: Oh no, I'm not giving you a date to put this off any longer, my queen.

He was right. I just needed to do it. I wasn't ashamed of us being back together. I was just scared how Kevin was going to react because he had been affected by our breakup too. I hadn't been the only one who had been on edge and angry for months.

Lanie: But he's going to be mad.

Jason: We have discussed this. He may be mad, but if it means that much to you, he will get over it. Now go talk to Kevin and call me when you're done.

Lowering my phone, I tapped it against my leg. "Hey, Kev, can we talk?"

"Yes."

"Will you listen if I talk?" I couldn't help the smirk that lifted my lips, and when he huffed a laugh, some of the tension left my shoulders.

"I will listen."

Sitting down on the other end of the couch, I pulled my knees up to my chest and wrapped my arms around them. "You know that I love you very much and that you will always be my first priority, right?"

His head moved up and down. "Because we are family. It's just you and me."

A ball of emotion sat in my throat. "Right. What do you think about having someone else in our family? Someone who cares for me very much?"

"You have a new boyfriend," he teased, and I couldn't help but smile. "I do."

His head tilted as he looked at me quickly before asking, "Why are you scared to tell me?"

"Because we were together before."

He stopped drawing on his notepad, and I saw his body go tight. "No. You can't be with Mr. Rathborn."

I lifted my eyebrows. "Why not?"

"He hurt us. No one is allowed near you if they hurt you."

Here it is. I let out a sigh as I prepared for the tough conversation I'd been expecting. "You know how much I cared for him."

Kevin stood quickly and threw his pencil across the room. "No. I don't want you with him. He was going to be my brother, and then he ran away. You cried all the time for a very long time. Kami had to help." His head started shaking back and forth. "No, sissy. No more hurt."

This was the most we had ever talked about the breakup, and while I knew it had affected Kevin, hearing him verbalize it was a punch to the gut. He was growing more upset and was having an increasingly difficult time being able to regulate his emotions right now. If I pushed this, it was going to send him over the edge. I unfolded myself from the couch and stood slowly, adjusting the direction of the conversation. "Kevin, you were okay with me having a boyfriend until I told you it was Jason. What is the difference?"

In a rare moment, he looked me straight in the eyes. "Other boys *may* not hurt you. Mr. Rathborn already did."

I took another deep breath and nodded at him. "You are right. He did. What if I told you he apologized and that he wants to make things right? If I'm willing to give him a second chance, can you?"

He was shifting from side to side, and his shoulders released some. I inwardly took that as a good sign. Kevin was looking down at the couch as he said, "He left us once. He will leave again. Everyone leaves. Only Sissy stays." A single tear slid down his cheek as he let out a determined breath.

My heart broke for him right there. I tried to hold back the tears myself, and my breath hitched with the influx of air. After attempting to swallow the lump in my throat and make myself sound as normal as possible, I said, "Jason is my boyfriend. I have told him that this is the only chance he gets to make things right. You know how when you do something wrong, you want to fix it? Try again so you can do it right?"

He nodded. "This is not the same."

"No, not exactly, but that is what Jason is doing. He is trying again. He wants to get it right this time. I promise you that I won't give him a third chance, okay?"

Kevin glanced up for a moment, studying my face intently before looking at the floor again. "You really want to give him this chance? You like him that much?"

"I really do. I don't think I've ever stopped loving him. I need to give him this one chance so that I can say I tried. If he messes it up, then that's it. It's over and he's gone. I promise."

His head lifted again, and as his gaze met mine, another tear rolled down his cheek. "Okay. One more chance, only because I love you and want you happy."

I reached out and took his hand and squeezed it. Only, he surprised the hell out of me and pulled me into a huge hug. Holding him close, I couldn't stop the tears from flowing. Since we'd moved into this apartment, there had only been a handful of times that he had wanted a hug. The touch was just too overstimulating for him.

This is really important to him.

Kevin held me for almost a minute before he pulled back. "I'm going to draw on the deck."

I just nodded as he picked up his drawing paper and got another pencil from his bag by the couch. Slowly, I took a long breath to calm myself down. Kevin was going to give it a try. That was all I could ask for.

Lanie: Done. He said he'll give you a chance.

Jason is going to have one hell of a challenge proving himself.

CHAPTER TWENTY-FIVE

LANIE

SAN DIEGO

"Hey, Sissy?"

I turned out of the Velas parking lot and toward home. I'd gone to dropping him off and picking him up either inside or right at the entrance door for a few weeks now, and Kevin seemed to adjust to the slight difference in normality pretty easily. "Yeah."

"Can we stop and get more blueberries?"

I chuckled. "Of course."

He loved those damn things. They were too tart for me, but Kevin loved them. He would deal in the off season with the frozen ones, but he always complained how mushy they were or that they just tasted weird. He didn't mind frozen ones in yogurt, surprisingly. When it came to fresh blueberries, though, the grocery store was fine, but when we would head up the valley, he loved to get them from the workers who sold them along the road. Strawberries, too. We always got the most delicious fruit and veggies from the stands along the road.

I kept noticing the same dark blue SUV behind us. Once again, it was turning where we did, and when it was the car behind me, I tried to see who was driving. About the only thing I could tell was that it was a man in a suit and dark aviators. When we pulled into the parking lot at the grocery store, it passed by us, and I took a bit of a breath. As we pulled into the parking spot, Kevin asked if we could get a pie from the bakery and vanilla ice cream while we were here. "Sure thing."

He narrowed his eyes at me and studied me for a long moment before we got out of the car and headed inside. "Why are you saying yes to everything?" He pulled me to a stop and crossed his arms. "What are you hiding?"

"I'm not hiding anything. I just don't think it's unreasonable for you to get more fruit, pie, and ice cream. I don't have any real reason to say no. You love your fresh blueberries, and we are already here, so it doesn't hurt anything to get pie and ice cream too."

He kept staring at me, which was a little weird because he always had a hard time keeping eye contact. "Okay."

I leaned over and bumped his shoulder. "Good job on your eye contact, by the way."

"Thank you."

When a dark blue SUV drove by between our parking space and the store, I swallowed hard and watched as it drove a bit farther down. Slowly, I tried to let out a long breath to calm down because I didn't want to worry Kevin over something that probably wasn't even a problem.

But how many times do I brush this off?

Heading inside, we went straight for the bakery. When we got there, they had just put a few new pies out. The sweetness filled the air as fresh baked bread wrapped around me like a warm blanket. Kevin was looking at each one meticulously as the attendant answered all of his questions. Finally, they smiled at each other, and he took one of the pies in his hand and headed my way. I couldn't help but notice the rosy cheeks on the attendant as she watched him walk toward me.

"Olallieberry. Jackie just made them. Feel the bottom, it's still warm." I felt the bottom, and heat radiated out of the box.

"The pie isn't the only thing warm. Her cheeks were awfully pink while talking to you," I teased.

He lowered his head as he put the pie in the basket. "She's nice. Jackie is at the center until noon on Monday, Wednesday, and Thursday."

I lifted my gaze a moment and saw her mindlessly putting bread on the shelf but looking in our direction. "She's still looking at you."

"Sissy . . ."

I smiled brightly. "Okay, okay. I'll stop. Now, do you want French vanilla or vanilla bean ice cream?" He just gave me an even look. "Yeah, yeah. Fruit pies get vanilla bean. All others get French vanilla."

"I'm going to get blueberries."

Nodding at him, I watched as he strode to the other end of the store. My eye caught Jackie's, and she blushed harder. I gave her a simple nod and wheeled the cart toward the bread aisle.

After picking up some cinnamon raisin English muffins, I slowly made my way across the store, collecting the different items we needed, including the ice cream. When I got to the produce section, though, there was a man in a dark suit talking to Kevin. As I rolled up next to him, the man in the suit nodded to me and then walked off.

"What was he talking to you about?" Kevin was casually looking at the baskets of blueberries as he moved them around to find the best selection.

"Nothing. Just said that I should be careful of who I let into my life. That I could get hurt." My heart stopped as I looked up in the direction the man had gone. He was standing by the drink aisle and gave me a little smirk before turning and going down the row.

"I'm just picking out my blueberries, so I don't know what that has to do with who I let into my life. They are just berries." He lifted another basket and studied it before he smiled. "This one."

"Okay then. Do you want whipped cream, yogurt, or just want to eat them plain this week?"

He made a show of thinking about it, but I knew the only real question was whether he wanted a tub or spray whipped cream. "Whipped cream. In a can."

I elbowed him and smiled as we headed off to get the rest of our groceries—canned whipped cream included.

THE
DEN

Don't Let Them Eat You Alive

CHAPTER TWENTY-SIX

JASON

TRENTON

It was a beautiful day today, and I couldn't stand sitting in my condo and grading papers another minute. As I locked my door and headed for the elevator, my mind went back to the discussion Lanie and I'd had about what we would like to explore to broaden our sexual horizons. She had surprised me a bit when we'd discussed having a threesome. It was one of those things that most guys have had the fantasy, but to have it offered on a platter to you? Have her agree to it and even offer to experiment to see if I'd like having a dick involved? Unthinkable. I shook my head as I stepped into the lobby and then out onto the street.

My feet carried me down the street, and before I knew it, I was standing before one of the adult entertainment stores. Shaking my head at myself, I sighed.

Jason, your mind knew exactly where you were going.

Opening the door, I headed for the counter. A woman who looked to be in her mid-forties with bright-red, short hair smiled at me and asked if there was anything she could help me find.

Nerves exploded within me, but I thought of Lanie and how she had a look of complete understanding on her face. I had been nervous about telling her some of the things I had thought about, but she had given me the opening so I'd taken it. Taking a deep breath, I explained to the woman behind the counter how I was thinking of exploring anal for myself.

"Of course. Right over here." She smiled and proceeded to show me a multitude of different options.

After selecting a trainer kit, she went over some basic prep and maintenance. She had even given me some ideas for the next time I saw my queen.

"It can be difficult on your own, but with the right equipment, you won't end up in the ER."

"If the base ain't flared, it don't go there." I chuckled.

"Exactly." She quickly greeted someone else who came in and then turned back toward me. "Just remember to go slow. Just like with your girlfriend, you need to prep and allow yourself to adjust."

"Will do."

"Realistically, do you think this is something you will enjoy?"

I thought about it and finally smiled. "Yeah, I think I will. Why?"

"You mentioned that she's in San Diego?" I nodded, and there was a wave of longing that went through me. I really missed her. The woman's voice broke through my thoughts, saying, "If things go really well, you could move into a harness for her to use. Give you more of the effect of being fucked."

The image of my legs on her shoulders, her tits bouncing in front of me as she fucked my ass had blood rushing to my cock. I swallowed and felt my entire body flush with heat. "Hook me up. We need to make sure it fits a plus-size woman though."

"Yes! I love a plus-size queen."

After selecting one that the trainers fit into and a dong that also snapped in, she asked, "Can I get you anything else?"

"I need some more clit stimulant, rope, and—" I looked down at the case I was leaning on. My eyes caught on a set of nipple jewelry with a clit clamp. I instantly pictured them on my little slut and smiled at the worker, pointing to a pair that were looped with hanging blue and clear crystals. "And those. Second from the end."

"I'll get it all wrapped up for you."

Five minutes later, I was walking out the store and heading toward Vispania Tower. It sat at the head of the business district also known as The Avenue. I had avoided the Avenue, just because it was so busy. Now that I was here, however, and I *had* checked just about every other antique and jewelry shop for the perfect ring for Lanie in Trenton . . . I hadn't been lying to her when I'd said I wanted her forever. There were a couple of shops down here, so I figured it couldn't hurt to look.

As I passed the large glass doors and lobby of Vispania Tower, I looked up at the expansive building and wondered what stories it could tell. It had been updated throughout the years, and floors had been added, but it had been owned by either the Vispania or Velarde family for as long as the town had been here.

Making the turn down the street, I stared down The Avenue. Tall buildings lined the street on both sides, housing the major businesses of the city, but the ground levels were always commercial, and each had penthouses and a few apartments on some of the upper floors. I wove my way through the crowd until I reached *Modern Memories*.

A small bell rang as I walked through the door, and I was inundated with the smells of polished wood, sawdust, oil, and all things old. I couldn't help but lean my head back and inhale deeply. I let it wash over me, and when I opened my eyes, a man was smiling at me. He was about my age, maybe a little younger, with brown hair and sparkling blue eyes.

"My grandfather does that every time he walks in."

I chuckled as I looked around the expansive room. "I teach ancient history, so I have a thing for the old. It just . . . Well, I feel like we are too connected to technology sometimes. I'm just as guilty as everyone is, and I realize how hypocritical I sound, but to have something made by hand a hundred or more years ago . . . you just can't replace that."

"They literally don't make things the way they used to." He tilted his head to the side. "Is there something specific you are looking for?"

"I'm going to propose to my girlfriend, and well, she isn't the kind to want something new and shiny. So, I'm trying to find something that suits her. I've been all over the place, and I haven't seen anything yet that screams her name."

He tilted his head as if he were thinking. "So, nothing traditional. Likely not a diamond center. Do you want diamonds at all?"

"I'm not sure. I think that will depend on the ring, but you are right that a diamond center doesn't really feel right."

He nodded and held up a finger as he disappeared into the back room. He came out a few minutes later with a few trays. "What's your budget?"

"I am more concerned about finding the right ring. Show me everything." He ticked an eyebrow up. "I'm not saying there won't be a limit, but right now, I just want to find the ring."

"I get that." He laid a few trays out and lifted the cloths over them. "I'm Jake, by the way."

"Jason."

"So, precious stones are here. I have some more, but I'm still waiting for the appraisals to come back." He gestured to the next tray. "These are lab grown gems or they have been re-pressed with the shavings of. So, these are all newer rings."

I looked them over, and while they were stunning and beautiful, none of them said they belonged to my queen. Shaking my head, I said, "I think we need older."

He smiled. "I figured but wanted to at least let you see these, just in case. Happens all the time that someone comes in looking for one thing but leaves with something completely different."

I had no doubt.

Jake put the two trays away and then pulled over three more, lifting the fabric from each. One was lined with beautiful rings that looked to be from the early 1900s. Mostly art deco in design. But nestled down in the bottom corner was a kite cut ring that I couldn't take my eyes off of. The stone was clear with black lines going in each direction. It was stunning, and I could immediately see my queen wearing it.

Slowly, my fingers moved toward the simple ring to see that it had a second band, creating a set. It had small petal-shaped stones that matched the center with smaller diamonds around it. Picking it up, I stared at it between my fingers. It wasn't traditional but still elegant and worthy of my queen.

I slipped it onto my pointer finger, knowing that it was close to the same size as her ring finger, and it was a perfect fit. "I'll take it."

"That easy?"

I smiled as I looked up and met his gaze. "It belongs on her finger. I knew when I saw it, it was a done deal."

"Very well."

THE
DEN
DON'T LET THEM EAT YOU ALIVE

Chapter Twenty-Seven

Lanie

San Diego

"Hey, Lanie," Vanessa said as she knocked and then opened my office door.

"Yeah? What's up?" I was looking through piles of papers for the profits and losses from the last months' worth of bingo but couldn't find the damn things.

"You have a delivery." She was holding up a brown bag and a to-go cup from Konnie's sandwich shop down the street. "There's a note on the receipt."

She came over and set it down on my desk and then hurried out of the room, fully closing the door behind her. I narrowed my eyes at her then looked at the bag.

Video call me when you get this. -Jase

Looking at the time, I sighed. I didn't realize it was so late already. *How is it almost two thirty?* I opened the bag and smiled at the turkey sandwich and caramel fudge brownie inside. I took a sip of the drink after sticking the straw in it and let out a loud, "Ahhh." Konnie's always had the best lemonade.

I propped my phone up and called Jase. It took a moment for him to answer, but when he did, he set his phone down and folded his hands in front of him. "Was I right that you hadn't eaten yet?"

There was no way I could control the eye roll. "Yes."

"Good, because I lost track of time working on my lesson plans and didn't eat either. You up for a lunch date?"

I blinked but realized I was smiling wide. "Absolutely. You have something to eat?"

"Yeah, but I'd rather have you." He winked, causing me to squirm in my chair a bit.

"Not fair, Jase. I'm at work and can't do shit about it. Not fair one damn bit."

"Maybe, but it's the truth." He smiled and reached over to grab his sandwich and drink. "So, how has your day been going?"

"Alright, I guess." I let out a bit of a sigh and took another sip of my lemonade. "Trying to get these budget numbers together for the program and have not able to get my fingers on the bingo numbers for the last month. I'm going to have to estimate it. I can get it pretty close, I think."

"Don't they want hard numbers?"

"Yeah, but bingo is pretty steady each month. That isn't something that they will look closely at. Now, the field trips and special events? Those I need the hard numbers for."

"When is it due?"

I had just taken a large bite of my sandwich and held a finger up as I chewed, and I instantly moaned as the sweet and tangy flavor of the honey mustard burst across my tongue. He was laughing at me and lifted an eyebrow, no doubt questioning the moan, and I didn't have it in me to yell at him for it. Jason waited patiently, and when I finally swallowed the rest of the bite, I took a deep breath. "This is delicious, by the way."

"So I hear, and you are welcome. Gotta take care of my girl."

"Getting back to your question, I need this by tomorrow night so we can get it printed in time for the meeting on Friday. I'm freaking out a bit about it, even though I know it will be fine. I love the event planning and seeing the residents' faces when they get to have fun. So many of them don't have visitors, and it's sad. They lived these lives and now that they are older and not doing so well, their families kind of tucked them away. So yeah, I love the events, but budget planning? Yuk!" I took a long drink of lemonade and smiled at him. He looked so adorable just sitting there attentively. "How has your day been?"

His whole face lit up at the question. "Actually, it's been fascinating. I just read a paper about how they have found more artifacts in Bulgaria that date back to the Copper Age. They were in sections of the country they didn't believe humans had been able to occupy, but there are clear indications of them using tools that we previously thought they couldn't possibly be using yet."

Watching him come alive and be so animated warmed my heart. It was the side of him that I thought I'd fallen in love with first. As he continued on, there were many pieces of information that didn't make much sense to me, but his love and excitement for history was infectious. I made appropriate confirming sounds as he continued, and by the time I finished my sandwich, he was wrapping up.

"So, this is really groundbreaking. It could change the timeline of the ages." He ran his hand through his hair and looked up at me. He gave me a shy smile. "Sorry. I've been talking nonstop for twenty minutes."

"Jase, you are excited. Never apologize for talking about what you love. Even though I didn't understand half of what you just said. I am taking joy in your joy. In your infatuation with history and the discoveries that are being made. So again, please, never apologize for geeking out on me."

"Why do you have to be so far away? I just want to kiss you." He shook his head and chuckled but kept his eyes down on his half-eaten sandwich. "Thank you for never making me feel like a burden. You didn't years ago, and you don't now."

I smiled and broke off a piece of the caramel brownie, popping it in my mouth. It was deliciously rich and buttery. I did it for him because he was important. Because he was someone that I needed. I also did it because I wanted to. Having him back in my life had me more even-keeled . . . more centered. "It's an easy thing to do because you aren't a burden. I never want to discourage you from enjoying or talking about your passions."

I could have sworn I heard him say, "Like you?" under his breath. A bright, wide smile crossed his face as he looked up and met my gaze through the phone. "I don't deserve you."

"No, you don't, but you are stuck with me anyway," I said, shrugging and acting nonchalant.

He just chuckled and shook his head again.

Someone knocked on the door, and I let out a sigh. "Come in."

Vanessa opened the door, sticking her head in. "Adrian wants to meet with you about the schedule for the fundraiser. Said he was sorry for interrupting lunch, but he would make it up to you."

I gave her a nod. "Tell him I'll be there in a few minutes." She closed the door, and I put my head in my hands, groaning.

"What's wrong, my queen?"

"I don't want to tell you," I muttered into my hands.

He didn't say anything, but I looked through a crack I'd made in my fingers and saw that he had crossed his arms and was giving me a look. "Why not?"

"Because I know how jealous you can be."

Slowly, I lowered my hands, and his entire body relaxed. "I trust you, Lanie."

"I know that, but . . ." I studied him for a long moment before deciding to tell him everything. "He's been pretty insistent for almost a year on wanting to take me out. I've shut him down every time. I just don't see him like that. Besides, even if I did, I am not wild about having a relationship with one of my bosses. This business is too much of a small world. I don't want to damage my career for a fling. Now I'm with you, and he just won't take the hint."

Jason didn't say anything, just sat there and listened. He didn't twitch or anything, and it was kind of freaking me out. When I was done talking, he took a quick breath and met my gaze.

"I won't lie to you and say that I haven't been with others since the last time we broke up, but no one can compare to you. And before your head gets too big to fit through the door, let me tell you, part of that is because of what we share emotionally. When it comes to Adrian, though, there just is nothing there. I have professional respect for him, but nothing else."

"Okay." His shoulders were relaxed, and he took another bite of his sandwich.

I blinked and tilted my head to the side. "Okay? That's it?"

He chuckled. "You are my queen, and I trust my queen. If she says there is nothing there, then there's nothing there. We have to have trust between us if we are going to make this work long distance. You are the most important thing in my life, Lanie. I'm going to do everything I can to make sure that this works long-term. Including trusting that we are going to stay faithful to each other."

My entire body heated. It wasn't just a sexual heat though. It was the feeling of being truly loved and cherished. "Okay."

"Now go to your meeting. Thank you for having lunch with me."

"Thank you for sending me lunch."

He smiled. "Of course, my queen. I will always take care of you. Talk tonight? I have class until eight."

I grabbed the files I would need for my meeting with Adrian. "Okay, talk to you then."

"Until then, my queen." Then he hung up.

I stared at the phone for a long minute. He trusted me. The old Jason would have been much more outwardly perturbed at that conversation. He'd said it though. There had to be trust between us in order for this to work. Sighing, I headed to meet with Adrian.

THE

D E N

DON'T LET THEM EAT YOU ALIVE

CHAPTER TWENTY-EIGHT

JASON

TRENTON

My hands were wrapped around my coffee, the heat seeping into my fingers. It was a bitterly cold morning, but the temp would likely jump twenty degrees by this afternoon. The sun was barely up, and the only reason I was vertical at this ungodly hour was because I needed to meet with Chase about what I'd found out at The Den almost a week ago. He'd wanted information right away but had a strict rule about info only being passed on verbally, and this was the first day and time that worked for both of us.

I didn't have to wait long for him to slide into the seat across from me at the bistro, a breakfast sandwich in his hand. "Sorry it's taken so long for us to see each other. How are you doing?"

"Oh, you know, just working and shit. It's not like you to wait so long for coffee." I lifted mine to my lips and took a sip, the bold, smoky flavor coating my tongue and waking my brain. I closed my eyes, savoring it.

"Yeah, sorry about that. Had some shit go sideways that required my attention. So, how was the game? Heard you made out pretty well."

I smiled because I had and had instantly put it in savings for Kevin. "It was fruitful for sure. Was interesting watching the merchandise swap around me."

"Oh? Tell me more." He took a bite of his breakfast sandwich while I took another sip of my coffee.

"Most of it seemed pretty on par for the business." I tipped my head side to side. "But when they got into sleep aids, I was a bit confused."

Chase's body froze for a moment. "Sleep aids?"

207

I nodded and leaned forward, wrapping my hands back around the paper to-go cup. "Yeah, people talk and don't realize their professor is listening. Apparently, they have some pretty serious side effects, like memory loss, making it really popular with those who don't like victims to remember things."

He was chewing his last bite slowly as he studied me. "I've heard whispers."

I nodded, glad he had caught onto what I was saying. Nightwhispers were highly sought after. When they hit the streets a few years ago, the number of reported rapes and assaults where the victims didn't remember anything had skyrocketed. From what I'd heard, Vispania had had a lot of work to do in order to keep the media from blasting it all over the place. I'd overheard some students talking about it as well, and how many were trying to be a lot more careful because apparently it was completely tasteless. One girl complained that it felt like she'd taken too many antihistamines, and then the next thing she'd known, she'd been waking up in her dorm with no memory of the night before.

Looking back up at Chase, I saw he was focused on the table, and I could see the wheels moving. "The fat one was pretty quick to bid a chunk on it."

His focus snapped up to me. "The fat one? Not the dame?"

I shook my head. "She was most accommodating, actually. Suggested that I tell you about it."

"That's good to hear. When you say a chunk . . ." He raised an eyebrow and leaned forward slightly.

"She said it was worth about three-fifty?" His eyes widened just slightly in shock. "Yeah, that's what I thought. I hear things around campus. It's my understanding it doesn't take much to help someone get a full night's sleep."

Chase's voice was low as he said, "That's true. While it's available, it's expensive. Five grams will easily cost a couple hundred bucks, and it only takes a pinch to put you out. That's why we are trying so hard."

I let out a long breath. "Fuck, man."

His head moved up and down. "The fat man, though."

"Yup." I brought my cup to my lips and took a large drink, letting it try to settle my nerves. My attention went to the large clock on the wall as I sighed. "Is it wrong for a professor to call in with *I don't wanna?*"

Chase chuckled. "I can tell you from a student's viewpoint, we would have liked a little more notice so we wouldn't have even had to get out of bed yet."

"Alright, fine. I'll make it worth it for your sorry asses to get out of bed." The smile that was slowly crossing my face had me looking at him.

He swallowed down the last of his coffee and wrapped up his trash. "I should get going. Wouldn't want to be late for class, and I need to stop by Dad's office before. Drop off some information he needs."

"Sounds good. Talk soon."

He got up and left, and I took a deep breath in relief. I stared at my cup of coffee and swirled it in my hands. Still feeling uneasy, I rolled my shoulders and neck, trying to loosen them up. Something felt like it was on the horizon.

CHAPTER TWENTY-NINE

LANIE

SAN DIEGO

Jason: Wear my present today.

   Lanie: What?

   Jason: Wear my present today. I didn't think that text was capable of stuttering.

   I stared at the message and groaned. Today? Of all days?

   Lanie: I have a meeting with the president of Halo Group.

   Jason: Wear. My. Present. Today.

   Pushy bastard.

   Lanie: As long as you agree no funny business between one and six.

   I waited nervously because I knew when it came to sex, he was the one in charge at all times. Public sex had been on my hard no list, but after our discussions up in Trenton, I was willing to try some new things. This, though, *this* was a pretty big ask of him.

   Three dots went across the screen.

   Jason: I will agree not to make you cum during the meeting. That is all I can agree to.

   That didn't mean that he wouldn't tease me and put me on edge.

   Lanie: This meeting is pivotal. I can't take any chances.

   Jason: I understand and promise I won't cause any problems.

   Lanie: Seriously, I have a job to do. Tomorrow. I can comply tomorrow.

   Jason: I will not bother you during the meeting.

   Lanie: Jason . . .

Jason: I promise.

I took a deep breath and ground my teeth together. I would just keep it off in my purse during the meeting, but the app would alert him to the device being turned off, and if I wasn't responding to him, he would know that it wasn't in place.

Jason: Have a great day, my queen.
Lanie: You too.

I set the phone down and leaned on the counter. *That man is so lucky I love him.*

That thought alone was what had me pushing myself from the granite counter and heading to the bedroom to finish getting ready. When I reached for the handle to the drawer the remote vibe was in, I wondered if I was being highly irresponsible and unprofessional for this.

You know you are! Are you going to do it anyway? Yes. Yes, you are.

I reached in and pulled the bright pink egg vibrator out. I felt my pussy tingle in anticipation. I would be lying if I said I hadn't tried it out on myself. That had been one of the fastest self-pleasure orgasms I'd had in a very long time. This thing on low packed a punch, and I pressed my legs together, knowing that he was going to have control. Before I could think much of it, I added a little lube and slid it in, groaning a little as it settled into place, resting the tail against my clit. I knew I'd probably regret the decision later. Activating it, I slipped on a pair of underwear.

Heading to the closet, I went to reach for a pantsuit but then looked at one of my navy sheath dresses. I pulled it from the bar and held it up. The capped sleeves and high neckline would be conservative enough to meet with the president. It gathered at my waist, accentuated the curve of my hips, and gave my legs some length. However, it was still going to make me feel sexy on a day I knew would have multiple orgasms involved.

I looked back at the tan pantsuit, but I was a little concerned about having a wet spot that I couldn't hide in the seam of the pants if I wore them. But then, a skirt could still leave a mess down my thighs . . . I smiled and went to one of my drawers, pulling out a pair of biker shorts. Problem solved.

Dressing quickly, I put my hair up then double-checked to make sure everything was locked since Kevin had left early today for a day trip with some of his students. Grabbing my things, I headed out the door.

Coffee. I needed coffee.

Luckily, there was a shop just a block from my apartment building. Hell, most of the city had a coffee shop on every corner. How else did the world expect us to operate?

Standing in line, I was scrolling through my social media, when all of a sudden, Jason started to play. The vibration was strong at first, and then he slowed it and had it moving in rolling intensities of low to medium. The man was warming me up, and I thought the anticipation was worse than the actual stimulation. I was trying to act like nothing was bothering me, but I couldn't help but shift on my feet.

"Morning, Lanie. Your usual?"

"Yahhumm," was all I could get out because what Jason was doing was just not fair. Hell, he had spiked the movement just as I'd tried to answer the barista. It wasn't like he knew I was ordering coffee at the time. I paid quickly with my phone and then headed to the waiting area.

Opting to lean on the counter instead of sitting, I closed my eyes and tried to hide all my reactions. I was certainly on edge, but of course Jason had a sixth sense about this sort of shit and backed off. I was just getting my senses back when a man came up and asked if I was okay.

"I'm okay. Thank you."

"Good to hear. A lovely woman such as yourself should make sure to take care with whom she associates with."

Alarm bells were going off in all directions. It was almost the same thing that had been told to Kevin the other day in the grocery store. Slowly, I turned my head to look at the man before me. Brown eyes lowered to look at me as he wrinkled his bushy eyebrows together, and just behind the hood of his sweatshirt, I saw a tattoo. I tried to figure out what it was, but the shadows and curve of his strong jaw distorted it so it was just long lines that stretched out along his neck.

"What?"

He took a sip of his coffee and smirked. I watched as his Adam's apple bobbed as he swallowed. "Be careful whom you associate with. Being tied to certain people will put a target on you."

Then, just as the barista called out, "Lanie!" I looked up to see the barista setting my coffee down on the counter for pickup. The man next to me tipped his head to me. "Good day, Melanie."

I blinked. *How did he know my name? No one calls me that.*

"Lanie!"

I shook my head and grabbed my coffee. Inhaling the scent, I let it calm my nerves as I looked at the clock, realizing I only had a few minutes to be in the office. I cataloged the encounter away for now and would tell Jason about it later. There was too much to deal with today.

Hours had gone by, and I had ignored Jason's little tease for the most part. However, then he had thrown it on full blast, bringing me to the brink before stopping completely.

Lanie: Asshole.

Jason: What?

Lanie: Bring me right to the edge and then stop?"

Jason: It isn't like I know whether you orgasm or not. I'm just having fun here.

Lanie: Yeah, yeah.

Jason: Now, don't forget to eat lunch. You will need your energy for your presentation.

Lanie: Okay.

That was until just before lunch, when I nearly jumped out of my skin while talking to Vanessa.

"You okay?" I adored that she was concerned for me, but there really was no need right now.

I bit my bottom lip and then said, "Yes. Fine."

It stopped, and I settled myself a moment before finishing my conversation with Vanessa. "I'll go get the replacement pages copied while you work on getting these ready."

I was halfway down the hall when Jason played with the vibration settings again. By the time I was in front of the copier, I was pretty turned on. Jason must have known because he turned that thing up on full blast, and I had to lean against the copier.

Adrian walked up then and was saying something about how he knew that I would kill it in the meeting with the president today and rested his hand over mine. The vibrating stopped for a moment, and I let out a hard breath before taking and releasing a slower one. I had to get myself under control.

"You okay, Lanie?" His hand lifted to move a piece of hair from my face, but I shifted away from him. "You look a little flushed."

"I'm fi—" It started vibrating again, and this time the vibration was strong enough that it was causing the tail to stimulate my clit. I tried to stifle the moaned whimper. "I'm fine."

"You sure?"

"Yes. Just trying to get these replacement pages copied for the meeting. Then I'm going to have some lunch and take a moment to try to relieve some stress beforehand."

His voice dropped as he took a step closer, running his fingers along my arm. It sent a chill through me, but I tried to act normal. His voice was sickly sweet as he said, "Why don't you join me for lunch? I'm sure we could relieve some of the stress together."

That was like dropping ice water on me. Regardless of what was happening between my legs, I stood taller and used my most professional voice to say, "As I have told you before, Mr. McFarland, I'm not interested and will gladly take lunch alone. I would appreciate it if you could stop these advances."

"Lanie, how long has it been for you? I'm sure it wouldn't hurt to clear out the cobwebs."

My eyes went wide at his words. "I'm sorry. Are you insinuating that I haven't had sex in a long time? Why would you make that assumption? Also, on what planet is this an appropriate conversation topic while at work *or* between a boss and their employee?"

The vibrating stopped, just as he said, "Well, you are a beautiful woman, but I'm not sure how many would want someone in your current condition. If you were mine—"

"Good thing I'm not." *What in the actual fuck is wrong with this man?*

He grabbed my wrists and pulled me against him. I felt his tic tac dick hard against my thigh, and I winced at the pressure he was putting on my wrists.

"If you *were* mine, I'd get you all the help you need to become the most stunning woman ever to be on my arm. What, about seventy pounds should do it?"

Blind anger filled me, and before I knew what I was doing, I pulled my hand from his and smacked him. He dropped my other wrist, and I took a step back. "Just because I carry a little extra weight doesn't mean I'm not beautiful or wanted or worthy of love. In fact, I think my boyfriend would have a few words to say to you if he were here."

"Well, he isn't."

Oh, my gods. This was the most forward and inappropriate McFart-face had ever been.

"Lucky for you he isn't. It would be a shame if you had to walk into the meeting with the president and have to explain a swollen jaw and eye. Now, if you'll excuse me, I need to finish getting ready for that meeting."

I grabbed my photocopies and stormed off back to my office. Handing them to Vanessa, I told her, "I'm going to lock myself in, eat lunch, and see if I can get a hold of J-Jason." The vibration, coming from deep within me, had me stuttering over his name.

She simply smirked. "Yes, ma'am."

As I stepped into my office, I slammed the door and locked it. My legs were a little wobbly as he played with the intensity. When I made it to my chair, though, I flopped on it and reached for my phone, instantly setting up a video chat.

"Hey there, gorgeous." He had one helluva smirk on his face, but then he noticed the lack of one on mine. His face blurred out for a moment, and then the vibration stopped completely just before he was back on my screen. "What happened?"

"I was a second from an orgasm when I was propositioned and insulted all in the same conversation."

His eyebrows shot up. "I'm sorry, what?"

"Adrian McFarland. He suggested that we take lunch together, that he could help me relieve some stress,' and then he made the assumption I haven't had sex in a while because I'm not a size four."

"Again, *what?*"

I glared at him, too angry to repeat any of it. My blood was thrumming through me, and I could almost hear my own heartbeat.

His eyes were wide, but he shook his head and said, "I'm not hard of hearing. I just can't believe he would say something so asinine."

"I smacked him and basically told him he could kiss my ass." I huffed a laugh. "Though, I did tell him that he was lucky my boyfriend wasn't here because it would have been a shame if he had to go into the meeting today with a swollen jaw and eye."

The murderous look in Jason's eyes matched the lethal tone in his voice as he said, "That would have been me taking it easy on him."

"You know what bothers me the most?"

"What's that?"

"He totally killed my mood. I'm not kidding when I said that I was on the edge of cumming."

He shook his head and chuckled. "Lanie, you are amazing."

It was my turn to look at him like he had rocks for brains. "I know, but why now?"

"You aren't mad because he gave you bullshit about your weight. You aren't mad because he propositioned you, at work no less—"

"Did I mention that he pulled me against him so I could feel his tiny, hard dick?"

Jason took a deep breath. I knew he was trying to hold it together and shove the anger down. He was a bit possessive of me, but he trusted me for the sake of our long distance. "You didn't. However, like I was saying, I'm still amazed that it's that you didn't orgasm that is contributing to this anger."

"Well, my boyfriend was working *so* hard to get me there, and it really wasn't fair that he couldn't finish it off."

His face went blurry again, and then the vibrations restarted. Leaning back, I just moaned and pressed my legs together. "Fuck."

When I looked back at the phone, he was smirking. "I can fix that from here, you know."

I rolled my hips to create more friction, and he alternated the sequence as I held his gaze. "Please?"

"Please what, my little slut? I love the look of you writhing in pleasure. Sure, I would prefer it to be either beneath or above me, but that is not the point. Fuck, look at how pink your cheeks are."

The speed changed as he got up and locked his office door. As he walked back to his desk, I had the perfect view of him undoing his pants and releasing his cock. My mouth watered, as I instantly wanted to have it down my throat again. "Jase . . ."

"Yes, my little whore wants this, doesn't she?"

"Yes, she does." The s trailed off as he hit the controls again.

He started stroking himself, and my tongue snaked out in anticipation of licking the pre-cum now sliding down his cock. A whimper came from my lips as I had to remind myself I wasn't going to taste it just yet.

We teased each other for another fifteen minutes, him bringing me to the edge and then backing off. I stood, pulled the shorts off, and sat with my legs wide so he could see all of me. When I moved my panties to the side, he groaned and stroked harder, the head of him turning purple with the force of his jerking and need for release. "Fuck, look at how wet you are."

I reached down and inserted two fingers along the toy for him to see and slowly pulled them out, a trail of my wetness leaking from my pussy to my fingers. He was licking his lips and stroking harder now as I reinserted my fingers. My hips rolled with the increased vibrations coupled with my fingers and the heel of my hand.

"That's right. My little whore loves to fuck that beautiful pussy while I watch." His other hand reached for the phone, and a moment later, the vibe was on full as he ordered, "Cum for me."

I pressed the heel of my hand against the little vibrating bulb and my clit, which instantly had me moaning in pleasure. I had to cover my mouth as I let out a loud groan. My legs were twitching as Jason pumped his cock harder, saying, "Yes, that's my dirty little girl. Fuck, keep cuming for me." Then he was spurting ropes of cum into his hand. "Yes, that is my good, dirty slut."

As my orgasm came down, I started twitching more and starting to rise to another cliff. I rolled my hips, pulled the device from me, and pressed it against my clit. "Fuck, yes. Again. Make me cum again."

"Fuck, you are beautiful begging like that." He cleaned up in one hand, and the other alternated the speeds.

I found the perfect spot to send me sailing and said, "Yes, right there. Fuck. Fuck. Fuck." I ground down just as Jason revved up the device. Then I was lifting my ass from my chair, and I felt my pussy and thighs quake in response.

Finally, I came back down and pulled the device from my core. It stopped moving after a moment, and I opened my eyes back up to see Jason putting himself away. I rolled my head to look at the clock hanging on the wall and realized I had ten minutes before I had to be in the boardroom.

"Dammit."

"Almost time to go?"

A large sigh came out of me as I tried to move to at least sit up. I needed to put my shorts on and clean up. "Yeah."

We stared at each other for a long minute, just relishing being together. Those three words sat on the tip of my tongue, but I reeled them back and instead told him, "I'm leaving this in my purse for the meeting. Turned off."

He smiled slightly but nodded. "That seems fair."

"Talk to you tonight?"

"Wouldn't miss it, my queen. See you tonight."

I nodded and hung up the phone.

My muscles were less tense at least, so I hadn't lied to Adrian when I'd said I was going to get some stress relief. Two orgasms with Jason. That would do it.

Now, it was showtime.

THE
DEN

DON'T LET THEM EAT YOU ALIVE

Chapter Thirty

Jason

Trenton

Reaching over and turning the alarm off on my phone, I groaned at the brightness coming off the display. I rubbed my eyes and made myself get up. Five in the morning was early, but it was finally the end of the trimester, and I couldn't wait to get on the road. It was going to take almost nine hours, but after Lanie and I body-doubled for a few hours last night, I finished grading everything and turned in my grades, packed my shit, and put away messages on everything. Nothing was going to take me away from spending a week in the southern California sun with my girl. I just hoped Kevin would be alright with my sudden appearance. He needed his schedule, and I knew that I was taking a huge chance here, but I was hoping it would help him understand just how much I was willing to put in the effort.

I was just through Stockton on the 5 when my phone rang, scaring the everliving shit out of me. I was surprised when I saw Kai's name on the caller ID. Answering it, I growled, "What is your happy ass doing still up at seven in the morning. Didn't you work the overnight tables?"

"Look, I don't need your shit right now." His voice was tight, and he really sounded like he'd had a rough night.

"What happened?"

I heard the deep breath he took and let out through the phone. "Don Kingsley came by tonight . . . last night? Whatever. He came by The Den."

"Okay. He's been known to come in and play a few hands."

"Yeah, only he was asking for you. When I told him you hadn't been in for a bit, he asked me to deliver a message."

"He has my direct contact number and so does Chase." Kai was one of the few people who knew what I did at The Den for Kingsley. There was silence on the other end for so long that I finally shook my head in confusion and asked, "What was that message?"

"He said he needed to talk to you regarding someone you both have special interest in." My heart was beating double-time.

"Didn't happen to mention *who*, did he?" Though, I had a pretty good idea since his son had a security detail on Lanie.

"He didn't. There is more, though. Cyress overheard him asking about you. Cyress is looking into people you have in common. Thought I would give you a heads-up."

I stared down the straight interstate, half zoned out, and thought about how Lanie had mentioned she thought someone was following her. It wasn't Chase's guys, but—

"Jason, you still there?"

I took a deep breath and rubbed my face. "Yeah, I'm here. Just trying to figure out why Cyress would have an issue with a Don who brings in so much cash to his business."

He huffed a laugh. "Oh, you know Cyress. He doesn't like anyone he loses money to. You are just over Don Kingsley. Likely because we are in his territory, so he plays nice to keep a bullet out of his brain."

"Cyress pays his penance, though."

"That he does." Silence hung in the air before he continued, "I just hope whoever it is stays out of the sights of Cyress, and whatever Don Kingsley wants with this person, it's for good reasons, not retribution."

"Agreed."

"When you get back, I'll get you the information he left. I suppose you don't have something to write with at the moment since you are driving?"

"That would be right. Now, go get some sleep, Kai."

"Already in bed. Drive safe, and see ya when you get back." He hung up, and with how tired he sounded, I would be surprised if he got his phone charging before he was conked out.

Taking a deep breath, I tried to push Kai's conversation from my mind. When I wasn't successful, I pulled over and looked through my audiobooks. My eyes stopped on one that Lanie had suggested. A human with demons.

Why the hell not. I could use some demon smut. Going outside the box is a good thing, right?

By the time I got it going and was back on the road, I leaned back as the book started.

"'Chapter 1: The Crossroads.'"

SAN DIEGO

Parking in one of the guest parking spots at the apartment complex, I took a deep breath, leaned back in my seat, and closed my eyes. I was beat. Every inch of my body hurt from being in the car for so long. Twelve hours was a lot of time to be on the road.

I should have just flown.

It was always a hit or miss with traffic coming through LA, but when it was eleven thirty and I hadn't even made it to the peak of the pass before I came to a complete stop, I'd known I was in for the long haul over the Grapevine. The fight over was excruciating. Not to mention the fast food that I'd picked up at the base of the hill had me feeling bloated and like a freaking slug. Rolling my neck, I picked up my phone and texted Lanie.

Jason: You home?
Lanie: Yeah.

I stepped out of the car and grabbed my duffle bag from the back seat.

Lanie: Just got home from picking Kevin up from his trip. Making spaghetti for him.

Jason: No problem. Wait, I thought tonight is a taco night? Pasta is on Tuesdays.

Lanie: You are right. He was pretty insistent upon it tonight. Give me about fifteen minutes and I can talk.

Smiling up at the building, I stepped into the center courtyard that had a giant lawn and a small playground for toddlers. Finding the elevator at the end of the courtyard was easy. I rushed toward it and hit the button to take me to her floor. There were a few other people in the car, and I couldn't help but fidget and shift my weight from side to side in anticipation of seeing her surprised face.

"You look nervous," an older lady said next to me. She was leaning on a cane and had a bag of groceries at her feet.

"Surprising my girlfriend."

She broke out into a wide grin. "I remember when my Richard used to surprise me. A jokester he was." Her eyes went to the buttons and she asked, "Eleventh floor?"

"Yes, ma'am."

"That's my floor, too." Her head shifted to the side. "Are you here to see that nice girl Lanie and her brother, Kevin?"

I could feel my smile brighten. "Yes, ma'am."

"You must be Jason."

"I don't know if I must be, but . . ." She chuckled. "I am."

"Her face brightens every time she speaks to me about you. It's wonderful to see her like that again. She was so sad for so long. Lanie kept up a brave face for that sweet brother of hers, though. He helps me with all sorts of things. Did you know he's a brilliant painter? I have a piece he made for me hanging in my bedroom."

I smiled at her. She was so enthusiastic about them, it warmed my heart. The elevator stopped and the doors slid open. I held them for her and took her bag of groceries for her as she hobbled out into the hallway. "Lanie is two down from me, and I am just about halfway down this hall."

As we walked, I couldn't help but think how this could be my every day. Talking to neighbors, coming home to Lanie and Kevin . . .

"This is me." She opened the door and took the bag. "I'm Ms. Langston. Tell those two I said to have a great night. It was nice to meet you, Jason."

"You as well, Ms. Langston."

I turned and headed down the hall and found her apartment. Knocking, I held my breath and heard her curse before footsteps hurried to the door. When she opened it, the chain caught, and a bit eased in me that she at least had that going.

"Yes—" Her eyes went wide, and then she shut the door, unhooking the chain and whipped it open to jump into my arms. "Jase, what are you doing here?"

My grip on her tightened around her waist, and I nestled into her neck, breathing her in. "I needed my girl, and it's break. I wanted to surprise you."

She leaned back and peppered my face with kisses, causing me to chuckle. "Mission successful."

I kissed her quickly before setting her down, and then she pulled me into the apartment. We had just gotten inside when Kevin stood from the couch, but quickly looked away and shifted on his feet. "Hi, Kevin."

"Hello, Mr. Rathborn. I didn't know you were coming today." His back was ramrod straight as he continued to shift, and I didn't see even a flicker of happiness on his face. Lanie had said he would give me a chance, but he also didn't like surprises. Kevin liked his routine, but he had always handled disruptions and changes to his schedule when he had been given a heads-up.

"I wanted it to be a surprise. I didn't mean to upset you." I knew me being here could upset him. "Is it okay if I stay here for a few days?"

Lanie tensed next to me, and out of the corner of my eye, I saw her look up at me, but I kept my attention on Kevin. His head tipped to the side, but he kept looking at the console controller on the table.

"Can I still play my video games?"

I chuckled and let a small smile lift the corner of my lips. "Of course. You still have to go to the center all week, though. I have no intention of disrupting your normal schedule."

He looked at me like I was crazy. "Obviously. I get up in the morning, have my breakfast, make Sissy coffee while she is getting ready, and then I go to Velas. I have lunch with Paul on Wednesdays."

"Good. Lanie said you are doing really well there. Do you like it?"

He nodded. "They are nice. They don't yell at me when I have to make sure my things are set up a certain way."

Lainie stiffened next to me as she asked, "Did they at your old school?"

"Yeah, but you said I don't go there anymore."

"That's right." I pulled Lanie into me tighter, and she wrapped her other arm around my waist. "So, is it okay if he stays with us for the week, Kevin?"

There was a mischievous sparkle in his eye as he said, "Yes. As long as I get to pick dinner every night."

Lanie laughed, looked up at me, and I shrugged. We both knew that there was a dinner schedule, so this wasn't really a big thing. "Deal, buddy. Now go and get cleaned up while I finish up the spaghetti."

We watched him go down the hall, and then she shifted from my side to in front of me. "Now, kiss me like you really want to say hello."

"Don't have to tell me twice." Cradling her head in my hands, I pressed my lips onto hers, tilting her head to the side, and slowly backed her up to the counter, pinning her in place. Our tongues danced with each other, and I couldn't believe I had forgotten how amazing my queen tasted. I let one of my hands slide back and tangled my fingers in her hair, gripping tight. She moaned deep and pressed against me. Kissing her softly one last time, I leaned against her forehead. "Did that meet your expectations?"

"It did." She reached up, kissed me again quickly, and hurried around the corner into the kitchen. I leaned on the counter, watching her as she pulled the bread out of the oven and drained the pasta in the sink.

THE
DEN
Don't Let Them Eat You Alive.

CHAPTER THIRTY-ONE

LANIE

SAN DIEGO

I had just walked out of a meeting where McFarland had laid it on thick in front of half the entire board of directors.

We work perfectly together.

Oh, you can count on Carley and me to make a stunning appearance.

I have all the faith in Carley being able to handle a big load.

On the surface, they didn't seem like much, but the winks that he'd given me after each statement, how he'd sat next to me, and how, on multiple occasions, he'd tried to put his hand on my thigh just made my skin crawl. Once the meeting had ended, Dezmond, our boss, had asked, "Lanie, can I talk to you for a moment?"

Taking a ragged breath, I'd told him. "Give me five minutes and I'll meet you in your office. Need to use the restroom. Shouldn't have had the large soda at lunch."

After he'd nodded, I'd grabbed my stuff and had ran out of the room and back to my office as quickly as I could. Once behind the closed door, I'd locked it and sat down at my desk.

Can't I just go home to Jason?

I swear that man wouldn't let up. What was it going to take? Not to mention the complete lack of respect during that meeting to insinuate a relationship between us. I could lose my job for that shit, and I wasn't even at fault. The office fraternization policy was fierce here. There was massive HR paperwork that would have to be filled out, and if it wasn't, both parties would be immediately fired.

There was a knock on my door, and Dezmond's voice came through. "Lanie, can you open the door, please?"

Taking a deep breath, I stood and opened it slightly, making sure that McFarland wasn't there with him. When I only saw my boss, I checked the hall to make sure no one was coming before closing it again and locking it. I looked at it for a long moment and then unlocked it, knowing that if I was in a closed-off room with my boss, that, too, could be an issue.

"Lanie, I need to talk to you about what happened in there."

I gave him a quick nod and sat down at my desk. "We are not involved. I promise you that."

"From the way you reacted to each of those comments and the way you rushed out, I thought that might be the case. Besides, Vanessa mentioned that you have a boyfriend up outside of Sacramento?"

There was no hiding the smile on my face when I thought of Jason. "Yes, sir. Jason surprised me earlier this week actually. Showed up at my doorstep. It's difficult with me needing to be around for Kevin and Jason being a teacher at the university up there. It's hard for us to get a common time to get away together." I snapped my focus to him. "But I can guarantee you, I have zero romantic interest in McFarland."

"Is he going to be a problem?" He lifted an eyebrow at me in question. "Does HR need to be contacted?"

My head moved back and forth. "Not yet. I just don't want it to affect my job. I don't want his sleezy comments to affect anything that I'm doing here. I just want to do my job and go home without being harassed. Plus, HR will only tell him to stop, and then he will do it more on the sly. Likely with more handsy stuff so no one else can say they heard it. It could really just make matters worse."

"But—"

My phone went off, and when I looked down at it sitting on the table, I saw it was the center. I didn't even tell Dezmond to wait, just picked it up. "This is Lanie."

"Hi, Lanie. Kevin is fine, but I wanted to call you because a couple of guys came in today, hung around the lobby for almost an hour before things slowed down enough that we could talk to ask them what we could do for them. My supervisor tried to get photos off the security cameras, but it was like they knew where to move their heads so they wouldn't be caught."

"The poetry reading," I said in understanding. The center had been planning the public event for months now.

"Yes, ma'am. Well, these two guys said they were here to pick up Kevin for you. Said you had gotten caught up at work and had given them instructions to pick Kevin up and take him to your office. As per our policy, I informed them they weren't on the list and that I would have to verify with you."

"I didn't send anyone. I'm planning on picking him up in an hour. He didn't want to take the bus today." My heart was racing so hard, I thought Dezmond would be able to see it through my shirt. "Kevin is not to go home with anyone other than those currently on the approved list or Jason Rathborn. Is that explicitly understood?"

"Yes, ma'am." There was a moment of silence before she asked, "Jason Rathborn? He isn't on the approved list."

I took a deep breath. "I know. I haven't gotten around to filling out his paperwork. And I highly doubt that Jason is one of the men standing there to pick up Kevin." I sighed.

"No one knows who they were, and they knew exactly where to turn their heads so no one could get a good look at their faces. We will put a complaint in his file."

"Thank you." I hung up the phone, and when I looked down, my hands were shaking.

"Lanie, you okay?" Dezmond put the papers he was holding down on my desk and reached out to take my hands. "You're shaking. What's wrong?"

My chest was tight, and I was trying to get air to come into my lungs, but it was like someone had cut off my throat. I couldn't even make myself swallow. "Som— Someone just tried picking up Kevin from Velas."

"Go. You aren't going to feel better until you have him and know he's safe."

"Thank you. I-I will be back tomorrow."

He nodded his head and held my gaze, and he had me breathe a few times with him before I nodded and headed out of the office. Rushing through the building, I texted Jason.

Lanie: Meet me outside in five minutes.

Just as I was getting to my car, my phone went off.

Jason: What's wrong?

Lanie: Just be downstairs in five minutes.

I threw my phone in the console, backed out of my spot, and didn't even stop on my way out of the parking lot.

Please tell me Kevin doesn't know that someone unapproved tried to pick him up.

Who would want to take him?

My mind was racing, and the only thing I could think of was I needed Jason to help me calm down, and I needed to get to Kevin. Luckily, the apartment was only a couple blocks out of the way, and when I pulled up, Jason jumped off the stoop and circled 'round to the driver's side.

"I'm driving." We switched quickly, and I had just closed the passenger side door when he asked, "Where are we going?"

"Velas. Someone tried to pick Kevin up who wasn't on the list." My leg was bouncing up and down, and Jason reached over, laying his hand on my thigh. While the heat from his palm helped to calm me as he pulled out of the apartment parking lot, my leg was still moving.

"What else?"

I swallowed and took a deep breath. "Velas has lots of security, which is one of many reasons why they are so highly rated. The men came in during the poetry reading and asked for Kevin when it was done, saying that I'd asked them to pick him up."

Jason's hand tightened on my thigh as he nodded. "And unless they are pre-approved by you, they won't let him out."

"Right. The problem is that whoever they were evaded the cameras. They don't have a clue who these people were."

The car sped up as I finished, and Jason nodded. He wove through cars quickly, and when we got to Velas, he inputted the number and was tapping his thumb on the steering wheel as we waited for the gate to open. Once we were parked, I went to jump out of the car, but Jason took my hand.

"Lanie, stop. You need to calm down. Kevin is only going to freak out if he sees you like this." His other hand reached up, cupped my cheek, and I couldn't help but take a calming breath.

"That's my girl. Again."

After I repeated the exercise a few times, he smiled after the fourth and leaned forward and kissed me. His lips were soft and warm against mine, and I felt more of the tension leave my shoulders. When he pulled back, his gaze met mine.

"You calm?"

"No, but I'm not panicking anymore. Can we go get Kevin now?"

He nodded, and when he reached my side of the car, he took my hand, lacing our fingers together. As the doors opened, Mrs. Brackworth, the director, met us at the check-in desk.

"Ms. Carley, it's good to see you. I'm sorry that it is under these circumstances though."

I nodded. "You as well, Mrs. Brackworth. Does Kevin know? Is he okay?"

"Kevin is fine. He's hanging out in the lounge." She looked to someone behind me and then said, "I'm sorry that we can't identify the people who came in."

I blinked in confusion, my heart beating faster as Jason's hand tightened in mine. "People? As in more than one?"

"Yes, ma'am. I'm sorry if that message wasn't received."

Jason spoke up and covered for me as I racked my brain. "I'm sure the information was, but sometimes we don't hear everything when we are worried."

Squeezing his hand in thanks, I nodded at her. "I'm sorry. I'm . . . Well, life has been weird for me lately. Not to mention there have been some changes, like Jason." I turned to smile at him. He smiled back, but I turned toward her and continued, "He's a more permanent fixture, and he surprised me by showing up earlier this week. Anything that isn't normal, I'm just worried how Kevin is going to react. Does he know about today?"

"He does not. I wanted to talk to you first, and I'm glad I did, considering what you've just said." Then she was looking behind me, smiling. "Kevin, it looks like you have two people to pick you up."

When I turned to face him, he smiled when he saw me and then he looked at Jason, smiling brighter. My chest loosened slightly as I noted that he was happy that Jason was here.

"Mr. Rathborn? You came with Sissy?"

Jason smiled and pulled our joined hands behind me, so that I was forced to stand closer to him. "Is that okay?"

"It is, but you are early. Is everything okay?"

Jason squeezed my hand, and I let out a big sigh. "I had a rough day. The meeting today was stressful and so I left early."

"Well, let's get you home and into a bath."

"Sissy loves her baths."

I looked between the two of them and shook my head. "Alright, let's get home. Good night, Mrs. Brackworth."

"Good night."

THE

DEN

Don't Let Them Eat You Alive

CHAPTER THIRTY-TWO

JASON

SAN DIEGO

I couldn't believe the blind panic she'd been in when she had pulled into the complex and I'd opened the door. I'd been thankful that I was there to help calm her down a bit before walking into Velas. Luckily, it appeared that Kevin had bought the tough day at work story, and when we got home, he said he was going to his room and to draw and have headphone time.

Lanie watched as he headed down the hall and shut his door. She rushed right back into my arms, sobbing uncontrollably and hardly able to breathe.

"Someone tried to take him. Who would want to take Kevin? He's innocent."

Rubbing her back and holding her, I murmured, "I don't know, my queen. I don't know."

It took some time, but I got her somewhat calm and in the bath, then I paced in the living room. This wasn't the first time something strange had happened, but the first time I had been here for it. Looking back toward the bathroom, I wondered if this is how she came home each of the times before or if she had stuffed it down so that she wouldn't worry Kevin.

Could this be tied to Don Kingsley looking for me at The Den? What if something followed me from Trenton? With my hands on my hips and my head tipped back, looking at the ceiling, I sighed. Chase. I needed to talk to Chase.

Pulling out my phone, I opened my contacts and sighed before pressing the button to call him.

"What can I do for you, professor?"

I inwardly groaned at the formal title but let it go. "You have your guys down here watching Lanie, right?"

There was silence for a moment before he finally conceded, "Yes. She isn't supposed to notice them, though."

"I don't know if it was your guys or not. She happened to mention that she had noticed some guys following her for some time. I was going to talk to you when I got back, but today someone tried to get to her brother. Someone came into Velas and tried to check him out of the facility."

"What?" His growl through the phone was unnerving.

"Chase, she called me and I met her downstairs to go pick him up. She came home completely freaked out. I've got her in a bath right now, and Kevin is in his bedroom, occupied, which is the only reason I can even make this call. So, if it is your guys, can you ask them to back off and stop scaring the shit out of her?" I ran my hand through my hair and let out a tense breath. "I'm glad I was here today, but I don't want this happening every time she leaves the house."

"Of course, professor, but it wasn't my guys. They know all about Velas's security and are simply keeping an eye out for suspicious shit. One reported in that they had rerouted some followers, but they wouldn't interfere in their lives so blatantly."

I took a deep breath. "Thank you for that, and I believe you." I waited a moment as I paced across the living room floor before I continued, "We were at dinner last night and she mentioned that she had seen a man sitting in the corner following her before. She has no idea who he is."

"Did you get a look at him?" It sounded like he was searching for something in the background by the papers moving and something heavy being moved. When someone hollered for him, he told them to wait a moment.

"He looked just like any other businessman. Brown hair, clean cut, glasses, in a blue suit. Sorry I can't give you more. Whoever it is, is using people who are forgettable. Only, she's scared, and it's getting

THE PROFESSOR'S BET

worse. I don't know why you care so much about my girl, but I want an answer to that."

"I know, man. I just can't yet. *Dad* says I can't."

I let out a frustrated breath. That only meant that this was personal. *What in the fucking hell is going on?*

"Just tell me something." There was silence on the other end, so I continued, "Is she in danger from you, as in the Kingsley family?"

"Good gods, no. She's going to be protected. Totally and completely. Lanie and Kevin are untouchables."

My shoulders sagged in relief, but his adamant promise that she was wholly protected still put me on edge. *Don't push it right now, Jason.* "Okay. I'll take that for now."

"I gotta run, but I'll talk to my guys, okay?"

"Thank you." Then the line went dead.

I leaned against the hallway wall and settled my racing heart before I headed into the kitchen to make Lanie a cup of hot cocoa. As the water was heating, I looked to the liquor cabinet. In another book series she loved, there was a lady who spiked the cocoa to help her people calm their nerves. *Why the hell not?* Heading to the cabinet, I pulled down the peppermint schnapps. Once her cocoa was ready, I poured a bit of the liquor in and headed to the bathroom.

The room was filled with steam as I pushed open the door, walked in, and sat on the edge of the lid on the toilet, handing her the cup. "It's spiked, so don't chug it."

She lifted an eyebrow and inhaled. "Mmmm, peppermint." She took a sip and slipped a little farther into the water. Her large brown eyes turned to look up at me as she asked, "Should I just take the week off and stay with you? I'm tired of this."

Smiling at her, I shook my head. "I admire you, my queen, but don't worry about all of the crazy for tonight. As for during the day? I knew you were going to have to work. It's okay. I just enjoy being in your space. Kevin and I are also going to get some time together, which is a good thing. And I am not mad about being able to snuggle up next to you each night."

"And the sex is great, too."

"Yeah, the sex is amazing."

Her head was leaning back on the tub as she let out a large breath, and I just stared at her. The strands of wet hair that stuck to her face and the reflection of the water on her face only made her shine. I was stunned once again by her beauty. The way her large brown eyes held so much emotion, the way her full cheeks cradled her fabulous smile, the way her whole being held my future. Leaning forward, I moved some of the hair stuck to her face and tucked it behind her ear. She leaned into my touch, and a content smile crossed my face. "I'm going to let you relax, okay? Kevin and I will figure out what kind of burgers we will have for dinner."

She nodded as I leaned forward and kissed her forehead.

As I left the room, I couldn't help but think, *I love you, Melanie.*

My mind was still reeling from my discussion with Kevin this morning when I dropped him off. He had been insistent that he stay the night at Velas. After a bit of probing, he said there was a girl, Jackie, that he really liked, and he wanted to have dinner and watch a movie with her at the center tonight. His face had been flushed as he'd admitted that he'd had a crush on her for a long time, but it wasn't until he and Lanie had seen her at the grocery store that he'd realized that she liked him, too. So tonight, they were going to have dinner. I told him it wasn't a problem and that maybe I would take Lanie out on a date tonight.

I was just finishing the dishes when there was a knock on the door. After toweling my hands off, I answered it to find a large bouquet of black roses with a dusting of red in the center in a pitch-black vase with a bloodred ribbon around the top, weaved in and out of the porcelain. They were beautiful, but when I crouched down to look at them, I saw an envelope underneath and a small fine wire sticking out through the envelope that was set under the bottom of the vase. Gently, I slowly moved it, only to realize it was too light and kept it in place. Moving a couple of the flowers over, I saw no water in the vase.

My heart started racing and I took a ragged breath. I didn't remember calling, but Chase was suddenly answering and barely recognized the fear in my voice. "Please tell me your guys have eyes on Lanie right now."

I heard him mutter a few things in the background and a phone ringing. "Eyes on the woman? Okay. Thank you . . . Yeah, I'll call you back." He brought the phone back to his ear, and with my heart in my throat, I waited for him to confirm one way or another. "They have her. What's going on?"

"Flower delivery. There is a slip of paper under the vase against the floor, but there is a wire looped around like it popped out just before the vase was set down. If I hadn't been paying attention and just slipped the paper out . . ."

"Where are you, Jason?"

I looked up and down the hallway, looking for anyone, but of course, they were long gone. "The apartment."

"Okay. Ismael will be there in a moment. He's overseeing the apartment building."

I sat down on my ass in the doorway. I wasn't going to take a chance that some nosy neighbor was going to take the sheet of paper and then be hurt. "Alright. It could be nothing, Chase, but I have a really bad feeling about moving it, in case it ignites something. Wires sticking out of the bottom of things? I've worked with the Kingsley family long enough to know better. I've learned a few things along the way."

"I rather you feel stupid for being over protective and cautious about this than be riddled with guilt if someone got hurt."

"Chase, why Lanie? Why do you and Don Kingsley have such a special interest in her? I let it go before, but I need answers!"

He took a long breath. "We need her alive and well, too. I know you want to know the connection, but you can't just yet. In time, Jason, in time. First, I need to find out if she's being targeted due to our affiliation or whatever else the fuck is going on if it's not us."

A tall, dark-skinned man I had seen on rare occasions since I'd arrived rounded the corner and nodded to me as he took the few steps up to me and said, "You still on the phone with Chase?" I nodded. "Good. Chase, stay on the line while I look at this."

I huffed a dark laugh. "Front row seats to the destruction."

Ismael smirked. "Not if this is nothing. And if it is, well then, it was nice to meet you in person."

"Likewise."

"Hey, Jason, put me on speakerphone." I did and set the phone down on the floor next to us, so I didn't have to sit here and hold it. "Talk to me, Ismael."

"I'm impressed with Rathborn. The fact he caught this is impressive." Slowly, he pulled out a knife and cut the wire section out of the envelope from under the vase. The wire section stayed in place as Ismael pulled the envelope out, pinched the end to open the letter, and pulled it out. I watched his eyes move back and forth, and his face stayed neutral before he gripped around the flowers and gently pulled them from the vase.

He handed me the roses, but the second the smell hit me, I recoiled. "Why do the roses smell musty?"

Ismael's hand froze, and as he gently set the bouquet down on the ground, he pulled out a pocket knife. I took a moment to look down into the vase, where there was a claylike substance in the bottom. "What is that?"

"If I had my guess, C-4, but let's worry about the flowers first." He cut open the ribbon holding the perfectly structured bouquet, and the arrangement spread out on the floor to show a fresh bustle of hemlock hidden in the center.

I narrowed my eyes at it, and when he went to lift a piece of it to his nose, I halted him. "Hemlock. It shouldn't be a problem to touch it, but you don't want it getting ingested in any way."

Ismael's head tilted to the side, and he looked at me. His eyes were assessing, and the wheels were definitely turning.

"Ismael . . ." Chase's voice came through the speaker of my phone.

"Hemlock was in the center of the bouquet. I'm not sure why, though. The note was a warning, but . . ." Ismael blinked at me and then looked back down at the dismantled bouquet before us.

"What did the note say?" I asked. He shook his head at me, and I asked again more firmly. "What did the note say?"

"Even the prettiest flower can be deadly."

"What does that even mean?" Then I looked at the phone, waiting for Chase to say something. When he didn't, I shuddered at the chill that went down my spine. "Will someone explain this to me?"

Chase's breath blew across the mic on the phone, then it sounded like he covered it before he started hollering in the background, but I couldn't make it out. A moment later, he said, "I'm sorry, Rathborn. This is actually on our side of things. I may have another game for you by the time you return. I'm really sorry. This shouldn't be affecting you and Lanie. Let us handle it. Good job on catching this. Ismael, is the vase safe to move?"

"It will be. Just going to need a minute." He looked up at me. "Can you get a trash bag for the flowers?"

Nodding, I headed back into the apartment, into the kitchen, opened the cupboard, knelt, grabbed a bag, and just as I was standing, there was loud pop, sizzle, and a cursed, "Fuck, that hurt!"

I rushed back out there, and Ismael was holding his wrist while shaking out his hand. Chase, however, was chuckling through the speakerphone. "Told you should have waited till you had all your tools."

"What the fuck happened?" There was a small char mark on the carpet.

Ismael rolled his eyes. "Fuck off, Chase, I'll talk to you in a bit."

Chase hollered, "Stay close to Jason and Lanie."

I looked between the phone and the man sitting on the floor across from me, still shaking out his hand, when the line went dead and the screen went dark. Reaching over and picking it up, I stuck it in my back pocket and helped Ismael clean up the mess in the hall. It took a bit of work, but even the char mark on the floor almost blended into the pattern. When we were done, I gave him a bottle of water from the fridge and asked, "Is it okay if I leave the apartment? I planned on heading out to have lunch with Lanie."

"Yeah. No problem, I don't want you to have to change anything you do. Just continue to keep an eye out for things like this."

I nodded as he took the bag from the floor, headed down the hall, and disappeared into the stairway. Walking back into the apartment and shutting the door, I was eternally grateful that none of the neighbors had come out during all of that. It being the middle of the day in a workweek was helpful. As I leaned against the closed door, my mind raced with all that happened and how little I knew of the details.

It's Kingsley business. Stay out of it, Jason.

Looking at the clock, I still had an hour before I needed to leave and meet up with my queen. Just enough time to get the laundry put up and take a shower.

THE
DEN
Don't Let Them Eat You Alive

The

DEN

Don't Let Them Eat You Alive

CHAPTER THIRTY-THREE

JASON

SAN DIEGO

Lanie's head was down as she worked, her hair up in a messy bun, strands falling around her face. She had a yellow wrap sundress on that complemented her skin tone beautifully. Long silver earrings hung and swayed as she moved, and at the angle I was at, I could see just enough of her cleavage to be professional, but also tease me to hell and back. I wanted nothing more than to walk in, slam the door shut, free her full breasts, and love on them until she came.

But she was at work. The last thing I wanted to do was get her in trouble, so I leaned on the doorjamb and knocked. Without looking up, she sighed. "Vanessa, I'm almost done. You can tell McFarland I have lunch plans and that he can fuck the hell off."

I lifted my eyebrows and smiled. "I'm not sure why McFarland would think you had lunch plans with him, but you can cancel them."

Her head popped up in surprise, and then her face broke out into a bright smile. "Jase."

"Hello, my queen."

Pushing off the door, I walked into her office and around her desk. I took hold of her chin between my knuckle and thumb, leaning down to give her a kiss. "Cancel your plans for lunch."

She chuckled. "Luckily, those plans were to hide from McFarland at the park and just read a book."

I smirked. "Sounds like someone needs to realize that you are taken."

She just shrugged and started putting her stuff away. "Give me like five minutes."

"Yes, ma'am." I went and sat in the corner, and just about the time she was done, a woman came to stand at her door.

"Lanie?"

My queen shook her head and looked up at her. "I have plans for lunch and am leaving right now." With a nod, the woman's gaze moved to me then back to Lanie, where she wiggled her eyebrows before she turned and walked away. Lanie stood, and when she rounded the desk, she reached her hand out for mine. Taking it, I entwined my fingers with hers, and we headed out.

Twenty minutes later, we were at a deli, sitting out on their patio. I had just taken a bite of my sandwich when a tall man with perfectly coiffed, blond hair, a large, bulbous nose, and fat lips poking out from a dark beard, dressed in a suit with the tie loosened, came up and leaned on her chair. "Mind if I join you?"

I glanced over, and Lanie's eyes blazed fire as she reached over and put her hand on my thigh. "Actually, I do. See, I'm here with my boyfriend."

"Oh, well . . . See,I thought maybe he was your brother considering . . ."

"Considering *what*?" I huffed a laugh. "I'm not sure why you would think I'm her brother. By the way you are looking her up and down, I can tell how much you're attracted to her, and well, I'm not surprised. She's fucking sexy as hell." I leaned over and nibbled at her earlobe and then kissed her neck, swirling my tongue along the skin. Her head tipped to the side as she pressed her legs together, and she hummed in satisfaction. "But my queen is very much taken, so I would appreciate it if you would back the fuck off."

"Well, she *could* be sexy as hell." He tipped back on his heels, and his gaze rolled over every inch of her.

I wrapped an arm around her and rested it on the back of the chair as I rubbed my thumb back and forth.

The man's eyes narrowed, and then an arrogant and lustful look filled his eyes as he focused on part of Lanie. "She just needs a few more pounds off her. It wouldn't take too much work to smooth out those curves and make her a true piece of eye candy."

She stiffened, and I kept moving my thumb, reminding myself that punching him right here wouldn't do any good. "You are such a child. You wouldn't know a piece of art if it hit you in the face, especially since she's already done it once." I shook my head at him. "You're so concerned with her looking like the image Hollywood declares sexy. This is why you don't deserve her. Hell, I'll be the first to admit, I don't even deserve her."

"Jase." Her voice was astonished as she turned to look at me, but I kept my focus on the douche in front of me. I had a point to make, and I was only getting started.

"There are so many things to love about her, so I understand your obsession. See, I love the fact that she loves herself the way she is. The way she does not question my love for her. She is smart, funny, and damn, she feels so good mewling under me. Something I'm sure no woman has ever done with you." I tipped my head to the side and really studied his face. "Have you ever considered another woman's pleasure? Or are you all about taking it?" He straightened and glared at me. Before he could say anything, I smirked at him. "Look, I would berate you about trying to compensate for something, but the fact is you're not worth the effort. You just piss me off for not respecting the fact that the lady is taken." I saw Ismael come and sit a few tables away, his attention going to ours with a nod. "So, this is the last time I will ask nicely. Leave my queen alone. In case I wasn't clear as to who that is, my queen is this spectacular woman, Lanie Carley. Understood?"

"And what are you going to do if I don't?"

I smiled brightly at him. "You have no idea who I have connections to and who has it in their interests to protect Lanie."

She stiffened next to me, and I leaned over and kissed her shoulder then muttered, "Don't worry. Everything is fine."

He straightened his jacket again, like he was putting his armor on, and looked down his nose at me. It was such a childish move that I had to try to hold back my laugh. Lanie coughed in an attempt to hide hers as he said, "She's no one. You can have the trash."

My muscles tensed and rage burst through my body. Lanie's hand tightened on my thigh. "Mr. McFarland, I believe you should leave before I have to collect bail money for my boyfriend, or he has to collect it for me. Have the day you deserve."

He lifted his chin and strode out of the seating area. A man in the matching suit to Ismael's looked to me, and I gave an imperceptible nod before he got up and followed him. Ismael smirked at me and then paid very close attention to his sandwich.

"Okay." She let out a long breath and shook it off. "Now, what was this about you knowing people?"

It didn't surprise me that it was the first question out of her mouth. My queen didn't miss anything. I shrugged casually. "Nothing much. I know people. Didn't say they were important people and didn't say they weren't. I just know people. And there are plenty of people who think you're important enough to protect. So, no lies were told. He just took them the way he wanted to take them."

"Alright." She shifted and faced me. "I have a question for you, and I need you to be completely honest with me."

My eyebrows came together. "I will tell you anything you want."

"There are two guys behind me. One of them is the guy who followed me the other day. The one to the left, in a pair of jeans and a black CSU Trenton hoodie, and one to the right, in a tacky brown suit, have not had their eyes leave our table since we first came in here. Do you know them?"

As discreetly as I could, I looked at them. They weren't Chase's men, so who in the hell are they? "No, I don't. Here. Take a picture with me." After I lifted my phone, we put our heads together, and I muttered, "The top right frame?" She hummed, and then I looked at the picture.

"The glare from the sunlight was bad. Let's try in the opposite direction."

When we put our heads together, she chuckled. "You sneaky bastard."

"Your sneaky bastard." I repeated what I did on the other side and then sent both to Chase with a note about who he should be looking for in the photos.

"Who did you send them to?"

I smirked at her as she leaned on my shoulder like she was looking at the photos we'd just taken together. "A friend of mine who knows how to get information back in Trenton."

"He isn't even smart enough not to wear a Trenton sweatshirt."

Turning my head, I kissed her temple. "These hired hands don't have to be smart, my queen. Now, are you done eating? We should get you back to work."

With a whimper, she snuggled into me. "I don't want to go back to work, Sir."

Using my finger, I lifted her chin, and there was a wickedness to the gaze she gave me. I thought back to the special item I'd brought with me from Trenton. "You remember our discussion about new things?" She nodded as she pressed her legs together and her pupils dilated. I leaned closer to where we were sharing breath. "How do you feel about preparing my ass, my queen?"

She blinked and pulled back just a smidge before she reined in her shock and kissed me. Her lips were still against mine as she asked, "Do I need to stop for a harness?"

I shook my head. "I picked up a few things before I snuck down here. So, after work, get home. Kevin and I already arranged for him to stay at Velas tonight. Don't worry, he said he wanted to. Mentioned something about spending time with a girl he likes."

Lanie jumped back and smiled. "I knew it. I knew there was something there. How did you get him to tell you?"

Shrugging, I leaned over, kissed her, and then started putting our trash together.

She was quiet on the way back, and when we arrived, she pulled me inside the her office and shut the door. "I have a couple questions that I want answered now."

I pulled her against me, bent down, kissing her neck, and ran my hands up her sides, unable to keep myself from moving her dress and bra aside and groping her bare tit and pinching her nipple. Her eyes glazed over as she met my gaze again. "Tonight . . ."

Kissing her neck and humming a response, I licked the skin along her artery up to her ear. "Yes, my queen?" God, I was already hard for her.

"You are usually in control. Hold the power. I'm your little slut to fuck and use however you want."

I smiled against her skin. "And tonight, I will be your little whore to fuck, suck, and use how *you* want, my queen. Your king will be at your service."

She swallowed, and I felt her breathing hitch. "You'll give me the power?"

"You've always had the power." With one hand tweaking her nipple, I lifted her skirt, my fingers trailing across her skin, along the line between her stomach and thighs till I hit the heat of her pussy. "All you've ever had to do is say the word and it all stops."

"Tonight, you will, too. If at any point—" Her breath hitched as I moved her panties aside and flicked her clit. "If at any point, it hurts too much or it's not the pleasure you want, you have to stop me."

"Fuck. I can't wait to watch you pound my ass." Then I thrust my fingers into her, pressing the heel of my hand against her clit. Finding her G-spot, I curled my fingers against it and rubbed. "Right now, though, I need to hear you moan as you fall apart in my arms, my queen."

Her hips rolled against me, and her nipples were hard against my shirt. "That's right, my slut. Ride my hand and fuck yourself."

"Oh, god."

"Fuck no. The only name on your lips will be mine, just as the only name on mine tonight will be the woman who will be fucking me to the best orgasm I've ever had. Come on, Lanie, fucking cum for me. Fucking cum like the slut you are."

Her pussy latched onto my fingers, but I didn't stop moving as she moaned my name. Her hips jerked a couple times against me, and I leaned forward, kissing her neck as she came down. When she had her breath again, I gave her one last caressing touch before sliding her panties back into place and bringing my fingers to my lips, licking them clean.

When her gaze met mine, I slowly put her dress back in the right place and whispered, "Tonight."

She was smiling as she pulled back. "I have ideas already."

"The night starts when you walk into the apartment. I will be at your complete mercy, my queen."

Fuck, I can't wait.

THE
DEN
DON'T LET THEM EAT YOU ALIVE

CHAPTER THIRTY-FOUR

LANIE

The afternoon crawled by as my mind kept running through different scenarios for the evening. Even seeing Adrian for a second didn't put a dent in my good mood. Jason was giving me the responsibility of taking over. I would be the one dictating orders. There was a part of me that was scared of taking that role, but also eager. This was a way for him to explore one of his fantasies, and I wanted to indulge. There had been times where I had wondered if pegging would be something that could be enjoyable. Some of my queer friends in college had said it was amazing, so yes, I was more than a bit excited to try this.

Taking a deep breath as I stood in front of my apartment, I unlocked the door and opened it. Nothing could have prepared me for what I saw when I walked in.

Jason was completely naked, sitting on his knees in the living room, head down, hands folded in his lap. My heart raced. I had no idea seeing him so submissive would be such a fucking hot sight.

Stepping toward him while taking slow, purposeful breaths, I put my keys in the bowl next to the door, set down my bag, and toed my shoes off. "Jase."

"Good evening, my queen. How may I serve you?" The man hadn't even lifted his gaze from the floor.

Fucking hell.

My clit heated at his tone.

A flicker of doubt went through me. This wasn't normal. This wasn't how we did things between us, but there was no denying how heady it

255

was. I pulled on everything he had done to me and felt the confidence settle over my nerves.

"Eyes on me, slave." A slow smile twitched the corner of his lips, and I didn't miss the way his cock twitched at my words as well. His eyes lifted their focus to me as I stood two steps in front of him. Untying my dress, I let it slide off my shoulders into a puddle on the floor. Jason's throat bobbed, his eyes heated, and I saw his muscles twitch in restraint not to reach out toward me. Slowly, I walked around him, lowering my breasts right in front of his face, but being the good boy he was, he didn't move. As I was bent over, my attention went to the coffee table, where three different sizes of anal trainers, a bottle of lube, along with a beautiful harness with a vaginal insert and sturdy cock attached to the front sat.

"You want this now?"

"I am yours to command until morning, my queen." His voice was deep, yet soft at the same time.

"Jase, this is new for both of us. We need to do check-ins."

His gaze lifted and he met my eyes and nodded. "Light system?"

"Green, good. Yellow, stepping to a line. Red, full stop. At any time. Red or safeword is a full stop."

"Agreed."

"And your safeword?"

Jason didn't hesitate. "Strawberry."

Smiling at him, I lifted my chin, and he lowered his gaze. "That's my little fucktoy." Jase's whole body froze, and I could almost see the shiver that went through him. Feeling a bit emboldened by his reaction, I demanded, "Pull my tits out of my bra and strip me of my panties." He started to lift his hands, but I stopped him with a quick jerk of my head. "With your teeth."

I sat on the edge of the coffee table and watched as his pupils became blown out with lust as he sat fully onto his knees in front of me. Using a single curled finger, I beckoned him to me. He knelt between my knees and, without breaking his gaze with mine, leaned forward and took the top lip of my bra between his teeth and pulled my breasts free one by one, licking and teasing the nipples to hard peaks. I moaned at the feel of his tongue. With it being the only thing touching my skin, it was almost all-consuming.

Once he was done removing my breasts from their confines, Jason kissed and swirled his tongue all the way down my stomach and then to each of my hips as his teeth latched onto the fabric there and pulled my panties down my hips. As he worked them down, he nibbled and kissed both of my legs. When I lifted my feet to step out of them, Jason looked up at me and licked his lips.

"Clothes are not allowed until morning. Is that understood?" Jason didn't take his eyes off me as he nodded once in acknowledgement. "Good boy."

A whimper came from him, and I smirked when I saw his cock hard and twitching in his lap.

"You like when I call you my good boy?"

"Yes, my queen."

"Then come here and kiss me."

Slowly, he stood and lifted his hand to hover over my cheek. "Permission to touch my queen?"

"Jase . . . ," I drew out as I studied his eyes. They were soft and filled with so much need. He had really drawn himself into this, accepted this as his position tonight, and was enjoying it.

Is this for real? How is he going to be when we get there?

"Yes."

His hand cupped my cheek as he pulled me closer, and he wrapped an arm around my waist. His cock pressed against my stomach, and I rolled against it, unable to stop myself from teasing him just a little. Jason whimpered and then deepened the kiss. This was where he had the control. In this kiss, he had everything. When he pulled back, he was breathing hard and slowly opened his eyes. "I need my queen."

"You'll have her." A flash of excitement went across his eyes, but then I smirked. "In time. First, I want to fill that ass of yours and make you beg for release."

I nipped at his bottom lip, and the huff of breath from him was enticing. "Yes, my queen."

"On your knees on the couch, hands on the back, bent over," I ordered as he took a step back, and I saw his chest vibrate with the ragged breath that he took.

Once he was in position, I stood behind him and admired how fucking hot he looked. Softly, I ran my hands over his back and the fleshy portions of his ass. Fuck, his ass was perfect. His breathing hitched as I reached between his legs and ran a finger over his hard cock. Gripping it in my hand, I stroked him as I bent over and kissed his back. "Safeword?"

He hummed in pleasure and then mumbled the word. I stopped my stroking. "Louder. What is my whore's safeword?"

"Strawberry, my queen. Strawberry. Please don't stop touching me." His legs quivered, and I kissed his back again.

"Look at you, all wound up. Who would have thought the man who used his woman like a whore, was a whore himself?"

"Only for his queen." He groaned as I pumped his cock a few more times, rolling my thumb across the head of him. "Only for his queen."

"That's right." I released his cock and swatted his ass softly as I turned to the coffee table to start my night. The whimper from him was like an electrical charge to my nipples and clit. Just then, I looked down at the coffee table and saw a set of nipple clamps with a long string with another clamp at the bottom.

"A present for me?"

"Yes, ma'am. It would do me a great honor if you would wear it while fucking me tonight."

"Then stand up and dress me in it."

Should I be loving all of this so much? I love when he treats me like this. He's said how much he enjoys me taking pleasure in it, but how was he able to let go of that dominant side of him? He would tell me if it wasn't working, right?

Jason crawled off the couch, turned, and picked up the nipple and clit clamps. Bending down, he sucked a nipple into his mouth, ensuring it was at its full peak before he removed his tongue and pinched the clip into place. He repeated the actions on my other breast and then dropped to his knees. I lifted one of my legs and rested my foot on the arm of the couch.

"Do you think you deserve a taste of what you are doing to me?" He shook his head.

Not the answer I expected. God, I wanted him to eat me out like this. I was feeling energized, empowered, and the fact he didn't think he deserved to taste hurt. "Why not? Why don't you think that you deserve to lick your queen's pussy? You've been so good tonight."

"I will never be worthy."

I ran my hands through his hair. "Eat my pussy. If you make me cum, though, I will stop all of this and you won't have your ass fucked."

His eyes widened in shock, but he must have seen the love and sass in my expression because he smiled and answered, "Yes, my queen."

With that, the man dove in like he was starving. True to his word, he tongue fucked my pussy, flicked my clit to the brink, but he pulled back the moment before I lost myself over the cliff. My legs were shaking when he lifted his head. I had to use all the bedroom training I had to not cum all over his face when he attached the clamp to my clit.

Still holding onto the hair on the top of his head, I bent down, feeling the pull and tension of the clamps, and kissed him. The taste of myself on his lips had heat blooming through me. When I pulled back, he smiled like a cat who had finally gotten the cream. His eyes were glassy, and there was a huge smile on his face. When I released his hair, he sat on his heels. "Back on the couch."

He stood in one fluid movement, and I gripped his balls and rolled them in my hand. His whispered, "Fuck," was more fuel for the fire. I let go of him and jutted my head to the couch. There was a tip of his head, and I took a moment to calm myself down from the edging that had just occurred.

I was a glutton for punishment of my own doing.

Looking at the coffee table, I thought about where I wanted to start. I took the lube and poured a little in my hands before turning toward him and smoothing over his ass and his cock and balls again.

Nervous but determined, I got onto my knees, leaned in, and licked from his balls up to the puckered skin that was waiting for attention. The moans and groans of pleasure that came from Jason encouraged me along, and I slid my hand up and easily pushed a finger in.

"Fuck, that feels good." Reaching behind me, I grabbed the lube and poured it down the crease of his ass, working more and more into it.

"Such a good boy," I said as I slipped another finger into him. His back muscles tightened, and then as my free hand soothed over his back, he relaxed. "Don't forget to tell your queen if it's too much."

Jason's head moved back and forth. "It's not too much. Just stretching and needing to get used to being so full, and I know there is so much more to come. It feels so good."

"Yes, there is, but remember your queen will only give you as much as you can take."

Nodding, he continued, "I trust you, my queen."

With those words, I started slowly twisting and stretching him out. Looking behind me, I didn't see what I wanted at first but realized it was in my toy stash. When I thought he was ready, I stood and told him to stay where he was. I heard a mumbled acknowledgement, but I was halfway down the hall. Slipping into the bedroom, I opened my toy drawer and pulled out one of my favorite toys. Grabbing the pieces to it, I headed back into the living room, where he hadn't moved.

Lubing the butt plug and then adding a little more to his ass, I slowly worked it in and out of him. "That's a good boy. You are taking it so well. Slow and easy." I rubbed the small of his back again, and before I knew it, the widest part popped in.

Jason moaned loudly as I twisted it back and forth within him. I lined the handle up to run vertically with his ass crack and then bent down and kissed each of his ass cheeks.

Standing, I lay down on the couch. His eyes widened at me in confusion. "Do you like your ass filled?"

"Yes," he drawled.

"Good. You are not to allow it to slip out under any circumstances. Understood?"

"Yes, my queen."

"Now, fuck my throat, but you are not allowed to cum."

THE

DEN

DON'T LET THEM EAT YOU ALIVE

CHAPTER THIRTY-FIVE

JASON

SAN DIEGO

I stared at her in disbelief. I was the one to be used, and yet she still wanted me to fuck her throat? "My queen. I don't understand."

"I am to use you as I see fit, am I not?"

"You are."

"And I need your cock down my throat. I want you to have pleasure at both ends. That plug in your ass and you completely sheathed as well. It will be hard to keep your ass filled, but I know my good boy can do it."

The pleasure that rolled through my body with every movement was unlike anything I had felt before, and I knew this woman was only getting started. She had said she had ideas about tonight after I suggested this, but me sliding down her throat was not one of the things I thought we would do. As I repositioned on the couch, the plug moved and I had to take a breath.

"I'm not allowed to cum?"

Her chin lifted as she said, "No. You taught me self-control. It's your turn."

How in the fuck am I going to pull this off? I'm already so close to the edge.

Her head lifted as she maneuvered my cock to her mouth. Slowly, my cock slid along her lips, the bead of pre-cum spreading like her personal lip gloss.

Fuck.

When she slipped her lips around the head and sucked softly, I gripped on tight to the couch. I was hers to use. I had to control myself. When her head reached higher as she took me, I reached down to cradle her neck. She tipped her head so that I could slide back down her throat.

"My queen. I . . ." She swallowed with my cock in her throat, and there was a strangled cry that came out of me as I tried to hold myself back from cumming like a virgin on prom night.

I rocked my hips, and the combo was pure ecstasy. When I moved my hand from the back of her head to her throat, unable to keep the bit of dominance within me away, she moaned as I tightened it, and I felt my cock through the thin layer of her skin as I slid in and out. Slowly, my cock rolled up and down her throat. If I moved any faster, I was going to lose it. She tapped my shoulder, and I slipped out of her, taking a moment to catch my breath.

Licking her lips, she smiled at me. "Such a good boy."

"My queen, can I please cum?" I was pleading and panting with the struggle to obey her. It took all my energy to not only keep from cumming, but also keep the plug in place. A ripple of pleasure rolled up my spine, and I tipped my head back, letting out a deep breath.

She leaned up and licked from balls to tip, sucking quickly before sitting up. "Not yet. Since I've had my appetizer, I think your queen would like some dinner please."

Whimpering, I replied, "Yes, Your Highness." When I stood, I looked at her, silently asking if the plug was to stay or go.

"It stays."

I nodded because I shouldn't be surprised. I'd done this sort of thing to her many times in the past. Dragged on the pleasure through the evening. Both of us on the verge of insanity before we finally released. The last time I'd edged her, we both had seen stars and passed out from the force of our orgasms.

Taking a deep breath, I tried to steady myself, knowing this was going to be a marathon. I went to make a salad with veggies and took some of the rotisserie chicken leftovers from last night and cut them into bits. When that was put together, I pulled out the cherry tomatoes, cucumber, olives, salami and a couple blocks of miscellaneous cheese and sliced it up, placing it on the board. Finger foods tonight. Something light and easy to eat that would still give us some energy.

I was laying out the different items on the charcuterie board when Lanie came up behind me, placing her hand between my shoulder blades. I leaned forward as she took hold of the base of the plug and wiggled it slowly back and forth before moving it in and out of me. My legs trembled with pleasure, and I felt my spine tingle as she repeated the motions over and over again. She pulled it from me, told me, "Don't move," and walked away.

Swallowing, I stood there letting the cold seep into my hands from the counter. Focusing on the fine lines of the stone work on the counter and breathing, I couldn't help but think about how much more I'm enjoying this than I ever thought was possible. A moment later, she came back in the kitchen after a moment and kissed my shoulder as she worked the plug back in. My cock bounced as I pushed against her, feeling the slight pain and stretch. Letting my head hang, I moaned at the pleasure that filled me.

With a giggle, she pushed the plug all the way into me and held it. Lanie leaned against my back and, with another gentle kiss to my shoulder, said, "Breathe."

Slowly, I let out a long breath and felt myself relax, but I reminded myself to clench my cheeks so that the plug didn't slip out. Even though I cherished the feel of her naked body against my back, I turned to her slowly and watched the humor dance in her eyes. My focus dropped down to her lips as they turned up in a half smile. "Feed me."

I picked her up and set her on the counter that separated the living area from the kitchen area, again keeping in mind to not let the plug move. Picking up a piece of salami, a cracker, and a slice of cheese, I held it before her. Her mouth opened, and I fed it to her slowly as she set her hands behind her.

Once she said she had enough, she jumped down and put the charcuterie board items into a bowl, added some olives, and then slowly dribbled the vinaigrette over the top. When she handed it to me, she reached up and kissed me. "How was your day?"

"It was majestic. I got to see my queen at lunch. She was accosted by some childish limp dick, but we were able to set things right."

Lanie leaned against my side as I ate my salad. "Did you find out anything about the guys at the deli?"

Shaking my head, I chewed on the chicken, and after I swallowed, I sighed. "Unfortunately, I haven't heard anything back. Once I do, I promise to tell you."

She nodded, picked out a piece of the chicken from the salad, and fed it to me. Lanie held my gaze for a long moment, reached behind her, and then my knees about fell out from under me when the butt plug that was in me vibrated.

"Oh, fucking hell." I groaned as my bowl fell to the floor and shattered. Only, I couldn't care less about it. I stared at my queen as she lifted her chin, holding my gaze. When the vibrating stopped, she crossed her arms under her boobs, pushing them up, and I couldn't help but let my attention drop to them for a minute. I swallowed and looked back up to her. "It's a remote . . . None of the ones I bought were remote controlled."

"True. Now, control. You taught it to me, and now you should have it as well." Reaching up on her toes, she kissed me softly, and I wrapped my arms around her, holding her close. My cock slid between Lanie's legs, and I had to force myself not to thrust my hips. "Now, have you had your fill of dinner?"

"Yes, my queen. My appetite is for something else entirely."

She lifted the small, oval, white device, pressed the black button, and vibrations radiated through me, making my eyes roll back into the back of my head.

"What do you want?"

"You, Your Highness."

Lanie's finger trailed down the center of my chest and then along the length of my cock. "What do you want your queen to do?"

"Fuck me. I want you to fuck my ass." I tightened my hold on her to keep pressure on my cock. I started breathing in long, nervous breaths, but I trusted her. My voice was pleading as I said, "Please."

THE

D E N

DON'T LET THEM EAT YOU ALIVE

CHAPTER THIRTY-SIX

LANIE

SAN DIEGO

The look in his eyes when he pleaded for me to fuck him almost brought me to my knees. I'd seen want and command in his eyes before, but this was something more. Something primal. It was like he needed it to breathe.

Pulling away from Jason, I took him by the hand, stopped the vibrating plug, and rounded the counter into the living room. Letting his hand drop, I went to the coffee table, and bent over so he could see all of me as I picked up the lube and harness. I looked over my shoulder to find Jason on his knees. Standing, I turned, met his gaze, and took a few steps to stand before him. Extending a finger, I lifted his chin so he had to still look at me. His pupils were so large and black, I could barely see the color of them against the whites. While I was used to the lust in his eyes, seeing him so completely consumed while waiting for me to act was not something I was accustomed to. It was a heady feeling. His arm started to lift toward me, but he lowered it. "See something you want?"

"Yes, Your Highness."

The way he was looking at me spurred a memory of when he'd had me crawl my way to him to suck his cock. Fuck, it had been hot as hell. I stepped back, put some lube on the vaginal plug, and stepped into the harness, surprised at how well it fit. The fact that he had ensured he'd found one that would actually fit a plus-sized woman warmed my heart. When the insert slid in, I moaned and vaguely heard Jason whimper. I met his gaze and asked, "Like what you see?" I finished

269

strapping myself in, and when I took a step toward him, the bulb jiggled inside of me. A wave of warmth spread through me, and I smirked. "Stand and follow me."

I strutted down the hall, making sure to sway and pop my hips out with every step. The movement heightened my own pleasure, along with the hiss and look on Jason's face when I looked over my shoulder to see him following me. Once I was in the bedroom, I placed the lube on my bedside table and ordered, "On your back, knees to your chest."

Before reaching the bed, he froze, looked at me again, and I reached down to stroke my light brown, silicone cock. It was soft and pliable in my hand as I caressed it, and his attention was solely focused on the movement. "Unless you want to suck my cock first?"

Jason's focus popped up to my face. "May I?"

"Color?"

"Green."

I smirked. "On your knees then."

As he came to stand before me, I saw the heat in his gaze. He lifted his hand, and it trembled with restraint. "My queen."

"If you want to suck my cock, then get on your knees."

He dropped hard on the hardwood flooring, and I tried not to wince. Stroking myself again, I stepped up closer to him and ran the head along his lips, lifting an eyebrow. "Jason, do you want this? If not, we can move on. This wasn't discussed. I will feed every inch of this into your mouth, but only if you want it."

His voice was soft and full of heat as he said, "Green." Then my little whore opened his mouth, slowly taking only the head of me in, tasting, exploring, and sucked a few times before pulling back. "You slave needs some practice. Next time you can teach me how to take your cock like you take mine. Right now, I'm about to explode. I might cum from the pleasure of sucking you."

"Very well. Up on the bed. Now," I ordered and watched him stand, not breaking my gaze. I was surprised at how much he'd wanted to try sucking it, but also not surprised that he'd enjoyed it.

As he climbed up on the bed and brought his knees up, the black base of the plug wiggled. I stepped up and took hold of the base. "Are you ready?"

"Yes."

As I twisted and worked the plug, his eyes glazed over. After slowly moving it in and out, I pulled it from him, and he released a large breath. Grabbing the lube from where I had put it on the bedside table, I stroked my cock and ran it along his ass crack, up to his balls, where his cock jumped and a small bead of cum pearled at the tip. I couldn't resist bending down and licking from base, up along the vein, and through the slit of him, gathering the saltiness on my tongue. I hummed as it filled my senses, and I actually had to restrain myself from swallowing him whole again.

I stood and lowered the bulbous head of my cock for the night to his ass. "Are you ready for your queen to take you?"

"Yes, Your Highness." The final *s* hissed out as I pressed against him tentatively, watching his face and letting my free hand run along the back of his thigh. I moved slowly, and once the head was beyond the ring of muscle, I waited until he nodded. "Green."

I put a little more lube on the shaft of the cock then pushed in more, pulled out to the head, and added a little more lube before pushing back in. Slowly, I thrust in and out of him, watching the pure pleasure and joy on his face. I was almost all the way into him when I reached for his cock and stroked him, rolled my hips, and finally lay balls deep within the man who'd trusted me with this. Trusted me to take his virgin ass and give him pleasure like he'd never experienced.

I was so worried that I'd hurt him that I just stayed there. Moving my hips like this was so different than when the roles were reversed. The bulb in my own pussy had been working to bring me pleasure, and between that and the sight before me, I wasn't sure how long I would be able to hold back from cumming. This was one of the sexiest things I had ever experienced. The trust and love in his eyes as his met mine had my pussy pulsing.

"Please move, my queen. Please fuck me?"

His head tipped back with a moan as I rolled and thrust in and out of him. I leaned over him, pushing his knees to his ears as he moaned and mewled under me. The sounds I heard from him were when he was unable to keep control of himself anymore.

"You like that, my dirty little whore? You like me fucking your ass?" I gritted out as my hips moved faster and harder with each stroke.

"More."

"Use. Your Words," I said with each thrust. "Do you want faster or harder?"

"Fuck me harder and faster, my queen."

Repositioning myself so that I could slip a pillow under his ass, I came up onto my knees and pounded into him hard and fast. I took him in my hand, and with every thrust into him, I gripped and jerked his cock.

"Yes."

"God, you look so good taking my cock. Such a good boy, taking every fucking inch of me." His hardness twitched in my hand. "My little whore, taking everything his queen gives him."

My nipples hardened at the movement of the dildo within me, rubbing against my G-spot, all fueled by my desire, and I could tell he was close. "Do you want to cum for your queen?"

"Yes. I've been trying to hold it back, but you feel so good." I wrapped my hand tighter around just the head of him and jerked him off with every thrust. "Please, please let your fucktoy cum."

I wasn't able to hold mine back much at all either, so I pounded into him and reached down to hit the small button on the harness. Vibrations shot through us, and the loud moan of pleasure that came from Jason was all I needed.

Faster, I thrust my hips. "Fucking cum for me, whore. Coat my hand in your release. Show me whose ass this is."

"My queen's. Only my queen's." He panted, and then he moved as much as he could in time with me. Taking his pleasure.

"Fuck your ass on my cock." He lifted his hips just as I slammed into him. "That's it."

He shouted as his orgasm hit him hard, and his legs spasmed. My hand continued milking his cock as I pounded into him, stretching it out for as long as I could.

His lips spread in an O as it washed over him, and seeing his body tense and twitch as he rode out his euphoria was like nothing else. When I thrust one more time into his ass, I ground myself against the vibrator, setting off my own release. Throwing my head back in ecstasy, I screamed, "Yes, Jason!"

When I could finally half think straight again, I pulled out of him slowly. Jason whimpered, and I smiled, knowing exactly how empty you could feel after being so full. "Color."

"So fucking green." His voice was soft, but there was no doubt he was still riding the blissful aftermath.

After removing the harness, whimpering myself when I removed the vaginal insert, I went into the bathroom, cleaned myself up, and got a warm rag for him. He had taken care of me so many times after sex, it was fulfilling to be able to give that back to him. He was lying on the bed half conscious, and I couldn't help but smile at him. This had been incredible for me, and I couldn't wait to hear if this was something he wanted to do again.

After wiping up the mess we had made, I reached down and grabbed a bit of jelly and lined the inside of his ass with it. "You are going to be sore. For your first time, I didn't take it easy on you, and I am sorry for that."

He shook his head back and forth as I tossed the washcloth into the bathroom and climbed on the bed to snuggle up next to him. "That was fucking amazing. Definitely want more of that." I couldn't help the chuckle that came out of me. "It was a little weird being the Dom tonight. As you know, I'm a bit of a princess."

"Not a princess. A fucking queen."

I shook my head at him, chuckling. "Not the point, but it was fun to switch it up."

He nodded. "It was. I didn't expect to enjoy it so much."

"Now you know why I love anal so much." I chuckled and snuggled closer to him. "Are you okay with the fact I was so forceful in taking over?"

He took a deep breath. "It was a little weird at first. Taking orders from you was hard, but then there was a point where I realized how freeing it was. I could just enjoy the experience. Don't get me wrong, I was watching to make sure that you were okay, but especially once we got here in bed, there was just absorbing the pleasure and the experience." He kissed my forehead and continued, "I love being your dirty little whore. I would be open to not only having you fuck me on the regular, but I am definitely open to a threesome with another guy if that is what you want. Have him fuck my ass as I fuck you. Have us both

273

fuck you. Two girls, I don't care. Whatever you want. I'll do anything to have you fuck me like that again."

Pride burst through me, and a bright smile sat on my face as I pushed up to lean on my elbow. "Anytime you want, Jase." I kissed him softly and whispered against his lips, "Now get some rest. I have more ideas on how to use my fucktoy before morning."

"As you wish, my queen."

THE

DEN

DON'T LET THEM EAT YOU ALIVE

Chapter Thirty-Seven

Jason

San Diego

"Sissy?"

Lanie turned at Kevin as he was looking in the fridge. "Yeah?"

"We are out of fresh fruit. Can you get more?"

"Are you asking because you know the farmers' market is today and I took the day off to spend with Jason?"

Closing the fridge door and turning to face his sister, he had a huge smile on his face. "When you go, can you bring home fresh honey?"

Her face was full of the love she had for her brother. "With honeycomb, yes. I'll also get some of the honeycomb candy."

"Honeycomb candy? Oh, I need to know more," I teased.

Kevin had been warming back up to me this week, but I was in this for the long haul and I needed him on my side. When we'd gone to dinner just last night, he had asked that I order his food for him. When he'd come back and realized that I had ordered him the four-cheese lasagna, he'd looked over at me and smiled. "You ordered the right food. Did Sissy tell you what to get?"

"Nope. It's pasta night, and I know how much you love a good lasagna. Thought about the fried lasagna, but it would probably be too dried out for you, and you can't get the cheese stretch." I'd shrugged and taken a drink of my iced tea.

Kevin had looked at Lanie and then back to me. "Okay."

It hadn't been so much what he said, but rather how he'd acknowledged it. There had been so much warmth and acceptance in his face and body language.

It would tear Lanie up to have us not get along, and there was no reason for that. Kevin was a good human. He was sweet, smart, and even though he had a different way of showing it sometimes, he cared deeply for his sister and just wanted her happy.

His whole face lit up and he was very animated with his hands, trying to show me all about it as he said, "The freeze-dried honeycomb dipped in dark chocolate is my favorite. You would love it, Mr. Rathborn."

Lanie's attention bounced between the two of us before she finally shook her head. "Kevin . . ." His smile got larger, and I chuckled at how firmly wrapped she was around his finger.

That makes two of us, bud. That makes two of us.

"Fine. I'll drop you off, and then Jason and I will head over and get some for you. Which fruits do you want?"

"Strawberries, raspberries, and blueberries, please. Oh! Can you please get some carrots, too? For crockpot day. I want stew."

She nodded and went to finish getting ready. We both watched her as she headed down the hallway, but when I turned back to Kevin, his head was cocked to the side as he studied me. "You love Sissy, don't you?"

I let out a deep breath and nodded. "Yes. My biggest mistake was walking out on the two of you. I'm a lucky man for her to give me a second chance."

"I thought you were going to be my brother. That you two would get married and you would live with us."

Warmth spread through my chest as I took in his words, but it was also set with pain. "I messed up, Kevin. I let the pressures of my job control my future. I would give it all up to have her by my side and you as my brother."

His gaze went to the floor, and I stood then walked over to the counter that separated the living room and kitchen. Slowly, I leaned against the cold tile and looked back at him. "I'm sorry for hurting your sister, and I'm sorry for letting *you* down. I know that just apologizing isn't enough. I only hope that in time, you will be able to move past it and recognize that all I want in life is to have your sister by my side, happy, forever."

His throat bobbed and his fingers were twitching just like he had done in high school when he'd been thinking through different scenarios. Lanie came back into the living room, and his eyes popped up to look at her. His attention flicked to me quickly before he headed toward the living room.

I simply nodded as he passed by me and then took a deep breath before turning for the door behind them.

Once we were in the car, Kevin talked to Lanie about his schedule for the day in the front seat, and when we got to Velas, he turned to me and said, "You can sit in my seat while I'm not here."

Catching Lanie's gaze in the rearview mirror, I smiled. "Thank you, Kevin."

He swung the door open and hurried into the building as I made my way around the car. When I got in, tears fell down Lanie's cheeks.

"What's wrong, sweetheart?"

"He's really trying, Jase. I overheard you two talking in the kitchen. I couldn't make out the words, but I heard you. He has a hard time talking about his feelings, unless they are big feels." Her gaze swung around to meet mine. "He said that you could sit in the passenger seat. Kevin doesn't offer up 'his spot.' Not that he has a say in that, but the fact that he *volunteered* his seat means he's giving up some of his space and making room for you in his life."

I looked back toward the front doors of Velas he had walked through. "Making room for me?"

My throat tightened, and I squeezed her hand. I really wanted him to see that his sister was my main concern. He had listened to me earlier, so I hoped he could see that. I couldn't explain the range of emotions going through me, but one of them was something that felt like relief.

CHAPTER THIRTY-EIGHT

JASON

SAN DIEGO

"Two bags of the dark chocolate honeycomb, please." After the vendor bagged it up and I paid, I reached over and took Lanie's hand, threading her fingers with mine, relishing in the normality of the moment.

"Remember when we went to the beach with Kevin and he was so excited to be there until he got to the sand and stopped?"

Chuckling, she leaned against me. "Yeah, he forgot how much he hated the feel of sand against his skin. I felt so bad for him. Adult Kevin is much more aware of his texture icks than teenage Kevin, that's for sure."

"We still had a good time there, even though he wouldn't go any farther onto the beach."

Lanie stopped at a booth that had some handmade pottery and was looking at one that was a swirl of teals and browns when something caught her eye beyond where I was standing. Her shoulders tightened, and she immediately became too invested in the cups she was looking at.

When her hands balled up, I took a few steps toward her, wrapped my arm around her, and kissed her temple while muttering, "What's wrong?"

Looking up at me with fear in her eyes, she said, "There is a guy who has been following us for the last thirty minutes. I thought it was a coincidence because the street is only so big, but he stops when we do and has kept an eye on us the entire time. He just smiled at me when our eyes met."

I kissed her forehead and casually looked behind us. Sure enough, there was a man in a dark blue hoodie staring directly at us, and every hair on my body stood up as unease washed over me. How had I not noticed him before Lanie? This was one of the same assholes from the diner. I should have seen him. Sure, he had a busted lip and was sporting a bit of a black eye, but I should have recognized him.

Fuck!

Slowly, I rested my cheek on the top of her head, wrapping my arms around her protectively as I met his menacing stare and held it. A slow smile crossed his face, and then he looked up across the street. I followed his line of sight, up to the top of a three-story building where a man in black lifted a rifle and rested it on the ledge.

Shit. Shit. Shit.

"Let's go."

Clay sprayed just as we left the booth with the handmade mugs. Keeping my arm wrapped around her, I hurried down the street toward the parking garage where we had parked her car. We passed several booths, trying not to knock over others as they, too, realized what was happening. Water sprayed in the air from one of the booths next to us, and people were screaming. We ducked into an alcove out of line of sight of the shooter. Quickly, I pulled her behind me so that I was on the outside. It wasn't big enough for us to stay there long, but it would work for the moment while I found somewhere better for us to hide.

From the sound of shots going off so close together, I figured there had to be at least two shooters, maybe more. If the guy we'd seen was one of them, was he after us? If so, why hadn't he just taken us out when our backs were to him? Why wait until we noticed him, and why show us the shooter on the roof?

I took a deep breath to calm my racing mind and heart before turning back toward Lanie. "Are you hurt?"

Her head moved back and forth against my back. Scanning down the street, I saw people were trying to find cover wherever they could. Some jumped behind large metal cooking stoves, took cover in alcoves, or were running to the alleys that were up and down the street. My attention went to a group of high school students hunkered down across from us. An older man, who one of them called coach, was screaming at them to get behind the large barbeque and stay low to the ground.

"Jase, how are we getting out of here?"

My heart raced, and I took a step out of the alcove, just as something bounced off the concrete wall. My attention jumped down the street and up to the rooftop where the shooter was pointing the rifle toward the opposite end of the farmers' market.

"On top of the bank building!" someone screamed as they rushed by, and my head snapped around to look at the roofline, and there was another one. So at least two rooftop shooters.

Fuck! Where can we go? We are too in the open here.

My eyes scanned all around us, looking for anything at all that could give us somewhere safer to hide. A woman sprinted past us, with a man a few steps behind her. Just as he caught up with her, he wrapped his arms around her waist. They hadn't taken more than three steps when blood burst out the side of her head and she went limp in his arms. His heart-wrenching scream was cut short as they collapsed to the ground. Blood spread on his back as he landed on top of her, protecting her even in death.

When I turned back toward Lanie, she was staring at the two of them. The fear written across her face tightened the breath in my throat. I pulled her into my arms and muttered, "That's not going to be us, baby. That's not going to be us. We will get out of here. I promise you that."

I held her for a minute, my mind racing on how I was going to be able to uphold that promise. She would get out of here, and I would give my life to ensure it. I kissed the top of her head, and she shifted in my arms before she screamed, and I caught her as she buckled.

"Lanie, talk to me!"

She grabbed at her thigh. "My leg."

I crouched next to her to take a look at it. Blood was spreading in the jean material at about the halfway point down her thigh, but as I looked on the backside, there was no exit wound.

"Can you put any weight on it?"

She hissed her breath through her teeth, but she nodded, standing and turning toward the street. San Diego PD hustled past us, telling people to get into the parking garage or off of the street. I scanned somewhere we would be able to take cover. With her leg, we weren't going to be able to make it three blocks to the parking garage, but if we could find somewhere out of the way, we would have a chance. Then I saw an alcove nearly double the size of the one we were in.

"Come on, my queen. Let's get out of here." I wrapped my arm around her and helped her walk. "There is a deeper alcove across the street and up a couple businesses. We need more cover than this."

She nodded, trusting me. We went past the high school athletics' booth to see six of the kids balled up behind the barbeque. I looked for the coach, and when I saw him, he had blood running down his arm, but he was working on two other students behind a table they had tipped over for protection. I briefly made eye contact with one of the older girls there, and while she was balled up, her eyes were empty. She had completely disassociated from the situation.

"Jason, the kids."

"I know, baby."

We kept moving, and we had just hit the sidewalk on the other side of the street when the window next to us shattered, sending glass raining down around us. I tried to protect Lanie as much as I could, but she tripped over the curb and went down hard. The sting of glass hit along my back and arm as I bent down to pull her back to her feet. Lanie turned her head up to me, and tears were streaming down her face and her jaw was set hard. When I wrapped my arm around her again, she whimpered. "My arm. I can't move it." We took a few more steps, and I noticed it was hanging limply by her side.

Shit.

As I pushed her forward toward the alcove, there were clouds of dust coming up from a flower garden in front of the kitchen store, glass and clay spraying into the air. Just before we got there, Lanie stumbled again. "Keep moving, baby. You're almost there."

I turned to look behind us, and I could hardly register the number of people who were dropping to the ground or jumping behind anything to protect themselves.

Lanie hissed again, and when I turned back toward her, she was falling into the alcove, where she hit the back of her head.

"Lanie!" Kneeling before her as she righted herself, I noticed blood seeping from her temple.

I knelt in front of her to protect her from any more potential hits, and her head leaned on my back between my shoulder blades. My hands reached around my back, and she took her good one and squeezed tight. "It hurts."

"I know, baby. We just need to hold on tight until we can get you to the car and I can get you to the hospital. I'm so sorry, Lanie." My heart was pounded quickly as she nodded against me.

"Fuck!" I cursed when there was a sudden, searing pain just above my hip. I ignored it, though, when Lanie jerked against me and her hand released from mine. Turning around, I saw her face was draining of color and tears filled her eyes. Lower, her hand was pressed to her side, red slowly making its way through her fingers.

Panic filled me as I reached around her and didn't feel an exit wound. Her lips moved but nothing came out, and when she tried again, her voice was filled with hopelessness and despair. "Jase."

"I know you are scared. I am too, but we are going to make it out of this, my queen. We are going to live long, full lives together. You will get to see Kami and Kevin again. Don't give up on me." I swallowed hard around the ball of fear and emotion in my throat. "You are going to run and chase our kids in the park, all while the dog bounces around, yipping and causing chaos. You understand? Just breathe, baby. Breathe."

I held her gaze and waited. There were a thousand emotions that passed onto her face, but I couldn't latch onto any of them before they were gone. "Okay?"

She nodded. "Okay."

While the alcove was much deeper than our previous hidey hole, it didn't take much to inch out to the edge. I looked for any emergency services, but there was still nothing.

Where are they?

Hating how we were essentially sitting ducks just lying here, I also knew that there was still too much chaos for us to try to go any farther. Turning back toward Lanie, I forced my attention to the woman I loved as more shots rang out, cutting off my words as Lanie winced and curled up tighter into me. Time slowed to an excruciating crawl as I willed my body to protect hers. Hot, burning pain ripped through my leg, but I ignored it as my arms tightened around Lanie in desperation to keep her safe and alive. Her whimper was heart-wrenching, but my body moved automatically to protect her.

I just got you back, my queen. I can't lose you.

"Jase." Her voice was tight and full of pain that I never wanted to hear from her. Her hands gripped tight onto the front of my shirt as I pulled her closer to me. "I love you. I need you to know that."

"Hold on, sweetheart. Don't give up on us yet." I was talking directly into her ear, trying to soothe her as much as I could. We were still in the main area of the farmers' market, and fear and rage gripped me as I heard more screaming, running, and gunshots nearby. I could feel wetness seeping into my shirt and I winced. Glancing under the booth we were lying next to, I could see people running down the street and falling to the ground. Wails of voices sounded all around us, but when I looked back at Lanie and the blood pooling under her shoulder, all of the world went silent.

"Lanie." I didn't think my heart could beat any faster, but seeing that much blood had me freaking out. "You're going to be okay. Okay?"

Her eyes were fluttering but they met my gaze. "Jase. It hurts a lot . . . and my arm is getting cold and numb. I . . . I can't—"

I gave her a quick kiss, hoping to comfort and distract her, distract myself. "I know, baby. But I need you to hold on."

Just hold on, my queen.

A tactical team hurried past us, and I held her tighter.

Please let them stop whoever this is. Please stop them.

"Who? Why?" Her words were soft and faint, and my stomach seemed to drop out from under me.

"I don't know. I don't know, my queen. I'm sorry, I don't have any answers. Please, just keep breathing. I'm sure help will be here soon."

There were at least four other people lying in the street or on the sidewalk bleeding. My focus went back to the booth with the kids, and they all seemed okay, considering the chaos around us. They were alive at least.

Looking at a few others on the street, I swallowed. Two of them were not moving at all as blood pooled around their bodies.

Fuck. Fuck. Fuck.

I looked up to the roofline as bullets continued to fly down, and more people fell next to their loved ones. A moment later, the gunman

I had eyes on stopped and hung over the edge of the building. Relief flooded through me as I saw Ismael take the rifle and aim it down the street. Concrete sprayed near us again, and I winced as pieces bounced off my arms.

Chase's guys were here. They were on it.

But why did they not take care of the creepy man on the street first? Why give him a chance to be so close to us?

Sirens blared in the distance, and time slowed again as we stayed in our little alcove. My heart was beating so hard, I swore Lanie could feel it against her chest. I twisted and kissed her forehead. "Breathe, sweetheart. Breathe. Look at me."

She did, and I moved back from her and pulled at her shirt to take a look at the wounds. Her shoulder was still limp, but there were no bullet wounds. Hopefully, it was just dislocated. She'd be fine from that. When I looked at her side, though, I cursed as terror shot through me. Blood was flowing pretty quickly from her stomach and back where she had been hit.

No. No. No.

My hands roamed over her, trying to see if there was anything else. I had to be able to tell emergency personnel as much as I could when they got here so they could patch her up again. In the meantime, I grabbed the bottom of my t-shirt, tore a long piece from it, and pressed it against the wound to hopefully slow the bleeding.

"Look at me, Lanie." Her head had tipped back against the wall and moved from side to side as she groaned at the pressure. I brushed some dirt and debris off her cheek, leaving a smear of red along it. I could care less if I was covered head to toe in her blood as long as she lived. When I kissed her hard, her body twitched slightly, and I thought I heard a whimper come from her. "Come on, my queen. Hold on."

"Jason," she muttered weakly before her eyes fluttered closed and she went limp against me.

"No. No. No." I smacked her cheeks gently, but then a little harder when she didn't respond. "Come on, baby. You need to stay with me." I choked out a sob as I rested my forehead against hers. "I need you here, my queen."

The street was getting quieter and the sirens louder now, but I just kept trying to get her to wake up. It felt like an eternity before the sound of shoes pounding the pavement grew closer to us.

It wasn't long before there was a paramedic within sight, checking for life.

"Over here," I hollered, trying to get his attention. He rushed toward us, and I hesitantly moved over to give him space to do his job.

"Shot on the side and leg. Also hit her head pretty hard when she tripped at one point," I rattled off.

He looked at me and scanned me quickly. "And you?"

"Grazed side. Same bullet that went through to hers. Just make sure she's okay." I ran my hands through my hair and tried to remind myself that she was with the EMT now and that he would do what he could for her.

There was someone else checking me over, and I felt pain as they pressed on a spot on my calf. They said something about me being shot there as well, but my world narrowed on her as her chest and shoulder were checked. Everything sounded like it was under water, but all I could do was focus on Lanie. She blinked a couple times before her gaze latched onto mine, and through tight, painful breaths, she uttered, "Kevin."

The paramedic looked up at me. "Who is Kevin?"

"Her brother. He's not here." Giving my full attention to Lanie, I promised, "I'll make sure he's taken care of, sweetheart."

There was more yelling and movement behind us, and she reached over for my hand as they put her on the gurney. I walked with her to the ambulance, pain radiating through my leg, but I pushed it away. She whimpered again as they lifted her into the back, and our hands dropped.

"Let's get moving." The EMT turned to me and added, "You should be with us. Get that leg attended to."

I didn't hesitate to jump into the back with them as the doors closed behind me. I sat on the bench by her feet. "Keep your eyes on me, sweetheart. Let them work."

The entire ride was a flurry of sounds and movements. At some point, there was an IV placed in her arm, but her focus never left my face. Those brown eyes were filled with pain and fear, and I knew I'd be having nightmares about this for a long time. The whole ride to the hospital passed too slow and too fast all at the same time. Before I knew it, we were pulling in as I looked through the back window to see a few more ambulances coming in behind us. Once we stopped, the doors flew open, and I climbed out and started following Lanie in.

"Sir, you can't—"

Lanie was calling for me again, and the nurse looked at her and asked, "Who is he?"

Her eyes flicked to mine, and my heart ceased at the panic there. "My husband."

I blinked at her, a huge smile filling my face. She was claiming me. *Her husband.*

That would never be enough to encompass what I was. I was hers, heart, body, and soul. I would be the one to protect her, covet her, need her, pleasure her, and give everything to her to ensure that Melanie Anne Carley stayed happy and healthy. That woman who was my everything had just claimed me as hers. Rushing to her side, I cradled her head in my hands.

Whispering against her lips, I said, "I love you, sweetheart."

Some of the pain lifted from her eyes as they softened. "I love you, too."

"Now hold on okay. I'll be with you soon."

The nurse turned back to me and placed her hand on my elbow. "This way, sir. Let's get you looked at, and you can give us all her information. Then we can get you back with her."

The pain in my leg was radiating up into my hips and lower back. Pulling back, Lanie whispered, "We can talk more later." I nodded, and then her gurney was being wheeled through a set of double doors. *Come on, baby. You can do this. I need you to do this. Need you to survive.*

They fixed my leg up pretty quickly. I really only needed a couple staples after they pulled the bullet out. While they took care of that, they had me fill out all the paperwork for the two of us. Now I was sitting in my own room, waiting for them to let me go to Lanie.

Kevin. I needed to make arrangements for Kevin.

Pulling my phone out, I called Kami, where it went to voicemail. I hung up and dialed it again, hoping she had it out and just sent me there because she was in class or something, but I didn't care. Voicemail again. One more time. When it went to voicemail the third time, I left her a message to call me right away.

Kevin. I needed to call Kevin. After finding the number for the center, I called and asked if Kevin could stay there tonight.

"I'm sorry, sir, but who are you?"

I took a deep breath because this was not going to be easy. "Jason Rathborn. I'm his sister's boyfriend, and unfortunately, there was an incident today."

"Sir, you aren't on the approved list."

"Okay. Can you tell me if Kamille Robins is? I have a call in to her as well."

There was a long silence before the woman on the line let out a big sigh. "She is."

"I'll have her call and make the request, but can you please have Kevin call me? He has my number programmed into his phone."

"I will deliver the message when he is done teaching his class."

"Thank you," I breathed and hung up.

One of the resident doctors came in and double-checked my leg. "Well, looks like it's good for now. I want you to keep it elevated, but I realize that is going to be hard to do since your wife is here."

My wife.

I swallowed and looked at him, trying to keep my anxiety under wraps for the moment. "How is she?"

"We've set the shoulder and patched up the leg, but she's being wheeled back for surgery on her side. We need to make sure that nothing was critically damaged, and if there was, make those repairs." He was soft-spoken and looked me in the eye as he delivered the news. "The OR just freed up, so she's heading back now. We are gonna have you move into the hall until she's out."

"How long do you think she'll be in surgery?" I swallowed and tried to tamp down the fear rising.

"I can't give you an estimate. It really depends on what the surgeon needs to do."

I nodded and played with my fingers as he walked out. One of the nurses came in right after and helped me into a wheelchair, where I could sit in the hall with my leg up. I sat there in a daze as I watched people go in and out of the doors to different rooms. For three hours, I sat in that hallway, imagining her dying in my arms in that alcove. Then I would force myself to remember that she was here, where she had called me her husband, connecting us. Then I would imagine her bleeding out on that table in surgery. I was beginning to panic when a nurse came over and stood next to me.

"Mr. Rathborn?" I looked up at her, trying to hide the fear that was tightening my chest. "Mrs. Carley is out of surgery, woke up in recovery, and is asking for you. She's being transported to her room right now. I'm going to take you there. Do you have anyone who can bring you a change of clothes?"

"No. Not till morning."

She nodded, turned, and a few moments later returned with a pair of scrubs. "I'm not supposed to do this, but for contamination reasons and with so many people here . . ." She handed me the clothes. "There's an empty room down the hall. We can get you changed."

"Thank you." I finally breathed as my chest loosened with the knowledge that Lanie was okay.

The nurse took hold of the wheelchair, took me into the room, and helped me get my pants off and the scrub pants on over the leg before turning her back to allow me to finish getting changed. Once I was done, she took me upstairs to the fourth floor. When we got to Lanie's room, they were just finishing getting her settled, so we waited outside.

Her gaze met mine and held until I was wheeled in and was able to hold her hand. "Hey, my queen."

"Jason." Her voice was hoarse and quiet as she smiled weakly.

"How are you feeling?"

"Better now that you are here."

While sitting in that hallway, I imagined not only her not being able to use her arm again, but also her possibly having medical adjustments made to her lifestyle or, worse, her dying in my arms and me burying her, then having to tell Kevin I wasn't able to save her.

Once the nurse had her settled, she turned to us and let us know the doctor would be in soon to talk to us. She looked up at me with nothing but kindness and compassion in her eyes, and I wondered how they did it. Today had been horrible, and yet they still found a way to be compassionate toward the patients.

Lanie's focus was on me, and I squeezed her hand. "I love you."

A soft smile lifted the corners of her lips, and I brought my hand up to kiss her palm as she mouthed the words back to me. Her eyes fluttered, and I took my free hand to push back some of the hair off her face. "Rest, sweetheart. I won't leave your side."

"Kevin?"

"I'm handling it."

She mouthed a, "Thank you," before her eyes fluttered closed again, and she drifted off to sleep. It was only about a half hour before the doctor knocked and came in.

"Mr. Rathborn," he greeted, and when he saw that Lanie was sleeping, he lowered his voice. "How are you doing?"

"Physically? Sore, but I'll manage. I'm more worried about my wife." I squeezed her hand, and the doctor nodded. "How is she?"

His face softened. "She's going to be okay. Mrs. Carley here is a lucky woman. The bullet went through part of her spleen, which had to be removed. She's going to take some time to heal."

"What are the long-term effects?"

"Her immune system will be weakened, and so in the short term, we want to monitor her bloodwork. Make sure she is fighting infections properly. As you were probably told, she dislocated her shoulder and it's going to be sore for a bit. She should be in that sling for a couple weeks. The leg will be fine, but much like yourself, she should keep it elevated." He lifted an eyebrow at me before saying, "Though, I have a feeling you are going to be up on it, taking care of her."

"I'll take care of myself, but she's my priority."

He nodded, acknowledging the statement. "She'll need to be here at least overnight. We will check her out tomorrow and see how she is doing. I'll have them bring in two meals."

"Thank you, doctor."

I turned and watched Lanie breathing for a few minutes before my phone rang in my hand. When I saw the caller ID, I took a deep breath and answered it. "Kami."

"What happened, Jason? You sounded panicked."

I took a deep breath and gave her a rundown of everything. After assuring her that everything was being done for Lanie, I asked, "Can you call Velas? We need Kevin to stay there tonight and my name isn't on the list to make that decision. The doctors said Lanie will need to be here at least overnight, so I'm not sure when she is going to be able to come home, and I need to keep him safe."

"Of course. I'll ask them to have him ready for me to pick up in the morning, too. We will meet you at the hospital. Which one you at?" I heard a thunk and then what sounded like clothes being thrown into a suitcase. "Don't even think about telling me not to come down. She's my best friend, and she and Kevin are closer than family, so shove it. I'll let Eric know where I am and ask him to let my professors know I had a family emergency."

I chuckled, looked at Lanie, and focused on the steady rhythm of her heart monitor. "I wouldn't dare. We are at Mercy."

"Okay. I'm assuming you won't be leaving her anytime soon?"

"Nope. The car can stay in the parking garage. I really don't care if it gets towed. I'll deal with that after I know Lanie is home and comfortable."

"Jason, I doubt they are allowing anyone in or out of the parking garage right now. Relax. See you in the morning. Oh, and Jason?" I hummed. "Thank you."

"Thank *you*, Kami. See you in the morning."

After ending the call, I turned my phone over in my hand a few times and let out a tense breath before dialing again.

"Please tell me that you two weren't hurt?"

"Sorry, Chase. I got hit in the leg, but they stapled it shut after digging the bullet out. Lanie had to have surgery. She's going to be okay, but we are laid up for a bit."

His words were tight as he asked, "What happened on your side?"

On your side? Then I remembered that I had seen Ismael on the roof.

"Lanie was in one of the booths and noticed a guy following us. When we turned around to look at him, he met our gaze and then looked up at one of the rooftop shooters. We took off running, took cover where we should, but she got hit in the leg, had a dislocated shoulder, and the surgery was to remove part of her spleen. So, like I said, we will be laid up for a bit, recovering."

"Thank the gods."

We sat in silence for a moment before I asked, "What is going on, Chase? You said we couldn't know yet, but for fuck's sake, we were shot at. Shot at and hit, multiple times, Chase. Lanie is asleep in front of me, fresh out of surgery from taking a bullet in the side. I could have fucking lost her today!"

"Don't you think I fucking know that? We don't want to lose her either. I don't know what happened. All I know is that Ismael was able to take out one of them, and when we got to one of the others, we interrogated him, but eventually he put him down like the dog he was after not being able to get much information."

I let that sink in. Chase had his guys in deep with Lanie. "Who is Lanie to you, Chase?"

His dad's voice bellowed for him in the background, and I sighed, knowing that Chase wasn't going to answer.

"I'll be in touch, professor." The line went dead, and I growled in frustration.

THE
DEN

Don't Let Them Eat You Alive

THE

DEN

Don't Let Them Eat You Alive

CHAPTER THIRTY-NINE

JASON

SAN DIEGO

I was dreaming of stuffing my face with eggs, bacon, pancakes, sausage, and fresh coffee. Then I was poked in the arm. "Jason, wake up."

Why is Kami in my dream?

Blinking against the bright lights as I came out of my delicious dream, I lifted my head to see Kami standing there with Kevin, who was staring at Lanie.

"Kevin." I waited for him to look at me, and when he did briefly, I said, "She's going to be okay."

He nodded before looking at his sister again, so at least I knew he had heard me. Shifting my gaze to Kami, I saw she looked relieved for a moment, then a stern expression crossed her face. Shoving a fast-food bag and a to-go cup of coffee at me, she looked like a woman on a mission.

"Something tells me that you haven't had a damn thing to eat except maybe a bag of chips and a bottle of water or can of soda since this happened. Please eat. You won't do her any good if you drop from starvation or dehydration."

"One day isn't going to do that to me, Kami."

"Eat and drink. It wasn't a request."

"I'm fine." I held Lanie's hand tight, not wanting to let go of the other half of my heart.

Kevin took a few deep breaths and muttered, "Sissy is going to be okay. Sissy is going to be okay. She is just sleeping. Her heart rate is good . . . . Oxygen levels are good . . . . Last blood pressure reading was good . . . . She's breathing on her own. Sissy is going to be okay."

My heart broke for him. He had to be so scared, but I knew it was important for both Lanie and Kevin that he be here. He would be calmer if he could see with his own eyes that she was alright.

Kami clocked it and went to her backpack. She pulled out a drawing pad and a few graphite pencils and went to him. "Why don't you sit down and draw for a few minutes? I'm sure Lanie would love to see one of your drawings when she wakes up."

Once she had pulled a chair up to the foot of the bed and convinced him to sit down and draw for a bit, she pointed to the bag of food. "Eat, Jason. Don't make me get mean."

I went to fight it again, but Kevin butted in without even lifting his eyes from the picture he was drawing, "Sissy is going to need you, brother. Will you please eat so that you can be strong for sissy and . . . me. Please, brother?"

Neither Kami nor I had moved as what he said sunk in. Taking the bag and coffee, I swallowed hard and shifted my gaze to him. Twice he'd used that word. "Brother?"

Kevin glanced at me and nodded. "You told me that you are sorry for hurting sissy and that you would be proud to be my brother." I nodded but felt Kami's attention still focused on me. "You said that you love Sissy, and that you want to have her by your side forever."

I turned my head to look at the woman I would give anything to have as mine for exactly that long, if not longer. "I did, if she will have me."

"Then you are my brother."

I needed to move. Standing, I tested the weight on my leg. It was achy and there was a little pull of the skin where the staples were, but it felt fine. I bent down and lowered the leg rest and switched spots with Kami. I moved to stand opposite Kevin. "Thank you, Kevin."

He shifted in his seat, and then his eyes were going in every direction. As his breathing picked up, I shifted my coffee and food into the same hand and leaned on the end of bed. "Want to take a walk with me? I need to stretch, and I would love your company."

He nodded and turned for the door. I looked back at Kami, and she had Lanie's hand in hers as she said, "Go. I got her for now. Take care of him. He's scared."

"Me, too. The three of us will get her through this, though."

"Oh, and Jason? Take the duffle at your feet and get cleaned up in the bathroom. You smell like shit. At least the hospital gave you something to change into, but couldn't they have given you one of their care packets? Deodorant at least?"

I smiled despite myself. "Thank you, Kami."

I hobbled out of Lanie's room, and Kevin stepped up next to me as we headed down the hall. "Thank you for the food and coffee."

"Kami said we should eat before we came to the hospital, and she figured you wouldn't have eaten anything. She was right."

"She was."

We walked in silence until we got to one of the little seating areas at the end of the hall with dark-blue, soft, fabric chairs and love seats, but the best part was the floor-to-ceiling windows in the corner and along the wall. The view was spectacular, and Kevin sat in a chair facing the window, so I sat in the one next to him and put my leg up on the table in front of me. We stared out through the windows onto the unobstructed view of the Sierra Mountains. White, poofy, decorator clouds were scattered throughout the sky. Taking a breath that released some of the tightness in my chest, I opened the bag of food. I pulled out the bacon, egg, and cheese biscuit and offered Kevin the crispy hash brown. "I know how much you love them."

"You need to eat."

"And I will be just fine with the biscuit." I pushed it toward him, and this time he took it.

"Thank you."

I smiled. "Thank you for bringing me the food."

When I unwrapped and took a bite of the biscuit sandwich, my brain didn't register any flavor. The texture was fine, but it was like my taste buds had been turned off. It was just blank, and I went through the motions of chewing and swallowing the food. I let out a long breath and leaned back in the chair. I would be lying if I said my back didn't bother me. Sitting in that chair all night and leaning over Lanie's bed had me sore in places I didn't think I could be sore.

"Thank you for letting me come to the hospital."

I narrowed my eyes. "Why wouldn't we? You have more of a right to be here than Kami and me. More so, you are her brother!"

He fiddled with the hash brown wrapper. "I navigate and picture the world differently than everyone else. I know that I process emotions differently and I can be a bit much. When we got here, the lady at the desk asked if I was going to be supervised the whole time I was here."

"I'm sorry, what? You are a grown ass adult who can handle himself. What is that bullshit?"

He gave me an even look. "To be fair, I was a little hysterical downstairs, but I needed to see that my sister was okay."

I tilted my head and thought about what he was saying. "Well, that is bullshit. Just because you think differently doesn't mean that you aren't capable of acting like an adult."

"Thank you." He stared out the windows for a minute, and just as I leaned back against the chair again, he asked, "You okay?"

I couldn't help but smile at him. "Yeah. I'm okay. Tired. Lanie is going to be okay and that does a lot for making me okay."

"Yesterday, when Kami called, she said that there was a shooting at the farmers' market and that Sissy got hurt. Said that she was on the way down, called and arranged for me to stay at Velas last night, and would pick me up in the morning.. Why didn't you arrange for it? You are my brother."

I didn't know if I was ever going to be able to get used to him calling me that. It made love and hope swell in my chest. I took a long drink of the coffee and winced at how bitter it was. It was always hit or miss with fast food, but caffeine was caffeine and I wasn't going to complain.

"Remember yesterday how we talked about how I made a mistake and that I was trying to earn her back?"

He looked at me with interest. "I remember. But she loves you. Always has. She was really sad when you left."

"I know." I squeezed his hand, and he took it back, putting it on his lap. "Well, because I'm still working on earning her trust back, I'm not on the list of people who can adjust your schedule."

"I will ask her to put you on that list. I trust you."

Smiling, I shook my head. I knew Lanie was in the process of it, but it took time. "Kevin, there are good legal reasons why I don't have that right. How would you have felt if she had put one of her other boyfriends on the list?"

He wrinkled his nose and made a noise of disgust. "Eww. I wouldn't have gone with any of them."

"Well, see, that is probably one reason why she didn't. I plan to be here for a very long time, so there is no rush. I'm here for both of you. She mentioned that she was working on it though."

"Are you okay?"

Smiling, I nodded. "Got my leg stapled back together, but I'm alright."

He shifted in his seat. "How bad did she get hurt yesterday? Everyone is glossing over it, but she had surgery. Surgery isn't for small wounds."

I took a big, steading breath. This was the hard part. Telling him just how seriously she'd been hurt. "You know we were at the farmers' market, and after getting your treats, someone started shooting. I don't know who or why, but a lot of people were hurt, including your sister and me." I waited to make sure he was able to let that sink in.

"People are dumb. Guns are not supposed to be used like that."

"That is true."

"It's my fault that she got hurt."

"No. We were going to be at the farmers' market anyway. Just because we happened to be working on getting your requests while we were there, doesn't mean it was your fault. Bad people are going to do bad things. She is going to be okay." His breathing was picking up, and I remembered how he liked details. "I can't tell you all the technical terms for all that happened to her. There was a shot to her leg, and they had to remove part of her spleen because it was damaged. She may have some autoimmune issues, but she will be fine."

His head was moving up and down in understanding. "And they made sure she wasn't bleeding internally anymore."

"Exactly. They did that. Everyone keeps telling me she's going to be okay. I believe them."

He gave a curt nod and leaned back in his chair, staring out the window. I was sure his mind was racing right now. So, I took this time to head to the bathroom to get cleaned up. "You okay to sit here for a few minutes while I go to the bathroom and get cleaned up?"

"Yeah."

Quickly, I limped my way down the hall and stepped into the men's bathroom. Tossing the duffle on the counter, I unzipped it and found a complete hygiene kit, along with a new set of clothes.

Thank you, Kami.

I worked quickly, and just ten minutes later, I was flopping into the chair next to Kevin and leaning back to sit in the silence. Kevin had his sketch pad out, and when I looked over at it, he was sketching out the landscape through the windows. Every few minutes, medical staff wandered the halls behind us, and I knew I would work until my last breath to prove to Lanie I was worthy to be here by her side. The panic that had filled me when we'd been in that alcove, not knowing whether she was going to make it or not, was something I never wanted to endure again.

Cherish every day because you never know when it will be your last.

"Jason?"

I gave a hum of acknowledgement and rolled my head against the back of the chair to face Kevin.

"Why do people do this?"

A huff of a laugh came out of me. "That is a really good question. There are lots of people who would like an answer to that. Do you know of anyone who doesn't like your sister?"

He shook his head and shifted in his seat. "I don't. Sissy is kind to everyone, but . . ."

"But you know something. Kevin, please tell me."

He shifted again. "I don't want sissy to get mad at me."

"Okay, that is understandable, but I can't help her if I don't know what is wrong." Slowly, he turned to me and took a deep breath. "She hasn't told you what is wrong, but you noticed something, didn't you?"

He nodded. "She doesn't tell me a lot of things because she doesn't want to scare me. I know that I have problems maneuvering around the world sometimes, but it has also made me very observant. I'm very smart in math and love art. I see colors as numbers, and it all comes together for me. I'm not dumb, and I wonder if sometimes she thinks that I am."

I blinked in shock. Lanie always gloated about her brother. How talented he was, caring, and smart. Dumb was the furthest thing that Lanie would say about him.

"She's protective over me. I am glad for it, but I'm also an adult."

I turned to look at him fully and watch him. Even when Lanie and I had been together before, Kevin had never talked this openly with me.

"You are, so what have you noticed?"

"She is more aware of everything around us. Usually, I'm the one that will notice the lady in the red jacket coming down the hall over there." I turned my head, and there indeed was a lady in a red jacket. I looked at him as he continued, "But she's been noticing more of that. More of who is around us. I see her check out the exits of a building like she is making sure of how we can get out in a hurry. Also, she used to just drop me off at the gate and I would walk into Velas alone. Now she drops me off at the doors."

I thought about how we'd seen the man staring at us at the market and then looking up toward where the shooter had been. How Lanie had said he had been following us. How she had noted all of that, but I hadn't. I was the one who should be picking up this stuff. How in the hell had I missed him following us. I had missed the guys at the bistro too.

"Okay."

His head tipped to the side. "You noticed something, too?"

"It's probably unrelated, Kevin, but yeah."

We sat in silence again for a bit, and I wondered if the shooting had anything to do with Cyress or Don Kingsley looking for me. Sure, Chase had guys on Lanie, but why hadn't they taken those assholes out? Why would anyone other than Cyress want to come after me? I'd taken a number of people for their money at The Den, but Cyress's sum had the most zeros after it.

Would he really sink so low as to go after Lanie? Would he also go after Kevin?

Fuck, I hope not.

My brain was starting to spiral down that well when Kevin's voice broke through. "I wasn't happy when she told me that she was dating you again. You hurt her. I'm protective over her, too."

I knew that. Lanie had told me how he'd reacted, but he ultimately had agreed to give me a chance.

"Mr. Rathborn, I've seen how you look at her. You have even taken over some of the things I do in the morning."

I sat up straight, concerned. "Are you upset about that?"

"A little. I get Sissy her coffee and fill her water bottle for the day."

I couldn't help the smile on my face. "Okay. You can do that again, but can I make your lunches while I'm here?"

His face broke out in a bright smile. "Oh, yes. I like your lunches better than hers. Your sandwiches are tastier, and you always put one of the fun-size chocolate peanut butter cups in there for me. But don't tell her that I like yours better, okay?"

"We got a deal. Ready to go back and see her?"

He nodded, and we got up to head back. When we got to her hall, though, Kami was walking out of her room, looking both ways, and when her gaze met ours, she shouted, "She's awake!"

I instantly hobbled faster, trying not to hurt myself getting down the hall. Kevin rushed past me and strode into the room first. I heard his shouted, "Sissy!" from the nurses station a few doors down.

One of the nurses chuckled. "That boy is so cute."

I smiled and made my way into the room. A bright, weak smile graced Lanie's lips, and then Kevin was hugging her. "You okay?" Her words were tired and strained.

"You scared me." He pulled back, letting her take ahold of one of his hands, tight.

He was really doing so much better with human touch since I'd had him as a student. Lanie had told me he still wasn't much of a hugger and had only recently started hugging her on a consistent basis, but it showed how much he needed her. They were my package deal. Two people I would protect with my life. My Queen and my Jack of Hearts.

"Mrs. Carley?" the nurse asked, getting her attention. "How is your pain? One being the lowest and ten the worst, like you were mauled by a bear."

"I'm real groggy."

The nurse smiled at her. "That's normal, but can you tell me how your pain is?"

Lanie blinked slowly and said, "Like a six? Most of the pain is in my side."

She nodded and then adjusted a few things before finishing up her vitals and telling us that the doctor would be in before too long. "Mr. Rathborn, can I speak to you outside?"

Lanie's voice was strained as she called after me, but I turned, strode back to her, gave her a kiss on the forehead, and then muttered, "I'll be back in just a moment. Comfort Kevin. He's been scared to death, and Kami? Well, she's been off her rocker with worry." She huffed a laugh, and when she looked at them, Kami was shaking her head.

When I got to the hallway, the nurse went through all that they had done again and that Lanie would likely be there for a few days for observation. The doctors wanted to watch the healing near one of the arteries before they could even begin to discuss physical therapy.

"She's going to need help around the house for a couple weeks for sure. The ligaments and muscles in her shoulder are going to hurt like hell, and her strength and motion will be limited. She needs to be very careful how much she bends. Limit showers to every other day at minimum, and no baths until the wound has sealed up on her side."

"It's not a problem. Whatever she needs. Just, thank you for everything you have all done."

The nurse nodded again as someone else walked up. "This is Jane from admin. She'll take over from here.

"Thank you, ma'am."

Jane smiled softly and shuffled some files around in her arms before finally opening one and looking at me. "Mrs. Melanie Carley?" I nodded. "And you are?"

"Jason Rathborn, her husband."

She looked over the chart and her finger stopped, showing my name as the contact. "You are listed here as the primary contact for billing?"

"Yes, whatever the insurance doesn't cover, we can cover it."

"Does she have secondary insurance?"

"No." I ran my hands through my hair and gripped my neck. "I'll take care of it."

"I'll note that. Thank you. Do you have any questions?"

"No, thank you." As she walked away, my gaze went to the ceiling as I thought about what the number could be that I would need to cover. There was no way I'd be allowing her to pay that portion. She had so much to worry about financially, and she was mine. That meant she was my responsibility. Her bills were my responsibility.

Kevin came out of her room and stood next to me. "Sissy is asking for you."

"Thanks, man."

"Mr. Rathborn?"

I looked at him as his gaze went to the ground and he shifted on his feet. "I heard what the nurse said. Thank you for everything. Thank you for taking care of us."

"Of course, brother."

A smile tugged at his lips, and then he followed me into the room. Lanie's focus moved over to me from where Kami was sitting in the chair next to her, and she smiled. "There he is."

"Hey there, sweetheart."

I stood at the foot of the bed, leaning on the bar at the end. My legs were tired, but I refused to show any signs so that I didn't worry any of them. Kevin walked around me and told Lanie, "I'm tired, sissy. If you are okay, can Kami take me home? Or I can stay at Velas?"

"I'm going to stay at the apartment while she's here. That way you can sleep in your own bed." Kami was confused, as was I.

"Where is brother going to sleep, then?"

Lanie's breath hitched, and when I looked at her, she was looking at Kevin, tears filling her eyes. I put my hand on her foot and squeezed. She looked at me quickly and blinked as a tear went down her cheek. I gave her a look that I hoped told her I would explain when he wasn't here, and she took a ragged breath.

"I'm going to stay here with Lanie. Kami can have her bed, and you can sleep in yours."

Kevin turned toward me and looked up at my face before looking away quickly again. "Promise me it's okay for me to sleep at home?"

"I promise."

Kami gave Lanie a kiss on the top of head and whispered a few things in her ear that had her chuckling before she switched places with me, and I took Lanie's hand again, threading my fingers with hers. She squeezed weakly as I sat down, and Kami asked, "Kevin, it's still early. Do you want to go back to Velas for a few hours?"

"I'm tired. I would like to sleep at home please."

"Alright then."
Kevin then said over his shoulder, "Love you, Sissy."

CHAPTER FORTY

LANIE

SAN DIEGO

"Love you," I whispered hoarsely at Kevin as he pulled back. Smiling, he moved out of the bed, and Jason took his spot. There were flashes of the market going through my head, but what I remembered most was Jason lying on top of me, protecting me.

"Hey, sweetheart." He reached up and ran his thumb along my cheek as his other hand gripped mine tight. I leaned into it and savored the warmth of his touch, reminding me that I was safe. We both were. "How you feeling?"

"I think the pain meds they gave me are starting to kick in." My words were slightly slurred, and I felt the weight of sleep pulling on me hard.

We held each other's gazes for a long moment, and I took a deep breath. "I've been in and out with the meds, but have you slept?"

"Got a few hours here last night."

My eyes narrowed. "You changed."

"Yeah, Kami and Kevin brought me clothes, toiletries, and some breakfast. So yes, I have fooded and caffeinated."

I couldn't help but chuckle. "I have always loved how you said that."

Jase brought my hand up to his lips and kissed it softly, maintaining the contact as he took a deep breath. "I was so scared."

"Me too. What happened? Does anyone know?"

He shook his head. "I don't know. I've sort of been worried about *my wife*."

I studied him for a reaction, and when there was a playful gleam in his eye, I relaxed a bit. "Sorry for surprising you with that. I knew they wouldn't . . . I mean . . . you would have been told to leave. I couldn't do that to you. They wouldn't have even told you anything."

He started chuckling and kissed my hand again. "It's okay, sweetheart. I'm not mad in the slightest. I've already told you, I'm here and not going anywhere. I'm right where I want to be."

The love and warmth in his eyes were everything I hoped and needed to see. "Jase, I know we haven't been back together long, but I love you. I never stopped loving you. When you asked if I would give you another chance, my only concerns were the distance and Kevin."

Before I even realized Jason had stood up, his lips crashed onto mine, and I held him there. After a moment, he pulled back slightly and whispered against me, "I love you, too. You are my everything. You always have been."

"Why did it take me getting so hurt for us to tell each other?"

"Stupidity. Fear. Technically, we both did once, but I don't think either of us wanted to draw attention to it. I know I didn't. Didn't want to make things weird. I'll say it again. I love you, Lanie."

I leaned forward to kiss him again. "Don't make me live another day without you."

"I'll see what I can do about that." His smile was electric.

He sat back down in the chair but didn't let go of my hand. We just stared at each other. Warmth spread throughout my entire body, and I was finally able to relax. Slowly, the pain in my shoulder and side started to fade, and I concentrated on the feel of his hand in mine.

He was here. And he was mine.

THE

D E N

Don't Let Them Eat You Alive

Chapter Forty-One

Jason

San Diego

We'd been discharged from the hospital a couple of days ago, and per the doctor's instructions, Lanie was allowing me to take care of her. Kami had been invaluable the last couple of days. It had really allowed me to concentrate on Lanie, all while she'd helped with Kevin and ensured I didn't take it too far with my leg. She was out grocery shopping and had asked if I could take Kevin to Velas this morning, and of course I'd agreed.

I leaned down and gave Lanie a kiss on the forehead. "You okay? Need anything?"

"Just you, *Sir*." Her eyes sparkled with mischief, and I groaned. "Don't worry. I realize I'm not going to be up for any extracurricular activities for a couple more weeks."

"Not unless I get *really* good at shibari and can suspend you in a way that would please us both and not hurt either your shoulder or side."

She chuckled and then whimpered as she held her side. "I guess you are right. Your loops are getting tighter and more consistent."

There was no holding back the groan that slipped out as I pictured her hanging by the ropes in the room. "Thank you. I'm going to leave now because you are making me hard, and I have to go out there and help Kevin get to Velas. I love you, sweetheart. Be good and rest. Your Kindle is fully charged right here."

"My water?"

I lifted the large bright-green jug and put it next to her Kindle. "Drink your water. Drink so much you have to get up and pee when I get back."

"You just want to carry me. You know I'm capable of getting up on my own, right? I wouldn't have been able to come home unless I could."

Mockingly, I clutched my pearls. "And allow you to do things on your own? My plan is going to fail if you do things on your own. You should be totally reliant on me."

Lanie shook her head, rolled her eyes, and smiled. "You are ridiculous."

"You know I just love having you in my arms, my queen."

She gave me a dramatic eye roll again before asking, "How long will you be gone?"

I kissed her quickly. "Not long, but seriously, drink your water." I reached over and handed her the Kindle. "Read something smutty for me. If you're a good little thing, then I might help you alleviate the ache."

"But you said—"

"We don't have to fuck for me to relive some of that pressure, sweetheart."

She turned bright red, and after swallowing a couple of times, she finally nodded. "No, no you don't."

"Alright then, so I think I can handle taking Kevin to the center. I'll see you soon." Then I took a deep breath and forced myself out of that room. As I stepped into the living room from the hall, Kevin was rushing around, muttering to himself.

"Kevin?"

He didn't pause at all in his movements. He frantically hurried by me, rushing down the hall and into his room. I heard things shuffling around as he chanted, "It's all wrong. It's all wrong. It's all wrong."

He let out a loud frustrated groan, and when he came back down the hall, I grabbed him by the shoulders. His arms instantly went to my chest to push me away, but I held him tight.

"Kevin. Stop." When he did, I loosened my grip on him and removed my hands, lifting them up so he knew I wasn't trying to restrain him. "I know you don't like to be touched. Now, please take a deep breath."

In and out.

"Look at me. It doesn't have to be in the eyes, but look at me." When he did, I nodded. "Good. I'll do it with you, now breathe again."

In and out.

In and out.

"Okay, I took two," he grumbled, but his shoulders were lower than they had been before.

"Can you try to, calmly, tell me what is wrong?"

"I can't find more."

Holding his attention, I asked, "Can't find more what? I'll help you find it."

"I'm out of drawing paper."

I went to where Lanie had told me that she kept extra and found it empty. "Shit." Turning to face him, I told him, "I'm going to take you to Velas. Then, while you are there today, I will pick up more paper. Do you need more pencils? What other supplies do you need? I will make sure they are here when you get home. I'm so sorry I didn't know you were low."

He sniffled and shook his head, shoving the emotions down. "It's not your fault, brother. You didn't know. Sissy always makes sure we never run out."

"It's okay. You are overwhelmed, have been drawing a lot in the last week since all this happened, and we ran out of the thing that helps you cope. I'm sorry. I know there are a lot of changes, but we are trying to keep things as normal as possible."

"I know. Just, nothing is right. Everything is wrong. Our morning routine is wrong. Sissy isn't drinking coffee and she can't have her usual breakfast."

His eyes were wide, and he was worried. "I know, Kevin. It's going to be okay though. She is healing. Once she is able to do more by herself, I'm sure she would love to be out here with us, eating and talking to you about your day over a cup of coffee."

He looked down the hall, where she was lying in bed. He took a deep breath, and I could see he was trying to calm down.

"Okay. Will Sissy be okay while we are gone?"

I couldn't help but smile at him. He was so worried about her. There were times like this that I was reminded just how big his heart was.

"Yes. She's able to get around on her own, but I'll only be gone for an hour. She will probably just watch *Avatar*." A small smile lifted the corner of his lips and he nodded. "Now, get your stuff. We need to get you to the center."

With a quick jerk of his head, he stood and grabbed his backpack and a sweater. I grabbed my keys, popped my head into the bedroom, and gave Lanie a quick kiss on the forehead.

"Everything okay?"

"Yeah, you rest. I'm getting him off to the center. Then I'm stopping by to get him more art supplies."

Her eyes went wide. "Oh no, he ran out of paper?" I nodded. "That explains everything. I'm usually on top of that. Check a couple times a week. Of course he's more anxious and drawing more."

"I got it, sweetheart. Rest. I'll be back in an hour."

When I got to the door, Kevin muttered, "Sissy okay?"

"She is. She feels bad about the supplies, but we will get it all settled, alright?"

He nodded, and then we headed out.

We were sitting at the light a couple blocks from the center when Kevin turned toward me, super excited. "Brother!"

"Yes?"

"I need you to pick up some things for Sissy when you get more paper."

The light turned green as I nodded. "Alright, what would you like me to get her?"

"A pink hand towel. She always laughs when she sees them because it reminds her of one of her favorite scenes in a book."

"Alright." I knew exactly what book that was. It was a great paranormal series. "Then she needs a fuzzy pillow and a weighted stuffy."

"Those are not two things I would have thought of, but consider it done. Any specific kind of pillow or stuffy?"

He thought for a moment and shook his head as he looked out the window. "No. Just get her something you know will make her smile."

He gave a sharp nod. "Kami is going to pick me up?"

"Yes. She wants to see you before she gets on her plane tonight."

"She can't stay for dinner?"

"No, she has to be at the airport at seven."

He lowered his head but nodded as he played with his fingers. "I like Kami. She's really good for Sissy, and she doesn't treat me like a child."

"That's because you aren't a child."

Shifting in his seat, he continued, "No, but a lot of people treat me like one because I'm different. Which isn't right either, but it happens. I'm really smart. I'm a really good artist, and I'm kind."

"You've mentioned how people perceive you differently a few times since I arrived here. Is there something going on?"

"No. It's just, with the strange things going on and the hospital." He let out a big sigh. "I'm just noticing it more. There won't be any way to change others' perceptions though. The only thing I can change is how I react to them. I'm working on that, but part of that is noting how others react so I can adjust."

"First, you have grown up so much in the last few years, Kevin. I'm really proud of you. Second, you don't have to change for others. I understand if you want to modify small behaviors that make your life easier, but don't change who *you* are just because society is dumb."

We pulled into the drive and pulled up to the gate. He smiled as I looked at him quickly before reaching over and punching in the entry code. "It hasn't been easy. That's one thing they have worked on with us here at Velas. Self-confidence and owning what we are good at. This place is good. I like it." He lifted his head to look up at the large white building as we pulled up.

When he looked over at me, I could see the wheels turning. "You know, if you and Sissy do get married and you officially become my brother, I would be okay with living here if she wanted to move in with you."

Shock rolled through me at his words. "Kevin . . ."

Without looking at me, he opened the door and got out of the car. He turned toward me and bent down. "Thank you for being here for us."

"Nowhere else I'd rather be."

He shouted back before the door shut behind him, "See you tonight!"

Two hours later, I was walking back into the house and setting everything down on the counter. I had stopped by the grocery store and picked up some fresh fruit plus a few other things we needed. Not to mention, I stopped by the florist next door and picked up a large bouquet of tiger lilies, daisies, cherry brandy roses, and some various spray fillers. It was colorful, and when I saw the bouquet sitting in the freezer, I knew I had to get it for Lanie.

"Jase?" Her voice was strong, but she sounded tired.

I grabbed the vase of flowers and headed down the hall. When I walked in, her face lit up. "They reminded me of you, and I figured you wouldn't mind something to brighten things up in here."

Setting them on her dresser, I turned around and was stunned to find she was crying. I rushed to her side and bent down over her, coming face-to-face with her. "My queen, what's wrong?"

Her watery gaze met mine, and the tears rolled down her face. "It was just so thoughtful."

Huffing a laugh, I met her gaze again and said, "Well, if the flowers brought you to tears, then the stuff Kevin asked me to pick up for you might send you into full hysterics."

Lanie sat up with a start, her eyes wide. "What do you mean? What did he ask you to get?"

I shook my head. "Oh no, I'm not spoiling the surprise for him. He gets to give you those things. And yes, I did stop by and pick up a triple stock of paper and notebooks for him. Once I told the lady at the store that it was Kevin I was getting them for, she went crazy, pulling the supplies from the back room for him. Said something about how they special order for him to make sure they always have it there."

She chuckled. "Yeah. They love it when he comes in."

I watched her for a minute, and when she slid back farther down the bed, she winced. "Do you need more pain meds?"

Shaking her head, she emphatically told me, "No. I want off the narcotics. I'm so done being fuzzy all the time. So, no more meds. Over the counter only, some ibuprofen wouldn't be a miss."

After getting her some and watching her take them, I asked her to drink some more water. When I took the jug from her, I set it back on the bedside table and set her Kindle next to it. "Want me to keep your mind off the pain while we wait for that to kick in?"

"I thought you said no shenanigans, regardless of any teasing that you have been doing."

"No sex, no eating you out, and no blowjobs . . . at least for a couple more days. I don't want to accidentally hurt you while you are healing."

A wide smile crossed her face. "That's it?" I narrowed my eyes at her. "There was no restriction on handjobs."

"Fucking hell, my queen." My cock grew hard at the image forming in my head. "Not today. Add them to the list."

Lanie let out a huff, and I stood, purposefully readjusting my cock in my pants in front of her. Her giggle enticed a smile to cross my face. "Don't move."

She pouted dramatically. "Not planning to go anywhere."

I headed to the bathroom, grabbing her favorite lotion, nail polish remover, a pale pink polish, and a clear topcoat. It took a moment to find the cotton balls, but when I did, I stepped back into the bedroom, placed the items on the bed, and told her, "Come on, let's get you into the recliner."

She looked at the extra-wide grey recliner in the corner, but slowly inched down carefully. When she got to the edge of the bed, I picked her up and moved her. "You know I can move myself."

"And like I said, I like having you in my arms."

When she was in place and I set her up with an ice pack for her side, she asked, "What are you doing? I was thinking of cuddling in bed with you and watching TV."

"Giving you a foot massage, and then I'm going to paint your toenails."

"What? You are going to paint my toes?" Laine's eyes were wide, and I couldn't help but chuckle. "I mean, I'm not going to complain about the massage because you give the best massages, but . . ."

"Oh, hush. I can paint your nails and not have it look like a disaster, and even if I do, no one is going to see it." I grabbed the remote to the TV and asked, "What do you want to watch?"

"*Avatar: The Last Airbender* of course. I can't believe you would ask something so ridiculous."

"Okay, sassypants." I flipped through the programs, and when I found it, I shook my head when I saw where she was. "This episode is so sad. Can we please skip it?"

"You just don't like when Uncle Iroh sings 'Leaves from a Vine.'"

I winced. "No. No, I do not. It's sad."

"Yes, we can skip it."

"Thank you." Skipping the episode, I hit play, turned to the bath-room again, and got two wet hand towels. Slowly, I started washing each of her feet and tossing the towels back into the bathroom. "Now, just sit there and enjoy the pampering."

Then, I took two pumps of the lotion and started on her left foot. The moan-like hum that came out of her was almost sinful. When my thumb ran up the arch of her foot and pressed just under the ball , I watched her entire body relax.

"That's my good girl."

THE

DEN

Don't Let Them Eat You Alive

Chapter Forty-Two

Lanie

San Diego

After Jason gave me one of the best foot massages I'd ever had then painted my toes, which came out much better than expected, he lay with me and cuddled for a while. Eventually, he got up, made me lunch, and did a few other things around the house while I napped in and out, but just having him here was heaven.

When Kevin got home, he came in with an oversized light green bag with white tissue sticking out the top of it. "I asked brother to pick up a few things for you today."

I took the bag from him, smiling. "Thank you, Kevin."

After pulling the tissue off, I looked in the bag and I cracked up at the pink hand towel laid over the top of it. Kevin's smile was bright as he said, "I know how much you love that scene in that book, even though I haven't read it yet."

He wasn't wrong. The male main character came in nothing but a pink hand towel to open the door to the girl he was head over heels for, and I had cackled every time I'd read the scene. Kevin was smiling when I pulled out the fuzzy pink pillow that was molded for my head to rest on. When I put it behind my head, I instantly felt the muscles in my neck and shoulders relax. "Oh, this is nice, Kevin. Thank you."

"I have one more thing for you. It didn't fit in the bag. It's silly, but I laughed when I saw what brother picked out. He is really good at picking presents for you." He was practically bouncing on his toes in excitement.

"Alright. Show me."

"Close your eyes." I did, and then he placed something heavy on my outstretched hands. "Okay, you can look."

Opening my eyes, I squealed in delight and smiled at the little guy. There was the cutest little grey hedgehog stuffy with pink stitching in his cheeks and a smile on his face. "Oh, my goodness! He's adorable! He's heavy, too." Hugging him close, I sighed as the weight pressed against my chest.

Kevin's eyes were bright as he smiled. "Now you have a weighted thing, too. It isn't the same as my blanket, but I've read studies where just having some weight on your chest can help calm you down."

My vision was getting blurry, and my chest was tight. "Thank you." I wiped at my cheeks and then asked, "You guys wanna get pizza and have a movie night?"

"It's Chinese night, though." His head tipped to the side, and then a big smile crossed his face. "We can switch pizza and Chinese food nights. I'll even let you pick out the pizza."

Jase walked in just then. "Pizza and a movie? It's Chinese night though?"

"We can switch the nights." Kevin shifted a little on his feet, and I saw his hands twitch some. He was trying to be flexible, even if it was difficult for him. I couldn't help the smile on my face.

"I don't care either way. As long as I have my boys on either side of me."

Jason's return grin was full of mischief and lust that I knew neither of us could act on. "What are we going to watch?"

Kevin and I answered at the same time. "*A Few Good Men* of course."

"Why *that* movie?" Jason was chuckling.

My brother's face erupted in a rare, huge smile. "Sissy and I love to shout, 'You can't handle the truth' at the same time. It makes Sissy laugh."

"Well, I'm all for Lanie laughing. Come on, Kevin, let's get the house picked back up while we wait for dinner to get here. Lanie, you call it in?"

"Yes, *Sir*." I couldn't keep the heat from my voice, and it was horrible because my brother was right there. But this side of Jason, the domestic caretaker, the one who put family first, it warmed me in places other than my heart.

As they stepped out, I brought up the app and ordered two medium pizzas. Once I saw the confirmation, I put my phone down, only for it to ring with a number I didn't recognize. It said it was from Sacramento, so I answered it.

"Hello?"

Nothing but silence greeted me on the other end of the line. No breath, no background noise of any kind.

"Hello?"

I swore I heard a gasp on the other end. "Is this . . . Is this Melanie Carley?"

"This is Melanie." My heart was racing.

There was a muttered, "Oh, holy fuck."

"Who is this?" I sat up and winced as I did so too quickly, but the line was still silent.

Hardening my voice, I demanded, "Who is this?" I kept my voice down but tried to keep it sounding like I wasn't rattled.

There was shouting in the background, but I couldn't make out what exactly they were saying. It sort of sounded like orders were being given, but then someone closer said, "Time's up. Let's move."

Then a smooth voice said, "Finally." There was a short silence that hung between us, and just as I was going to ask what the hell was going on, he continued, "All in due time, Melanie. It won't be long now."

Then the line went dead. Lowering the phone to my lap, I stared at it. There was something familiar about the sound of that voice, like a distant memory being rumbled through drums. It was the cadence in how he'd said my name.

Instead of being scared by the call, there was something warm and comforting about it. I ran through the entire thing again and couldn't figure out why.

Why do I have such a warm and fuzzy feeling?

Did something break inside of me when I got shot that an anonymous call, that on the surface, was super creepy, gave me warm fuzzies?

None of it made a damn bit of sense.

My mind must have been reeling for a while as I stared at my phone because Kevin was coming in with drinks and Jason with the pizza. "Don't worry, if the bedding gets greasy, I'll change it out."

As we settled into bed, Jason leaned over and kissed me on the temple. "What's wrong? Need some pain meds?"

I shook my head. "No. I'm okay. Just had a strange call." I handed him my phone as Kevin handed me a couple pieces of pizza.

As Jason looked into my call history, his lips went thin and there was the slightest line of confusion on his face. If I didn't know any better, I would have missed it. "You know the number?"

"Maybe. Don't worry about it." He kissed me again, and I leaned my head on his shoulder.

"Okay." I waited a minute. "Just so you know, while the call was weird, there was something comforting about it. Like I knew the voice and I wasn't scared. It was just strange."

He nodded as Kevin hit play on the TV for the movie.

THE

DEN

DON'T LET THEM EAT YOU ALIVE

CHAPTER FORTY-THREE

JASON

SAN DIEGO

Lanie stopped and leaned on the counter. She'd able to get up and move around much better the last couple of days, but she still couldn't go very far. "I swear this fucking rib is going to be the death of me. My shoulder doesn't hurt near as much as this damned thing."

She smirked at me as Kevin got up and headed for the kitchen. "Sissy, sit down. Jason and I are going to make you a cake."

"We are?"

Kevin nodded emphatically. "I've already checked. We have everything to make it from scratch."

I lifted an eyebrow to him and then looked at Lanie, who nodded. "Kevin makes the best chocolate cake."

"I have two secret ingredients." He was going through the cupboards and pulling everything down as I helped Lanie to the couch.

She sat sideways so she could still watch us, and as I gave her a kiss, I muttered, "I'm nervous."

"Why?" she asked as she wrapped her good arm around my neck, holding my face close to hers.

My eyes flickered to Kevin. "I don't know if I can live up to that kind of hype."

"You make a mean box cake, Jase. From scratch? I have no measure. But Kevin's? Yeah, it's just that good. The only thing you have to do is what he asks. He basically just needs you to hand him things. He will measure it all out and do the work."

"Alright then."

I headed back to the kitchen, where Kevin was grinding some coffee beans, and when they were at the consistency he wanted, he moved over to where he had a sifter over a bowl and dumped them in to combine with the dry ingredients. Once he had measured out the flour and other dry ingredients, sifting them all together, he set them aside and went to work on mixing the wet ingredients.

Kevin was in the zone, and I loved how I was just doing something so normal with Lanie and Kevin again. She just sat back watching us. While her brother worked away in the kitchen, here I was, just hanging out, helping where I could.

Nothing pleased me more. When our gazes met, I couldn't help the lust that filled my eyes. She was the sexiest thing on the planet. If we weren't having family time, I'd definitely take her back to her bedroom and try to please her in every way possible.

"Can you get me one cup of water, please?"

I nodded at Kevin's request and went to the filter to get some water. Once done, I took it over to him, where, without looking, he continued to combine the wet ingredients, then he took the cup of water, reached up, and dumped it on my head. "Maybe that will cool you down until you two go to bed tonight. And I don't want to hear lies about you two not doing anything."

I stared at him in astonishment. Lanie, however, was trying not to laugh and chastised, "Kevin!"

A moment later, he smiled and asked for two eggs. "You aren't going to crack them over my head, are you?"

"No, I wouldn't ruin good eggs that way."

I smirked and grabbed a glass of water that was still on the counter, and pour it over the top of his head.

In shock, he bent over, quickly wiping the water from his face and head, and gasping. "Brother!"

Kevin turned his head toward me, droplets of water still falling from his hair onto his face. However, the spark of glee there had me stepping back. He stood up, and quicker than I could register, he had picked up the bowl of dry ingredients and started throwing its contents in my direction. Flour, chocolate, coffee, and everything else that had been in there rained down on me, covering my upper body.

Trying not to tip my hand, I dove for the sink, ignoring the pain in my leg, as he continued to throw powder from the bowl. I was quickly becoming caked in the stuff, but I grabbed the nozzle to the faucet, flipped the water on, and sprayed him.

He took a step to the side, and water sprayed all over the kitchen as I tried to chase him down. Next thing I knew, he had the bowl of wet items and tossed them toward me. Closing my eyes, I moved to get out its path, but I winced as the liquid splashed on me, causing my shirt to stick to my skin. When I lifted my head, looking like I was the beater for the mixer, Kevin froze.

I just stared at him, stunned, but when he started chuckling, I couldn't help but follow in his footsteps. Pretty soon, we were both laughing so hard we were holding our sides. I didn't know the last time I'd had this much fun. Sex had been an easy way to get some release until I was back with Lanie. Now it was so much more.

But this? *This* was just good, organic fun. I ended up sliding down onto the floor and laughing for another five minutes. We eventually pulled ourselves together enough to start cleaning up the mess. At one point, Kevin looked over at me and started laughing, telling me how the chocolate and liquids now made it look like I had a brown booger on my face. I had my revenge of laughter when he slipped on the wet floor and tumbled down.

"You two still okay over there? I can't see you, and it hurts to get up," Lanie shouted from the living room. The laughter in her voice had both Kevin and me looking at each other and smiling.

I maneuvered myself so I could see around the counter and told her we were fine.

She smiled back at me and mouthed a, "Thank you," before I looked back at Kevin and told him that we should probably finish cleaning up. After getting up, I washed my face and shook off my clothes as much as possible, wincing as a twinge of pain went through my leg from where I was still healing. Kevin went and got the broom and mop, while I worked on scrubbing down the counters.

After the kitchen was sparkling again, I went to shower. By the time I was out, Kevin had a new cake in the oven and was preparing the ingredients for the frosting.

Lanie's gaze met mine as I sat down on the couch next to her and asked, "*Avatar: The Last Airbender* or *Twister?*"

She and Kevin answered at the same time. "*Twister!*"

THE

D E N

DON'T LET THEM EAT YOU ALIVE

CHAPTER FORTY-FOUR

LANIE

SAN DIEGO

The next morning, I sat up in bed, pulled the sling off, and threw it across the room. Jason lifted an eyebrow at me as he sat up in bed and crossed his arms. "I hate that thing."

He stared at me a moment and then sighed as he got out of bed, came over, and picked me up, carrying me to the bathroom. "Come on, let's get you in the shower."

The man lifted me like I weighed absolutely nothing as I wrapped my arms around his neck. "How are you even able to do this? Your leg is still healing."

"It's fine. I promise."

"You know I'm capable of walking, right?"

"A king never lets his queen walk anywhere."

Dramatically rolling my eyes, I let him have this.

Taking a deep breath, I cemented my resolve as I told him, "I want to go back to work. Despite you wanting to carry me everywhere, I get around fine." He lifted an eyebrow at me. "Look, I just tire easily."

"Which is why the doctors have you out for a few more weeks, my queen." He set me down and lifted his hand to cradle my cheek. "I could call out for a family emergency for the rest of the trimester. There isn't much left. Could even finish out via video chat or online if the school would let me."

He slowly lifted my nightdress off while his fingers trailed lightly up my sides, and he stared deeply into my eyes.

Fucking hell, this man is my kryptonite.

"I've kept you from work long enough, Jase." My breath hitched when he bent down and kissed along my neck and then gently around my aching shoulder.

His lips pressed on the tender skin below my jaw, and then he murmured, "I don't care. Being here with you is what I want. If you want me to stay, I'll stay."

"I don't want you to go, but you have a life and a job up there." I really didn't want him to go. I loved being pampered by him and enjoying the little things. Watching movies, cooking, and even doing everyday chores felt right with him.

With a groan, he pulled back and leaned his forehead on mine. "I do, but my true life, the one I'm meant to live, is right here in my arms. I'm yours, Lanie."

My heart went into overdrive, and I could feel my pulse beating in my head, my ears, my fingers, and, most of all, my clit. Lifting my good arm and resting my hand on his cheek, I smiled. "I love you, Jason." My attention bounced between his eyes as I found the strength to say, "But it doesn't change the fact that you have a life you have been living in Trenton, and I've already kept you from it long enough. I'm okay to do day-to-day things here. I love how you and Kevin have repaired much of your relationship with each other, and having you here is a dream, but we've been living in a bubble."

"That bubble doesn't have to pop." His eyes were pleading, and I knew that if I asked him, he would quit his job and move in here with us permanently.

"I can't ask you to leave everything in Trenton. Not yet."

"Lanie . . ."

I reached up and put my finger on his lips. "I know that you would leave everything in a heartbeat, but let's get into the summer and we can discuss taking things further, okay?"

His chest expanded in what I assumed was a calming breath. "As you wish."

"Now, are you going to help me shower? Or are you just going to stand there and look at me like I kicked a puppy." I shook my head. "I'm sorry. I didn't mean to hurt your feelings."

As he turned on the shower, he undressed and then tested the water with his hand. "It's not that you hurt my feelings. I'm just all in, ready to go. I'm just disappointed you aren't there yet, my queen."

We stepped into the shower, and I wrapped my arms around his waist. "It's not that I'm not all in, Jase. I'm scared."

He rested his head on top of mine, and I felt a smile spread across his face. "You have every right to be. It's okay. I'm patient, and you're more than worth the wait."

I knew that. I just felt bad because I really wanted nothing more than to jump into the deep end with him and live happily ever after. I just . . . couldn't yet. When I'd tried to talk about the future a few times over the last couple weeks, the words had died before they would reach my tongue.

"What are you thinking?" I whispered as he held me in the shower.

"I'm confused." He kissed my forehead. "I've told you exactly where I stand with you, my queen. I'm all in and, as you said earlier, would pick up and move in a heartbeat to be here with you. You called me your husband at the hospital, but was that just so I could be there with you? What is holding you back from me?" There was a lump of emotion in the words, and it made my chest tighten.

"I don't know." He let out a heavy sigh, grabbed some of the shampoo, and started working it in my hair. "Seriously, Jase. I don't know what is stopping me. You've done everything you possibly could to prove that you want to be mine forever and don't ever want to put me through what happened before again. I know that, but I can't yet. Time. Just let me have a little more time."

He tipped my head back, nodding, and helped me wash my hair, and after he put the conditioner in it to set, he took a washrag and methodically washed every inch of my skin. When he got to my still-healing side, he was extra gentle and kissed the skin around it, as it was still tender where they'd removed the stitches.

His mouth trailed the washcloth, and he knelt as he worked his way down my body. When Jason got to my core, he lifted my leg and rested it on his shoulder. He met my eyes, asking for permission, and I smiled at him, giving him a nod. That was all he needed. His tongue snaked out and circled around my clit, teasing me before he flicked it.

A moan spilled from me, and my head tipped back as I threaded my fingers through his hair. His tongue tasted every inch of me, dipping into my entrance, and his nails dug into my skin as he moaned in pleasure. Vibrations rattled through me, causing my body to ignite, and my orgasm to hit hard and fast. My fingers tightened in his hair, and my hand shot out to grab the tiled wall to steady myself. I vaguely felt the pain in my shoulder, but I didn't care.

Only, Jason didn't stop. He continued to lick and suck me, overwhelming my senses. "Jase."

His only response was to slide two fingers into me and curl them with every withdrawal before thrusting back in. With a quick flick of his tongue, he pulled back while his fingers continued fucking me.

"That's it, my little slut. Cum for me again. I can feel you on edge. Fuck my fingers and ride my face." Then he dove back in, sucking and licking me with a renewed enthusiasm.

"Sir. Fuck."

The pleasure and pain were blurring as his fingers stopped thrusting but instead curled and teased my G-spot repeatedly, and I felt my whole body become weighed down with pleasure before Jason sucked my clit into his mouth, pressed it against the roof, and rolled it with his tongue. There was nothing I could do to hold back the orgasm as sound ceased to exist. It was just Jason's tongue and his fingers teasing me ceaselessly as his free hand slapped my ass. Vaguely, I heard him grunt and groan, but the pleasure ripping through my body overwrote everything.

Slowly and methodically, he released his hold on me and kissed his way up, his arms circling around my waist so I didn't collapse. When he reached my neck, he buried his head there and kissed me softly as my breathing returned to normal.

"You are the picture of perfection when you cum, my queen."

I chuckled against him as his softening cock pressed against my stomach. I leaned back to look at him and raised an eyebrow.

He smiled at me, kissed me softly, and whispered against my lips just loud enough I could hear him over the water, "As I said, you are the picture of perfection when you cum, my queen. I couldn't hold it back anymore with the taste of you on my tongue, the sound of you coming undone, the feel of you against my face and fingers. Perfection."

"I love you so much."

"Love you, too. Now let's get your hair rinsed out and you can start drying off while I wash up."

THE

DEN

DON'T LET THEM EAT YOU ALIVE

CHAPTER FORTY-FIVE

JASON

SAN DIEGO

She nodded and tipped her head back. My fingers massaged her scalp as I ran my fingers through her long black hair. The silky strands ran through my fingers as the conditioner rinsed out. Once I had it all clean, I turned the shower head toward the wall and helped her out of the shower, wrapping a large white towel around her. "Go get dressed. I won't be long."

She nodded and kissed me gently before sliding the shower curtain back into place. I heard her moving around as I cleaned up. Before long, she stepped out of the bathroom, and I heard one of the drawers close to the dresser in the bedroom. When I was done, I turned off the wate,r that had long since gone cold, and reached out for a towel, only to be met with a bare rack.

Opening the curtain, I looked above the toilet, where I had just grabbed one for Lanie and knew there were a couple more there, to see it was empty. Looking around the bathroom, I chuckled when I saw the lone pink washcloth hanging on the rail by the sink.

Of course she would. Well, ask and you shall receive, my queen.

I shook off as much of the water as I could, so I didn't get everything wet while walking around, and I stepped out into the bathroom. Grabbing the pink washcloth, I covered myself and strode right for Lanie. Her eyes went wide, and I saw her pupils dilate as I smirked at her. Backing her against the wall, I leaned on my forearm above her head and said softly, "Hello, darling."

Lanie stared at me a moment, her cheeks blooming red before she started chuckling. "You are such a dork."

"Yeah, but I'm *your* dork. Besides, you knew exactly what you were doing, leaving only this washcloth in there for me." I leaned down and kissed her softly. She moaned into me as I deepened the kiss and thrust my tongue into her mouth. Hers fought for dominance with mine, but it quickly relented as I tasted every inch of her. There was a deep moan that rumbled through her body, and I had to wrap my arm around her as her knees gave out.

"Okay. Okay. You've made your point."

Grinning, I pushed off the wall and grabbed a towel in the linen closet, knowing she was watching my ass the entire way.

THE

D E N

DON'T LET THEM EAT YOU ALIVE

THE

DEN

DON'T LET THEM EAT YOU ALIVE

Chapter Forty-Six

Jason

Trenton: Two months later

Cyress was sitting there, staring me down from across the table for far too long. I didn't relent my gaze and waited for him to call the bet. He was bluffing. He was being too aggressive and drawing out the bet for far too long considering it was just three of us at the table now. Not to mention, he'd highballed the bet without even looking at his cards.

He placed his bet, I immediately called, and his eyes went wide. "Why would you call on that?"

I smirked because I knew I had the hand, even with just the three of a kind. It was sad really. "Cyress, you run a gambling and poker den. What is wrong with you today? You are playing and acting like a fucking amateur."

"We all have our bad days, Rathborn," he gritted but nodded to the croupier, who dealt the next round. After we had a quick look at our cards, I waited for the flop. When nothing came of it, I folded and waited. I was a patient man when it came to poker, and I was curious what else I could pick up from his erratic body language. As I watched the next few hands play out, my confusion only amplified. Cyress seemed to be playing desperate. He was sweating, and instead of taking too long to bet, now he was betting almost immediately, his fingers tapping on the felt and his leg constantly in motion. Cyress had always been calm and collected while playing. Now, he just seemed . . . anxious. Sure, he'd had a couple good hands, but he'd played them all the same. Wild.

I knocked out the player sitting to my left, and he simply nodded his head before taking his place behind his chair, leaving just Cyress and me. When after several more hands, I knocked Cyress out, his eyes blazed with anger. "Watch it, Rathborn, or that pretty lady you care so much for might just get hurt."

Standing, I kept my head up and my expression neutral, although I wanted to punch the man for threatening Lanie. "Seriously, what is with you today?" I was actually a little worried. Even some of the bouncers around the room gave him wary looks. Shaking my head, I went to the cash office, and when Kai was done transferring the eighty thousand into the special account I had set up for Kevin, I headed upstairs. I nodded to Ashley, the bar manager, as she was putting away glasses before the rush tonight and headed out the front doors to the street.

I wasn't to the corner of the building before Cyress jumped out and swung. "You son of a bitch!"

My arm went up automatically to block the swipe of steel that came at me. I felt the sting before I kicked out. Metal clanged to the ground, and he fell backwards into one of the light poles on the street. The bouncers outside of the bar looked at each other and then away.

What the hell is going on that even his bouncers are turning a blind eye to a fight that involves him?

"Rathborn, tell me how you are cheating!" Again, his arm swung toward me in what appeared to be slow motion. I grabbed his wrist and twisted it too easily, pushing him against the wall. It was as if he didn't have any strength in him. I was a shit fighter, and the fact that I had the upper hand on him weirded me out. "How are you doing it?"

"I keep telling you, I'm not."

His body jerked, he twisted his head to the side, and he projectile vomited all over the sidewalk. I jumped back and looked at the bouncers at the door. They hung their heads low, and when they played rock, paper, scissors, I couldn't help but chuckle. The tall, bald, darker-skinned one cursed and then slumped his shoulders as he made his way over.

Cyress was still violently vomiting and was completely passed out.

"Jason, I'll take over from here."

"What the fuck is with him tonight?"

His huge shoulder lifted a smidge as he crouched beside him. "I didn't say shit, but there's a rumor he's been hitting some new product on the street, and he has complained about money issues. If it weren't for Kai, none of the workers in the bar or The Den would get paid."

"That would explain why he's after me so hard."

Cyress rolled onto his back and lay there still completely out.

The bouncer looked at me and lifted an eyebrow. "You have taken him for more money than anyone has. He's right pissed. Has tried to see about banning you from The Den because of it."

"Why hasn't he? I would."

Cyress started heaving again, and the bouncer growled, "I should let you choke on your own vomit, you piece of shit." My eyebrows went up in shock as I waited. He rolled Cyress back onto his side. "As for why he hasn't? Kingsley. Somehow this fuck bubble has it in his head you are protected by him."

"Not to my knowledge." Not explicitly. Sure, Kingsley had transferred funds into a shell account for me to play on when he needed to, but Cyress shouldn't know anything about that. That didn't mean I was untouchable—nobody was. Well, except for Lanie apparently.

He nodded, and without looking up from Cyress, who was heaving on the sidewalk, he said, "I'll get him taken care of. Get out of here."

Without saying another word, I headed to my car, pulled out my phone, and skipped over my usual contact, dialing Don Kingsley directly.

After four rings, Don Kingsley answered, "What can I do for you, Rathborn?"

"I need some answers."

He sighed through the phone. "That's what you have Chase for."

Shaking my head as though he could see it, I opened my door to the car and slid in. "Not this time. Sit down and talk to me for a few minutes."

"What do you want to know?"

"First, did you figure out who it was at the market?"

A light chuckle came through the phone. "What am I, an amateur? Of course we did, and I'm working on it. That's all you need to know."

The tone of his voice had the deadly finality to it that if I pushed, I'd likely have some "bad luck" come my way. Taking a deep breath, I asked, "And what is it that has you so centered on Lanie?"

"Chase already told you she's safe with us. She has our protection."

"I realize that is what Chase told me. I want to hear it from you on your word. And tell me why you jumped on board so quickly. It can't be because I'm on the payroll. I only collect information over cards for you, sir." I took a deep breath. I could feel my blood pressure rising, but I tried to remember who I was talking to. "So, what is it about my queen that has you all but locking her up in a tower?"

"She's important."

No shit, Sherlock.

I waited for him to elaborate, but when he didn't, I asked again, "Don Kingsley, why are you protecting my girl? To you she's just some random connected to one of your men."

"She's not a random. It's a coincidence that you are connected to her, but it's a family matter. I won't say more at this time."

"A family matter. Is she related to you or something?"

"Rathborn, I said I won't say more right now. However, rest assured that she is safe in our hands. I'm going to make the assumption you are going to ask her about it?"

"See, that is what I don't understand, sir. When we were together before, she didn't have any family, so I'm struggling to see how the dots connect."

His voice was serious as he said, "Because you don't have all the information."

Every ounce of anger at being given the run around and all the fear for my queen came to the surface as I yelled, "Then give it to me!"

"Rathborn," he shouted through the phone, and I knew I really had pushed my luck.

"Fine." I took another breath. "Will you eventually tell me why you have a special interest in Lanie?"

Silence stretched out on the line. "In time, Rathborn. There are things that need to happen before . . ." There was a heavy sigh that came through the speakers of my car before he continued, "Before all is revealed."

"You realize that sounds like a villain monologue, right?"

He chuckled. "Hey, there are a lot of people in this city who think me the villain, and I'm okay with them believing that. Trust me, Jason. It won't be much longer before I'll tell you everything."

I leaned my head back on the headrest of my seat and let out a long breath. "Fine. Do you need me anytime soon? I sort of just took Cyress for a buttload of cash, and he's currently puking his guts up in the alley on some new sort of drug. Bodyguard said he's been trying some new shit on the streets and he's draining The Den dry. Kai's making sure that everyone's getting paid, but Cyress is losing it."

"Not for now. Probably best for you to lie low for a bit then. Be safe."

"Will do." Then the line went dead.

Well, fuck. That didn't lend any answers.

CHAPTER FORTY-SEVEN

LANIE

SAN DIEGO

"Thanks again, Ms. Jones."

A strand of her long grey hair whipped in the wind as she chuckled. "It's no problem to bring you down here." Her attention shifted to my brother, who was shifting on his feet. I reached out and took his hand as she continued, "You know how much I adore Kevin. He will sit with me for hours and do impossible puzzles when he's not busy at the center."

Nodding, I squeezed Kevin's hand, and he looked up at me "Everything is going to be okay."

"Sissy, your shoulder still bothers you."

A corner of my lip lifted. "I'm okay, and you will be with Ms. Jones. My shoulder feels really good, too." I moved my arm around as the muscle ached and pulled. Even months later, I still had it wrapped for support, and the doctors had just asked that I take it easy for a bit on it. In reality, it was my side that hurt more than my shoulder. I'd bend the wrong way and it would hurt like hell.

"I'll miss you." He pulled me to him and held me tight. I couldn't help but wrap my arms around him and hold him as his chest hitched.

"Oh, Kev." I rubbed my hand across his back until his breathing evened out. Since the incident at the center and the shooting, he had seemed to withdraw into himself and didn't want to be left alone. Someone he trusted had to be somewhere close to him. Not necessarily in the same room, but within a close distance. I pulled back slightly and rested my forehead to his. "I'll call you when I get to Jason's, okay?"

He pulled back, nodded his head, his eyes focused on the ground, and wrinkled his nose. The airport drop-off was loud with people yelling, cars honking, and the beeping of the crosswalk signals, and I was sure that he was getting overstimulated.

"Okay." I looked behind me to the ticket counters then over to the security line. "I need to get going. Even with TSA clearance, it's going to take a minute to get through security."

When I turned back to them, Ms. Jones asked, "Why aren't you just driving?"

"I needed to finish up some things today at work, and while driving would have been cheaper, I didn't want to get there in the middle of the night. This gets me more time with Jason. Plus, I can get a little more work done on the plane this way. Jason will still have to work the rest of the week, but then he's mine."

She smiled and then looked at Kevin. "I just got a large white circle puzzle for us to work on. Afterwards, you can draw or paint something on it."

My brother's face morphed from being concerned about me into happiness, and he started heading toward the garage.

"I love you, Kevin!" I shouted after him.

He lifted a hand and waved to me as Ms. Jones chuckled and trotted on after him. I couldn't help but smile. He really did enjoy his time with our neighbor.

Grabbing my suitcase, I headed toward security. After putting my carry-on in the bin and emptying my pockets, my phone pinged. Looking at it quickly and seeing it was Kami, I tossed it into the bin and waited my turn for the scanner.

It never ceased to amaze me what they could pick up. Of course, they picked up the small piece of metal that was still in my hip from a childhood accident. I explained to them what it was and exactly where it was located. When they cleared me, I grabbed my things out of the bin and looked at my phone.

Kami: Jason is picking you up.

Lanie: You okay?

Kami: Don't you know it. I'm lying in bed next to Eric, who has completely rocked my world.

Lanie: Well, good to know the bestie had a good orgasm or six.

Lanie: Does he know I know he's picking me up?
Kami: No. So act surprised. He has the whole visit planned out.
Lanie: Bestie, care to explain?
Kami: No. He swore me to secrecy.
My heart started racing as I headed down the terminal toward my gate.
Lanie: Kamille . . . is he proposing? If so, I've got to see if there is somewhere here that I can at least get my nails done.
Kami: Not to my knowledge, but he is going to lay things all out. It's okay, Lanie. I promise. Jason and I had a long talk. I'm not telling you any more. I've already said too much.
Jase: You at the airport yet? Please don't miss your flight.
I sighed. He *would* tease me. *You miss one connecting flight because you have to pee and you never hear the end of it.* I flipped back to my text string with Kami. Jason could hold tight for a minute.
Lanie: Love you, Kami. I'll see you tomorrow.
Kami: <3 you too, bitch.
I chuckled as I made my way to the gate with a few minutes to spare and found somewhere to sit. The sun was still barely coming through the windows, and there were a few kids running around with different memorabilia and hyped on consuming sugar all day. I couldn't help but smile as I pulled my headphones out of my backpack to call Jason.

Sticking them in my ears, I started the video call. When his face popped up on the phone, the sounds of the gym filtered through. He was dripping sweat and shirtless, all while running on the treadmill. I couldn't help the breath of air that burst out of me. If he had been in front of me, I would have dropped to my knees instantly.

"Cat got your tongue there, beautiful?"

"Jase, you did this on purpose." Heat bloomed across my cheeks, and I pulled my shirt out and in, billowing air in to cool me down. "That wasn't fair."

He grinned, clearly pleased with my reaction to him. "Well, I wasn't planning on you video calling me."

"I have a few minutes before my flight starts boarding."

The roll of his eyes was gold medal worthy. "That means you got there ten minutes before boarding. You like to cut it close, don't you?"

"Listen here. I'm at the gate with time to kill. I don't see the problem."

He reached behind the phone then jumped off the treadmill. When he grabbed his phone, he gave me a spectacular view of his chest.

"Jase," I chastised as the woman sitting next to me shifted in her seat. My attention flicked to her, and she was beet red and crossing her legs, taking a deep breath.

Yeah, I know. He's all mine too.

His chuckle filtered through my headphones, and when he lifted his phone, there was a playful heat in his eyes. "You heard from Kami?"

"Yeah. She was hanging out with Eric. Okay, well, lying in bed exhausted with Eric." I rolled my eyes. He chuckled, and then he was walking into the locker room. Naked men flowed across the screen behind him, and I saw his lip lift slightly. *He's doing this on purpose.* "I swear you love to tease me."

"What are you talking about, sweetheart?"

I just glared at him as he set his phone in his locker and started toweling off. "I am going to hang up now," I warned, but then the airline was calling for people to start lining up. I let out a long sigh. "Seriously though, they just called for boarding. I'll see you in a couple hours."

"Or sooner," he mumbled just barely loud enough for me to hear.

"What was that?" I teased.

He shook his head, smiling. "You didn't eat dinner yet, right?"

"No. Figured I'd have dinner with Kami after she picks me up." There was a twitch of his lips, and then I saw the side eye he gave the camera. Narrowing my eyes at him, I thought about what Kami had been saying about him having the weekend all planned out. "What are you up to?"

"Nothing. I'll see you soon. You get on that plane, and I need to get in the shower. Love you."

"Love you, too." Then he hung up the phone, just as they called my boarding group. I grabbed my things and lined up for my flight.

TRENTON

Two hours later, I was walking out the doors to the pick-up line when strong arms wrapped around me from behind and a kiss was placed on my cheek before Jason buried his head in my neck. "Fuck, I've missed you."

"It's just been a few weeks, Jase." I leaned back and cherished the feel of him holding me. "Decided to surprise me, huh?"

He turned me to face him and cradled my head in his hands. "I moved the meeting I had to last night so I could be the one to pick you up. I didn't want to miss a minute of you being here."

His lips brushed against mine, causing my entire body to heat. Leaning in, I kissed him, melting a little at how good it felt to have my body pressed against his. Jase's hands slid down and grasped my neck as his tongue pushed through my lips, tasting every inch it could reach. When his hand gripped my neck tighter, a deep moan crawled out of me, and I pressed closer to him. My body was alight with his kiss. This one felt different, like it meant more.

When he pulled back, he placed a quick kiss on my nose and then pulled me into his chest to hold me close. We stood there for a long minute, just cherishing the moment. The erratic beating of his heart against me rooted me to my spot. "What's wrong, Jase?" His head moved back and forth before a kiss was placed on the top of my hair. "Don't lie to me. I can hear your heart beating faster than usual."

I stepped back from him and looked him square in the eye. His focus bounced between both of my eyes before he let out a long breath. "I've missed you and want to talk to you about a few things."

Blood drained from every cell of my body, and I felt numb. Why kiss me like that just to break it off? I swallowed around the tightness in my throat, and his face became too blurry.

"No. No. No, sweetheart. Don't think for a minute that we are done. I will never be done with you. You are my forever." He kissed me hard, and I wanted to believe him but . . .

His lips left mine as he said, "I love you with everything I am, which is why we need to talk. First, though, let's get dinner."

Jason's arm stayed tight around my waist as we walked to the parking garage. Memories of him taking me in the back seat of the top floor last time I'd been here popped into my mind, and I tried to suppress a smile. We paid for parking, and then when we got to his car, he opened the door and helped me inside, kissing me quickly before shutting the door. Once he was settled, his gaze met mine and there was a mischievous glint in his eye.

Within minutes, we were merging onto the expressway. My hand roamed up and down the inside of his leg, making him shift in his seat. After about five solid minutes of me teasing him, he groaned. "Lanie . . ."

"Yes, Jason?" My voice was light and teasing, but he growled at me again. "What?" I turned to face him and leaned my head on his shoulder. It was a little awkward with the center console, but I lifted my head and kissed his cheek while running my finger up and down his very hard cock.

"Lanie." His voice was a tense whisper. A smile spread on my face as I sat back into my seat and noticed how he sped up a little.

"Where we going?"

"You want trouble this early in the trip, I'll give you trouble." A smirk lifted at the corner of his lips as he made his way down the road and took the next exit. Before I knew it, we were in a parking garage, and he had me over his shoulder and was heading inside the elevator.

"Put me down, Jason."

"Nope. You wanted to play with fire. My little slut is going to get burned." The elevator opened, and he rushed down the hall. The door was barely shut when my feet were on the ground again and he was ordering, "On your knees, my queen."

I dropped, unable to ignore his command, and looked up at him through my eyelashes, licking my lips. His eyes stayed focused on me as he took his jacket off, toed his shoes off into the corner, and then slowly started unbuttoning his shirt, before laying it over the edge of the couch. Quickly, I shed my sweatshirt, leaving just my T-shirt. When I went to remove it, he commanded, "Don't you dare move. You want to act like a whore with no patience in the car, then I'll treat you like one."

He disappeared for a moment, and when he came back, he ordered, "Hands behind your back."

I did as he'd said. Jason circled behind me, looped the rope around my hands, bent down, and kissed my neck. "Safeword."

"Strawberry, Sir."

"That's a good girl." Then he pulled the rope tighter and down around my ankles. Once I was effectively hogtied on my knees, he circled back around to the front of me and asked, "Do you mind if that shirt is ruined?"

"No, Sir." While I really liked this shirt because it was comfortable as hell, I was too horny *not* to allow him to do anything that wasn't a hard line for me right now.

He smiled but continued in an almost pained voice, "Good, and I'll buy you new jeans. Anything you fucking want."

When his gaze met mine, I saw the lust and restraint in his eyes, so I simply responded, "Yes, Sir."

He grabbed a pair of scissors and cut up the center of my T-shirt, careful not to get my bra, letting the cool metal slide against my skin. After slicing the shirt off, he moved to my jeans. Grabbing the front, he unbuttoned them, slowly sliding the zipper down. Then he trailed the tip of the scissors along my skin, to my hip, and cut my jeans down one leg.

The cool metal was enticingly erotic, and I wanted to press my legs together to relieve the pressure quickly building in my clit. Slowly, my breathing became more methodical, and my stomach tightened with every glide of steel across my skin. Kneeling before me, he kissed me softly as he slipped the scissors between my stomach and my clothes. The first cut was made, and then another before he stopped and pressed the blunt end of the scissors against my clit.

"Sir." My nipples hardened, and I whimpered.

"Control," he whispered against my skin as he made another cut, and another before he had cut through my jeans through the center of me. As he stood, he took his belt off and set it on the coffee table next to me.

Once behind me, he cut through the rest of my jeans so that he could remove them from my body. He was more careful with my bra and unclipped the straps in the back and then the band so that it could come off without damaging it. He quickly tossed it to the couch and then helped me down to the floor. With a few strategic tugs, Jason had my feet closer to my hips with my legs spread, so I was sitting much like a frog, with my hands in the small of my back.

"Damn, you look good like that for me. All tied up, your beautiful pussy all out and ready for me to devour. The only thing I need is for your ass to be blushing red as I pound into it."

As the vision burst through me and my core pulsed, my nipples tingled. Wrapping my hair in his hand, he pulled me forward so my chest was leaning against the couch. Then leather snapped, and I took a deep breath. Just as I let it out, a sound of the belt hitting skin went through the air, and the painful pleasure rocketed through me.

"One for teasing me in the car."

A hit on the other ass cheek and I was moaning.

"Two for looking up at me with those fuck me eyes."

Smack. Smack.

"Three and Four for those tits that just beg to be sucked. Five for those beautiful nipples that stick out straight and hard for my attention."

Smack.

"Six for being such an amazing caretaker for those you love." His hand caressed each orb of my ass before a soft kiss was laid on both of them. "Always giving what you can to your people."

He pulled away, and the belt landed hard against the already sore skin. I couldn't hold back the scream that came out, but it wasn't one of pain. Well, it was, but the pleasure of him whipping my ass was all-consuming. I shifted my shoulders, and he lifted my hips, so I was in a modified doggy style position, before running his hands over the globes of my ass.

"Seven for being so wet for me that I can't wait to see the puddle on the hardwood." His hands pushed my legs farther apart, and then he licked me from clit to ass. As quickly as his tongue was on me, it was gone.

Smack.

"Eight for tasting so divine."

Gods, I was so close to cumming. "Sir, please." The belt ran over my spine and down my back.

When it left my skin, there was a pause before it came down on my pussy. That was all I needed to fall over the edge. My orgasm rolled through my body, and even my legs were shaking.

"My queen. My slut. My whore looks so good cumming for her Sir." Then he was thrusting into me, prolonging my orgasm as he pounded nonstop. The pain of the spankings, heightening each thrust, quickly pushed me toward another release.

"Fuck, yes, Sir. Please, fuck me hard."

Jason didn't disappoint. He turned me and laid me down before gripping the rope holding my hands in place. With each pull, my body jerked with the power behind each stroke. My shoulder was getting angry, but it only heightened the pain to pleasure going through my body. My back bowed as he held me in place, my boobs swaying so that my nipples brushed the floor, and I was so damn close. Jason's grunting and groaning filled the air, and then he smacked my ass.

"Damn, slut. You love me using you, don't you?"

"Yes."

Another smack. "Do you want me to fill this pussy with my cum?"

"Yes, Sir."

"That's it. Take my cock, you cumslut. Fuck yes, I'm going to fill you with my cum until you get pregnant."

"Fuck!" I groaned as my orgasm took over, and he quickly followed. Stars danced before me and a flash of cold went through my body before my vision tunneled and everything went black.

The next thing I knew, I was untied and cradled in his lap.

"There you are, sweetheart. I wondered how long it was going to take for you to wake up." He kissed my temple, and I looked up to smile at him.

"How long was I out?"

He shrugged. "Just a little over a minute. Long enough for me to catch my breath, untie you, and put some cream on your ass to help with the sting."

"Thank you."

"For what?"

"Taking care of me. You always do." I snuggled up into him, and he held me tight. I was lying there processing what all had just happened. "Hey, Jase."

He gave me a kiss on the forehead and hummed.

"Did you mean it when you said you wanted to get me pregnant?"

He took a deep breath and then let it out slowly through his nose. "I did." He waited a moment, and I just sat there. I didn't hate the idea. I had always thought we would have kids together. "Was it too much?"

The sudden vulnerability in his voice made me love him even more. "No."

"You sure?"

"Yes, Jase. I'm sure." I shifted so that I could look him directly in the eye. "You said once you were all in and that you wanted to create a life together. I just never thought you would have a breeding kink."

He nodded. "Having a life with you hasn't changed. I'm not sure it's a kink, but . . . well, maybe it is. I can't wait to see you growing our child. To know that we made them."

I took a scared, ragged breath but made myself say the words that my heart knew were true. "I want that for us. I want us to create a life together. Kids, a home, the whole bit."

He was kissing me instantly. It wasn't hard and desperate, but instead was filled with something more than need. I could feel the love in it.

When he pulled back, he simply said, "One day very soon, I'll wife you up and make it all happen."

"Nothing would make me happier."

THE —

DEN

DON'T LET THEM EAT YOU ALIVE

Chapter Forty-Eight

Jason

TRENTON

A few days later, Lanie and I were finishing up dinner out on the patio of a restaurant after a long day of hiking up near Lake Jackson, when Cyress stepped up to the table, glaring at the two of us. "Looks like your girl came out okay." His gaze trailed up her body, and I tightened my fists. Lanie's face went from annoyance to anger.

She met his gaze and spat, "You!"

He smiled at her. "Me."

"Lanie?"

"Remember that night I was at the bar with Kami and you picked me up because a guy mentioned you and other things he shouldn't know about?"

Rage filled me as my head snapped toward Cyress. "You fucking asshole."

Cyress blew off both of our anger and smiled at us. He met Lanie's gaze and continued, "That night at the bar, I didn't get a chance to introduce myself. I'm Cyress Dazar." Her eyes narrowed at him, and just as she was going to say something, he persisted. "I warned you that you need to be careful who you associate with. So glad something worse didn't happen in San Diego."

Just behind Cyress, I saw Don Kingsley coming out of the restaurant with Chase just behind him. Our gazes met, and he raised an eyebrow. I wasn't sure what he saw in my face, but Don Kingsley came to stand just behind Cyress, who stiffened when the Don asked, "Is there a problem here?"

Lanie looked like she had seen a ghost as she looked right past Don Kingsley to Chase and whispered, "Chase."

I couldn't help but reach over and take her hand, which she squeezed tightly. Her focus switched over to Don Kingsley and didn't move as she hardened her expression. So, I met Cyress's gaze and said, "No. He was just leaving."

"Your connections won't prevent the inevitable, Rathborn." Without a look in Don Kingsley's direction, he strode off.

"Mr. Rathborn," Don Kingsley greeted with a nod before his eyes met Lanie's, and he smiled softly. "Melanie."

I narrowed my eyes in confusion as she breathed, "It's Lanie."

"What's Cyress's problem today, Rathborn?"

I looked back and forth between Lanie and Don Kingsley, her eyes full of a longing and sadness I couldn't quite understand. I also couldn't help but notice how Chase looked at Lanie like she was an angel come to life. "He still doesn't like to lose money. He also talked about what happened in San Diego."

Don Kingsley lifted the corner of his mouth. "You've bested him more than a few times at the table, and he's none too happy about it."

A laugh bubbled out. "You could say that."

"Jase, what are you talking about?" Lanie whispered. She was staring at me, but I refused to look at her, keeping my attention on Don Kingsley.

Lifting an eyebrow, Don Kingsley smirked at me. "Melanie, does— I'm sorry, Lanie doesn't know?" I shook my head, hearing her groan. His bows crunched together as he studied her, fire burning in that gaze. *Why would he be so angry? She's the one who got hurt.* "Best bring her up to date soon."

"Someone want to tell me what the fuck is going on here?" Lanie asked just above a whisper. When no one answered her, she growled, "Jason Hill Rathborn, answer me."

Her tone and use of my full name almost made me wince, but my attention stayed on the man in front of me. When Don Kingsley held my gaze and raised an eyebrow, I finally looked at her and squeezed her hand tightly. Rage was rolling off her in waves, and the frustration in her eyes had me swallowing hard. "You mentioned something about him possibly being connected to what happened in San Diego?" He nodded once. "Cyress is the only one I've pissed off."

Don Kingsley put his hands in his pockets as he lifted his chin. "And we took care of the four idiots in San Diego. We just don't have the connection between them and Cyress yet. Anyone else you could have pissed off at the table?"

My focus held Lanie's questioning, worried gaze. Her hand was holding mine so tight, the tips of my fingers were starting to tingle. "No. I know everyone I've sat across from, and we've always ended up joking and laughing." Looking up at the Don, I hardened my expression. "He's the only one who is pissed I've taken him for so much. As you, I'm sure, are aware, he's also the only one who I've come to blows with over his inability to manage finances. Cyress likely didn't expect for me to be as good as I am."

Don Kingsley looked at his son, who nodded. Chase looked between his father and Lanie again before reaching into his wallet and giving her a business card, saying, "We will talk soon, Lanie." She swallowed but nodded. When Chase got to the gate at the entrance of the patio area, he jerked his head to some guys who were standing there to follow him.

What was that about? How do they know each other?

I watched him rush off but then brought my focus back to Don Kingsley. He was watching his son, a small smile on his face.

"He's a good kid."

"He is. He'll follow in the family business, but I wanted him to get more of an education first." His gaze met mine again as his smile brightened slightly. "He loved your class. Wanted to add a major, and even though I told him I didn't care if his degree was in basket weaving, he decided to get a minor in history but keep the business degree. Said he still wanted to have a degree that would help our family."

I just nodded as Lanie's hand squeezed mine. "Jason. Answers." She was purposely not looking at the man next to us.

"Well, I'll leave you to your evening, Mr. Rathborn. We will be in contact soon."

I looked between Lanie's fiery gaze and Don Kingsley's stoic one. "Any chance you'll tell me the connection between you two now?"

Don Kingsley held my gaze a moment before he looked to Lanie, who stared him down and said, "Sit your ass down."

My eyes went wide as I watched her glare at him. Without taking his eyes off her, he reached behind him and grabbed a chair and whirled it around to sit in it. She lifted an eyebrow at him, and I was scared and proud of my queen basically making the Don do her bidding.

"Don Kingsley?" I asked.

Lanie's eyes widened for just a second. "Don? As in a mafia don?" He lifted his chin and nodded once. "Is that why you left?" He shook his head and pulled on the end of his jacket at the wrists. "Are you going to actually explain? Say something? It's been over fifteen years, and you can't do anything but shake and nod your head at me? If you can't have the fucking balls to tell me, then I believe Jason asked you a question. Maybe you would dare to provide him an answer?"

If I didn't know any better, I would think that Don Kingsley was actually nervous about talking to her. He shifted in his seat, foot tapping on the ground irregularly, and he took a little larger breath than he usually did.

"Lanie . . ."

She lifted her eyebrows and gave him a look that clearly said, "I'm waiting."

He swallowed and shifted again.

"Fine." She spat and turned to me. "Jason, while you know him as Don Kingsley, I grew up knowing him as Uncle Thom. He is my mother's brother."

I blinked in shock. "Don Kingsley. The man who has almost as strong of a hold on the underground as Max Vispania . . . is your uncle?"

"Estranged, but apparently they are one in the same." Her breathing hitched as she turned to face him. "I didn't know you were here. Didn't know that Chase was here."

Kingsley's gaze softened. "I am sorry for that. We should have reached out to you after your parents died."

I lifted my hands in a wait motion and asked, "How could you *not* know that, Lanie?"

"What part of *estranged* doesn't that beautiful, handsome brain of yours comprehend?" She turned to Kingsley again and, while still addressing me, watched his reactions as she told her story. "There was a huge fight between my mother and *Uncle Thom* when I was about thirteen. Mom said it had nothing to do with me, but rather it was about Kevin. I didn't understand why, though. I knew he could be a lot to handle sometimes, but she didn't elaborate on what the specific problem was. She just told me that Don Kingsley was never going to be in our lives again and to forget he ever existed."

"That is one version of the story." Kingsley leaned against the table and folded his hands together and watched them. "The other is much more complicated, and we will have to cover all that another time, but please know that once Rathborn told me what was happening to you, we immediately had people watching over you. You are known as an untouchable. Anyone who tries will be removed from existence."

I saw her eyes grow large, the breath she took in realization, and then finally the rage that was about to burst from her, so I cut her off. "My queen, you didn't notice those guys. It was Cyress's assholes that were following you. Chase's guys tracked the others down and . . ."

"Disposed of them," Don Kingsley said matter-of-factly.

Lanie crossed her arms. "So kind of you to step in and help after we fought *for years* to stay afloat."

His gaze hardened as he looked at her. "Things were in utter chaos after your parents died."

"Yeah? Tell me about it." She mocked him by leaning forward on the table. "Tell me about the utter chaos of my parents dying and me trying to sort things out like a roof over Kevin's and my head, food on our table, continuing to get him to school, keeping his programs going, supporting his art, getting him to pass high school at all. No, no you didn't have to do any of that. I did. So tell me about how I had to go to my boss and beg for a flexible schedule because I am all that Kevin has left. How I had to stuff and manage all my own grief of them dying to make sure that Kevin, my little brother, *your fucking nephew*, continued to grow and thrive."

I swallowed, and my eyes were a little wide at her going off on him. I'd never seen anyone lay into him like that. Turning to look at Don Kingsley, I was shocked to see he was taking it from her.

"It wasn't that easy."

She threw her hands up into the air. "Then *do* explain, *Uncle* Thom. Explain to me *how* it wasn't easy for to you to leave Kevin and me to fend for ourselves after both my dad and my mom, your sister, died. You could have contacted us then. Mom was dead. There was nothing stopping you."

"There was some fallout—"

Her voice smoothed out to become the tone I had heard him give people one step from becoming nothing but a meat suit. The problem was that he had unlocked Lanie's rage. She was going to say her piece.

"Fallout. Okay, let's talk about fallout. How many times did you have to lie to Kevin about why you had a screaming headache because you hadn't eaten anything more than a piece of toast all day because you made sure he never went hungry? Oh right, that was me. How many times did you take on freelance accounting work on the hope that you would be able to get paid on time to make rent that month? Oh right, me again. How hard did you have to work to get the slightest increase in pay, knowing that even just a three percent raise was going to help ease the budget just the slightest? How many times did you have to open up emails and mail to find out you are just over the threshold for financial assistance and realize that you are too rich to get help from the state and county, but too poor to be able to put food on the table for both people in the house every day? As the Don to a section of Trenton, I am willing to bet you haven't skipped a meal on purpose."

"Lanie, that isn't fair." Don Kingsley's voice broke at the words. I blinked at him, still in shock that this was coming from my queen. It also didn't escape my notice that everyone around us had gotten very quiet and were trying not to make it obvious they were paying attention.

"Fair." She tipped her head back and laughed. "Fair. That's rich. You know what isn't fair? How about going *years* thinking no one gives a shit about you or your brother when you know there is extended family, but not a single one of them thought to reach out and offer a damn bit of assistance. Even if it was just to come over and hang out for emotional support. To know that you weren't alone. How was it fair that I had to make the decision whether to get new work shoes because my toes were peeking through the bottom or get Kevin a warm jacket for the winter? That was me, multiple winters in a row actually. Thank goodness we live in Southern California and we don't get snow and freezing temperatures. I understand you and Mom had a falling out, but it also wasn't fair that I lost both of my parents and had to become the parent to my younger brother. I love him with everything I am, but I shouldn't have had to be the person that was completely responsible for raising him. I did it though, with no complaint. I would break down occasionally from the stress, sure, but I don't regret one damn moment of it. Not. A. Single. One." She jabbed a finger on the table, emphasizing each word.

She stared at him, almost daring him to say anything. The man so many feared just swallowed. Honestly, I didn't know what to say to all of that either. Lanie had never told me it had been that hard. She had smoothed so much of that out before we'd met. She'd had a stable, good paying job and had a disposable income of sorts, or at least enough to get Kevin extra art supplies.

"Now, if you two don't mind, I'm going to go to the bathroom." She stood, and I watched her weave through the tables and step inside the main restaurant.

My heart broke for her.

"Did you know?" Don Kingsley asked me.

I shook my head. "I had no idea it had been that bad for them. By the time we met, Kevin was excelling in high school, and while we were dating the first time, she had life stable and consistent." Forcing myself to look at him, I saw a man who was ashamed. "There's more to the story than she knows, isn't there?"

He took a deep breath and ran his hand through his hair. "Yeah, and she needs to know, but this isn't the place to have that discussion. It's a very tangled web that will completely reshape her childhood and how she views her parents."

"You have to tell her, sir."

His gaze met mine and there was true pain there. "I don't want to hurt her any more than she already is."

I took a deep breath and saw her come back out into the patio area. "If you want to mend this relationship, you have to give her all the information and let her sort it out."

When she got back to the table, she put her hands on her hips and looked at me. "Now, you are going to take me home and explain what he was saying about tables and all the money that Cyress apparently thinks you owe him. You have some explaining to do as well."

"Yes, my queen." There was no way I was going to disobey her at that moment. She was owed answers from me. She wasn't wrong about that.

I stood and put the cash on the table to cover the bill. Lanie reached over and took my hand in hers, lacing our fingers together and holding them tight.

Don Kingsley stood and looked between us. "I hope that you will give me a chance to explain my side of things to you at some point soon. In the meantime, we still have people watching over you."

She nodded and then pulled me out of the restaurant. When we got around the corner, I pulled her to a stop and into my arms. Her arms swung around me, and her hands gripped my shirt tight. She took a few hitched breaths, and when she pulled back a few minutes later, I wiped her tears away, kissed her forehead, and wrapped an arm around her to lead her to the car.

We sat in silence the entire way back to my condo, and when we were finally back inside, she sat down on the couch and stared at the floor. There was confusion, longing, and sadness all flicking across her features, and I didn't know what to do.

"I didn't know he was so powerful here in Trenton. I knew, even then, that he was well off, and partially because of some shady shit, but I was too young to care enough to ask questions. Dad always said that he had done really well in real estate and other business. He also told me not to ask any about it and never mention him to my mom." I waited, letting her think through her thoughts. "Seeing him today . . . it brought up all those questions from my childhood, and then there was such longing in his eyes as he stared at me. He tried to cover it up, but I saw it."

"Do you want to talk to him?"

I sat down next to her, and she took my hand in hers. Lanie's fingers played with mine for a moment, and then she let out a heavy sigh. "I don't know. I want to respect my mom and dad's wishes, but at the same time, they *are* dead. Besides, I sort of unloaded on him. I don't care who he is here. I didn't say a single thing that wasn't true. He's had over ten years since my parents left to reconnect." She looked up at me, and there was conflict but determination in her eyes. "But what if he has the answer as to who Kevin's biological dad is?"

"The fact he said that you two should talk soon . . . that gives me the feeling you don't know the whole story. You were just a teenager. They've been gone for years. You are a grown adult able to make your own choices."

Not to mention the way Chase thought he had seen a ghost and just wanted to pull you into his arms and hold you.

She nodded. "Chase and I used to be really close growing up. We used to text each other all the time, even after Uncle Thom and Mom stopped talking, but then Mom found out and started checking my phone monthly to make sure I wasn't still talking to him."

"That's sad. You lost your best friend when she ostracized them from your part of the family."

She gave a quick, affirming nod before saying, "I want to go shower. Then when I come back out, you need to tell me what that conversation with Uncle Thom was all about as well."

My throat bobbed as I swallowed hard. "Yeah, I owe you an explanation."

Chapter Forty-Nine

Jason

Trenton

Lanie had a lot to sort through. The day had been wonderful until Don Kingsley had stepped up and revelations had been made that had turned most of what I knew into a mud pit. Once she came back from taking her shower, I was about to tell her that I'd paid for my parents' expenses, my house, and car by gambling and winning most of that money from Cyress Dazar.

I wasn't ashamed of it. I hadn't become a junky, and while the rush of betting and winning was addicting, I was one of the lucky ones who didn't let it destroy my life. Mostly because I was good at it. I hadn't been to a game for myself in weeks. I would, of course, continue to play as Don Kingsley needed me to. Anything that I won was for me to take home and put into the savings account for Kevin. There was more than my great grandkids would need for their retirement, if they were smart. Hell, Lanie and I very well could live on just the interest right now.

Sitting down on the couch, I leaned forward with my elbows on my knees. Clasping my hands together, I looked over my shoulder toward the bedroom. I wouldn't lie to her nor hide anything from her ever again. This was my second chance, and I had no plans on living another day where she wasn't a part of it. I had walked away from her once. I wouldn't survive doing it again.

I didn't hear the water turn off, but while I was lost in my own thoughts, Lanie had come back into the living room and sat down on the couch, feet under her butt, watching me. I didn't dare break eye contact to take in how fucking beautiful she was with her wet hair and the thin-strapped sleep dress she had on. She had her shoulder wrapped, and I swallowed, wondering just how much it still bothered her.

I sat there leaning on my knees and looking at her, waiting for her to start. I had no idea where to begin. We just sat there staring at each other for a minute before she said, "Two questions."

"Two answers." Her eyes rolled, and a small smile twisted her lips. *Well, good to know we aren't starting this off as a fight.* I nodded for her to continue.

"How do you know Uncle Thom?"

"Chase, actually. He was in one of my classes a couple years ago. Then I met Don Kingsley in what seemed to be a random encounter shortly after that. One day, he asked me to meet him at his office after he saw me at The Den. He said he had a proposition for me, and we've been working together, in a way, ever since. It's been mutually beneficial."

"Okay. Now, what were you two talking about? Why does this Cyress creep have a vendetta against you? What's The Den?"

"That's three questions."

She gave me an even look. "Don't be an ass."

I chuckled and let out a long breath, leaning back on the couch. "I told you already that shit went downhill when I got to Trenton. Dad's cancer set in hard, then Mom died in the crash, and I was left holding the reins on everything." She nodded. "I had picked up extra classes to teach, sold off everything I could of my parents' to pay things off, but it wasn't enough."

Swallowing, I studied her. She was guarded, but she was listening. "I was approached by Cyress Dazar at the hospital while dealing with my dad, and he suggested I come and play cards at The Den. It's an exclusive club for those who want to play poker. You have to be invited in. The buy-in levels are high, and there is a full background check done before you are allowed at the tables."

"You gambled." Her voice was careful, and I could tell she was trying to hear me out but wasn't sure where I was going with this.

"Yes."

Her chest expanded with the large breath she took. Her eyes flashed with fear and disappointment. It broke my heart to see her like that. The last thing I wanted to do was disappoint her. "How much are you indebted to him for?"

I chuckled, shook my head, and smiled at her. "I'm not. Turns out, I'm good. *Real* good. I've taken him for a lot of money. Bought the car and this condo with my winnings. I've even started a bank account for Kevin to help pay his living expenses."

Her head snapped up, her eyes wide and jaw tight. She hissed through her teeth, "You *what?*"

"There is about a hundred forty thousand in a savings account held in trust for Kevin should he need extra cash for his everyday expenses. When you told me you had a benefactor to help pay those costs for him but were still trying to pick up extra shifts to make up the difference, I wanted to help."

Her body completely froze, her chest barely moving from the shallow breaths she was taking as she stared at me. Finally, she blinked a couple of times and muttered, "Why?"

"Because I love you, Lanie. You are the woman I want to spend every day with. I want to wake up with you by my side. Have you tell me what kind of a shit day you had and then hold you while I assure you everything will be okay. I want you to come to me when you are tired and frustrated. I want to work with you and help Kevin out wherever possible. Change diapers in the middle of the night and try to console our kids so you can get some extra sleep. Sit with you at Little League, dance recitals, or whatever the kids want to do, cheering them along. Share that workload. I want to take care of you. Both of you."

"Jase." Lanie's expression was full of awe as she was studying my face, but I didn't know what she was looking for. *Is she second-guessing my dedication for her? Does she not believe that I want to help her with Kevin? Maybe even have kids of our own?*

I had laid it all out on the table for her.

Leaning back, she let out a long breath. "That's a lot."

Shrugging, I took ahold of her hands and squeezed. "It doesn't change anything."

"Jase . . . you set up a savings for Kevin."

Lifting her hand, I kissed her knuckles. "You two are a package deal."

"Okay." She leaned into me, and I wrapped my arms around her. "Promise me that this gambling thing isn't a problem."

"No addiction to it. I play games to relieve stress or cure boredom for myself. However—"

"You also play for Don Kingsley."

My girl was smart. It didn't surprise me that she'd picked up on that, so as I let the smile cross my face, I said, "I do."

"Okay." She held onto me a little tighter and sighed. "Okay."

THE

DEN

DON'T LET THEM EAT YOU ALIVE

THE

D E N

DON'T LET THEM EAT YOU ALIVE

CHAPTER FIFTY

JASON

TRENTON

It had been a couple of days, and Lanie had continued to ask questions about my relationship with Don Kingsley and what I knew of him. I'd told her what I knew from working with him and what was considered public knowledge, but there was really only so much I would be able to tell her. I couldn't tell her if he was a loving family man outside of what I knew of his and Chase's relationship, which frankly wasn't much.

She was processing, and I was okay with that. I would give her the time she needed, but she needed to know that I was in this for the long haul. I thought about the ring in the top drawer of my bedside table and how while sitting at breakfast this morning, I'd looked down at her bare hand, envisioning it there.

I'd almost gotten up and asked her right there, but instead we'd just chitchatted and eventually moved to the couch, where I sat grading papers, and she had been reading on her Kindle for the last few hours. The comfortable silence between us was glorious. It helped solidify just how perfect we were for each other. Not that there had been any doubt for me, but here, right now, looking over at her as I finished the last of the homework assignments, this was a peek into our future.

"My queen?" She hummed in acknowledgement. "Have any of your dreams for the future changed since the last time we were together and discussed it?"

"Not really. Before, Kevin was still in high school, and I didn't know what his adult life would be like, so I always factored him into my future living arrangements. Now, I know how much he has grown and is completely capable of living on his own. He's foraging his own path in life. Though, I will leave it his decision to stay with me or move out on his own"

"He was a good kid back then, and to see how much he's grown into a good human is a testament to you. You gave him stability after your parents died."

She let out a big sigh. "I didn't have a choice. He's my brother. Of course I had to step in and become a pseudo parent. You saw how much I struggled with that."

"You did, but I'm just saying that you did beautifully."

"Thank you. At least if we have kids, I've had some practice." Closing her e-reader and putting it on the coffee table, she tipped her head to the side and smiled. "Do you still want kids?"

"With you, yes. One hundred percent." Her cheeks flushed, but when she didn't say anything else after a moment, I got up, went into the bedroom, and pulled out the ring I had bought her when I'd gotten back from San Diego. I opened the box and looked at the kite cut, black, rutilated quartz ring sitting within the silver satin.

I took a deep breath before I turned the corner back into the living room, my gaze meeting hers. I knelt before her and opened the box for her to see it. "The hardest thing I ever did was walk away from you, Lanie. I promise never to do it again. When I saw you standing in my classroom doorway, I thought for sure I had died and was looking at my biggest regret. I pinched myself, and when you still stood there, I knew I wasn't going to let you get away again. I will always be here to protect you *and* Kevin. All I need is your love. Will you marry me?"

She just stared at me, surprise and happiness shining back at me. Her smile grew larger as she lifted her hand, plucked the ring from the pinched satin, and slid it on her finger. "Yes."

I crashed my lips on hers. Lanie's arms wrapped around me and held me tight. She opened for me, and as our tongues danced together, the sweet taste of honeysuckle filled my senses.

Sliding onto the floor, I pulled her with me, positioning her so she was straddling my lap. Her hips moved against me, and I gripped her thighs hard, a moan slipping from me.

She pulled back, declaring, "I will be your wife. I will be your dirty little slut. I will be yours to use until my last breath."

THE PROFESSOR'S BET

Nibbling on her neck and running my tongue along the area under her jaw made her head tip back as I slowly lifted her nightshirt up her body, letting my fingers lightly tickle her skin. Sliding the shirt over her head, I pulled it taut, pinning her arms in place.

"Jase." Her whispered plea had me chuckling as I bent forward and kissed along the skin of her collarbone. As she rolled her hips, my cock hardened even more for her, and I growled at her as I bit just above the artery in her neck. My tongue circled the spot, feeling the blood pulsing quickly.

"Jase . . ."

I sucked her skin in deep and scraped my teeth along it. As her breath rushed out of her, she ground herself against me, searching for any kind of relief.

"Please."

Biting a bit harder before releasing the skin, I licked and nibbled my way up and against her jaw. "Please, what?"

She whimpered as I leaned back from her, tightening the nightshirt in my hands to pull her back and away from me. When she opened her eyes and her gaze met mine, they were heavy and glossed over. The corner of my lips lifted as a spark of defiance flashed in her eyes.

"Please, *what*, my queen?"

"Please use me, Sir." Her head tipped back as she pleaded with me.

I thrust my hips against her at the sight of her giving herself so willingly to me. Damn, it was sexy as fucking hell. When I leaned forward again, my lips whispered against her skin. "How do you want me to use my naughty little playtoy?"

Lanie's head came up, and she had nothing but fire in her eyes. "I want to be your personal cocksleeve. I want you to fuck me until I can't move or walk straight for days."

Slowly, I let my gaze trail between our bodies, taking in the smooth tan skin that lightened at her breasts and stomach. The way her chest and stomach expanded with each breath she took. The wet spot on my jeans where she had been grinding against me. I hummed, bringing my focus back to her pleading face, and studied her as she waited for my response. "Stand up."

She practically bounced up onto her feet, where the nightshirt she'd been wearing dropped to the floor behind her. Letting my gaze slowly trail up her body and back down, I reveled in the sight of her squeezing her legs together.

Fuck. How was I ever so stupid as to walk away from her?

I dropped to my knees before my queen, tapped the inside of her knees, and she widened her stance. I kissed up her legs, and as I got to her core, I kissed just above her clit and looked up at her. "Put your leg over my shoulder." When she did, using the couch to rest her foot, I wrapped an arm around her then held her gaze as my other hand opened her up and I licked her from end to end, flicking over her engorged clit.

"Mmm." I licked my lips. "You are so wet for me, my little slut. So wet for Sir." I didn't wait for her response as I dove in and licked and sucked every inch of her delicious pussy. Nothing stopped her from grinding herself against my face, and I couldn't help but moan against her.

"Yes, Sir. Fuck yes."

I felt her pussy lips tightening as she inched closer and closer to her release. I flicked my tongue around her entrance, teasing her with what she wanted, what she needed, but refusing to give it to her. When I licked farther back against her rosebud, she moaned. I teased her relentlessly from her ass to clit, and she rolled her delicious pussy against me. Her hips moved faster and with less rhythm and just before she exploded, I pulled away and blew on her clit.

A loud, frustrated cry came from her as I slowly made my way up her body, kissing and nipping her stomach. With a quick flick on each of her hard nipples, that I had no doubt were aching for attention, I stood up, stripped my shirt off, and said, "Knees on the couch, hands braced against the back."

When she did, I kissed each ass cheek before telling her I'd be right back. I ran to the bedroom and got a few items that I needed for this particular scene. When I returned, I grabbed the silk strip and walked back around the couch so I was facing her. Leaning forward, I kissed her softly, letting it linger. "Safeword."

"Strawberry."

"That's my girl," I whispered against her lips, and as I pulled back, I slipped the silk blindfold over her eyes.

THE
D E N
DON'T LET THEM EAT YOU ALIVE

CHAPTER FIFTY-ONE

LANIE

TRENTON

Once the silk caressed my eyelids, I took a deep breath and lowered my head so that he could tie it in the back. I was trying to keep my breathing even as he walked away. When his hands rubbed up my spine, I jumped, and he chuckled. My hands gripped the back of the couch, and I forced myself to relax for him. Slowly, the tension in my muscles relaxed the longer he ran his hands over my body.

It was driving me crazy, and I pushed back against him. A gasp of air rushed in as he swatted my ass. "Easy there or I may have to show my whore who is in charge."

The sound of his belt sliding through his jeans and then a snap rang through the air, and a shiver ran up my spine in anticipation. "Yeah, look at you. Already trembling."

He wasn't wrong. My muscles in my arms and legs were already twitching as I waited for the next sensation to rocket through my body. When I tried to move my legs closer together so I could relieve some of the pressure building in my core, Jason's belt landed on my ass hard, a second strike landing on the other cheek in quick succession. My ass was already tender from our session last night, but it only seemed to gloriously amplify the pleasure rolling through me. My back arched, and I heard his hum of satisfaction behind me just before another burst of pain hit. Over and over again, never hitting the same place twice, that belt landed on my skin.

The delicious pain radiating through my body had my own juices rolling down my inner thighs and dripping onto the couch. The muscles in my thighs were quaking, and I didn't think I'd be able to handle Jason so much as blowing on my clit without exploding. Only, that was exactly what he did after ordering, "Cum for me, slut!"

My climax burst through me so fast, I screamed as my muscles spasmed in pleasure. Every ounce of me zeroed in on the pleasure that went through me as my nipples tingled and hardened and my body stiffened except for my inner thighs and pussy, which were spasming. After a moment, I gulped down a deep breath before resting my head on the back of the couch. I bit down on my bottom lip and tried to remember how to breathe.

Jason kissed each of my red-hot ass cheeks again before I heard his footsteps walk away from me and away from the living room. A moment later, I thought I heard the fridge close, and then his cool hand was on my ass, rubbing over the tender skin. The sting spread across both cheeks, but then his tongue licked from clit to ass again.

"Fuck, you are delicious. Don't move your hands."

Once I was steadied, he spread me wide and stuffed his face back into my core. His tongue was working overtime, but he avoided my clit, only circling my opening. When he had me on the edge again, something cold, hard, and smooth pressed against my ass. I focused on not clenching as he pressed what felt like an ice cube inside of me. He immediately latched onto my clit and finger fucked me. Once again, the orgasm hit hard and fast, and Jason licked up each and every drop of me.

My arms trembled, unable to hold my weight anymore, so Jason wrapped his arm around my waist and pulled me against him, twisting so that I landed on his lap. My ass stung as he held me tight against his bare skin. His hard cock seated between my ass cheeks. I didn't even have the strength to move against him. I just leaned back, resting my head against his. He kissed my hair and then hummed in my ear. "Such a pretty, dirty whore for me."

I could hardly muster a verbal response, only able to give him a contented sigh. His chuckle reverberated against me, and one of his hands moved to cup my center. We sat like that until I was able to make a coherent thought, and when I felt like I had my breath again, I rotated my hips against his length behind me. There was a slight hiss from his lips at my ear, then a nibble before he pressed a finger against my clit, halting all movement from me. He, however, thrust his cock against the crack in my ass and kissed my neck as I tilted it to the side to give him room.

"Fuck, Lanie."

"Please fill me, Sir. Please?"

He lifted me without a word, sliding between me again, and then with a simple roll of the hips, he filled me with a hard thrust. "Damn. You feel so good."

"Use me," I growled. Slowly, I started moving my hips, and it didn't take much longer for him to start meeting me thrust for thrust. After a few minutes, he pushed me off, and I turned around to face him. With my knees on either side of his thighs, his cock slid back into me without any effort. He tore the blindfold off, and I met his gaze with determination. "Fuck my pussy like I'm your doll. I told you, make me so I'm raw and can't walk in the morning."

There was nothing slow and sensual about this. He lifted my hips and pounded into me hard and deep. At this angle, he was hitting my G-spot on every slide in and out, and I whimpered in pleasure as he continued. The sound of our skin connecting and the tang of our sweat filled the air.

"Yes, that's my cocksleeve. Gonna fill your little pussy with my cum and make it so you never forget who it belongs to."

His words sent a thrill through me. Only he could say these things and have me moaning like a whore in church.

Between the spanking and the way his thighs and balls were slapping against my core, I was going to have a hard time sitting later, but right now I didn't care. Looking down to see the pure pleasure and heat on his face was all I needed. It took only a few more strokes for him to groan loudly and spill his hot cum into me.

Rolling my hips as he slowly came down from his release, he brought his arms tight around me to hold me close. "Damn, baby."

Chuckling as I buried my head in his neck, I kissed him softly and snuggled into him. We sat there for a long time, his cock slowly softening and sliding out of me. "I hate when that happens."

"Me too, but I think that is my cue to get a towel to clean us up and something to sooth that ass of yours. It is gloriously red, and with the pounding you just took, we need to take care of you. Lie here on your stomach, and I'll be back in just a minute to take care of everything."

"Yes, Sir."

I rolled over onto my stomach, just as he had instructed, and pulled one of the pillows under my head. When he returned, he cleaned me up, kissed me, and then opened a jar, setting it down on the coffee table with a clank. After scooping a handful of the cream into his fingers, he rubbed them together before smoothing his palms over the tender skin, instantly cooling it.

I took a deep breath and let it out slowly, cherishing the feel of his hands on me.

CHAPTER FIFTY-TWO

LANIE

TRENTON

A couple of days later, I was sitting on the couch, double-checking work emails to make sure there wasn't anything that needed to be taken care of, when Jason kissed the top of my head and said, "I'm going to jump in the shower. Promise not to get into any trouble for a few minutes?"

"I think I can entertain myself for twenty minutes."

He smirked at me and winked as he headed down the hallway. My gaze went to the beautiful ring that now sat on my finger. I still couldn't believe that he'd asked me to marry him. I hadn't had to think about saying yes, just needed to make sure that he was in it for Kevin, too. He'd shown me what other boys in the past hadn't. Not to mention that the two of them had gotten along great once they'd had their initial hash out. Jason had made sure that Kevin was taken care of and everything was good while I'd been in the hospital, while still making sure that everything had gone well with me. The man had even completely taken over at home for the few weeks after I'd been released from the hospital. Kami had told me how impressed she'd been with how he'd just jumped in and taken care of things. Even if she'd had to remind him to take it easy with his leg.

A chuckle bubbled up as I recalled all the ways that Kevin and Jason had interacted. The way Jason hadn't hesitated to get what seemed like an odd list of things at the store, just to make me feel better. And then there had been the cake food fight. That had probably been one of my favorite moments. It had really cemented how much Kevin had reaccepted Jason back into our lives.

When I'd told Kami about our engagement, she had shrieked so loud that I'd had to pull the phone away from my ear. She'd immediately gone into wedding planner mode, and I'd told her that the maid of honor could just chill out a minute. Of course, that had been when the shrieking had started up again. After getting her to a normal volume, I'd told her we would start talking about planning in a month or so. I just wanted to enjoy it for now.

My focus went back down the hall where I heard the shower running, then out the wall of windows to see out over the city. Could I make Trenton my home? What about Kevin? Would he want to relocate? He was doing so well at Velas, though. I really didn't want to pull him out of there. And there was no way I was going to make him live there full-time without me if he wasn't okay with that.

Standing from the couch and sliding my phone into my back pocket, I walked to the slider, opened it, and walked out onto the balcony. I leaned on the railing and took a deep breath. While the air was still filled with the sound of a busy city, it didn't smell like San Diego. Sure, it was still concrete, food vendors, and the like, but there was a freshness to it. I was sure that it had everything to do with the Sierra Mountains the city sat below.

"What could it hurt to look? To just see?"

I dialed my department head, and when Dezmond picked up, I couldn't help but smile. "I swear, Lanie, if you are calling about work, I'm going to put you on mandated vacation."

"Oh, chill your goats, mister." He chuckled in the background. "I'm calling about work, but in a different aspect."

"Okay." A moment later, I heard the door to his office shut. "What can I do for you?"

"I got engaged."

"Congratulations! I'm so happy for you, Lanie. You've been so much happier since Jason came back into your life."

"Thank you. Thank you." I took a deep breath, but as usual, he knew exactly what I was thinking.

"You are wondering if there is a position available for you in the North Valley?"

Swallowing, I let out a long breath. "Yeah, is there anything in the Trenton, Sacramento, or Folsom facilities?"

"I don't want to lose you, Lanie. You are by far the best program director here at Jade Forest, on all of the West Coast actually."

I laughed. "Just the West Coast? I should feel insulted that you didn't say in the company."

"You are such a smart ass." I heard the breath he let out as it breezed across the mic on the phone. "Let me call Jannie up in Sac. She oversees those three facilities, and I'll get back to you later today, alright?"

"I would appreciate it, but it's not a done deal for me to move. Jason and I haven't even talked about our permanent living arrangements yet. I just want to see if the option is there."

"As I said, I would hate to lose you, but I understand if you need to relocate. Only, don't think I'll give you up easily."

"Loud and clear, Dezmond."

"Oh, and Lanie?" I hummed in recognition. "Thought you should know that McFarland was terminated at the end of the day yesterday. Sexual harassment. He was fired for repeatedly groping another employee. He thought it was you, but you said you didn't want to file the complaint yet with HR. Just thought you should know that he said you had begged him for services and that he was innocent, but we know better. Have it on video. He also mentioned something about you assaulting him, which is why he had a black eye a while back?"

I blinked. "Seriously? As much as I would have loved to give him one, it wasn't me, Dezmond."

The shower turned off in the bathroom, and I turned my head to look in that direction. *Did Jase do it? One of Chase's guys he had following me?*

"Yeah. I've told you too much, but I felt like you should know."

Still a little shocked, I muttered, "Thank you. Thank you for telling me."

"No problem. Have a good day, Lanie, and congrats again on the engagement."

He hung up, and I called Kevin to see how he was doing. He stated he wanted to stay at the center for a couple of days before heading home with Ms. Jones. Kevin was so excited, I had to ask him to slow down when he told me all about how he was put in charge of formulating an art program for the younger kids and how much fun he was having planning it and pulling it together. He couldn't wait to teach art to them.

"I think that the pencil's running out of ink, though."

Suddenly, Jason's arms were wrapping around my waist behind me, and I hummed. "I bet. You've been away from the apartment for a few days. Ms. Jones will pick you up today from the center, though, and you can sleep in your own bed."

Someone was calling for him in the background. "I gotta go, Sissy. Jackie needs some help."

"Jackie, huh?"

"Sissy . . ."

I could imagine how red his face was right now. "Hey, you give me shit about Jason all the time. Even dumped water on his head because you wanted us to stop just looking at each other. So, are you and Jackie getting closer?"

"Maybe. I don't know, Sissy. I don't know if she would want to go to dinner with someone like me. Could I even go to dinner without you, Kami, or Jason?"

"Of course you can. You don't need your big sisters or brother to chaperone a date for you. You are a bright man. You are kind, sweet, and very considerate of others. I also saw the way she looked at you when we were at the grocery store, Kevin. She likes you."

"But—"

"No buts, buddy. If you really like her, then go for it. If you are worried about it, though, Jason and I can go with you, but it won't be for a couple weeks."

Jason whispered in my ear, "Have you told him yet?" I shook my head. "Tell him."

Smiling brightly, I pulled my phone from my ear and switched it to a video call. His face was indeed bright red as it popped up. He instantly recognized Jason over my shoulder. "Brother!"

"Hey there, Kevin."

He smiled brightly, his eyes flicking toward me before he tilted his head and his focus went back to Jason. "Did you do it?"

Jason nodded. "I did. It's official."

Blinking, I watched Kevin's face light up. "So, you will legally be my brother now?"

I turned to look at Jason. "Kevin knew?"

"Of course I knew, Sissy. He wanted to make sure I was really okay with him being part of our family."

My heart warmed at the two of them smiling back at me. "I love you two so freaking much."

Jackie hollered for Kevin again, and his head turned to look off camera. "Just a moment, Jackie."

"We will let you go. Just remember what I said, okay?"

With a nod, he said, "I will. Love you."

Jason and I told him that we loved him too, and when I hung up, I wrapped my arms around Jason's shoulders. "Thank you."

"For what?"

"Everything. My one concern was Kevin, and you included him in the whole decision-making process."

He leaned his forehead against mine. "I don't know how many times I have to tell you. He's part of this. You two are a package deal."

My phone rang again, and I saw Dezmond's name come up. "Work. Be a minute." He nodded and headed inside. "Hey, Dezmond."

The man let out a loud sigh. "I have good news for you, but bad for me." I chuckled. "Jannie Aika said there is a position at the Trenton office. The director there is retiring at the end of the year and would like to cross train the new person, since the position is more than just the activities program director, but also the main director for that facility since it's a bit smaller. It would be a step up for you and, yes, a pay raise as well."

I looked out over the city, a smile spreading across my face. "Okay, I'm listening."

"I have recommended you for the position, and she is waiting for your call to schedule an appointment. I'll text the number to you."

"Thank you, Dezmond. I really do appreciate this."

"Of course, Lanie. Don't worry, I told her you were still feeling things out and no firm decisions have been made."

"Again, appreciated. I'll give her a call. Can I get a couple extra days off?"

"Of course. See you Thursday. Congratulations, Lanie!"

Hanging up the phone, I slid it into my back pocket and crossed my arms. Everything and nothing went through my mind over the next few minutes as I stared off into the distance. I felt my phone go off and knew that it was likely Dezmond sending me the contact info for Ms. Aika. I'd heard about her. She was strict, but fair. I would call her after Jason headed off to his morning classes. That way I could discuss it without getting Jason's hopes up before we even talked about it. Taking a deep breath, I headed inside.

"I'm about ready to head out. Thought I was going to have to interrupt your peace to let you know." I couldn't help but look him over in his fitted jeans, dress shirt rolled up to his elbows, and freshly shaven face. When he stood in front of me, I ran my thumb over his cheek and reached up on my toes to kiss him softly. His hand covered mine as his focus bounced between my two eyes. "What's your plan for today?"

"Make a couple phone calls and then get ready for our dinner with Don Kinglsey." I tried not to let it get to me that the uncle my mom had pushed away from me was also one of the mafia leaders of the city.

"He's not all that bad."

I narrowed my eyes at him. "What *exactly* is that mutually beneficial arrangement you two have?"

"I get to play poker and keep the winnings. All I have to do in return is give him the information I find out during those games." He leaned forward and whispered against my lips, "I'm not one of his henchmen, Lanie."

Then he kissed me softly and sweetly, and I deflated against his chest, letting myself just take in the feel of his body against mine. His hand skirted up and down my back, and he kissed the top of my head. The entire exchange warmed me to my core, but when he leaned down to kiss just below my ear, my knees went weak. When I pulled back and took a breath, I slowly opened my eyes and glared at him. "No fair, mister."

There was a smirk on his face as he gathered his things. "I should be back by three."

I nodded, and he gave me another quick kiss before walking out the door.

Chapter Fifty-Three

Lanie

Trenton

I had called Jannie Akia and spoken to her on the phone for a few minutes before she'd suggested a video chat at two. When we met, she said that Dezmond had highly recommended me and that he would hate to lose me as his employee, which was one of the highest recommendations she had received for an applicant. We went over the job description, and I was actually pretty excited about it. My only hesitation was that it was down in the business district known as the Avenue, but she assured me they had their own parking facility, so I wouldn't have to walk through a throng of people to get to the office. She had basically said the job was mine if I wanted it, but she understood I was still sorting out which direction to go.

That afternoon when Jason got home, he kissed me, took my hand, and pulled me into the bedroom, where he stripped me bare, then himself, before pulling us into the shower. There, he thoroughly worshiped every inch of my skin and fucked me against the tile hard and fast. He let out a long breath and rested his head on my shoulder until the water ran cold.

By the time we dried off and made it back to the bed, he seemed more centered and relaxed. Curled up on the bed and running my fingers up and down his chest and stomach, I looked up at him. "Now that you've calmed down, mind telling me what had you all wound up?"

He stiffened for a moment, and I sat up on my elbow, raising my eyebrow. He studied me for a moment before letting a harsh breath out of his nose. "I'm nervous about tonight."

Blinking at him in confusion, I asked, "Why? You've worked for Don Kingsley for a while."

Jason shifted and then pulled me on top of him. As I positioned myself so that I was straddling his hips, his hands ran over my thighs. "I have, but I'm going to dinner with my fiancée, who happens to be his niece. It's a different dynamic."

I let out a slow breath. He wasn't wrong, and I stared at the blank wall above the headboard of his bed. "It is, and I have no idea how to feel about it. On one hand, we had a great relationship until he left. On the other, Mom must have had a real good reason for removing him and Chase from our lives, right?"

"I don't know, my queen. You agreed to dinner, so you're willing to hear him out, right?" I nodded. "Okay, then. We suck up our fears and nervousness and go see what he has to say."

I leaned down and kissed him quickly. "Thank you."

A sassy smile lifted the corners of his lips before he said, "You're welcome. Now, we should get dressed and get you some water. I'm sure you haven't had enough for what I have planned for tonight.

"Yes, Sir."

Hours later, we were walking into Le Fronton, a French restaurant decorated as if we were in a brick alley, with vines and trellises hanging over our heads. Twinkle lights lit the ceiling around the restaurant. It was pretty quiet, but when we met the host, he bowed and said, "Mr. Rathborn, Ms. Carley. Right this way, Mr. Kingsley is waiting."

He led us through the restaurant, where a number of people were enjoying their meals in peace. I grabbed Jason's hand and squeezed tight, centering on the feel of him to calm my nerves. He pulled me closer and kissed my temple. "Everything is going to be okay."

I knew he was trying to reassure me and make me feel better, but aside from the accidental run-in the other day at lunch, I hadn't seen my uncle in over fifteen years. As we reached the booth, Chase's eyes lit up and he stood up quickly. "Mel—" He shook his head and restarted. "Lanie."

"Chase. It's really you?" He nodded, and I let go of Jason's hand, leaping for my cousin. His arms wrapped around me, his head bending down into the crook of my neck, and I swore I felt his chest shutter as he held me a moment before he pulled back and stared at me. "I can't believe it . . . after all these years. I've missed you so much. When—"

"Hold up on that, Chase. Let's at least sit down before we tell her everything," Jason said, and with his hand on the small of my back, he gestured for me to sit down across from another man I hadn't seen in over fifteen years before this trip.

"Don—"

"I swear, Lanie, if you call me Don Kingsley, I'll put you over my knee like I did when you were five and got into the cookie jar for the tenth time that day." His eyes were warm and soft, not an ounce of harshness the words might have conveyed. I studied his olive-brown skin that was wrinkling slightly at the corners of his eyes, forehead, and around his mouth. His dark hair was starting to grey at the temples, and I had flashes of the fun-loving uncle that I'd had all those years ago.

But so much has changed since he was the tickling, laughing Uncle Thom.

"Mr. Kingsley." A flash of hurt in his eyes had me sighing. "I don't know what to call you right now. It's been so long, and I don't fully know who was to blame for all contact being cut off. I blame my mom for cutting contact with Chase, but with you, I don't even know where to start."

He brought his hands up to the table and leaned on his forearms as he studied them, sliding his fingers between each other while he gathered his thoughts. His skin was tanned and calloused, which made the scars that covered them stand out. Swallowing the uneasiness in my gut, I reminded myself that he was a mafia don. That meant that he likely had done lots of unsavory things. If books had taught me anything, he had hurt people, and by the look of those hands and the small scar that sat just below his left eye, he had probably inflicted most of it.

The waiter came up and took our drink orders. When he got to me, I asked for a pear Moscow mule from the bar. "I'm already getting the feeling I need a drink for this, or will need one by the time we are done."

Jason's hand rested on my thigh while his thumb moved back and forth in comforting sweeps as my uncle looked to him and then back to me. Finally, he sighed. "What reason did your mother give you as to why we weren't around and why you couldn't talk to Chase anymore?"

I studied my hands as I played with my fingers in my lap. "Not much. She just told us we weren't allowed to talk to you or mention your name in the house again. And when she caught me texting with Chase . . ." I let out a long breath. "She read me the riot act, took my phone, said I was lucky to not be associated with *the likes of you,* and left it at that."

He nodded a couple times in thought. "What about Kevin?"

I instantly tensed. "Don't bring Kevin into this."

Chase's face fell and he looked at his dad. "Not possible, Lanie. He is sort of at the center of it all. An innocent kid at that."

"Sort of? Either he is or he isn't. Answer me straight." My chest was getting tight, and it was hard to breathe through the rising panic.

"He is."

My attention switched between the two of them, looking for answers. I was gritting my teeth so hard I thought they would crack, but I reined it in. "Explain."

Don Kingsley leaned on the table and collapsed his hands together. "What do you know of Kevin's dad?"

Breath halted in my lungs for a moment as I realized they knew Mom's secret. My attention bounced between the two of them as Jason put his arm around me and rested his hand on my back, rubbing his thumb back and forth.

"Our dad was kind, loving, and extremely supportive in everything we did. He adored Kevin and treated him as if he were his own blood. So, if you are asking if I know whether or not Kevin is my half-brother, then yes, yes I do. Kevin does not. If you are asking about who his biological father is, then I don't know anything."

My uncle leveled his focus on me and said, "I need you to listen and let me get all of this out. It's a bit of an information dump, and it's going to be really hard to accept all of this. Can you sit there and listen? I promise you can ask all the questions when I'm done, but I need you to fully listen."

"I'm not a fucking child," I spat. Jason's hand tightened on my leg, and I suspected he didn't agree with my tone. Too bad.

"You aren't, but I'm trying to tell you that you aren't going to like a fucking thing that comes out of my mouth, but I need you to hear it all."

I huffed and sat back like the petulant child I was claiming not to be. Yes, I realized the irony in that. I stared him down but finally nodded. "Why is Kevin at the middle of it all?"

Kingsley's lips tightened. I was sure he didn't tolerate people snapping at him like this, but he swallowed his frustration as he sighed. "You were eleven when it started. I don't exactly know what was happening between your mom and dad. All I know is that Monica was spending a lot of time with Heath, my second-in-command at the time. Your dad was taking you to all your activities while working long hours."

"I had come over to pick up Chase, who was outside playing in the backyard with you, but when I walked by the bathroom, Monica was crying. I asked if she was okay, and she looked up at me and told me to mind my own business. I was shocked because it was unlike her." He bowed his head, and I saw the lines of sadness that settled on his face. "That's when I noticed the three pregnancy tests on the counter. I picked one up, and when I saw it read positive, I looked back at her and asked if it was Heath's. She told me it was because she and your father hadn't had sex in well over a year."

I opened my mouth to ask a flurry of questions, but Jason's tap on my back and gentle rub was a silent indicator to wait and let him finish. I looked at him and pinched my lips together before looking back at Kingsley.

"We fought. Full-on screaming match. I told her she had to tell your dad, but she refused. Said that it wasn't like Heath was going to step up to take care of both you and this kid. That she couldn't let the baby be raised in a mafia family, regardless of the fact that I had made it work." He took a breath and ran his hands through his hair before continuing. "Then she told me she didn't love your father anymore. She loved Heath but lamented that your father wouldn't deserve all of the hell that would rain down if the truth came out. She told me to get Chase and never come back. She didn't trust me to not tell your dad. I said I would honor her wishes not to tell your father, but I was telling Heath because he had a right to know he had fathered a child. He had a right to be given the opportunity to provide for it. Monica had just looked away from me and nodded, saying she was okay with that, but insisted that your dad couldn't know. I honored her wishes from my side of things and told Heath about the baby. A few years later, she was tired of me trying to get her to open up to your father about Kevin. That's when she told me to get out and that Chase and I were never welcome at the house again."

I didn't understand. I looked over at Chase, who sighed. "Dad isn't lying. The entire way home, he told me he was sorry that I wasn't going to be able to see Aunt Monica anymore and that he was going to try to find a way for you and me to still hang out. It's why he let me keep texting you, until your mom took your phone away and changed your number."

Jason's hand was tight on my leg, and the physical touch was the only thing keeping me from completely coming unglued. "But Dad knew Kevin wasn't his biological son. Mom said so just before she died."

Kingsley nodded. "Heath talked to him not long after she told us to get lost. Heath told Monica that he was going to, and they fought over it, too. In the end, your father promised to raise the baby as his own, blaming himself for the fact Monica fell for Heath. He loved Kevin with everything he had. Your father even sent regular updates to Heath and me on how Kevin was doing after he was born. Even made sure that when Monica was at work and you were at school, Heath had a chance to spend some time with him, too. He really wanted him to be part of raising his son, but Monica wouldn't have it. When she found out . . ." He let out a low whistle. "Oh boy, the fight those three had together. She didn't know what to do when your father and Heath ended up pairing up against her. I don't know what happened, but shit went sideways there, and Heath was in the middle of it. It had nothing to do with you or your brother. Your parents were still friends in the end. They cared deeply for each other, but your mom just was in love with Heath. He said that they had talked about Monica divorcing your dad, but she couldn't do that to him. She had already put him through so much. She just couldn't do it."

"All those girls weekends . . ."

He nodded as he dropped his gaze and played with his glass. "She was with Heath."

I sat up straighter and tipped my head to the side. There was a sadness in his eyes that I knew too well. It was the look of someone who'd lost someone that meant the world to them. "What happened to Heath?"

"He was interrogating a kid, early twenties maybe. The kid was as tight-lipped as they come. Heath went too far and ended up killing him. We found out the son was the secret lover of one of the other Don's sons. When they found out Heath killed him, war broke out. Don Jaques's son raged, and just before we found out about your parents being killed, Jaques told us that since Heath had taken the one he loved, then he was taking what was most precious to Heath."

My heart clenched, as I knew where this was going. "My mom."

"Heath panicked and tore ass to San Diego, only to find out that your father had been killed instantly and Monica had died two hours before he'd arrived from her injuries. On his way back to Trenton, he set things in motion to fake a bunch of life insurance policies to be funded from his assets."

"So all that life insurance money from my mom and dad was actually Heath's?"

He nodded, and it took a moment for it to register. The life insurance policies on both Mom and Dad that I couldn't find any paperwork on at the house, that kept coming out of the woodwork, were from Kevin's biological father. It had literally saved us from being on the streets. "It helped a lot. Paid the medical bills, covered the funeral expenses, and helped Kevin and I get back on our feet."

"He would be glad to hear that." He lifted his gaze to the ceiling and then continued, "When he returned, though, he was so destroyed by the grief of losing your mother, he went after Jaques. He lost that fight, but so did Jaques."

I was stunned. We all sat in silence for a few minutes. The waiter came back over, and I vaguely heard people ordering. My head was reeling with everything I'd just been told. *What in the hell?* Eventually, I was able to pull my thoughts together, and I sat up straight, glaring at my so-called uncle. "Why didn't you tell me?"

He took a deep breath and leaned back. "I would have told you sooner. Chase would have told you if I didn't. If your mother hadn't . . . If we hadn't caused her death . . ."

"It doesn't sound like you caused their deaths," Jason said beside me, but then he looked at Chase. "This is why when I told you that I was back with her, you took special interest? Had guys protecting her again in San Diego?"

"What?" I sat up. "I'm sorry, *you* are the ones that had guys following us at home? Guys have been threatening us left and right. Telling us to be careful of who I let imto our lives and telling Kevin to be careful whom he associates with."

Chase's mouth tightened and he balled his fists as Kingsley's face was quiet rage. "Again, those were not my guys. You never would have noticed anyone employed by me."

"Well, I noticed."

It was Chase who said, "We are very careful."

Kingsley's voice was low and borderline lethal as he ordered, "Describe one of the ones that talked to you."

I described the man at the grocery store and then told him about all the other instances where I had been followed or told to be careful about being attached to Jason. "It's all moot. I'm marrying him, whether some random piece of shit thinks it's okay or not."

Kingsley's eyes went wide, then slowly, a bright smile spread across his face. "You two are going to get married?"

Jason took my hand in his and laced our fingers together, lifting them to his lips to kiss them, effectively showing off my beautiful ring. "Don Kingsley, she is everything I've ever wanted, and the day I walked away from her all those years ago is my single greatest regret."

"First, damn straight she's one of the best things on this earth. Second, you aren't allowed to call me Don Kingsley unless we are talking business. Understand?"

"Yes, sir, but what should I call you?"

"Uncle Thom works just fine."

I looked between them and then at Chase, who was just shaking his head. "Okay, well, now that that is settled . . ."

The waiter came up and set food down before us, and I looked down and saw a plate of duck confit over scalloped potatoes with fresh green beans. It looked delicious. "Thank you for ordering for me," I muttered to Jason, who just leaned over and kissed my temple again.

We were silent for a moment as we started to eat, and when I took my fork to the duck, it literally fell off the bone. Taking a bite, I sighed at the rich explosion of flavor that went across my tongue. Duck could be done so wrong, but this was perfectly tender and the balance of the sweetness from the fat, thyme and garlic was perfection. I might have eaten it a bit faster than was proper, but when you had good duck, you ate. The potatoes underneath had obviously been cooked in some of the fat and drippings from the duck, as it gave many of the same notes, sweet and salty all at once. I didn't know the last time I'd had a dinner this delicious.

The others were talking, but I forced myself to enjoy the meal and tried to process all that they had told me. When I was done, I placed my fork down and looked up at Kingsley. He had a bright smile on his face. "You seemed to enjoy your duck."

"It was so good. I haven't had duck that delicious in a very long time."

He smiled, and I looked over at Jason, who was finishing his up as well. I leaned my head on his shoulder and put my hand on his leg under the table. I leaned into him as I asked, "So, what happens now?"

"In what aspect?" Uncle Thom asked as he put the last of his food into his mouth.

"Kevin, us. Everything. Did Mom know that you were a Don? Can we at least get your old second's medical history for Kevin? What happens to Kevin and my life now that you are back in it? Hell, I don't even know what to ask or what is happening. Jason and I haven't even talked about where we plan on living after the wedding, let alone the who, what, when, or where of it."

"My queen."

Turning toward him, I crossed my arms over my chest. "Well, we haven't, Jase."

He chuckled and rubbed small circles on my back. "We haven't, but there is plenty of time for all of that. None of it has to be decided right here and now."

"No. I guess it doesn't." I looked back at my uncle, who was a freaking Don, and cousin. "However, my questions stand when it comes to Kevin and our relationship with you."

Uncle Thom nodded. "I'll get Heath's medical file for you. He was a reasonably healthy man. It was the bullet that killed him. Otherwise, he was good." I nodded and took a deep breath. "As for us, well, that's a little more complicated."

"How so?"

"Your fiancé *technically* is on my payroll." I groaned, but he smiled before he continued, "He's not really a problem. Jason has probably has already told you, but he gathers information for me when I ask him to and reports back to me. When I find out that information is going to be exchanged or meetings are going to be had at the tables, Jason goes in and plays for me. Becomes my ears. He can play on his own however much he wants to but doesn't all that often. We've agreed that he gets to keep the cash he wins. It's his payment for winning his hands. If he doesn't win—" He shrugged. "There is a base payment arrangement for still obtaining any fruitful information. No guns and not intentionally in any line of fire, Lanie. He's one of the safest people on my staff."

"You said you had people following us down south?"

Chase nodded. "They are my guys. They have explicit instructions not to interrupt your day to day. When you were shot, they ensured that the media stayed away from you at the hospital, left Kevin alone, and stayed away from your apartment. They will continue to do so. I'll be talking to them about keeping a better eye out for anyone following you."

Kingsley took over from there. "Whether you want to have a relationship with us or not, we will continue to protect you because we want to. I will continue to help with Kevin's well-being and—"

"I'm sorry, *what*?" I exclaimed.

He narrowed his eyes at me. "Oh, I thought you knew."

I raised my eyebrows in question as if to ask, "Knew *what*."

"I'm Kevin's benefactor for Velas. I really thought you knew about that. I am also fronting the bill for his math and art education. I will take care of my family."

It was Chase this time who looked at his father. "Dad, you knew where they were this whole time?"

"Of course I did. I wasn't going to let Heath or Monica leave them high and dry. Sure, Heath gave everything to Kevin, so he is taken care of for life, but that money hasn't been touched."

I wasn't sure how many more surprises I could take at this point. If I hadn't been sitting already, my knees would have given out a long time ago. "What do you mean that money hasn't been touched? What money?"

Uncle Thom chuckled. "You know there were the insurance plans to get you guys on your feet, but there were also the stocks, properties, and other things in Heath's estate. Kevin is the beneficiary to the entire thing. He will never want for anything. I simply wanted to provide for Kevin until he could access everything. Make sure he had all the opportunities that he wanted to take."

I wanted to rage at him. Yell, scream, and shout how he hid from us all these years. He had to know that we'd longed for us to reconnect, but maybe not. So I just said, "Thank you."

Chase was staring at his father with confusion and a tang of hurt. "You could have told me where they were. I've been asking about Lanie for years."

I widened my eyes, surprised that he had been. "You have?"

"Of course. We are family."

I looked between two people who had missed out on fifteen years of our lives. "Family." They both sat there looking at me. It seemed that they were waiting for my response. "I have been extremely careful about who I let into my and Kevin's lives. I've had to become a mother of sorts to him, but ultimately, we are brother and sister who had to rely on each other very much. My friend Kami has been amazing and loves Kevin like her own little brother. Now I have Jason in my life again. Even with him, I still have to think about Kevin first. I'm lucky he understands and accepts that my brother and I are a package deal."

I looked at Jase, who just nodded. Taking that to mean he would support whatever decision I made, I turned to face my cousin and uncle again, but someone walked up to our table.

"You fucking bitch."

My heart stopped as I looked up to see Adrian McFarland standing there. He looked like he hadn't slept in days, likely hadn't since he was terminated yesterday. His hair was greased back, his dress shirt was rumpled and uneven, and there was food dripping down the front of him and onto the thighs of his slacks. "Adrian?"

What in the fuck is he doing here?

Jason turned to block me from him, and at that movement, my uncle said calmly, "What do you want with Lanie?"

His dark eyes burned into me with hatred and something wilder. "This fucking slut—"

"I would watch what you call my fiancée." Jason's voice was low, and I wasn't sure what look he was giving him, but if it was half as lethal as the looks coming from Uncle Thom and Chase, the man should be burning in hell right now.

Taking a deep breath and resting a hand on Jason's back to calm him down, I bristled. "What did I do?"

"You reported me to HR. *You* got me fired." He hissed the words, and I didn't fail to notice how Uncle Thom and Chase now looked at me with mirror images on their faces. Each had a dark eyebrow raised and were questioning what the hell was going on.

I'd like to know that too. Well, if he wants a confrontation, I'll give him one. Yes, I knew I was feeling emboldened by the fact I had Jase with me. I knew he would do whatever he could to protect me. At this point, I had no idea about Uncle Thom and Chase. I didn't take my eyes off Adrian though. I'd never seen him this haggard, and when I took a deep breath, I realized the entire restaurant was dead silent. I swore I even heard people on the other side of the partition that I was leaning against being ushered out of the restaurant. In my peripheral, I could see there were definitely people being removed from the area.

Was this normal being around Uncle Thom?

Steadying my resolve, I sat up straighter and said, "That's cute. You think that after you flirt with me at work and off, me denying all of your advances, you degrading me by saying how I would only be pretty if I lost fifty to seventy pounds, and my fiancé putting you in your place, going to HR and getting you fired was my course of action? You really are dumb. I figured it was done and over with after you got your face rearranged that day at the bistro." I lifted a hand when he started to say something. "Which I did not ask anyone to do. If you got the shit beat out of you, then you got it of your own accord. Besides, I knew that if I went to HR, it would only embolden you and make matters worse."

"You are the one who was flirting with me. Then, when I gave you the attention you so desperately wanted, you played hard to get . . . then you reported me and got me fired."

"I didn't get you fired. How did you even find where I'm at? I'm across the damn state! Why did you drive nine hours to come and throw false claims?"

"Everyone in that office knew you were coming to Trenton. I had to call in some favors to find out exactly where you would be tonight, but having dinner with a Don . . ." He smiled, and it sent a chill down my spine. "You are more intriguing than I thought."

Chase went to say something and stand, but Uncle Thom reached over and put his hand on his forearm. Chase looked at his father before taking a breath and sitting back down.

"It would be best for you to leave. Go home. Find something new and learn how to treat women with respect."

Adrian stared at me, and when he didn't move, Uncle Thom stood and reached for him, likely to force him to leave, but Adrian was quick. He pulled a gun, and then there was a deafening sound in the restaurant and Jason was lying over top of me.

Panic filled me, and then I heard someone screaming. Fight or flight had kicked in and I was going to run. My heart was beating so fast, and I wasn't able to take any deep breaths as I kicked and jabbed at whatever was within reach. Flashbacks of the market raced through my vision, and it was like I was there again. The smell of blood in the air. The screams all around me as people ran for cover. The prideful look the man in the hoody had given us before all hell had broken loose that day.

Another loud gunshot went through the room, arms tightened around me, and then Chase was leaning over the table, grabbing me by the shoulders. I swung, but he caught my arm before I made contact.

I blinked, and then Jason had my head in his hands. "My queen. You are okay. You are safe. We are both unharmed. Now breathe with me. In and out."

Forcing myself to hold his gaze, which was oddly calm at this moment, I took a slow breath in and mimicked him as he blew out. After repeating the exercise for a few minutes, he asked, "Better?"

I nodded and turned toward Chase. He nodded and then said, "Take her home, professor. We will handle things here."

"Got it." He helped me out of the booth, and when I saw Adrian lying on the floor, blood pooling from his chest, I realized what had happened. My gaze dragged up to meet Uncle Thom's, whose head was held high and a gun was in his palm.

"No one fucks with my family and lives to tell the tale. You are untouchable."

Those words loosened something deep in my chest, yet it took a moment for me to breathe. He was making a statement I didn't fully understand, yet I knew it was monumental. My attention stayed on him, and he let a small smile lift the corner of his lips. It was so much like the uncle that I had seen as a kid. So much of the uncle that had been ripped away from me.

Taking a deep breath, I nodded. "You can be in my life again, but I have one condition." Uncle Thom lifted an eyebrow. "If Kevin gets hurt in *any way* because of either of you or your business, we are done."

Neither Uncle Thom nor Chase hesitated. "Done."

Without another look at Adrian, Jase wrapped an arm around me and took me home.

THE

DEN

Don't Let Them Eat You Alive

Chapter Fifty-Four

Jason

Trenton

Dinner with Don Kingsley, or Uncle Thom, as I guessed I was supposed to call him outside of work, had been . . . different. Before everything had gone to shit, it had been interesting and very enlightening. I was so proud of Lanie. She'd sat there and taken everything they'd had to say all in stride, until that douche from her job had shown up. Still, she'd proved herself a badass by standing against him. After the shots had been fired, though, I'd seen the same fear in her eyes as from that day at the farmers' market. It hadn't surprised me one bit that she had started to freak out. Adrian McFarland had lifted that gun and fired it at my queen. I'd thought my heart was going to cease beating in that second, but I hadn't hesitated to cover her body with mine again. Out of the corner of my eye, I'd seen Kingsley pull his gun before McFarland had dropped dead. I doubted he ever saw Kinglsey. Once Lanie had somewhat regained her composure and Chase and I had convinced her that we were okay and no one was hurt, she'd let me take her home. The whole way back to the condo, she'd gripped my hand tight and held her stomach with her free hand.

After parking, I went to get out of the car, and she gripped harder on my hand. "You need to let go so I can circle around the car, and then you don't have to let go of me for the twelve hours, okay?"

Her eyes met mine, and they were still a little wild, but her grip loosened, and I got out of the car quickly and to the passenger side. Once she was out, her arms wrapped around me and held tight. We leaned back on my passenger door for a long while as she continued to take long, slow breaths. I pulled back to look at her, and there was mascara running down her cheeks.

I didn't even notice her starting to cry.

"Let's get you upstairs and into your comfy clothes," I muttered, kissed her softly on the top of the head, and led her to the elevator. The garage was silent, and the sound of each of Lanie's high heels clicking on the concrete even had my shoulders tightening slightly.

A shorter guy, who looked to be in his early twenties, rushed in with an armful of groceries and joined us in the elevator after we stepped in. Lanie held me a little tighter as she trembled slightly, and I nodded to him. He mouthed if she was okay, and I nodded. I recognized him as one of the guys who rented a space a few floors down from me. The car stopped at his floor, and he stopped for a moment. "You sure you guys are okay?"

"Yeah. It's just been a long, rough night. Thank you though." With a quick nod, he turned down the hall. The doors squealed shut, and Lanie winced against the sound. "It's okay, my queen. Everything is okay."

The car was hot, smelt stale, but other than a few handprints from kids, I was thankful that the building's maintenance kept it clean. Lanie just kept her head down and pressed against my chest, her arms tight around me, taking slow, measured breaths. I looked up above the doors where the numbers continued to climb. "Almost there," I murmured and then kissed the crown of her hair.

Cooler air swept into the car as the doors opened on my floor. I bent down and lifted her up into my arms.

"Jase . . ."

"Shh. I got you, my queen."

Quickly as I could, I got the door open and shut it behind me with my foot.

"I can walk."

Kissing her cheek, I lifted an eyebrow at her. "But you won't tonight." I carried her back to the bedroom, set her on the bed, and started to undress her. "You are going to let me take care of you. Now, I'm going to get you undressed, into some jammies, and into bed. Do you want some cocoa?"

Shaking her head, she met my gaze. There was fear, hurt, and confusion, but I saw the appreciation in those brown depths. "Thank you. Once you are ready for bed, can you just hold me?"

Her throat bobbed, and I kissed her forehead. With my lips against her skin, I said, "Absolutely. Once you are tucked in, I'll close down the house and be here."

Ten minutes later, I was locking the front door and turning off the lights as I headed back to the bedroom. When I walked in, she was lying on her side, eyes wide open, waiting for me. There hadn't been any more tears up to that point, but once I was curled up around her, she let the brave mask drop and cried. The last few years had been so hard on her, and I certainly hadn't made it any easier. So much had changed in five years. So freaking much.

Now her family had grown by three in no time at all.

I wanted her to stay here with me. I needed her with me. Could I really ask her to give up everything down south and uproot Kevin, or even ask him to live at Velas full time?

No. No, I couldn't. I needed to provide for her, be there for her, and I wanted to do all of that. Even if that meant giving up my position here in Trenton. Eventually, she stopped crying, and her breathing evened out. Pressing my lips to her forehead one more time, I whispered, "I love you," before allowing myself to drift off to dreamland.

There was a knock on my office door, bringing me out of fixation on the tests I was grading. "Come in."

When the door opened, I didn't expect to see the dean standing there. I stood and walked over to shake his hand, and he took it. "Dean Winston. What can I do for you?"

Sitting back down, he asked, "Heard through the grapevine you got engaged? How does it feel?"

"Great. Went to dinner with her uncle last night. That was an enlightening discussion."

The dean chuckled and nodded. "When your uncle-in-law-to-be is Don Kingsley, I can only begin to imagine how enlightening of a conversion that was."

I froze. "I'm sorry. How do *you* know who her uncle is?"

He leaned forward and let out a long breath. "I received a message today. One that explained how you were wrapped up in a whole bunch of unsavory things, including the fact you are now involved with Don Kingsley on a personal level. The message then gave me that detail along with the fact that you've been known to frequent a poker den."

I lifted my eyebrows at him. "First, unless my connections affect my ability to do my job, which is teaching ancient history to college students, I don't see why my dean would need to come in to talk to me about any of that. Second, what I do in my free time is none of the school's business, as long as it doesn't affect the school."

"Listen, Jason, the fact is that your association with anything illegal affects the image of the school."

I studied him as he took a shaky breath. When I saw his hands trembling, I tipped my head to the side. "This isn't about the school, is it, John? It's the angle whoever sent you that message told you to take to try and strong-arm me out of my job. Out of the school." He froze to a point that if I hadn't been watching him so carefully, I would have thought he was a statue. "The fact is that even if I *were* visiting an illegal club, I haven't been arrested, I'm not in any kind of debt, and I have kept my nose clean around this campus. Which is better than about half of the faculty of the university. How do I know? Because people talk. The accusations of sexual assault, by professors and adjunct staff, that are pushed to the side because the school doesn't want the bad publicity . . . the number of drinking and driving arrests just in the English and art departments . . . or how about the fact that the FBI was here not two months ago asking questions about one of the professors in the mathematics department about insider trading. No. This isn't about my image with the school. Now, can you tell me exactly who sent that message? I think this is something I need to handle myself." His hands were shaking harder now, and there was legit fear in his eyes. "Since you seem to know so much about my family, how about you tell me what your little informant has on *you?*"

My phone buzzed next to me, but I didn't dare take my eyes off the dean. He swallowed and stood, somehow looking even more rattled now. "Thank you for your time, Professor Rathborn. It appears my information was wrong. I assume there will be no issues moving forward."

"I can't promise that, but I don't foresee any immediate concerns."

After he stood, he leaned a little closer to me and whispered so quietly, I almost missed it, "Careful of Cyress. He's pulling some strings to fuck shit up. You may want to reach out to your family about that." After he stepped back and got to the door, he said, "Try to have a good night."

After teaching my last class of the day, I called Lanie, who said she was going to take a nap while I finished up and then we could go to dinner tonight. After hanging up, I turned on my laptop and started looking for teaching positions in and around San Diego. There were a couple that were lateral transfers to UC Irvine and another one at San Diego State. It took some time, but I processed the paperwork for consideration. After spending a couple hours on them, I figured that even if I was offered the position, I could always turn it down if Lanie and I decided to do something completely different.

With that, I packed up my stuff and headed home to Lanie.

Chapter Fifty-Five

Lanie

Trenton

I had been having an amazing dream of Jason and me on some private beach with him fucking me in the water. The waves were crashing around us, and Jason was doing everything he could to keep us in one spot. He was holding me tight against his body, kissing his way down my neck, when a hand slapped down over my mouth.

What in the . . .

Someone was holding my feet down, and something sharp was on my neck. A scream ripped from my throat as I jerked awake.

My eyes flung open to see a man leaning over me with dark hair, dark eyes that had a wild edge to them, and a short scruff of a beard. The man from the bar and dinner.

"Hello, Ms. Carley. I'm sure you remember me. In case you forgot, I'm Cyress Dazer. Your fiancé owes me a bit of money, and you are going to help me collect it." I shook my head, but he smiled. "Now, I'm going to take my hand off your mouth, then you are going to tell me where to find it."

After he slowly removed his hand, I looked around the room, only seeing a few of Cyress's guys with him. Jason wasn't home yet. Good. "I-I don't know what the *fuck* you are talking about."

My muscles tightened as if ready to spring into action, but the fear coursing through me had me unable to move. He pulled me up into a seated position, while someone else pulled my arms behind me and wrapped my wrists in something thin and plastic. When I heard the familiar sound of a zip tie, I tried to remember the videos I'd seen online on how to get out of them.

"Now, tell me where the money is!" Cyress demanded, but when I kept my mouth shut, he pressed the knife against my throat. "Don't think I won't spill your blood and leave you here for Rathborn to find you."

Finding an ounce of my ingrained sass, I glared at him. "That would be dumb. You know that, right?"

"What are you going to do?" Then he pitched his voice into a childish whine. "Call your uncle to save you?"

I rolled my eyes. "In case you haven't noticed, I'm not exactly capable of calling him right now. You have a knife to my throat and my hands zip-tied behind my back. I'm saying it would be dumb because you would be killing someone who doesn't know anything, and then you would die because of it. It would turn into a race to see who would kill you first, Uncle Thom or Jason."

"Oh, to see the look on his face when he gets here to see how I sliced up this pretty face. Just tell me what I want to know."

I chuckled, trying to hide my fear. If I could stuff it down enough, I could get through this without freaking out and falling apart. "I don't know where or how Jason has his finances organized."

"You can't be serious. You two are getting married. You've certainly had the finances talk. So again, where. Is. My. Money?"

The knife tip pressed harder against my skin, and I felt the prick as it broke through. I winced but tried to not move. My muscles were tense, and I knew that if I relaxed them the slightest bit, they would start shaking, and I refused to give this man the satisfaction.

He lifted the knife up by my eye, smiling. "Would Rathborn still love you if I sliced all the way down your cheek? Removed your eyeball?"

I wasn't surprised when he pressed the knife against the skin right at my cheekbone. I stared at him and refused to flinch as he cut into the flesh. My attention stayed focused on him as the sting registered along with the warm liquid rolling down my cheek. He shook his head as he lifted the blade. "I will continue to cut you until you tell me."

"Well, I'll either bleed out or wear the scars proudly for the rest of my life. I don't know how I can tell you something I don't know. How many times do I have to say that in a five-minute span?"

His arm moved fast as he sliced down my arm. Intense pain pierced through me as his fingers dug into the cut, spreading it, widening it. He was growling at me. "Tell me."

Stubbornness took over to keep the fear at bay as I shook my head. Cyress took the knife, cutting into my leg while someone put clamps on some of my fingers. As much as I wanted to look around, I refused to break eye contact with Cyress. He would not see weakness if I could help it. That was, until his associate started tightening the clamps. I thrashed against the pain, trying to move away from it, but I couldn't. Flexing my hand and trying to dislodge the clamps from my fingertips did nothing, and I whimpered as the pain dulled slightly.

"You would be a pretty thing if you weren't so . . . plump."

"Fuck off. Why would I give a shit about your opinion?"

And what is with people being so concerned about my weight? Unless I'm sitting on your face, it has nothing to do with you.

"I could give you so much more than Rathborn."

I lifted my eyebrows, trying to distance myself from the pain that was bursting through my body. "If that is so, then why are you going after Jason for his money?"

Someone loosened the pressure on my fingers, and my nails pulsed painfully with each heartbeat. Cyress looked at me, his eyes wild and crazed as he growled, "That money is mine. I don't know how he did it, but he cheated. You want to live with a cheater?"

I closed my eyes and breathed through the pain as he pressed his finger into the slice he had created on my leg. "Is it that he cheated or that you are just that shit at cards? One would think the owner of The Den would at least know when to stop playing."

"Tell me where my fucking money is." His eyes widened even more, and spit flew through the air as he said the words.

I sighed deeply, my breath hitching a couple times as whoever was behind me tightened the clamps back down on my fingers. Even though I tried to sound brave, the words came out as a whimper. "I can't tell you something I don't know."

My eyes met the guards who were standing a few feet behind Cyress, and one of them had this look in his eye that looked as if he were conflicted. Cyress's phone rang and he answered a video call. Cyress chuckled. "Well, maybe this will change your mind."

When he flipped the phone around, my heart fell into my stomach. Kevin was sitting there with a gun pointed in his direction. His name came out of my mouth, and even I heard the fear and horror in my own voice. I tried to take a deep breath, but the air caught in my throat. Swallowing, I told myself I had to keep it together for Kevin.

"Kevin, you okay?"

His eyes shifted quickly back and forth as he brought the console controller up to his chin. "Yes. I was playing video games, but the pencil is out of i-ink, and these guys burst in and knocked out Ms. Jones."

"Is she okay?" He nodded. "Okay. Good."

Cyress spit. "What does that even mean? Is he stupid? Pencils don't have ink."

I had to remind myself it was in my best interest not to kill the man . . . right now. "It's a phrase between us. Means he's overwhelmed and scared. Do you blame him? You've got someone there with a gun to his head." My gaze slid over to Cyress, and I glared at him. He held my stare, and that was when I noticed his pupils were blown out. It made him look even more unhinged, and I wondered if he was strung out on something.

When I looked back at the screen, Kevin was shifting in his seat. "I'm working on that right now, okay?" His head moved up and down quickly, and his breathing was picking up. He was shutting down. My attention flicked to Cyress and quickly back to Kevin. I needed to distract him. "What video game are you playing?"

His voice trembled slightly as he told me, and by the way his head was ticking, I knew he was feeling very overwhelmed. "Sissy, who are these people?"

"I don't know, Kevin. I'm sorry." My eyes quickly shifted to Cyress, whose lips lifted in a smirk. "Have fun with the video games, and don't forget to eat and drink your water, okay? I know how you can get."

"Yes, Sissy." His eyes shifted around him, and he tucked his arms in closer and leaned forward. "But the pencil is out of ink."

"Just a little bit longer, okay?" He swallowed hard, but he were wholly focused on the controller. "Eyes on me."

He slowly looked at me, and I saw the fear in his eyes before they shifted to the side again. My brother knew this wasn't in my control, but he didn't know how much to say.

"Someone will be there for you as soon as possible. Then I want you to get a lemon cookie."

Kevin's gaze snapped back to me, and I hoped that he remembered the phrase for him to get to Velas as soon as he could. I could see his mind working, and a moment later, he looked in the direction of the bedroom, not the kitchen, and I knew he understood.

"Can I get two?"

"You want one for Ms. Jones when she wakes up?"

He nodded his head. "Yes, please."

"I think that is a brilliant idea. I'll talk to you soon, okay? Boop snoot."

"Boop snoot." He curled up into a ball in the chair he was sitting in and brought the controller up to his chin again, just as Cyress said, "If you are a good boy, we may even tell you who your father is."

I whirled to face him, not caring that the knife at my neck was slicing the skin as anger flooded me. "Shut your mouth."

"Sissy?"

With the knife pushing against my throat, I couldn't move, so I moved my eyes so that I could see Kevin in the video. "You know who your daddy is."

"Matthew Carley."

Cyress laughed. "That pathetic man wasn't your father."

"I said Daddy, not father." I spat the words at Cyress.

"Sissy? Was Dad not my dad?"

I held Cyress's gaze as an evil smile spread on his face as he said, "No, Kevin Carley. He was not. The man whom you called your father was nothing but a spineless twit having to deal with the damaged offspring of a sloppy second."

My shoulders sagged. "Kevin, I need you to listen to me. Dad was your *dad*. He loved you with everything he had. He didn't care that you were not biologically his."

"You knew?" The confusion and twinge of hurt in Kevin's voice made me swallow the lump in my throat.

Cyress pulled the knife from my throat, apparently content with the fact he was destroying the carefully cultivated world we had surrounded Kevin with. I turned to look Kevin in the eye again. "Mom told me just before she died. Wanted me to know so there wasn't any issue with blood transfusions or anything else. DNA has nothing to do with who your father is."

"But that means Dad didn't make me the way I am."

I blinked at him in wonder. Kevin fascinated me at the strangest times with the way his brain worked. "What?"

"This other person did. Dad loved me even though I was not of his blood. Dad is the one who taught me how to ride a bike and how to be kind. Like Sissy taught me how to be kind."

A bright smile lit up my face. *Take that, Cyress.* "That is right."

"Turn it off," Cyress snapped.

When Kevin was no longer on the video call, I looked up at Cyress. I kept the smirk on my face as I sassed, "That backfired, didn't it?"

Lashing out, he sliced down my arm again. I tried to hide the wince as it cut into the flesh and warmth ran down to my wrist. "I suggest you tell me where Rathborn is hiding all my cash. Now."

Glaring at him, I pressed my lips together. I didn't know shit, but he wouldn't believe me even if Jason had said something. I was terrified I was pushing my luck with him, but I really didn't care at this point. He had fucked with Kevin. It was a line that wasn't to be crossed. Fuck with me all he wanted, but I wasn't ever going to tolerate someone using Kevin against me or Jason. I would endure all of this if they just left him out of it from here on out.

I didn't see the fist that swung for me, but I certainly felt the pain that burst through my face, and I ran my tongue along my teeth as the taste of iron filled my mouth. Finding that all of them were still in place, I spit the blood onto Cyress's shoe.

He sneered just as the front door opened, and Jason's voice rang through the air. "Hope you are hungry!"

Guns were raised and pointed at him as he froze just beyond the threshold into the apartment. My heart was racing at the sight. I tried to convey that despite how I might look at the moment, I was okay. Jason swallowed and gave me a quick nod.

"Cyress, what are you doing in my house?" Jason was hiding the fear in his voice really well, but it was there.

"It's time you give me back all that you've stolen from me." Cyress stood from where he was kneeling before me and slipped his knife under my chin again. Cold seeped into the hollow part just behind the jaw as the blade pressed against the skin, and I carefully swallowed.

Jason's eyes were locked on mine as he growled, "I won it fair and square."

The jerk behind me pulled on my shoulders to hold me back as Cyress shouted, "You cheated. You've won millions. You've rarely lost. No one is *that* good."

Millions? Holy shit!

Jason's chuckle went through the room as I tried to hide my shock at that little tidbit of information. "So, you want me to throw games because I'm better than everyone else at cards? Yeah, no. And before you ask how I did it, again . . . I have never counted cards. I'm just *very* good at reading people."

"Where are you hiding that much cash? She hasn't told us anything about a safe in the house, despite our *encouragement*, nor have we found one."

"Well, that's because I don't have a safe in the house or any other safe house. Seriously, where do you guys get your information? I live a simple life."

Any other safe house? What is going on?

Cyress pressed the blade against my throat again, and more warm, wet liquid rolled down my throat. Jason was trying to stay where he was since there were at least three guns still pointed at him, but his muscles twitched in restraint.

"Tell me what bank the funds are in."

"Boy, you guys *are* real dumb. I'm not hiding it. Anyone with more than ten brain cells should be able to trace every dime." When he looked at me, I could see the fear there, but there was something stable in his demeanor. His attention shifted to Cyress, and he stared him down. "You and I need to settle this once and for all, Cyress."

"I want my money back. You stole it from me."

Jason crossed his arms over his chest and leaned against the doorframe, giving off an air of bored indifference, though I knew him well enough to know it was an act. "I won it from you fair and square in your own club, by your own rules. I'd win it all again, too."

Cyress looked at one of his guys, who swung his gun around in my direction as Cyress stood. "If you are so sure, then be at The Den tonight. Eight o'clock. I'll close it down. Let's settle this once and for all."

"All the funds on the table, and you leave us alone forever."

Cyress laughed, pulling the knife from my neck and waving it around. "Oh, we are playing for the cash alright. Plus your Queen of Hearts. If you win, then you keep the cash *and* your queen." He circled the couch, my heart beating hard in my chest, before he leaned behind me and whispered in my ear, "You will be mine to do with as I wish, little girl."

My stomach twisted and went sour. "In your dreams."

"And if you win?" Jason asked, oblivious to the taunting and bringing Cyress's attention back to him.

He stood back up and made his way in front of Jason before answering. "If I win, then I get your girl, your cash, and your brother-in-law. I can guarantee neither of them will live through the weekend, and your girl will be begging for death before I put a bullet in her brain."

Jason's eyes met mine, and I saw the question in them. I set my shoulders back, telling him it was okay. I could see this was the only path. If we could get ahold of Uncle Thom, then we might be able to get out of the game alive tonight, no matter the outcome.

Then, it was as if the word echoed through the room with the finality of it. "Deal."

CHAPTER FIFTY-SIX

LANIE

TRENTON

Once the deal was made, the man who had been standing behind the couch removed the finger clamps and forced me to stand. My digits burst in pain at the release, and I winced, scrunching up my face in agony. When I opened my eyes, Jason's attention was solely on me as I stood and felt the sting of the slice down my leg that Cyress had inflicted earlier. They forced me forward, and I limped my way toward the door, my heart pounding.

"She's going to come with us . . . as an insurance policy."

Jason shifted to stand between us and the door. "Cyress, I'll be there."

"You're right. If you ever want to see her again, you will be."

I mustered up some courage because I wanted to calm him. The worry and fear were heavy in his gaze as he studied me, so I said, "I'll be okay. I'll see you tonight. If not, please kill him."

"Watch it, woman," the man behind me said, tugging on the zip ties around my wrists, causing them to dig further into my skin.

Jason took a step closer, but when two of Cyress's men raised their guns to him, he stopped. He gave them a simple nod as his hands balled into fists, and he rolled his shoulders back to restrain himself. When he met my gaze again, I gave him a small nod.

Our gazes held as I tried to sound confident. "I'll see you tonight. I love you."

"Love you, too."

He leaned forward and kissed me softly, but when Cyress scoffed, the shithead behind me pulled me away from Jason. I hissed in pain as I stumbled backwards onto my injured leg. My heart was pounding and blood pumped through my body as they hauled me out of the condo. Everything felt tingly as they pulled me from Jason, and I tried to stifle the panic rushing through me. One of Cyress's goons stayed back with Jase, and I wondered if he would be ensuring that he showed up tonight and that Jase didn't try to get extra help. Jason's attention didn't leave mine until we got into the elevator and the doors closed.

The ding of the elevator signaled its stop, and I was pulled forward, wincing at the pain in my arm and leg. As we walked, the cold tile under my bare feet, I could hear the sounds of their boots in the large, empty entry. The smell of the city breezed by as we made our way outside, just before I was stuffed into a car. I didn't know the town well enough to even have an idea of which direction we were going, let alone pay attention to the turns that they were taking to get us to wherever we were going. Immediately, a dark-colored bag was put over my head, and even through the fear, I thought, *How cliché.*

It seemed like forever before the car came to a stop and they opened the door. Fresh, cooler air flowed through the vehicle and into the loose fabric around my neck before they ordered, "Slide to your right and put your feet on the ground."

I did, and then they were taking me by the elbow into the building. The floor creaked under our weight, and the air was filled with a mixture of fresh baked bread and chocolate chip cookies. We stopped, and the hinges on a door creaked as they opened it then gently pushed me inside.

When they pulled the hood off, I was standing in a room lined with a few metal shelves, holding various baking supplies, a metal commercial sink, prep table, and a floor covered in rubber mats with holes in them to drain water. Inhaling deeply as they cut the zip ties, I winced as the hard plastic dug deeper into my wrists and the delicious aroma filled my senses again. "You took me to the back of a bakery?"

"Shut up." Then the tall, muscular, bald man turned and walked out of the room, closing the door behind him.

My whole body hurt as I tried to get full circulation into my hands again and stretched my shoulders. I reached up and touched the cut on my cheek and winced. Looking around, I only hoped that they had left Kevin alone and that he was okay. In a few hours, I would have confirmation that Jason was okay, and then I stared at the door.

Gods, I hope I made the right decision.

THE

DEN

DON'T LET THEM EAT YOU ALIVE

CHAPTER FIFTY-SEVEN

JASON

TRENTON

Once Lanie was in the elevator, doors closed, the gun jammed in my back pulled away, and the burly man stepped into my field of vision. He holstered the gun, and I vaguely recognized him from The Den. I tipped my head to the side and let out a long breath. "Noah."

"I'm sorry, Rathborn. I'll do what I can to make sure Cyress doesn't lay a finger on her." His hands were up in a pleading manner. "Seriously. I'll guard her where I'm supposed to meet up with them."

"Where are you meeting them?" I popped my head up and glared at him.

Noah shook his head. "No. If I tell you, then you'll get Don Kingsley, and Cyress will kill her. You have to play the game tonight. I promise I'll be protecting her."

I ran my hands through my hair and let out a frustrated sigh as I paced the room. "I don't understand. Why would you do that if you work for Cyress? Why is it important for me to play the damn game tonight?"

"Because I work for Kingsley, not Cyress. I've been playing Cyress's loyal bodyguard for a year but reporting everything to Don Kingsley. So, I promise you I will do whatever I can to keep that idiot and his slimeballs off of Lanie. As for why? I don't know why. I have orders from my Don. That's all I know."

I took a breath and let it out slowly, nodding. I needed to check in on Kevin. I needed to make sure he was okay.

"I believe you have a phone call to make." Noah raised an eyebrow at me.

"What are you talking about?"

He leaned in close and whispered, "Kingsley will need a heads-up about tonight. Let him know that Noah will be there." I looked behind him at the closed elevator doors and then back at him. "I am in deep and can't take the chance to get a message out to him right now."

"Let her know I'll make sure Kevin is okay and I'll see her tonight."

He nodded once more and then sprinted down the stairs. Turning, I strode back into the house and called Kevin.

"Hello, brother."

"Kevin, are you okay?" I took a deep breath, trying to keep myself calm.

"Yes. They left."

My shoulders sagged as relief rushed through me. "Is Ms. Jones alright?" There was silence for a moment before he said, "Yes. She's awake and drinking water. Is Sissy there?"

"No, she's okay, though. I'm going to pick her up in a few hours." My throat was tight as I said the words. I hated skirting the truth for him, but one of us panicking was enough. Having him upset wasn't going to do any good.

"Sissy told me that she wanted me to go to Velas and that I should take Ms. Jones, too. So I'm packing an overnight bag."

"Good." I ran my hand through my hair again as I resumed pacing in the living room. "Good. Wait, how did she tell you to go to Velas?"

"She told me to have a lemon cookie."

I waited, and when he didn't elaborate, I asked. "I don't understand. What do lemon cookies have to do with going to Velas?"

"After Mom and Dad died, there were a few key phrases that we created so things don't sound rude. *The pencil is running out of ink* is when I'm overwhelmed or scared. *Go get lemon cookies* means that I need to go to Velas and stay there until she picks me up. *Can we get ice cream on the way home* is to say I want to go home right away. There are a bunch more. We will have to teach you."

"Okay." I was pacing faster now, and my stomach started flipping as doubt filled me.

Could I do this?

Could I win tonight?

Sure, I am really good, but I have to get the cards. There is only so much I can do reading him. If he gets the cards and I don't . . . I'm hosed.

I seriously bet the queen of my heart.

Kevin's voice was full of trepidation and concern when it broke me from my thoughts. "Brother, who were those men? I didn't like them. Why were they in my space?"

Fuck.

He was trying to put on a brave face, but I could tell he was half a second from shutting down. *How much do I tell him?* "Kevin, there are some things we need to sort out up here before we can come home. I played a game with some people, and one of them isn't happy that I won. Unfortunately, he was trying to use you as a way to get what he wants. I'm pissed they used you and hurt the people we care about. I'll make sure they know just how mad I am and that they never do that again."

"Brother, are you involved with bad people?" His voice was short and clipped, and it broke my heart.

"I didn't think so, Kevin. I didn't think they would impact you or Lanie's life at all. I'm so sorry all of this happened." My heart was racing again at everything at stake, and my breathing was becoming quicker.

"Okay. I trust you."

My hands were shaking, and no matter how hard I tried, they weren't stopping.

"Text me when you get to Velas, okay?"

"Yes, brother. Give Sissy a hug for me."

Smiling and letting out a long breath, knowing that he was settled and no longer in danger, I hung up, grabbed my keys, and raced out the door, texting Chase that I was on the way.

As I went through the gate at the Kingsley compound, there was motion at the front door, and Chase was at the bottom of the stairs as I parked in the circle drive. I stepped out and looked up to the limestone and black-steel mansion with floor-to-ceiling windows as everything crashed down on top of me. My heart was beating out of my chest, and I was starting to feel lightheaded.

"Professor?"

Closing the car door, I circled around the vehicle and rushed up to Chase.

"I need Don Kingsley's help. Now." Every muscle in my body was vibrating. I wasn't sure how I'd gotten here without crashing, I was shaking so hard.

Chase's response was immediate. "Done. Let's go see Dad."

I took a shaky breath and rushed in behind him. He had to listen to me. We had to get to Lanie. Every breath was becoming tighter the longer she was unreachable. What if they killed her? What if they . . .

No. Don't think of that. They wouldn't, would they?

Of course they would. "Chase, you need to—"

"Wait," he barked as he led me through the estate, and after a couple of turns, he stopped at a door and knocked in three quick connections. The entire house was an elegant, simple beauty that worked together to show the down-to-earthness that the man of this house held, but also the power you didn't test.

While we waited, I tapped my foot and rolled my shoulders. I had to calm down before facing Don Kingsley.

"Come in, Chase." Don Kingsley's voice was muffled but strong.

When we walked through the door, his head was resting in his hand as he studied something on the computer screen. His attention flicked to where we were standing just as Chase closed the door.

He must have seen the panic in my face because he instantly stood and asked, "What happened to Lanie?"

The pure determination on his face strangely checked my anxiousness. My hands balled up into tight fists as I met his gaze. "The short version? Cyress has her."

"The slightly longer version, please." His voice had dropped to a deadly calm, and my breath caught at the tone. I'd only heard that once and I was thankful it hadn't been directed at me at the time. The man that had been the recipient, he'd peed his pants almost immediately.

Glad that I was able to control my bladder, I willed my voice to be steady as much as possible while I looked him in the eye. "I came home from work to find Lanie bound on the couch, sliced up, with fingertip clamps on her fingers. As you know, Cyress is still insisting that I cheated." I rolled my eyes dramatically at the utter bullshit of it. "I'm meeting them at The Den tonight at eight for a playoff. Cyress has Lanie as insurance that I'll be there."

"The stakes?"

"Every dime I've won from him." I swallowed before his eyes widened slightly, like he was waiting for me to continue, somehow knowing there was more. "And my queen."

Don Kingsley's face went blank, and the death in his eyes almost had me peeing my pants. My stomach hollowed out and my body felt numb as my nerves short-circuited at the realization of how I could lose my queen forever.

I'd just gotten her back.

She agreed to be my wife.

My heart aches at the thought of not sharing a bed with her.

We are going to have that wedding she always dreamed of.

The sun setting behind us on the beach as we say our vows.

Kevin as my best man.

Kami standing next to Lanie.

My vision tunneled for a moment before I shook my head to clear it.

Kevin is going to become an accomplished artist, and we are going to stand in the corner of a gallery together, proud as hell of him.

We are going to have kids running around the house that are the perfect mixture of the two of us.

A little boy with her bright eyes and full lips, and a little girl with my brown hair braided in two little pigtails with her long lashes.

I reached out and leaned on the chair in front of me and concentrated on the tufted buttons of the seat as I thought of losing her again.

Hands clamped down on my shoulders, and Chase's face came into view. "Rathborn!"

I blinked, but my vision blurred slightly at the thought of having to tell Kevin that she died on my watch. At the thought of standing over her grave with him at my side.

I barely registered a hand swinging before the sting on my left cheek registered as Chase yelled, "Jason!"

My eyebrows pinched together as I stared at Chase, finally seeing the man in front of me. "You called me Jason?"

"Well, nothing else worked." He shook his head. "Now, sit the fuck down. We need to plan for tonight. We only have a few hours."

Chapter Fifty-Eight

Lanie

Trenton

A tall, burly man came in much later and with a tray with a plate of food and a glass of water on it. There was also a small duffle bag he sat down next to me. His voice was low as he said, "I'm Noah. Nothing will happen to you. The bag has a change of clothes for later."

I looked at the plate he had outstretched toward me and then back at him. "What's in the food?"

"It's a bag of kettle onion chips and a grilled turkey, bacon, and cheddar cheese sandwich on freshly made sourdough bread."

"And in the glass?"

Impressed, he smiled. "Water. Nothing else. I'm impressed you are questioning it. If you would prefer, I can get you bottled water." His voice lowered as he continued, "Your uncle would kill me if I gave you back to your fiancé dehydrated."

My attention snapped up to meet his gaze, and he raised an eyebrow at me. *What in the hell?*

"Will you please eat? We have no idea how long the game is going to be tonight, and I don't think anyone would be happy to see you pass out from hunger. I'll be right outside the door. No one is getting in here until it's time to go to The Den."

"Why are you being nice to me?" I muttered as I took the tray from him.

He knelt in front of me and tilted his head as if to listen for anyone outside the door before facing me again. "Not all of us are aligned with Dazar. Some of us have allegiances to those much higher on the hierarchy."

It took me a split second to realize what he meant. I mouthed, "Uncle Thom." He gave me a small nod and lifted two fingers as if to indicate that there were two of them here who were on his payroll.

He stood, went to the cabinet next to the door, and then pulled out a first-aid kit and started tending to the different injuries Cyress had inflicted. I was sore, but mostly in my shoulders, where they had my arms bound behind me. He cleaned up the cut on my cheek and used some wound glue on it to keep it shut, promising that the scar should be minimal, not that I cared at the moment. When he got to the one at my leg, he cleaned it, and that stung like hell, but when he was done, he used the glue again to close it up and added some butterfly bandages to help keep it closed. He repeated the process for my arm and anything else that was more than a couple inches long.

I took a deep breath and let it out slowly as he finished up. "What happens if Jason loses tonight?"

Standing, Noah said, "Dazar won't touch you no matter what he has planned or regardless of what happens with the game. Now, eat and change your clothes. I'll be back in a couple hours, and we will head out."

True to his word, Noah came in, and I was thankful for the pair of jeans, tank, and pair of cheap flip flops that he'd given me to change into. At least I wouldn't have to walk on my bare feet anymore. Noah looked me up and down and then nodded as he apologized before putting the hood back over my head. He took me by the elbow, and I heard multiple sets of feet this time, where before I was pretty sure there were only two.

Only, as he led me out of the bakery, we didn't get back into a car, but instead walked through what I assumed to be a back alley. It smelled of beer and piss mixed with the bakery and the sound of a dumpster lid closing. The pain in my leg was menial, but that didn't mean it didn't hurt. Trying to distract myself, I asked, "Where are we?"

Someone I didn't recognize snapped for me to shut up, and then there was a hand on my ass, rubbing and squeezing. I kicked out in the direction of the voice and made contact with what felt like a knee. Pain burst up my leg, and I was quickly reminded of the cut Cyress had inflicted on me. The man cursed, and then Noah was pulling me behind him. "Don't touch her, Martinez."

"Boss already said I could have a turn with her. Was thinking I would go sweet with her, but after that, I'm gonna ram her hard and fast. Teach her to follow a man's instructions." Chills went down my spine as my stomach churned. "She's going to be passed around like the fat pig she is."

"Martinez!" another voice from behind me bellowed as someone's hands landed on my shoulders. I tensed, but his thumbs moved back and forth. "You won't touch her."

The man whispered in my ear, "I'm with Noah."

That simple phrase lessened the tightness in my chest. One in front. One in back. I wasn't exactly sure how many men were around me, but I had two on my side. "Sandavol, take her inside."

The man who was behind me slid his hand down to take ahold of my elbow, and we walked about twenty feet before we stopped and a metal door creaked open. Once it was dark again, I heard the tinkling of glasses and noticed the smell of . . . whiskey? The hood came off, and standing in front of me was a man a little taller than I was with dark hair, a goatee, and warm brown eyes. He smiled at me and tipped his head to the side toward the grey metal door at the end of the storeroom. "Rathborn is waiting for you just on the other side of that door. Go. Have a couple minutes with him before the game. Don't think of running off, though. Cyress is losing it. If you run, the next time he sees you will be the last time."

I looked at the door and back at him. He nodded, and I rushed over and flung it open to the bar on the ground floor, Jason standing there, eyes wide in surprise across the room. I ran to him, weaving through the bar tables, and once his arms were tight around me, I breathed a sigh of relief.

"You okay?" I nodded. "Anyone hurt you?" I shook my head and held him tighter. I felt him relax some as well, and his breathing was becoming a little more even as we stood there.

He pulled back, kissing my forehead, and looked into my eyes. I could see the fear, worry, and determination in his gaze, but most of all I saw his love for me. "Everything is going to be okay."

I looked over my shoulder and saw Noah and another man who I suspected was Sandavol standing just behind us. Turning back to Jason, I sucked in the corner of my bottom lip in worry. "How do you know?"

He smirked, and there was a spark of mischief in his gaze. "I have a wild card in this stacked deck." He reached up and pinched my chin between his knuckle and thumb and made me face him. "I will do everything I can to protect you downstairs. I have no idea what Cyress is going to do. Do everything that Kai tells you to. Follow his instructions, and you will be fine. He will be the moderator."

He looked me over, and I swore I felt some of his muscles relax. I gave him a small smile. "Noah gave me a change of clothes."

Jason looked behind me and nodded. I assumed it was to Noah. "I'm glad. He the one who bandaged you up?"

"Yeah, my leg too. The pressure from my jeans is helping with the pain, oddly enough."

Jason pressed his lips to my forehead and kept them there for a long minute. I concentrated on the feel of him and let it relax some of the stress in my shoulders. I hoped that Uncle Thom would be here tonight. He wouldn't leave me to this fate, would he? My heart was racing, and Jason's free hand slid down my arm and threaded our fingers together. I knew my palms were sweaty, but he didn't let go of my hand.

"Uncle Thom?" I tried to keep my voice low so no one could hear me, but my blood was racing through my veins.

He lifted my chin, leaned in, and whispered against my lips, "He's downstairs, my queen. The ultimate wild card."

"Thank the gods. I love you, Jason."

"I love you, too." He pressed his lips against mine, kissing me languidly. My lips trembled slightly as I held back the lump in my throat and the tears in my eyes. I was walking into a lion's den, and I didn't have a clue who the king was. I could only hope that it was going to be Jason.

When he pulled back and our foreheads rested against each other, I whispered, "Realistically, what are our odds today?"

"If he hasn't paid off the croupier, which is the dealer, then eighty percent I win. Remember, I know Cyress's tells and can read him most of the time. It's not perfect, but I usually win against him. What scares me, though, is if he has been playing the long game, and now that there is something I'm not willing to lose, he will take me for everything." He shook his head. "If he has paid people off, then I'll only have the cards in my favor. I don't care if I lose every penny, but I won't lose you."

"If he takes me, I won't—"

Jason's lips slammed onto mine, and he wrapped his arms tight around my waist, pulling me close. As one of his hands smoothed up my back, his fingers tightened possessively in my hair. I felt every ounce of his want and love for me in that kiss. He pulled back and kissed me again quickly before threading our fingers together once more and leading me downstairs.

"It won't come to that."

My whole body hurt like hell, so I had to take each step slowly. Jase didn't say a word, but I could feel the rage at the cause of my pain rolling off him in waves. Eventually, we made it down. At the base of the stairs was a small room where each of us was searched from head to toe for weapons, and I saw Uncle Thom just past the threshold. Even though Jase had told me he was going to be here, seeing him in the flesh helped ease my anxiety.

We have a chance of getting out of here alive tonight.

I didn't think for one minute that if Cyress lost, he would let Jason and me just walk out of The Den alive and well, but if anyone could make it happen, it was my uncle. Right?

I went in first, Jason watching the hands of the burly, bald-headed man checking me over. After I was cleared, Jason stepped forward and grumbled, "Not sure why you are even checking for weapons. We all know that Cyress, Don Kingsley, and all of their guys are carrying."

"Sorry, Jason. Boss's orders."

"I get it, Kole. Just saying, it's dumb and petty."

Once he was cleared, Jason rested his hand on the small of my back again and steered me to the sign-in counter where a man with shaggy, dark black hair and warm eyes greeted us. I tilted my head and took in the thin nose, fine facial features, pale skin, full lips, and straight eyebrows. There was something in those eyes that told me I could trust him. His attention flicked to the center of the room before he looked back at us and swallowed. "Jason."

"My queen, this is Kai Dae-Jung. He handles the cash office and the contracts upon entry."

I reached my hand out and shook his.

"It's nice to meet you, Ms. Carley." Between our palms was a small, smooth item and a piece of paper that, when he pulled away, he left in my hand. As carefully as I could, I slipped them into the pocket of my jeans. "Jason, I have your paperwork here. Please sign and initial. This is the standard contract with a couple of different provisions. Please make sure to review the winnings section for allocation purposes and the disqualification clause that has been added, since this isn't our standard game."

Jason was muttering angrily under his breath as he read through them. There was a moment where he lifted his gaze to Kai, who swallowed hard and nodded once. Leaving them to discuss the contract, I took the moment to take in the room. I had expected some dingy, dirty, shoddy basement dive. This place was elegant with its medium grey walls, grey, black, and brown artwork, black iron sconces on the walls, and a black iron and gold chandelier over the table in the center of the room. There were about eight others that circled the space, and I assumed that they all hung over the tables that had been removed from the room. The floor was wide grey plank, making the room look much larger than it was. On the far wall was a bar with dark grey and brown accents in the padding, with bar stools lining the edge.

A tall Black man came up to us and nodded to Kai and Jason. "Reynolds."

"Rathborn."

Kai tipped his head to him and then turned to me. "This way please, Ms. Carley." He led me to the lone poker table in the center of the room. As he pulled a chair out for me, he muttered, "Don Kingsley has staffed most of the security. You won't be harmed."

After sitting down, I ran my hands along the grey, plush padding around the edges. The pitch black felt gave the illusion of a black hole ready to swallow us up, and there was a part of me that wanted to jump into the nothingness. Just because security said I'd be safe didn't mean that Dazar wouldn't pull the trigger himself. My gaze roamed over the table, where there were chairs on opposite sides, and I was strategically placed between the two of them. I shuddered at the way I was being treated like a prize to be won, sitting in the middle, right before I looked back at Jason standing with Kai, who gave me a little nod.

I sat there with my hands in my lap for a moment and then slowly slid the palm-sized piece of wood that Kai had given me out of my jeans pocket. When I pulled it out, something sharp pricked my palm. Looking down, I saw a small bead of red seep from my skin in my palm, next to a hidden knife. I quickly pulled out the faux sheath and stuck it back in my pocket. I took a deep breath and pressed my finger against the wound to get it to stop bleeding and leaned back in the chair, trying to look bored.

Cyress came up a few minutes later and stood behind me, bending down to smell along my neck.

"I would appreciate it if you would stop doing that," I ground out through my teeth.

Rancid onion breath flowed across my skin and assaulted my senses. "You just wait, my little peach. I am going to have so much fun with you."

Jason came and stood by my side. "You'd have to actually win a game against me first."

When I looked up, his eyes were hard. A dark chuckle sounded on the other side of me as Cyress stepped back and took his seat. My attention didn't leave Jason, though, as he bent down, gripped my chin, and kissed me softly. I melted into his touch and focused on the warmth of his hand as he held me in place. "That's my good little slut." His voice was so soft, I barely heard it, but I did and I whimpered, pressing my legs together.

"Not fair, Sir."

He winked at me and turned to sit down at the table. I carefully pulled the sheet of paper out of my pocket that was with the knife and opened it out on my lap, hiding it under the table. It simply read, "Kevin is safe." Relief once again flooded me, and I looked up to Uncle Thom, who nodded.

Once Jason was seated, Kai called out, "The game has officially started. Line up."

Six women walked out from the back corner and stood side by side, all looking forward. Each was dressed in a metallic gold halter mini dress with a cowl neckline, the fabric hugging every perfect curve of the six women. With a twist of Kai's finger, they circled, and you could see the dresses were bare-backed to the curves of their asses. "You will each pick a number from the hat. That number will be your assigned number for this game. With the roll of the dice, the first croupier will be selected. Every three hands, the dice will roll and we will switch out to a different croupier. If your number comes up just as you finish your round, we will roll again. You have all signed a contract that states you have accepted no bribes or received threats to assist one player or the other. This is your reminder that the penalty for breaking that contract is death. Your blood will be spilled on this floor, regardless of standard house rules. Is that understood?"

They spoke as one. "Yes, sir."

Kai took a hat that was handed to him and lifted it to each of the ladies, who each pulled a slip of paper. After stating the number they were assigned, they lined up in numerical order. Kai nodded to them and walked up to the dealer's spot at the table. Kai met my gaze and held out his hand. "Ms. Carley, you will roll the die."

"Oh, okay." I reached out, and when he saw the spot of smeared blood on my palm, his lip twitched as he dropped the die into my hand and nodded. I pulled it back and rolled the die between both hands. I met Jason's gaze, and he nodded that he was ready.

"At your discretion, ma'am."

I looked up at the gorgeous man who smiled at me as I dropped the die.

"Croupier number four."

A blonde walked up and took hold of the cards, shuffling them effortlessly three times before setting them on the felt.

"Let's get started, gentlemen."

THE

DEN

Don't Let Them Eat You Alive

CHAPTER FIFTY-NINE

JASON

TRENTON

Round after round we played, our chips staying pretty even until the last few. It had been hours since we'd started, and I was in desperate need of the bathroom, but if I left the table without a break being called, I forfeited the game. *Ain't no way in high hell that I am doing that.* Not with her on the line.

Lanie rolled the die between her palms again and lifted her hands up in a prayer motion, getting ready to let the numbers fall where they may. Just before she did, though, Kai announced, "Before you roll, Ms. Carley, we are going to take a fifteen-minute intermission. Player 1 can use the restroom on the south end of the room." He indicated the room to the left. "And Player 2, the one on the north."

When Lanie made to stand, Kai halted her. "I'm sorry, Ms. Carley, but you will need to wait here. Once Player 1 returns to his seat, you may use that bathroom."

My gaze met hers, and there was a worried expression on her face. I knew that I couldn't touch her during the game, one of the fine-print, bullshit things Cyress had put in the contract. I nodded to her and watched as she sat down. Before I went around the corner, I looked back and saw her attention flick between the two piles. I had purposefully allowed him to win a few hands and folded to let Cyress think he had a chance. The relief on his face had been minimal when I'd folded the last hand, even with the three of a kind that I'd had.

I rushed to the bathroom, relieved myself, washed my hands, and splashed some water on my face. Leaning on the counter, I looked at my reflection in the mirror. I knew I could do this. I had to. My queen was at stake. My heart was thudding loudly, and I took a moment to inhale a ragged breath before letting it out just as ragged. Inhaling and exhaling, I repeated the process until I could actually breathe normally. I met my own gaze in the mirror again and whispered, "For my queen."

Straightening, I rolled my shoulders and headed out the door. Kai was crouched and talking to Lanie, but nodded and stood when he saw me coming back in. Cyress wasn't back from the bathroom yet, so I looked over to where Don Kingsley was standing next to a pillar not far to the right of where Cyress's seat was. He wasn't quite at the right angle for him to give me indications of Cyress's hand, which I was thankful for since the last thing I wanted to do was be called for cheating. That would forfeit all of our lives.

Lanie stood and headed for the bathroom, rubbing the back of her neck, right where Cyress had been holding her at knifepoint earlier today. Balling my hands up into fists to restrain myself from reaching out and squeezing her hand, I took a deep breath to settle myself. I was surprised when she didn't reach out to get that ounce of comfort, but her gaze met mine and I saw the range of emotions that flitted across her eyes. I wasn't sure what hit me more, the love in them or the fear laced with trust. As she rounded the corner, I let out a long breath. "Thom." I felt the tension in the room tighten as I called the Don by his first name. This wasn't about labels or who had more power than who. This was a man wanting to protect his queen. Slowly, I lifted my gaze from the hole in the center of the table to meet his. "No matter what happens in the next few hands, make sure she gets out of here alive."

There was a quick jerk of his head. "On my life. I've already told you that."

My chest loosened slightly as his words sank into me. Just as Cyress was walking out of the back bathroom, I mouthed a, "Thank you." We both continued to stay standing in our respective places at the table until Lanie returned. She had run her wet hands through her hair and put it up with a pencil. She took a shaky breath and then looked at Kai as she stood in front of her chair.

"You may be seated." Once we were settled again, he looked at me, and I saw the plea in his eyes. "When you are ready, Ms. Carley."

My queen lifted her head, put the die between her fingers, stared at it for far too long before she dropped it, and let it fall onto the blackness of the felt. Her attention hadn't left Kai's as she leaned back and folded her hands on the padded grey edge of the table. I wondered what they had been talking about. She hadn't looked at me since she'd come out of the restroom.

"Croupier three to the table."

Becca, the redhead who had looked at Lanie like she'd wanted to devour her, came to the table and nodded to both Cyress and me. "Your blinds, please."

I flicked the required chips into the center and waited, tapping my finger on the felt. Lanie's gaze stayed on the redhead, who winked at her and dealt our two cards. Lanie simply kept her attention straight ahead with no emotion on her face at all. My queen lifted her hands onto the padded grey ledge and picked at her nails and sighed dramatically. She was trying to look completely unbothered by any of this, bored almost. If it were not for the occasional twitch of her shoulder, I would have believed her act, but there wasn't a part of her body that I didn't have memorized down to the last hair. Her muscles twitched in her back, and her feet would twitch before she would consciously try to keep them from moving.

Another four croupiers rotated through, and I was quickly and quietly handing Cyress his ass back to him on a silver platter. The cards were good to me, and I had taken him down to almost nothing.

When Lanie rolled the die again, Becca strode back to the table, winked at Lanie, and then looked at me, giving me a smirk. Only, when her left hand reached down for the cards, my attention froze on the roughly drawn gun on her wrist. Becca's eyes didn't move, and I just dipped my head as I looked at Cyress's chips before lifting my gaze back to her.

Shit. Is she trying to warn me that Cyress has a gun?

She rubbed her wrists together and the scrawl was gone. My attention flicked to Don Kingsley, who had moved, carefully studying Cyress as he shuffled his two cards over and over again.

I hadn't looked at my own hand yet but watched as Becca laid down a ten of hearts, three of diamonds, and six of clubs. My fingers tapped on the felt, so that Cyress had to lay the first bet.

"What, you aren't even going to look at what is in your hand?"

With a shrug, I watched him. I would look if the bet was big enough. I had most of his pot anyway. If I was lucky, this would all be over while Becca was at the table.

Cyress stared at his dwindling chip stack before taking a large handful and tossing it into the pot. "Fifty thousand."

My eyebrow lifted in consideration. Fifty with *that* on the table? The best that he could have was a three of a kind. Tens, no less. Slowly and methodically, I looked at my hand and then back at him where he twitched his shoulder.

Well, that is new.

"Call." I moved fifty thousand in chips to the center.

Becca looked between us, and without looking, she laid the next card down. The ace of hearts. Becca kept her focus on Lanie, whose mind was racing at the potentials on the table.

Cyress leaned against the table and tapped his fingers on the felt. "I think it's time to put an end to this and make the bet more interesting, for me that is. You already have everything on the line."

"I'm listening, Cyress. There are a multitude of options on the table, and as you said, I have the only thing of value in my life already at stake."

Lanie's breathing hitched as her focus snapped to mine, and in my peripheral vision, I saw the love and fear there. I looked down at my cards again, making a show of me being worried about the hand.

Wouldn't you know that in order to save the queen who rules my heart, I would need the Queen of Hearts.

"All in, plus the bar upstairs."

I took a deep, smooth breath and did the calculations on what the bar could be worth. I could cover that in savings. "Call."

Again, without looking, Becca pulled another card from the deck and placed the Queen of Hearts right in front of Lanie. I stared at it and looked at Becca, wondering if she had placed the card there on purpose. It was as if she knew exactly what card was going to be next. How could she, though?

My attention went to the deck and then back to the table. Cyress's chuckle floated through the air. "Don't look so disappointed, Jason. I'm all in, including the bar and the ownership of The Den itself."

There was a collective intake of breath in the room, and even I narrowed my eyes at the odd bet. "You seem pretty sure I won't call it. That's a hefty price tag."

"When you have the hand . . . and a beautiful girl to spend the evening with, it's hard not to." He looked at Lanie with a smile across his face that sent shivers up my spine. "What are you going to do, Jason? I'm all in. Everything I have is now on the table. That is how sure I am that no matter what I have in my hand, you can't beat it. That means this is the last round. Do you call?"

I looked around the room, leaving my gaze on Don Kingsley a bit longer, drastically swallowed, and looked over at Lanie. "I love you, Lanie, but I have to call this. I have to bank that the best hand he has is what's on the table . . . or a pair of aces. He's too smug." Keeping my cards flat on the table, I looked up at Cyress and lifted my chin as I said, "Call."

I held my breath as he turned his cards over, leaned back, crossed his arms over his chest, and looked way too pleased with himself. "Flush."

My gaze met Lanie's, and I apologized to her silently. As she nodded, the corner of her lips twitched up.

Letting out a long breath, I leaned on the padded ledge of the table. "That's a shame."

As Cyress lifted a gun, six more were aimed toward him. Cyress didn't seem to mind it and, with a malicious tone, ordered, "Lanie, come with me. We are going to have so much fun before I kill you and send you back to the professor in pieces."

"Now, now," I said softly as he met my gaze. "Game isn't over. You haven't seen my cards."

"You can't beat a flush with what's on the table." He turned toward me, and there was a flash of uncertainty in his eyes.

"There are at least a few things that beat a flush. Full house, four of a kind for example. Both have low possibilities, considering the community cards. Regardless, the odds are in your favor. Now, a straight flush? That's a possibility."

"Straight flush? Still aren't the best odds. It wouldn't be smart to play that."

I chuckled. "And neither is you betting the bar *and* The Den on a *flush*. That's a bit of a desperate play. No doubt the way to try to push me out of the game. Here is the thing. There is one play here that, while the odds are low, still has a possibility to ruin your day . . . and your life." Without changing my expression, I tossed my two cards into the center. The Jack and King of Hearts landed right next to the queen in front of Lanie.

"Royal flush."

THE

DEN

DON'T LET THEM EAT YOU ALIVE

THE

D E N

DON'T LET THEM EAT YOU ALIVE

CHAPTER SIXTY

JASON

TRENTON

Cyress stared at it for a long time, his face falling in disbelief.

Straightening my spine, I lifted my chin and stated, "I expect the deeds to both the property and The Den to be delivered, signatures notarized and ready to file by three tomorrow afternoon."

"How? How did you do it?"

"Same way I have done it every time. I read you. I played the odds and read you. No tricks up my sleeves. No bribes. No intimidation." I held his gaze as I held to my truth.

Red-hot anger creeped up his neck as his face morphed into rage. Cyress stood with the force to knock the chair back eight feet before he swung the gun toward me and fired. There was a stinging sensation on my cheek just as two more guns went off, and I saw Cyress twist around, cussing.

Don Kingsley was in front of him, gun to his forehead. "You take a shot at my niece and nephews ever again and I'll be the one putting a bullet in your brain. Now, leave with your tail between your legs and get the fuck off my nephew's property."

Cyress wordlessly holstered his gun and strode out of the place.

The entire room stayed quiet until the door upstairs slammed shut. Lanie immediately stood up and threw herself at me. I kissed her with everything I had. My hands were everywhere when I pulled back, making sure she was okay. She was shaking, but she hadn't gone into a blind panic at the gunshots this time, so I was proud of her for that.

"Jason, I'm fine. You, on the other hand . . ." Her finger swiped across my cheek, and then she brought it into my view, where there was bright red blood on the tip. "You are bleeding."

None of it mattered. I had what was most important right here in my lap. "I'm fine, my queen. I'm here."

"But you almost weren't. He almost killed you!" Her voice was getting higher and more panicky, so I kissed her again, pulling her against me, letting her feel every inch of my body. When I pulled back again, I took that hand with the smudge of blood on it and placed it over my heart.

"I'm still here. I'm yours forever."

Lanie turned toward Don Kingsley, tears in her eyes. "Thank you for everything."

"Of course. We are family." He looked over to one of his guards and tipped his head toward us, who went to the back room and a moment later came over with a first-aid kit and took a look at my cheek.

"It's just a flesh wound." Then the guard proceeded to clean it up and put some glue on it. I didn't really feel much as my attention was fully on the queen before me. Reaching up to Lanie's face, I ran my finger over where someone had done the same to the cut on her cheek. She gave me a small smile and leaned into the touch, letting out a sigh.

When the guard was done, Don Kingsley came to stand next to us. "I'll meet you at the condo at noon tomorrow to pick you up and bring you back here to sign the paperwork. Get some rest. It's been a long day."

Lowering my hand and trailing it down Lanie's arm, I took hers and threaded our fingers together, squeezing tight. She did the same, and we made our way upstairs and out of The Den. The bar on the main floor was full of college-aged adults dancing with the lights low, and I wondered if the bass on the music was up so high because we'd been downstairs and there'd been the potential for gunfire. As we walked through the throngs of people, it didn't appear that anyone was the wiser of what had occurred on the underground level.

Neither of us said a word as we hit the cool night air and rushed to my car. Once I had Lanie buckled in, I leaned in and kissed her before closing the door and rounding to the driver's side. In less than a minute, we were pulling out onto the boulevard toward home.

THE

DEN

Don't Let Them Eat You Alive

CHAPTER SIXTY-ONE

LANIE

TRENTON

My mind raced the entire way back to the condo. By the time Jason was unlocking the door, I was dancing on my toes. I needed to check in with Kevin. The door was barely open before I barreled past him and found my phone on the table next to the couch. Reaching for it, I called via video chat, and two rings later he was picking up the phone.

"Sissy?"

Relief flooded me with that simple word, and I sat down on the couch. "Are you okay?"

"I am. Are you and brother, okay?" I could see his eyes moving across the screen, and I suspected that he was looking over the injuries he could see.

"We are fine, Kevin. I promise. We are a little banged up, but we are alright. Is Ms. Jones still there with you?"

He nodded. "In one of the guest rooms on the second floor. She has a headache, but they checked her out and said she would be okay." Kevin shifted a bit in the chair he was in and looked off beyond the camera. "Sissy, who were those people? There was even a guy who came and said that he was a friend of yours. He was just checking to make sure I got here okay. He had Kami's safe code, so I knew it was okay to talk to him, but who were they? And what does this have to do with who my father is?"

I let out a long breath. "I can explain it more when I get home, but the short version is that Mom and Dad . . . Well, Mom had a boyfriend and became pregnant with you. Dad knew, and your biological father was a very close friend to . . ." I looked at Jason, who was smiling softly at me, leaning against the door. "He was a very close friend of Uncle Thom, Mom's brother."

His head tipped to the side in confusion. "We have an uncle?" I nodded. "Why haven't we seen or heard of him before?"

"Mom ordered him out of our lives when you were an infant. We also have a cousin, who I was close to at the time, Chase. I think you will like him a lot."

He blinked at me, and I could see him trying to process what I had told him. "Are we going to spend time with Uncle Thom and Chase?"

"I want to. He seems to want to be very involved in our lives. Already is in ways. Has been in others. It will ultimately be up to you if you want to have them more involved in your life. I can explain everything in full later, okay?"

"Okay, Sissy. You look really tired." He did too. His shoulders were slumped, and he was sitting cross-legged in his bed under the blankets.

Was he waiting for me to call?

My shoulders were so tight they hurt, and I was super mentally drained. "I am."

"Get some sleep, and when you get home, you can tell me everything, okay?"

I smiled at him. "Of course. Boop snoot."

"Love you, too."

When he hung up, Jason was kneeling in front of me, placing his hands on my thighs. He held my gaze for a long moment before sighing. "Come on. Let's get you in a bath."

As he pulled me up, I leaned into him. "My leg and arm, though. They're wrapped up."

"True. So, a shower. You need some water therapy to help calm your brain before you even remotely try to go to sleep."

"Jase—"

"Lanie." He pulled me against him before lifting me up bridal style. I wrapped my arms around his neck as he looked down at me. "Let me take care of you."

I stared at him and realized he needed this. He needed to do something, so I nodded. I kept my focus on him as he carried me into the master bath and sat me down on the counter. The man was sex incarnate, and my heart sped up as he reached in, turned the shower on, and slowly started to undo the buttons on his shirt. As he held my gaze, he unbuttoned his pants and thumbed the waist of both his dark jeans and his boxers, sliding them down his legs and off, tossing them into the corner.

I swallowed as I reached to take my tank off, but he lifted an eyebrow and said, "If my queen tries to take off her clothes, there will be punishments." Smirking, I hooked the hem of the tank in my finger. "They won't be anything enjoyable. Won't be a damn thing my little slut loves. Now remove your fingers."

Heat flowed through me as I uncurled them. Jason took a step toward me and slowly ran his hands up my thighs, over my hips, and under the fabric of the tank, bringing it up with him as his fingers danced along my skin. My nipples hardened at the touch, and as he pulled the tank over my head, he nibbled down my throat and along my collarbone. His hands circled around me, unhooking my bra and removing it a moment before he had both of my breasts in his hands and his tongue circling the right nipple.

"Jase . . ." I hummed as he bit down and then ran his tongue over the pain. "I thought you said water therapy."

"Oh, we will get there, my little slut. First, Sir is going to make sure that every moment of this is pleasure. Now, get down from the counter, carefully."

I did, and then Jason was undoing my jeans, holding my gaze. "Such an obedient little whore."

Slowly, he kissed down my body, sliding my jeans over my hips, down my thighs, and then he lifted each foot and pulled them free. Sir tossed them into the bedroom behind him and licked, teased, and groped his way up until his nose nudged against my core.

His gaze met mine as he leaned forward to kiss just over my clit. I was so wet, I had no doubt that the man could taste me through the fabric. Growling, Sir slipped his fingers between the fabric and my skin and tore it straight from my body before leaning forward again and slipping his tongue through the crease and circling my clit before flicking it once more and standing.

Groaning and letting out a little whimper, I glared at him as he walked over and checked the water temperature before taking my hand and pulling me in. "That was mean, Sir."

"That's what you deserve for tasting so fucking delicious. Now, come here so I can get you cleaned up before I turn you into my personal fucktoy."

Heat flowed through me, and I pressed my legs together, but he swatted my ass and muttered, "No release for you until I give you permission. Is that clear, my queen?"

"Yes, Sir." I sighed as he threaded his fingers through my hair and tipped my head back into the warm spray. I closed my eyes and let my head droop as he worked the water through my long, dark hair. I could feel him hard against me, but he just went to wash my hair and then put a conditioning mask in it. Twisting my hair up and securing it to the top of my head, he reached over and grabbed the silicone body scrubber, put a generous amount of body soap on it, and slowly, methodically washed every inch of my body. Sir was careful around where the bandage glue and butterfly bandages were, yet the care and attention was incredibly sensual as he worked over every inch of my body.

Kneeling before me, he lifted each foot, scrubbing and rinsing them before gently setting them back down. In every action, I could feel his love for me. It was in the soft, careful way he worked over me. He took his time working his way up the other leg and to my core. His soapy fingers slipped between my legs, rubbing against me and circling my clit. I couldn't help but to bite my lip and moan at the pleasure that rolled through me.

"That's my good little girl. Sir is going to make you feel good before he uses your body to please himself."

"Yesss." My back bowed, and his arm wrapped around me as he continued to work my clit.

"Do you want Sir to use you for his pleasure? Like the idea of me pounding into you, smacking your hot ass with your hair wrapped around my fist?"

My mind was starting to scramble as he pushed me closer and closer to the peak, but I was able to mutter, "Yes. Please use me."

His hand dipped deeper into me, two fingers sliding into my pussy as I lifted a leg and rested it on the lower shelf. His fingers found my G-spot quickly, and then he was pressing his thumb against my clit again. Sir's free hand gripped my chin and pulled my head up, taking me right to the edge. Just as I was holding off my orgasm, soft lips moved against mine as he demanded, "Fucking cum for me. Cover my hand with your wetness."

There was nothing I could do at that point. The pure demand had my orgasm ripping through me, screaming his name as he bit down on my shoulder, the pain mixing with my pleasure gloriously.

Lifting his head, he licked the area where he'd bitten me and met my gaze. "God, you are sexy when you cum for me."

My legs were trembling as he removed his hand and began rinsing me off. I was in such a daze, I hadn't registered him releasing my hair until he was massaging the mask out.

His eyes were full of love as he finished cleaning me up. Then he was rinsing his own body and hair out. Sir gripped my chin and gave me a soft kiss as he turned the water off and reached around for a towel. He immediately went to drying me off before towel drying my hair. "Go lie down on the bed."

As I turned to walk out, he smacked me hard on the ass. The sound of it rang through the rooms. I stopped to brace myself on the doorjamb and tried not to whimper as the pain and pleasure went straight to my clit and nipples. The act helped settle my brain some, centered my world again. Standing there for a minute to make sure I would be able to take the few steps to the bed and not collapse as a pile of gelatin, I heard him chuckle behind me before his fingers were threading through my hair again, and he gripped tight.

"My little whore liked that, huh?"

The words came out breathy as I said, "Yes, Sir."

"Well then, over my lap you go." Sir pushed me toward the bed. As he sat down, he turned me and pulled me down over his lap. His hand pushed my head down, while his other hand slipped through my core. "Brace yourself, my queen. I'm going to give you exactly what you want."

The smack as his hand landed on my bare, wet ass rang through the air, and I groaned again as another wave went right through me. Again and again, his hand made contact with my ass. With each connection, I felt my brain settle down and my cheeks heat. My thighs were becoming slick, and when I wiggled, my arm hit the bed frame, causing a stinging pain to shoot up my arm into my shoulder. It was hard enough that I winced and gasped at the connection.

Jason completely froze. Every muscle under my body was solid rock. He didn't move, and when I called out for him, there was no reply. Carefully, I pushed myself up, knelt before him, grabbed the arm that was still hanging in the air, and put his hand in mine. His breathing hitched as he continued to stare off into nothingness. My stomach bottomed out at his reaction. What had happened for him to change his demeanor so quickly? Slowly, his gaze lifted, and there was a line of tears in his eyes.

Pain throbbed in my arm and shoulder, and realization dawned on me. He had ensured I was physically okay while in the shower, and when I bumped my arm, the reminder of what I had gone through must have hit him.

"Sir." Jason just stared at me, so I reached up and cradled his head in my hands. "Jason."

He blinked, and a single tear dropped onto his cheek as I registered the fear in his eyes.

Oh, baby.

"Jason, I am here. Look at me. Really look at me."

He swallowed and blinked again. His eyes moved as if he were studying every inch of my face, and his mouth tightened as he lifted his hand to run a finger along the seam of liquid bandage.

"Alright, we are done for tonight. Get in bed." He blinked at me and his head tipped to the side, confusion evident on his face. "Are you going to say it or am I?"

His voice was soft as he scrunched his eyebrows together. "What?"

I leaned forward and kissed his forehead, and his arms wrapped around me tight. "Strawberry."

His arms stiffened, and his head popped up so that he could look at me. "What—"

"Shh. Not for me, but for you. You are not okay right now." As I rubbed my thumbs along his cheeks, he let out a long breath, finally resting his head on my chest and giving me a single nod. "Thank you. Now, up in bed. Do you want water?"

He shook his head and held me tighter.

"Okay." I forced him to stand and pulled him over to his side of the bed. "What do you need from me, Sir?"

He looked up and met my gaze. There was so much vulnerability there that it hurt my heart. I ran my fingers through his hair and waited for him to answer. The fact that he would trust me with how he was feeling right now solidified why I was his. I pressed my lips to his forehead, letting him feel the connection. Finally, he sighed, and a little of that tension released from his muscles.

"Can I just hold you? I need to know that you are safe in my arms."

I smiled and kissed his forehead again, realizing that I really needed to pee. "Of course. Climb into bed. I'm going to go to the bathroom, and I'll be right here."

His arms tightened, and I pulled back. "Jase, if I don't go to the bathroom, it's not going to be a pleasant situation."

Slowly, he released me, and I hurried off. I rushed in, went to the bathroom, washed up, and then leaned on the counter for a moment and took a breath. I heard him climb in under the blankets and looked up at myself in the mirror.

My dark hair was in every direction, so I grabbed one of the hair ties from my toiletry bag on the shelf and put it up in a messy bun before taking my face wash and squeezing some of it into my hand, rubbing it together until it foamed. Rubbing it on my face, I was careful not to aggravate the slice on my cheek but winced at the tenderness of the wound when I got to the edge. I could hear Jason shifting around just before he called out for me.

"Lanie?"

Quickly, I splashed water on my face and rinsed off all the soap. "Be right there. Just washing my face." I patted my face dry and then turned back into the bedroom to him gripping the comforter on top of the bed.

Jason's eyes were full of worry, so I gave him a reassuring smile. My feet padded across the soft carpet to my side of the bed. Sliding in, I wasn't even fully lying down before Jason went completely koala on me. "Jase, I need to scoot down a few more inches, and then you can hold on as tight as you need."

He looked up at me and loosened his grip slightly. I swallowed as I wiggled down into the blankets, wrapping my arm around him. He laid his head on my good shoulder and put his arm and leg over me. I felt him take a deep breath and let it out slowly against me as I rubbed his back. When he did it again and his breathing hitched, I kissed the top of his head. "We are both here and safe. You did an amazing job protecting me today. I'm home *with you*."

"I almost lost you today."

I tried to curb my own fear, but there had been a chance that I wouldn't be lying next to him right now. Tightening my hold on him, I hummed in agreement. "But you didn't. I'm here because you saved me."

"We are lucky that I got the right cards, that Cyress was unhinged. It could have turned out so much worse."

I swallowed and let out a shaky breath. "I know, but it didn't. There were contingency plans. You said so yourself. You had a wild card . . . Uncle Thom."

"You still got hurt."

"Yeah, and? Did you expect for all of that to happen today and for me to come away without a scratch?"

Jason tightened his grip around me. "You aren't supposed to get hurt because of me."

I chuckled. "While I prefer I never have to go through what I did today, you can't protect me from everything. Hell, one of the Dons of the city is my fucking uncle. At some point, trouble will likely be at our door."

He looked up at me and glared. "Not the point."

"It is though, Jase. You can't protect me from everything."

Nuzzling back into me, he grumbled, "I can try."

A chuckle bubbled out of me at his fierce determination and declaration. "Just lie here for a bit. If you need anything, let me know and I'll get it for you."

"I love you, my queen."

"Love you, too, Sir."

THE

DEN

DON'T LET THEM EAT YOU ALIVE

CHAPTER SIXTY-TWO

JASON

TRENTON

The next afternoon, Don Kingsley woke us up banging on the door. Apparently, he had been knocking for over a minute before he'd started banging and hollering for us. I crawled out of bed, threw a pair of pajama pants on, and trudged into the living room, exhausted, and when I opened the door, he was glowering at me.

"Another thirty seconds and I was going to just take the door off its hinges," he grumbled as he pushed past me. "Now where is Lanie? We have lots to do before we leave."

"Like what?" Lanie said as she repositioned her hair on the top of her head and came around the corner in a pair of jeans and a T-shirt that said, 'I'm a goddamn delight.' I couldn't help but giggle. She glared at me, put her hands on those luscious hips, then had the audacity to demand, "Coffee."

"You are lucky you are a goddamn delight because I should put you over my knee for demanding things from me like that." I pointed my finger at her as I was talking, but there was no way to keep the smile off my face.

"Rathborn, let me tell you now. Keep her happy and you will live a long, healthy life. And I highly suggest you do that. So get her some coffee."

"Would you like a cup too, sir?"

She blinked, shaking her head, and went to sit down at the table. He sat down next to her, and a few minutes later, the three of us all had our morning . . . well, afternoon IV drips and were going over an abundance of paperwork. I wasn't awake enough to make sense of it, but it basically signed over The Den and the bar, Jack Jacks, over to us. Lanie read through some of the documents, and she was asking questions, but after a while, even she just signed and passed the page along. There were so many pieces of paper, I wondered if we were actually buying a house, signing away all of our children, or flying to the moon.

Once we were done, Don Kingsley notarized them and started giving us an overview of how things were going to go when we got to The Den. When he was done, he leaned forward on the table and clasped his long fingers together. "Lanie, I don't want you in Cyress's presence any longer than absolutely necessary."

"Then why do we need to be there at all?" I asked as Lanie's hand found mine and squeezed tight.

He sighed and said, "Dazar won't sign unless you are there, and I don't think you are willing to take my niece out of your sight for long right now."

Nodding because he was right, I leaned back in my chair. "Alright. Let me get dressed and we can head out."

We had discussed the businesses in the car on the way over here and decided Lanie would handle Jack Jacks and I would help Kai with The Den. We weren't able to make a decision on whether we were going to make it our full-time jobs up here yet or not, though. We needed to talk to Kevin first. Needed to see how he felt about everything and whether he wanted to leave San Diego or not. If not, then we might live there, but that was all a discussion for after I had to deal with Cyress Dazar. I wasn't sorry I'd met him. He had made me a made man. If it weren't for Cyress, I would be drowning in debt and working through the mountains of paperwork trying to sort out bills.

We made our way through Jack Jacks and down the stairs in the back to The Den. It felt different now that some of the tension had left my shoulders and I had my queen at my side, but we still had to get out of The Den alive and with paperwork in hand. There were a couple of Cyress's guys at the door to the bar and another one at the door that led downstairs. I was glad that we had a Don at our back, considering I had no idea who was on whose payroll here today. Had Don Kingsley stacked the deck for us?

Lanie's hand tightened slightly as we made our way downstairs but relaxed when Kai greeted us. He gave us each a hug, and we went into the main room. "Jason. Lanie. Glad to see you in one piece."

"Say that again in a few minutes, after Cyress hands us certified documents."

Kai chuckled and then looked at Don Kingsley, who moved past us. "That is why Don Kingsley is here."

A file dropped on the poker table about fifteen feet away. "Can we get this done? I need to go and try to put my life back together since you—"

"Won your businesses fair and square?" I hollered back at him. "Again, you really shouldn't play games you can't win."

Cyress's lips and jaw tightened and shifted back and forth as he nodded curtly. And when I turned back to Lanie, she was handing a small, palm-sized, wood object back to Kai. "I'm thankful and happy I didn't have to use this."

"It was a real possibility that you might have. Don't get me wrong, your man here is one of the best, but if for some reason he didn't win, I wanted to give you something to defend yourself." He looked at me quickly then smiled, covering her hand as he met her gaze again. "Keep it."

"What is it?"

Lanie smiled as she pulled one end off the wood item and showed a little knife. "He gave it to me when we first walked in yesterday. Then during the bathroom break, while it looked like he was giving me a pep talk, he was telling me some of the provisions that would have you automatically losing the game, like if we touched."

Realization dawned. "That's why you didn't reach for me when you headed to the bathroom."

She nodded at me and smiled. "I may have gripped my neck a little harder, letting the pain from the cut center me a bit as I walked by.

He also gave me a few tips on using the knife so I didn't prick myself again."

Tipping my head to the side, my eyes widened as I asked, "Again?"

Lanie's lip curled up. "Yeah, when I first took it out of my pocket to look at it at the table, while you two were preoccupied, I *may* have pricked my palm. It was tiny, you worrywart." She patted my cheek and then kissed me softly. "Anyway, he gave me a few tips in case I needed to use it."

I looked at Kai and nodded, appreciating him looking out for her, and then turned toward Cyress. He stood there with his arms crossed and shoulders back. "Kai, can you show Lanie her office upstairs? I think I saw Ashley up there."

"Sure thing. Right this way, Lanie. Ashley Renee is the manager and a fucking rock star when it comes to managing the place. I don't think Cyress has had to worry about shit since she took over."

She leaned against me and squeezed my hand tight. "We don't own it until he signs the papers, Jase."

"Cyress shouldn't have bet things he wasn't willing to lose."

Cyress sounded almost bored as he groaned. "Says the man who literally played a game to keep his woman."

I lifted my eyebrows. "You didn't give me a choice."

"There is always a choice, Rathborn."

He wasn't wrong, but to me, the only choice was to save her. Now that I had her again, I was never going to let her go. "He *will* sign the paperwork, Lanie." She looked at Don Kingsley, but my gaze held Cyress's. I chuckled when the note of fear filled his eyes.

That's right, you bastard. Threaten my queen and I come with the royal cavalry to ensure her safety.

Wanting to get Lanie out of here as soon as possible, I said, "We should get back to the matter at hand."

"Ashley is a wonderful, efficient woman." Kai shot daggers at Cyress as he continued, "I know it's probably too early for this, but we should look at the books to see how much of a raise you can give her. She deserves so much more than what he's been paying her."

Kai continued to gloat about her as he and Lanie headed upstairs. Once they disappeared, Don Kingsley nodded to the guards, who went to stand at the top of the stairs. Turning back to Cyress, who was still standing at the table defiantly, he commanded, "Sit."

Cyress went from glaring at me to looking at Don Kingsley, and there was a distinct swallow as his throat bobbed before he sat down. "Let's get this over with."

He had been allowed two guards in with him, which didn't bother me much when there were at least eight that came with Don Kingsley. Two of which had gone up with Lanie and Kai, but that still left us with an overabundance of protection. His guards flanked him on each side and stared beyond us.

Don Kingsley, who took his jacket off and hung it on the back of the chair, sat across from Cyress, and I took the chair to his right. Once we were both settled, he opened a folder and pulled out the deed to the property and the two business transfer documents. "I'm assuming you have reviewed these documents in their entireties."

Gritting his teeth, he glared at me. "Yes." Then he leaned forward on his forearms and asked, "Doesn't Melanie also have to sign to take ownership, or are you going to be a man and keep it to keep your woman in line?"

Rage flowed through me at the disrespect he gave my queen. "Unlike you, I respect women, *especially* my woman. We are here to have *your* signatures notarized by Don Kingsley. Ours have already been notarized, as you can see on the documents."

He glared at me but pulled his wallet out, handed over his license, and went through the motions of signing everything over. It took over an hour as Don Kingsley notarized the signatures in the business transfers and the deed to the property. When Don Kingsley closed the portfolio and handed it to one of the men behind him, he didn't take his eyes off of Cyress as he commanded, "Take this down to the county and get it filed and recorded immediately."

Cyress stood, the chair squeaking across the floor, and his two bodyguards stepped to the side and behind him slightly. I didn't fail to notice that Noah and another one of Kingsley's men were his guards for today. If he noticed, he didn't show it, but the bite in his tone was harsh as he asked, "Are we done now?"

Kingsley stood, chuckling, and flattened out his shirt. "Just one more thing to finalize."

He moved so fast I didn't register him pulling a gun before a deafening sound filled the air. It was just a single shot, but the sound echoed through the room as I covered my ears and watched as Cyress dropped to the floor. I blinked quickly and shook my head to clear the rattling of my brain and the ringing of my ears. Both of his guards stood just as every other guard in the room did, blank-faced and facing ahead. There was a touch of smugness on their faces as the man lay bleeding on the floor between them. My attention swung around to Don Kingsley, who was lowering his gun and holstering it.

"Jason, it's getting a bit late in the day. I'll have this mess cleaned up. Why don't you head upstairs to Lanie and Kai."

"Yes, sir." I looked to Noah, who winked at me before going emotionless again.

"Oh, and Jason? Three things." I waited, and he took a deep breath. "It's Uncle Thom to you, just as it is to Lanie. Second, if you need anything, just let me know."

"Of course, Don . . . Uncle Thom. And the third?"

"You and Lanie should meet me at the house for dinner tomorrow night. Six o'clock. I'll have your copies of the documents ready for you then. We can video chat Kevin where I can formally introduce myself to him, and then we can sort out how we move forward."

"You would include Kevin in those discussions?"

His eyebrows pinched together at me in confusion, then cleared as he shook his head. "That's right. You both sort of glazed over and just signed everything I gave you earlier, didn't you?"

I blinked and realized that was exactly what I had done.

Note to self: read full documents when I get home tomorrow.

"Look, there was a lot, we were in a hurry, and it wasn't the smartest thing I've done in the last twenty-four hours, alright? I'll fix that once I get copies. You better not have screwed us."

He took a step toward me and smiled. "No, but we are business partners now. Half a percent went to me for the hassle."

"But of course." I couldn't help but chuckle and roll my eyes. Honestly, I would have agreed to more if he wanted. "What does that have to do with Kevin, though?"

"Nine and a half percent went to Kevin, with the other ninety percent in your and Lanie's names." He let out a long breath. "There is one little problem."

"What is that?" I narrowed my eyes and tilted my head.

"I *may* have put that ninety percent into the Rathborn Family Trust, with Jason Rathborn and Melanie Rathborn as trustees."

My heart stopped. "I'm sorry, what?"

"I may have also taken the liberty of drafting a basic trust where, should anything happen to you, the trust's assets would be passed on to Kevin, with Kamille Robins as the trustee and me as backup if she could not. Please read them over. They won't go into effect until you have executed them. Let me know if there are any changes that need to be made. The dates will be fudged for legal reasons. My lawyer was up all night getting all the documents together. I will need to have you sign the documents for the condo to be put into the trust, though . . . as well as a few other things to iron out."

"Sounds like we have more than a few things to discuss." I took two steps toward the stairwell before stopping and turning back toward him. "Thank you again, Don . . . Uncle Thom."

After he gave me a quick nod, I turned to the stairwell and left.

THE

DEN

DON'T LET THEM EAT YOU ALIVE

CHAPTER SIXTY-THREE

JASON

TRENTON

After a delicious meal at the Kingsley compound the next night, we spent hours on the phone with Kevin, sorting out all sorts of details. He had been intrigued with having an uncle, then pride surged through him when we told him he was an owner of a business and we had some discussions to make together. Lanie and I went through the trust paperwork, gave Uncle Thom some changes to give to his lawyer to make, and gave him a finalized list for the transfer of some of my personal property into the name of the trust. I didn't care if Lanie's name hadn't been legally changed yet. It would be soon enough.

Especially since after we finished the discussion of the trust, The Den, and the bar, Chase immediately started diving into wedding plans.

"Jason and I haven't even started to discuss things."

"The trust is made, so it needs to happen soon," Chase pushed.

"And just how soon do you think we need to get married?"

Chase made a show of thinking about it, and I tried to give him a look not to push it.

"Years ago, but it's okay. We can have a civil signing here at the kitchen table to make all the paperwork legit and then throw you a massive wedding." He looked at his dad and asked, "What about four hundred guests?"

Lanie looked at me, back at Chase, and then quickly pulled her long, dark hair up in a messy bun before putting her hands on those curvy hips of hers. "Are you fucking kidding me? I don't even know that many people. So if you think we are having any more than a hundred, I'll cut your dick off, shred it, and make you eat it as pasta."

Her sass had blood rushing to my cock. I loved it. Loved "punishing" her for it even more. There was even a moaned whimper I had to hold back at it. My fingers tightened against the table I was leaning against, and Uncle Thom chuckled.

"Shoosh," I told him.

Uncle Thom's chuckling morphed into full laughter, and when Chase and Lanie turned around, I shook my head.

"Jase, what is so funny?"

It was Uncle Thom, though, who answered, "Unless you want to embarrass the hell out of your cousin, I suggest he doesn't answer that."

When her gaze met mine, they were full of that fire I love so much. Even with her cheeks a little rosier than usual, she turned back to Chase and groaned. "Seriously, not only do you and I have a lot to catch up on, but Jase and I haven't even talked about what kind of wedding we want."

"You at the altar saying I do. Outdoor. Fall or spring. I don't want snow or for people to melt. Other than that, I have no require-ments. Okay, well, don't you dare put me in highlighter colors or pink. Though, I know you aren't much on pink, so I think I'm safe there." Lanie stared at me, and I took a few steps to stand in front of her as she held my gaze, and I lifted my hand to put a finger under her chin and looked at her. "As long as at the end of the day you are legally my wife, I don't care about anything else. Don't worry about the cost. I don't care if it's us, Kevin, these two, and Kami there or if we have eight hundred people. I just want you to be mine."

"I'm already yours. You know that."

The hum that came from me was unholy as I pictured all the ways she was mine and I was hers. I leaned forward and kissed her softly, taking my time. When I pulled back, I thought I had forgotten that her uncle and cousin were just a few feet from us because I whispered, "I can't wait to get my sexy slut home and show her just how much I love her."

She moaned and leaned against me. My arms wrapped around her waist, and I smiled. We stood like that for a minute before Chase said,

"Well, I think I just found out more about Lanie's sex life than I wanted to know."

Chuckling, I smiled as I leaned my head against the top of hers. "Don't worry, everything we do is consentual."

"Is that true, Lanie?"

She pulled back and glared at her cousin. "Of course, you moron! Do you really think I would tolerate anyone else calling me a slut, his dirty whore, or using me the way he does? Fuck no. I'd rip their balls off!"

Chase put his hands up in surrender. "Noted. I'm sorry I asked. Back to wedding stuff. Since he has given you guidelines, let's get started."

"Are you a mafia commander and wedding planner?"

He grinned. "Not for everyone. Just for you."

I kissed Lanie again on the forehead before stepping back to let them head over to the couch and continue talking about our wedding.

I leaned on the doorjamb and watched as they got started. They sat on the edge of the soft leather couch as they started thumbing through a few binders that Chase had sitting out. They talked about style options, with Chase pushing for the more formal since many of Uncle Thom's associates would be there.

"Look, Lanie, Dad is practically obligated to invite Max Vispania, Calus Velarde, and their wives. It's going to be a formal affair."

"I don't care if the president himself comes to the wedding. I want a softer look. It can still be black tie, but there has to be a way that we can put them both together. Grey tie affair."

They continued to bicker, and I let my gaze flow around the room. There were elements of the formal and the casual throughout the space. The fireplace was straight, dark stone lines but had photos of Uncle Thom, a woman who I expect had been his wife before she died, and Chase on the black stone mantle, along with other family photos on the more contemporary tables. While the house was very formal looking, they had decorated it with wood aspects that worked with those lines to bring warmth and comfort to the house. Standing there, I studied the row of windows at the front and was wondering how they'd manage that if someone decided to attack the house.

I must have been studying them longer than I expected because Uncle Thom asked, "You wondering about the windows?"

"Yeah. What if someone attacks?"

Uncle Thom chuckled. "First, they would be stupid to do so. Second, with a click of a button, steel slams down over every window on the house. Whether it's zombies or another family, no one is getting into the compound. If you ever need to hide away somewhere, come here."

"Okay, though I hope we never have to take you up on that offer."

"Agreed, and I'll do what I can to keep you guys out of it, but there is no way I can guarantee that."

"That's all I can really ask." I looked back at where Chase and Lanie were sitting and I couldn't help but smile. She was without a doubt the best thing that had happened in my life . . . twice. Thank the gods she'd been willing to give me that second chance.

Uncle Thom stood beside me and watched her as well. "Thank you for making her so happy."

"You are welcome, but I know I don't deserve her. You haven't said that, but I want you to know that I am quite aware I'm leveling up here. I just hope I never give her a reason to second-guess that second chance. I still can't believe how stupid I was."

"Know how you feel there." He let out a deep sigh. "I located them about four years ago. She was in a dark place. She was working so hard to make things work and take care of Kevin. Not only am I Kevin's sponsor for Velas, but also for his education."

I looked at him, and he was smiling at Lanie. "Kevin's a real smart, good kid. She's done an amazing job with him since their parents died."

Uncle Thom's attention went to the floor as he nodded. "I wish Heath were here to see him." His phone rang and he excused himself for a minute. He was trying to keep his voice down, but I heard mention of "nightwhispers" and "'Westwood," and I recalled the game I had played where Westwood had bet something called "nightwhispers." From the conversation I'd overheard as I'd played that game, I knew the information had been useful to Kingsley. When he returned, he acted like nothing had happened at all.

"I take it Westwood isn't a problem anymore?"

He smirked. "Your information was beneficial. During the game, she figured out who you were about halfway through. Well, it wasn't until after she kicked Westwood out of the game. Which is why she quickly ended it."

"Why would that matter? I don't understand. I also understand that I don't have to, I just have to do the job, but I am curious."

He watched Chase and Lanie as they discussed invitations and flowers, and I chuckled when Chase suggested an *Avatar: The Last Airbender* theme. Lanie's eyes lifted, and I shook my head, smiling.

"Well, while that sounds amazing, I don't think we can do that sort of theme and have your fancy formal wedding you have demanded. Just remember, this is our wedding, not yours, Chase. When you get married, you can make it as childish as you want."

"Brat, but there could still be subtle nods and touches to it." He bumped her shoulder, and they went back to looking at venues in the Trenton area. While I was sure they were beautiful, I suspected it would be in San Diego so her friends down south would be able to attend. Uncle Thom could just have his business associates travel if it was that important. I was truly fine with whatever she wanted. He kept his voice low and said, "I've been working with Mr. Velarde." His eyes swung to look at me, and I nodded, indicating I knew he was the right-hand man of Mr. Vispania. "We've been trying for years to get nightwhispers off the streets. It's a long and hard process."

"So, when I found out that Westwood had an abundance of stock . . ."

He nodded. "It was really more of a confirmation. We suspected that he did, but when we thought we would have the location, we would show up to an empty warehouse. Knowing which Don had the supply, though, was helpful because we could pool our resources. That call was just confirmation of removing Westwood from the market."

"But not that the product isn't still available." He gave me a simple nod but changed the subject. Jerking his head to Lanie and Chase on the couch, he said, "Go and make a few decisions on the wedding."

"We haven't said it yet, but thank you for everything you've done for us."

"You are family. It's what we do. Protect those we love."

THE

DEN

DON'T LET THEM EAT YOU ALIVE

Jason

After signing off on some paperwork for Kai, I leaned against the counter and looked out over The Den. Since we'd taken over, we'd doubled the money on the books and had a waitlist for time at a table. Where Kai used to have to call people in to fill spots, we were now having people put deposits down to hold their chairs, and if they no showed within ten minutes of that table's start time, then they forfeited and one of the people on the waitlist would be substituted in. There was one table, though, that always sat unbooked. The Don table was only used when the Dons needed to settle something. If someone wanted in on a Don game, there were separate contracts for it, and the table fees were doubled. The house was making a killing in comparison to how Cyress had run the place.

Kai came to lean against the counter next to me after he filed the things away. I glanced up and looked around the room. "Hey, Kai, how long have we been friends?"

Letting out a sigh, he said, "Too long by the sounds of *that* conversation starter."

"Okay, how long have you worked for this hellhole?"

He leaned back and looked at me. "Since I was eighteen. So, fifteen years? Fuck, what am I doing with my life?"

I chuckled and reached into my jacket, pulling out an envelope and handing it to him.

Confusion filled his face. "Are you firing me?"

"Oh, hell no. You are stuck with me for good, man. Just open the envelope, will ya?"

He did, and when he pulled out the letter and photocopy of the legal paperwork, his eyes sped across the paper. When he finally looked up at me, his face was in pure shock and tears lined his eyes. "Jase . . . You . . . You can't do this."

"Why the hell not? Lanie and I can do whatever the fuck we want. You deserve this. Now, you just have to realize that you are now officially a business owner as well as a business partner with Kingsley."

Kai's eyes went wide. "What?"

"That LLC that I've told you not to look too deep into that owns half a percent of The Den? The one you send a check to each month?"

He nodded, and then his eyes went wide as he finally put the pieces together. "Oh, fuck. Ummm. Okay."

"I'm not letting you say no, which is why the copy of the deed you have there has already been filed with the county. If you want to set up a corporation of some sort or a trust to hold title, it's fine, do it, but you've worked too hard for too long here not to have an interest in it."

Kai's mouth gaped like a fish.

"Now you can feel good about finally asking Ashley to marry you. Lanie's giving her an interest in the bar as we speak."

It had been an easy decision for both of us to give them each their own slice of the pie. Kai had been in love with Ashley for years, but only after we won the businesses had they finally taken the plunge into starting a relationship.

Thundering footsteps came down the stairwell, and guns were pulled from three different spots in the room. Kevin's, "It's me!" echoed down the hall. He'd made the mistake once of not announcing himself while running down and had almost pissed himself when he'd been met with six guns aimed at him.

The guns were lowered, and when he broke through the doorway, he yelled, "Brother, Sissy's water broke!"

I blinked at him, my heart racing as I just stood there. I had stood before multiple Dons, stared down numerous people at the tables in this very room, but my wife's water breaking was what left me paralyzed. She'd been having contractions since six this morning, so we knew we were getting close and wanted to give Ashely and Kai their presents before we were rushing off to the hospital.

Kevin's hands were on my shoulders, and I saw Jackie come in a moment later, her eyes wide in excitement. "Brother, you need to get Sissy to the hospital now. She had a really big contraction, and then her water broke."

I nodded and looked at Kai who was gesturing for me to leave. "Go. I've got it covered here."

As I ran up the stairs, I found Ashley standing in front of Lanie, who was leaning over a chair, taking deep, slow breaths. She looked relieved to see me. "They are only a couple minutes apart. Don't worry about the bar. I'm assuming Kai's good downstairs?"

"Yeah." I came over and rubbed Lanie's back, which was hard as a rock. "You're doing amazing, my queen". When it loosened slightly, she took an easier breath. Turning to look back at Kevin, who had an arm around his wife, Jackie, I asked, "Can you two go and get the hospital bags from the house? We thought we would have time to stop by there first before things got this far."

They nodded in understanding.

Lanie stood up and let out a slow breath. "Let's move before another hits. Kevin, can you call Uncle Thom and let him know?"

"Already texted him when he didn't answer his phone," Jackie said, smiling. "Come on, Kevin, let's get their stuff and then head over to the hospital."

"Thanks, everyone," I said as I helped my wife get to the car. "Ashley, I'll update you and Kai when the twins are here."

She nodded as Kevin opened the door to help us outside.

It was almost one in the morning, and the grip Lanie had on my hand was so tight, I thought she might break my bones, but if all I got was a broken finger, I was still coming out ahead. "You are doing great, sweetheart."

"Don't call me that." She panted through another contraction as the nurses and doctor were rushing to finish getting set up for the babies to be born. One of the baby's heads was in position, and my wife was finally dilated enough. "You don't call me sweetheart."

"I didn't think you wanted me calling you what I normally do in the bedroom, my queen. Not in front of all these nurses and the doctor."

She huffed a laugh, and when the doctor was there, she looked up at the monitor and said, "Okay, Lanie. You ready?"

She nodded, and the doctor walked her through the most effective way to push. "Push like you are trying to take the biggest poop you've ever taken. You probably will, and that's okay. Now, here comes another contraction. Three, two, one, push."

Over and over again, my beautiful wife pushed like the badass queen she was. The first baby came through with no problems at all. We had both decided early in the pregnancy that we didn't want to know the gender of the babies. We figured the surprise of finding out during labor was part of the experience of birth.

The doctor lifted the first baby up and announced, "It's a girl!"

Handing her over to the nurse, who started cleaning her up, the doctor looked back at Lanie. "One down, one more to go. You ready, Momma?"

Lanie looked over at me, and I leaned down and kissed her. Whispering against her lips, I said, "You are a badass. I love you so much. Ready?"

"Yes. Get this kid out of me. I'm fucking exhausted. Where is Mikayla?" Her voice was a bit panicked. Mikayla was one of the girl names we had picked out. I wasn't going to complain that she had immediately named her.

"She's with the nurses. You can have her, along with her sibling, once you push them out. Deal?"

She nodded, but her hand was shaking. I looked back at the doctor, who smiled at me. "Okay, Mom, push!"

Mikayla's sibling came out much faster, and then the doctor lifted the baby. "A boy."

Lanie looked at me and raised an eyebrow. "Christopher?" I nodded and smiled at her. "Mikayla and Christopher." She breathed and looked back at the nurses, who placed Mikayla on her chest, and then after wiping Christopher down, they placed him there, too. Lanie's breathing instantly evened out. I was mesmerized by the two tiny humans lying across her chest.

Twenty little toes.

Four adorable, little, wrinkly feet.

Four stubby little legs.

Two long, little cords from their tummies.

Two perfect, little rosebud mouths.

Two button noses that matched their Mommy's.

Mikayla's eyes opened slightly as she fussed, and I was met with the deepest brown eyes with long black lashes. "Oh, you are so damn beautiful, young lady." I reached up and let my fingers play with the long curly hair on the top of her head.

Lanie chuckled, and Christopher kicked his legs.

I looked over at him and said, "Patience, little man. And be careful with those legs." Leaning forward, I kissed Lanie softly. "You did an amazing job, my queen. Our little princess and prince are here."

"Mrs. Rathborn, I need you to give me one more large push, okay?" She nodded, and when the doctor counted down and got to one, she pushed. There was a plop sound, much like when you dropped gelatin on the floor, and when I swung my attention to the doctor, she had what I assumed was the placenta in her hand and was putting it into a tray on her right.

Christopher pumped his legs again, and I looked over at him, smiling. "You are a demanding little one, aren't you? Don't worry, you will have all of Mommy and Daddy's attention very soon."

A bright smile crossed her face, and then Lanie winced. I looked down at the doctor, who mouthed, "Sorry," before she finished stitching Lanie up. Meanwhile, Lanie and I just stared at the twins. We just lay there with the twins as they got Lanie's bed set back up.

"Mrs. Rathborn, we need to check them over and do some quick tests and measurements. They won't leave the room, and you can watch what we are doing from here, okay?" She nodded and gently handed each of them over as they put them in a cart next to the bed.

We watched for a moment, and I couldn't help the raw, primal feeling of needing more. "I can't wait for us to have more kids. The

K.M. RINGER

sight of you growing with them was something I'll . . . Fuck. I really can't wait to put another baby in you."

"Jase, can you at least wait until I heal from these two? Shit."

There was a devilish smile on my face as I leaned in and whispered against her lips. "Oh, I'll wait, but then I'm going to fuck my little slut until she is swelling with another one of our children. You lying here with our daughter and son in your arms is by far the sexiest thing I have ever fucking seen."

"Fucking hell, Jason. At least wait a couple days to say that shit." Then she play slapped my shoulder. "And not in front of the babies."

The nurses placed Christopher in Lanie's arms and Mikayla in mine. After kissing Lanie one more time, I kissed our daughter's head on the top. "Your mother is amazing, little one. One day, you will see."

Just as the last nurse was walking out, she asked, "Are you open to family coming in?"

"Sissy, I need to see my niece and nephew!"

Lanie laughed and then bellowed, "Then get in here. Jackie too, if she's still here."

They walked in, and behind them were Uncle Thom and Chase. All four of them had huge smiles on their faces. Handing Uncle Thom Christopher, Lanie readjusted how she was sitting as I handed Mikayla over to Kevin.

"Where is Kami?" Lanie was looking behind them for her best friend.

Kevin's focus never left the twins as he said, "She'll be here before too long. She was going to go to the condo to straighten up for when you get home."

"A boy and a girl," Chase muttered as he pulled the blanket down slightly on Christopher. "What are their names?"

"The girl," Lanie said as she smiled at me. We had both decided that if they were girls, she would pick middle names, and I would pick the middle names if they were boys, so I knew Mikayla's first name but not middle. "Is Mikayla Jane Rathborn."

I blinked. "Jane?"

She smirked. "After your mother."

"Where did the name Mikayla come from?" Jackie asked.

"Well, I wanted Lyla and Lanie wanted Michelle, so when we saw Mikayla, we thought it was a great compromise," I said, still staring at our daughter.

Kevin cooed at her and was whispering about all the trouble they were going to get into together. How he was going to teach her all about art, how Jackie was going to teach her to read and write by the time she was three, and all kinds of other promises I couldn't bring myself to dispel. He was absolutely smitten with her.

"Now, my son." I met Chase's gaze and smirked. Uncle Thom was still studying his nephew. His eyes were shining with pride and love. "I'd like to introduce you to Christopher Thomas Rathborn."

Uncle Thom wasn't moving, and Lanie's hand slipped into mine and squeezed tight. His eyes slowly lifted to look at us, and I dared to look at Lanie, who was smiling brightly. "Seriously?"

Lanie smiled brightly at him. "I'm not surprised by Jason's choice. You've been there for us longer than we knew. You never forgot about Kevin or me. Though, call me a bit of a nerd, but maybe we can call him Toph?"

I started laughing. "But Toph was a woman."

"Oh, don't you start on that misogynistic bullshit, Jase. Toph was a fucking badass earthbender. One that was constantly putting that kind of behavior behind her. You saw how hard that boy was kicking his legs earlier. I have no doubt he's the reason for my bruised ribs."

She wasn't wrong, and I looked around the room at my family; Everyone was smiling back at us. My gaze fell to my son, who was pumping his legs, losing the blanket wrapped around him, as a smile stretched over my face. "Toph it is."

Epilogue Two

Lanie

"I've got it, Sissy. I've watched the twins before," Kevin complained for the hundredth time.

"I know. I know." He had, many times in fact, and this wasn't the first time he and Jackie had had them overnight either. My emotions were all over the place, and now I knew why. The little stick in the bathroom with two lines on it had given an answer, but that didn't mean I had to enjoy the mood swings.

Jason, my ever-patient husband, came over and wrapped his arms around my waist and kissed me on my bare shoulder right next to my tank top strap. It helped settle me, but I was antsy. I wanted to tell him. Couldn't wait to let him know, but I also wanted to give him the news privately.

It took no time at all for us to get the twins into the back of Kevin and Jackie's SUV. I gave Mikayla a kiss on the cheek and Toph a kiss on the forehead, who immediately asked, "Aunni Jackie, ice cream?"

As I pulled back out of the car, she was smiling at him. "If you eat your dinner and are a good boy, we will get you some ice cream."

Mikayla, though, the smart, little, sassy cherub, nodded her head and smiled at her Auntie Jackie, saying, "But baby in belly want ice cream. Yes, baby do."

I sighed and shook my head. "Auntie Jackie already gave you an answer. We don't behave like that to get people to do what we want, do we?" They both bowed, mocking shame as they shook their heads

They would get their ice cream, and the point was made regardless of whether they felt shame or not. "Thank you. Behave. Boop snoot."

"Boop snoot," they said in unison, then Toph was asking Kevin for chicken nuggets for dinner.

I shook my head as Jackie turned to me and rubbed her belly. At six months, she was showing pretty decently, which made Kevin very happy. He was very much looking forward to being a dad and was going to be an amazing father.

When I raised an eyebrow at Jackie, she said, "Don't start with me. All this baby wants to do is eat ice cream. Kevin keeps a pretty steady supply in the freezer. That and honey barbeque corn chips. Oh, and put them together, I am in heaven."

"Yeah, tell me about it. Those two only wanted salt and vinegar chips, peanut butter, brie, and orange soda." I blanched slightly at the thought. This one wanted none of that. I'd been craving nothing but potato rolls, apple juice, and cucumbers. Not to mention my sex drive was through the freaking roof.

I looked over at Jason, smiling at the thought of telling him I was pregnant again, but Kevin wrapped me up in a hug and whispered in my ear, "Have a good night, Sissy. You two deserve it."

"Don't give them too much sugar, Kev. If you bring them back hyped up like you did last time you had them, I might . . . Well, I don't know what I'll do 'cause you need to be around for your little one, but anyway, please don't."

"Fine. I'll limit how much they have, but we are going to the planetarium tomorrow. Won't be back until at least four or five."

"You'll keep them through their naps?"

He nodded. "Wear them out in the morning, and they will go right out. You need to rest, too. You look tired."

I was exhausted actually, so I squeezed him tight and stepped back, waving at the kids. Jason came over and wrapped an arm around me and as they drove off before pulling me back into the house. He gave me a quick kiss when we got back into the living room and turned to head into his office. "Need to finish up some paperwork for Kai. Give me a few minutes, and I'll make you some snacks and we can get a movie going."

I nodded, and as I watched him stroll back down the hallway, I bit my bottom lip. That ass of his was one of my weaknesses. There was a part of me that wanted to go to the bedroom, grab the lube and harness, and fuck it till he was screaming his release. I shook my head to get the image from my brain.

A few minutes.

I could wait a few more minutes.

Occupying myself with picking up the kids' toys around the house, I heard Jason take a few phone calls. After about forty minutes, I was taking the last load of clean clothes into the kids' room when I heard him get off the phone with a sigh across the hall. Quickly, I hung Mikayla's dresses and put away their pants and shirts in the dresser. Suddenly feeling nervous, I dropped the laundry basket on the floor next to the door and went into our bedroom, undressed, and tossed my clothes on the bed before walking down the hall and striding into his office.

"Almost done, my queen. I just need . . ." His gaze lifted just as I reached his desk and he froze. Only his eyes moved as he looked me over from head to toe. "Fuck, that is a beautiful sight."

I gave him a bright smile, walked around to his side of the desk, and turned his chair to face me. Straddling his lap, I rolled my hips against him and wrapped my arms around his neck.

"Did I not do a good enough job this morning? Was my little slut not as satisfied as she should be?" His hand sat on my waist, and I could feel his fingers pressing tight against me. As he licked his lips again, I could almost feel it against my clit.

"Sir did amazingly this morning. Is it a problem if his whore wants more of him?"

He shook his head as he slid his hands up to cup my breasts. When he pinched them, I let out a gasping moan at the pleasure that went through me. "Oh, my whore is delectably sensitive today."

Humming as he leaned forward and kissed along my collarbone and up my throat, I could feel him getting hard underneath me. There was no way I wasn't leaving a wet spot on his pants, and I had zero shame about it. I couldn't help but tip my head back at the feel of his tongue swirling up my neck and the little nips of his teeth.

"Use me, Sir," I begged.

He chuckled against my ear as he sucked the lobe in and growled. "Do you think you could handle me right now?"

I whimpered. "Give me everything you have. Just fucking use me like your personal fucktoy."

"You are my personal fucktoy. All mine."

My nails dug into his shoulders as I jerked my pussy against him, looking for any relief from the throbbing in my clit. "Touch me. Use. Me."

"Fuck. You haven't been this insatiable and demanding since you were . . ." His gaze popped up to meet mine. "Are you pregnant?"

A huge smile crossed my face. "I am. Now, are you going to make me cum, or do I have to get one of the toys you bought me for my birthday a few months ago and make you watch."

"My little slut will do no such thing." Kissing along my collarbone, he chuckled. "You know I love a great teammate, but I want this one all on my own." Wrapping his arms under my thighs, he stood and set me on the edge of his desk. "Now, you are going to sit here and enjoy every moment. Is that understood?"

"Yes, Sir."

Slowly, he undressed, tossing clothes behind me until he was completely naked before me. When I reached out to take his cock into my hand, he slapped it. "No. You are giving me another child of yours. I am going to show you just how much I appreciate that."

Taking my breasts back into his palms, he nipped and sucked on my nipples. Desire flooded my body, and I was soaking his desk. "Sir. Please."

Once he lowered to his knees, his hands roamed all over my stomach. Jason pressed his lips on the area above my womb and smiled as he looked up at me. "I told you I was going to put another baby in here. I can't wait for when you start showing. You are the best mom I could ask for for my kids. You are an amazing wife and partner. Best of all, you are *mine*."

It wasn't that he hadn't said that before. Hell, he reminded me constantly, and it may have been the hormones, but love swelled inside of me. His hand ran down my thigh, and once it was behind my knee, he moved it wider and over his shoulder.

Closing my eyes and leaning back on my hands, I sighed as his tongue licked from one end of me to the other before circling my clit. "My fucktoy is so delicious. She's so fucking wet for me."

I was about to demand he do something before I lost my mind when he plunged his fingers deep into my pussy, hitting my G-spot. The guttural groan of ecstasy that came out of me sounded inhuman. He chuckled against me before he flicked my clit as he widened his knees.

Jason ate me like a starved man. He licked, sucked, and finger fucked every inch of me. When he licked around my asshole, my thighs twitched, and his chuckle reverberated against me. Sitting up slightly, I looked down at him, and my pussy pulsed as I watched him stroke himself before me.

"Fuck."

His eyes met mine as he beat himself and slipped three fingers into me, curling them against that spot again that had me groaning. "Sir likes eating his dirty little whore's pussy so much he can't keep his hand off his own cock."

Groaning in response, he bit my clit but then licked as the pain shot through my body, and I wasn't sure how much longer I would be able to hold off my orgasm. Reaching down, I threaded my hand through his air and ground my pussy against his face, his bearded scruff adding just enough stimulation to bring me to the edge.

"Yes." I knew I was close, and I reached up, taking my tit in my hand tweaking my nipple.

Jason's hand moved faster up and down his shaft as he groaned into me, licking and sucking.

"Cum with me, Sir. And fucking make me cum all over your face."

Pleasure rocketed through me as he attacked my clit with his mouth, sucking and licking as he focused all his attention on my G-spot with his fingers. It took mere moments before I screamed his name into the room. His grunt against me as he lapped and drank me up was music to my ears.

As I came down from my release, Jason reached up as he stood before he wrapped his hand around my throat and commanded, "That's my good girl. Now lick my hand clean, cumslut."

He lifted his hand to my mouth, and the warm saltiness of his cum filled my senses. I held his gaze as I licked and swallowed every drop on his hand. His eyes were full of love, pride, and pure happiness.

When I was done, he kissed me softly, threading his hand in my hair and holding me against him. "Thank you for giving me a second chance all those years ago. You have made me the happiest man on the planet. I love you, Lanie Rathborn."

"I love you, Jase."

BOOKS REFERENCED IN THIS STORY

BLOOD ON MY NAME
K. ELLE MORRISON

GORGEROUS, ARMED & DANGEROUS
ELISABETH GARNER

MODEL ATTRACTION
SCARLETT TEAGHRAN

THE ASTRAL'S BONDED
KIMBERLY M. RINGER

Other Books by K.M. Ringer

Weekend Series

Weekend with Rylie
Weekend with Malcom
Weekend with Desiree
Weekend with Bethany
Angel's Shadow

The Ashstrike Sanctorum

The Ashstrike Sanctorum: Orgin Story
The Astral's Bonded
The Exorci's Touch
My Kismot Savior
The Kismot's Undesirable
My Kismot's Beloveds

Other Books

Ashes and Flame
Otter Be Saved
Under the Needle
Dedicated in Ink

ABOUT THE AUTHOR
K.M. Ringer

K.M. Ringer lives in California with her husband, little human, and two furballs, Wall-E (a Jack Russell mix) and Pippin (a Pomeranian Terrier mix). Always loving a little (or a lot) of spice she just might have you reaching for that "extra little help" to cool down.

Contact K.M. Ringer:

www.kmringer.com

Instagram: @kimberlymringer

Facebook: Kimberly M. Ringer

Sign up for my newsletter on my website
and receive freebies, coupon codes, and stay up to date
on all things Kimberly M. Ringer and K.M. Ringer

WEEKEND SERIES

BY K.M. RINGER

WEEKEND WITH RYLIE
Book One

Luci's whole life changes in one weekend with her boyfriend, Rylie Allen.

Of course, there was the mind-blowingly good sex. It always was, but then there are secrets revealed, and a new job opportunity that would change everything between Luci and Rylie. When her ex-boyfriend comes back to haunt her, it threatens to throw their lives into further upheaval.

WEEKEND WITH MALCOM
Book Two

Malcom Henderson has been obsessed with his Project Foreman for months. When she's disrespected at a bar he steps in and after an enjoyable night, he hopes to have it turn into something more. The next morning, she's convinced that as much as she wants him, it was only a one-night stand, and tries to protect herself by kicking him out. A torturous week pulls between them when unexpected problems are occurring on the job site that ends up being tied to the Chicago mafia families, and it's not long before Malk and Raquel find themselves in the middle of a brewing war.

WEEKEND WITH DESIREE
Book Three

With threats against the Don Supreme and his family lurking around every corner, Jensen Maloy, the most feared man in all Chicago, has been working overtime to ensure everyone stays safe and alive. Desiree Hernandez loves and trusts Jensen with every fiber of her being, and while she understands the reason, they need to live in lockdown, it doesn't mean she's happy about it. Even if she is living with her best friend and honorary sister, and her fiance.

Jensen and Desiree aren't used to being apart for such long stretches of time, and despite all the support from friends and coworkers, tensions rise, and morale drops to an all-time low. When the enemy takes drastic actions to finish the deal, they forget to factor in two very important things. Desi is not to be underestimated, and Jensen will stop at nothing to make sure his Princess is safe and in his arms. Who will still be standing when the dust settles?

WEEKEND WITH BETHANY
Book Four
Her strength will save them all.

Weekend with Bethany is the explosive conclusion to the Weekend Series. The war between Dallas and Vaux has become deadly, and no one is safe. When Beth is captured, she was shocked to learn that her Wes was the one and only Wesley Backnoff. Sure, she knew the name. Who didn't? Can she reconcile the compassionate man with whom she fell in love, with the killer who stands before her?

After rescuing Bethany, Wesley Backnoff, second to the Don Supreme of Chicago, can't hold back his feelings for her any longer and is bound and determined to keep her.

Old secrets come to light and threaten to destroy them all. Who will pay the price? Will Beth and Wes survive the night or has their time run out?

ASHES AND FLAME

ASHES & FLAME

KIMBERLY M. RINGER

After working as an Advisor for the Roman Empire, Tiberius Maximus Vispania returned to Herculaneum in 79AD to start over. When he meets Sidonia Regilla, a fire instantly ignites between them. She would be allowed to choose her future husband. Could Sidonia be happy with Tiberius?

Just when happiness finds a way, an epic tragedy occurs and the entire village is wiped out. Only Tiberius and his best friend survive, courtesy of a curse that's provided them with immortality.

2,000 years later, Kelsey walks into his bar and lights a desire within him that only Sidonia had ever done. When their dark worlds collide, an overwhelming need to protect her takes over, and he realizes there may be more to Kelsey's ability to get under his skin than he thought. When Kelsey is kidnapped and tortured, unknown old rivals and secrets come to light.

When Max rushes in to save her, he vows that either all of them would come out alive, or none of them.

THE ASHSTRIKE SANCTORUM

THE ASHSTRIKE SANCTORUM:
CREATION STORY

When the Dark Witches of Moesia go rogue, and start creating immortals, will the paranormal creatures allow the new beings to live, or will they be out to destroy them? They have tasked Benjamin, an Ovexa, with finding three of these immortals to be interrogated to determine if they can be trusted to keep the paranormal world a secret from the humans.

Jorgen Hegland has found himself newly made but quickly learns being an immortal isn't worth it. When Benjamin finds him and demands he meet with the other creatures of the world, he agrees, but it isn't until he finds his mate, that he decides he will fight for his right to live.

THE ASTRAL'S BONDED
THE ASHSTRIKE SANCTORUM:
BOOK 1

EVEN ALPHAS HAVE TO ANSWER TO SOMEONE.

It was supposed to be a simple assignment. Astral Jade Romero was supposed to fix the werewolf problem at the Porter Ranch.

Only there was a problem, she hadn't prepared herself for, the human foreman Kolton Webster. He occupied all her thoughts and sucked her in like she never had been before.

When the wolves attack and Jade is injured will it be Kolton or the wolves that destroy her?

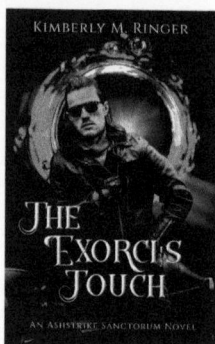

THE EXORCI'S TOUCH
THE ASHSTRIKE SANCTORUM:
BOOK 2
WHAT DO YOU DO WHEN YOUR ASSIGNMENT DOESN'T
DIE.

Exorci Jesse Westbrook can't touch anyone with his bare skin. If he does, they die. Such is the curse of an Exorci, the executioners for the Ashstrike Sanctorum.

His job is as simple and complicated as that. Receive the name and location of the person, and with a simple touch, the extermination is complete.

Jesse's life isn't all death and destruction. He has Maddie Taylor. The woman is his forever, but he's never dared to truly touch her. When her brother dies, her life spirals out of control, to the point she pushes Jesse from her life. Now... Now she's his next assignment.

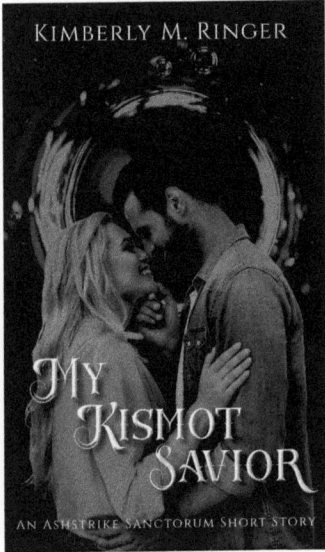

MY KISMOT SAVIOR
THE ASHSTRIKE SANCTORUM:
BOOK 2.5

Angelica's life has been nothing but hiding from her parents and trying to make ends meet. It's been hard, but worth the freedom it afforded her from her family.

Morgan would have never guessed he would have found his queen just walking down the streets of Carmel, California, but there she was, arguing with the most despicable of women.

When Morgan intervenes, chaos ensues and Angelica and Morgan's secrets come to light quickly. Only Angelica seems to have one more...

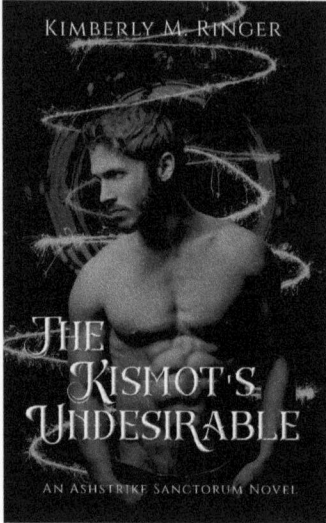

THE KISMOT'S UNDESIRABLE
THE ASHSTRIKE SANCTORUM:
BOOK 3

Masen Cartwell was the son to the pride's king. It was his responsibility to ratify the treaty by marrying the Los Padres pride's undesirable, Veronica Aktins. There is something about her though. Something that pulls at his protective instincts and calls to his tom.

Ronni was the daughter of traders to her pride, an outcast, the Undesirable. Used and assaulted by the princes, the King has demanded that she marry the rival pride's prince and kill the Ventana Prides ruling family. Only, when she meets Prince Masen, his possessiveness over her and the adoration he showers her with sings to her heart.

When Prince Edwin steals Ronni, Masen will do anything to get her back. He had promised to protect her and keep her safe from her old pride.

Masen Cartwell won't let anything happen to what is his, and will stop at nothing to have his Queen back.

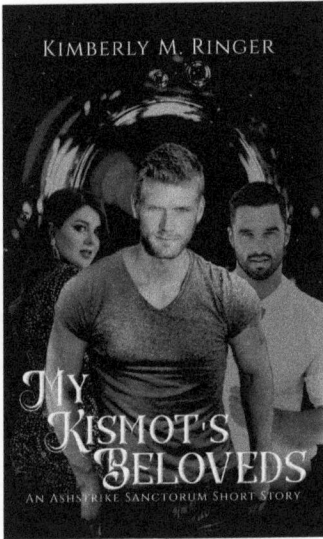

My Kismot's Beloveds
The Ashstrike Sanctorum:
Book 3.5

Leo Banks has watched his best friend and his prince find their mates. As hand to the crown prince, he was okay with that. They found their happiness and now his princess, and a woman he considered a sister, was pregnant with twins. He vowed to be her protector through the troubled pregnancy. He was happy with just being Uncle Leo.

Then when her pregnancy takes a turn for the worse, Dr. Marie Fuller and her nurse, Hadrian Fuller, come to Landow to care for her. When they arrived, Leo was not expecting to find his mate, let alone a queen and tom.

Can he balance the stress of protecting his princess, and welcoming his mates into his life?

Milton Keynes UK
Ingram Content Group UK Ltd.
UKHW031144121124
451094UK00006B/488